Secrets and Summonings

E.K Earle

MIDNIGHT ATELIER PRESS

Book Cover© by Adara Frances

Illustrations© by Sonja Liszewski

Editing by Nicole Evans

1st edition 2025

ISBN for paperback: 978-0-6457344-5-4

ISBN for ebook: 978-0-6457344-6-1

ALSO BY

Wraiths and Wanderings Saga:
Wraiths and Wanderings

To all of you who feel like you need to wear a mask—

I see you.

Content Notes

Dear reader; when reading or engaging in media, I always find it best to be mindful of the content I am consuming and what it may contain, for my own safety. Therefore, I present you with what I hope is a comprehensive list of content notes of *Secrets and Summonings*. Please remember to take care of yourself.

Blood

Bodily harm

Body gore

Breaking bones

Burns

Death

Demon summonings

Desecration of non-human corpses

Drowning

Fire

Humanoid monsters

Melting flesh

Mirror horror

PTSD symptoms

Public urination

Religious paraphernalia being used on monsters

Smoking

E.K EARLE

Vomiting

CHAPTER ONE

HAZEL

It was dark in the old farmhouse, but that wasn't anything new to her.

The shadows skirted their feet, shying away from the pan of their flashlights across the hardwood floor. There were no noises save for the creak of their feet—one, a heavier crunch of a pair of boots, the other, a more cautious, light-footed step. No scampering of mice, not even a chirp of a cicadas in the space surrounding them. The flashlight bounced over the eclectic knickknacks in the kitchen; a Victorian-era wood-fire stove, a fifties blender, tins from before the war. An odd mishmash of different lives and different stories.

"If I was going to be murdered anywhere, this would be the place."

Hazel broke the silence as well as the concentration of her companion, who flashed her a scowl.

Charlotte Blythe was wan, even by the pale lights of their flashlights in the shuttered house. Her long, chestnut brown hair was held in place by a braid that swung as she pivoted, returning her attention to their investigation.

"Is this really the place to make those sorts of jokes?" Charlotte whispered, glancing about. Hazel shrugged a shoulder nonchalantly, the black leather of her favorite jacket squeaking where it rubbed. Charlotte might have been an amazing witch and expert ghost vlogger, but she wasn't nearly as collected as Hazel was. At least, not yet. Hazel reasoned she could train her up in due time.

"If the set of one of my favorite movie franchises isn't the place to haunt," she grinned, "then where is?"

Charlotte pinched the bridge of her nose, drawing in a deep breath. "We have a job to do. Maybe we should focus on that instead of becoming a crime scene?"

"Sure, babes." Hazel moved past Charlotte, heading towards the main hall. "It's not like I'd go down without a fight, anyway."

They were currently in a Hollywood studio, on the set of one of the newest releases in a supernatural horror franchise. It was one of Hazel's dreams to be here, to see how the magic was made. Unfortunately, the circumstances in which they'd been asked to come were less than ideal. The director had contacted Charlotte directly through her channel, *Wraiths and Wanderings*, asking for their help. Something weird was going on. Creepy things that made the cast feel like they were in a horror film, and not just acting.

Everyone denied playing pranks, said that they weren't the ones making creepy laughter, weren't the ones slamming doors in an invisible wind, or breaking things that were nowhere near edges. It hadn't seemed legit—there was a whole establishment he could have contacted her through. Even Charlotte's business email would have been more credible—and yet, here they were. Two in the morning, hunting for the source of dread that had been filling cast and crew.

"I bet we aren't the only channel they asked to come," Hazel commented, pointing her torch around the thin hallway, noting the peeling wallpaper. The set design was on point. "I bet the ghoul boys are gonna come in after us."

"That means if something is here," Charlotte sighed, "that we better find it. I can't stand the idea of a single precious hair on their heads being harmed."

"My boy could take it," Hazel argued as Charlotte followed her out. "He's a demon unto himself. I bet he could vanquish them with a single word or some shit."

Charlotte rolled her eyes. "That's just a meme, Hazel! He's still a normal human, you know. He isn't like us. And he has way less common sense about ghosts than *my* boy. 'Come fight me, demons'," Charlotte deepened her voice, mocking Hazel's favorite ghost hunter. "He'd get sideswiped by something and be down for the count, while my boy would be outta there, safe and sound."

Hazel spun to face Charlotte, hands planted on her hips. "You're lucky Gran doesn't like us betting, or I'd crush you. I would totally wait for when they're let in and see."

Charlotte muttered something she couldn't hear, but sounded suspiciously like 'whatever you think, dummy'. Hazel ignored her friend as she did another glance around, looking for anything out of place. She wished she'd brought her polaroid camera with her; she could have gotten some cool shots for her journal.

"Hey, babes? Could I grab a cam and a mic? I think I could get some pretty sick shots."

Charlotte clutched her video camera protectively, shrinking back. "We have a strict NDA. Plus, I don't trust you not to break it. Sorry, not sorry." Hazel let out a huff at the other woman's words but didn't press it.

The hum of the exit sign and the shuffling of the crew in the distance became audible once more as they approached the front of the house. They'd done a full sweep of the set and had found nothing yet. Nothing that screamed supernatural or occult, anyway. Hazel cocked her head towards the door and Charlotte nodded in response. As they slipped through it and out onto the concrete floor of the studio surrounding the set, Hazel remarked, "At least we're the coolest ghost hunting channel in existence, right?"

Charlotte laughed, a breathy and easy sound that reverberated around them. Hazel joined in, warmed by the naturalness of Charlotte's joy. It had taken time, but she was getting there, becoming whole.

"Did you find anything?" Their moment was cut short by the director hurrying over to them. He was slightly shorter than Charlotte, with a thick Australian accent that sometimes had Hazel laughing. Especially with some of the nonsensical colloquialisms he used. The amount of times he'd said he was 'keen as' that evening had bewildered the girls.

Charlotte was immediately in 'head of the Blythe family mode', answering his questions with a detailed rundown. Hazel's attention drifted as the twosome spoke. She wasn't the details person, after all. Her attention was quickly snagged by one particular sign: 'dressing rooms'.

"See you in a bit, babes," Hazel murmured before slipping away.

 No one noticed her sidle off, and by the time she had reached the corridor that marked the dressing rooms, the sounds of people had petered away.

Hazel scoped out the names on the dressing room doors. It wouldn't hurt to peek, to have a look at their lives, she reasoned with herself. Just a glimpse. Charlotte could keep the skeleton crew and Jay, the director, safe if something came up. Just five minutes, in and out. *Besides*, she told herself. *Someone has to check and see if nothing bad is in here, anyway.*

She was slipping her hand into the inside pocket of her jacket to pull out the mini lock-pick kit she kept—just in case of emergencies, she swore—when she spotted it. The door with the movie's star actress' name. Hazel's heart skipped a beat. She paused, hand poised in her pocket. Vee was one of Hazel's top celebrity crushes—so much so that she had even gone to a comic book convention to see her panel once. It hadn't been worth it in the end though, what with the lack of personal space and the sparse use of deodorant by other con-goers. *This* was a much better opportunity. No nerds in sight. And it wasn't like the actress was around. So who was she bothering, really?

She didn't even need her kit to break the flimsy lock. With a sharp twist of her wrist, the lock mechanism made a brief, resounding *crack* and the door swung open. With a quick glance around her, Hazel slipped into the room, clicking it shut softly behind her.

Pulling her torch free again, she quickly scanned over the contents of the room. Nothing seemed out of the ordinary. *But you never know.* A lamp sat on an end table by a velvet, oversized chair. She pulled the chain on the lamp and illuminated the room in a soft, golden light that had Hazel keenly aware of the late hour.

Stifling a yawn, she rubbed her eyes under her glasses and set about examining the dressing room.

It seemed about how she expected. Several empty water bottles lay scattered across the low coffee table, a robe hung on the back of a coat rack, and some empty takeaway sat in the bin, waiting to be emptied. Her eyes were playing tricks on her in the late hour; shadows flickered at the corners of her eyes as she swept through the room. She scolded herself. She had been in this business way too long to be had by tricks of the light.

Padding across the plush navy carpet, Hazel headed for the vanity. Taking up an entire wall, it was lined with various makeups, wigs on stands, perfumes, and hairstyling tools. Hazel picked up one of the hairbrushes, turning it over. Seemed ordinary enough. As she went to return it, she froze, eyes darting toward the mirror.

She swore she had seen Vee's face in the mirror, staring at her with a haunted expression. *Jesus fuck, I need to sleep more. I'm turning into Lottie.* She stared at the mirror for a few seconds. Nothing. She spun away, then quickly turned back and looked at it again. Still, the reflection remained the same. Taking a deep breath, Hazel pushed away from the vanity, before glancing up once more.

There Vee was again in the reflection, standing by the shut door, staring at Hazel with wide eyes. Hazel spun on one foot, crouched, ready to spring into action.

No one was there.

"*For fuck's sake*, Hazel. Get your shit together. You're a goddamn Hunter, not a tween in a horror film." Hazel slapped her cheeks, groaning at herself in exasperation. "There's nothing there, look!" She stormed to the door, then back to the mirror, gesturing to her reflection. "There isn't shit here. *Grow* up."

With a frustrated sigh, she rubbed her eyes under her glasses again. She would go find Lottie and see what she'd found out. She shouldn't have snuck off from her, anyway. Her vision blurred—a combination of over-tired, strained eyes and a lack of eye drops—but despite that, she could clearly see what was now staring at her from the mirror, where her reflection should have been. It was Vee, but she was *wrong*. Her skin was sallow, with deep purple smudges under her eyes that almost looked bruised, cheeks hollowed out. Her mouth was a maw, her jaw distended and her teeth razor sharp. Worst of all, it was contorting itself as it crawled out of the mirror.

"You've gotta be fucking with me," Hazel groaned as the creature launched at her, its slender, elongated fingers wrapping around her throat. Hazel was more agile, though; whatever this thing was, it was no match for a seasoned Hunter. Without a thought, Hazel grabbed its wrist, twisting hard with a sickening crack. It screeched and loosened its grip as Hazel shoved it hard back at the mirror, cracking the glass.

"Try me, bitch," Hazel snarled as they lunged at one another. The pair crashed into the vanity, a flurry of limbs and angry hisses. Vee—or whatever was pretending to be her—was still halfway in the mirror as Hazel grappled with it. *How am I meant to stop this goddamn thing?* Hazel tried slamming it against the mirror again, but it wouldn't go back in. *Plan B, then.*

Witha grunt, Hazel succeeded in grappling it in a headlock and *yanked*. She pulled until her biceps strained and sweat pooled at the back of her neck. The creature clawed at her, raked its hands wherever it could reach as she slowly but steadily pulled it from the mirror. Bracing a foot against the vanity, she pried it free with a curse and a yelp.

They tumbled together to the carpeted floor, two flailing bodies fighting for control. It snapped at her as she tried to reach for the dagger strapped to her thigh, narrowly missing Hazel's forearm with its teeth as she twisted out of the way. She tried again, only for it to do the same thing. It leaped at her with reckless abandon and preternatural speed for the third time. It slammed Hazel into something—the coffee table, maybe—and she felt it crunch beneath her, her lower back throbbing. They rolled, and it knocked the glasses from her face, ripped at her curls, but Hazel wasn't going to let up. With a snarl, she flipped the creature onto its stomach, climbing on it with one swift movement.

"Let's see how you like this," she hissed, grabbing two fistfuls of its hair and yanking until it howled. "Bet that feels pretty fuckin' bad, doesn't it?" It bucked beneath her as she drove a knee into its spine. As it thrashed, the door to the dressing room slammed open.

"About time you got here," Hazel joked weakly as Charlotte barged in, the director in tow. She could see that Lottie was about to scold her as Vee-not-Vee managed to dislodge Hazel with an almighty heave. It slammed her into the vanity chair, smacking the same spot in her lower back as Hazel had just done to it.

"Guys, get in here!" The director already had a camera whipped out, excitedly filming the nightmare before him as Charlotte whipped into action. Much slighter, and less fit than Hazel, she was still capable of holding her own as she vaulted over the broken coffee table, hand thrust into her satchel.

"Grab it, Hazel!" Charlotte yelled. Hazel was up in a flash; the creature, distracted by new prey, had lunged at her friend, making it wide open to the Hunter. Hazel landed on its back, securing it in a headlock once more. It reared up, thrashing against her grip. She gritted her teeth as her bones ached.

"Whatever you're doing, hurry up, babes," Hazel hissed as the creature reached back, clawing blindly at her face. It grazed her jaw, leaving a shallow but stinging bitch of a scratch. "Before it claws my fucking eyes out." She caught sight of Charlotte as the creature thrashed again. She dashed across the room, a glint of silver in her hand.

"This will hurt a bit," Charlotte quipped as she splashed the creature in the face. Hazel got a glimpse of the tell tale vial of holy water as it let out an unholy shriek—leaving its mouth wide open for Charlotte to ram a silver crucifix down its throat. "And might have a metallic aftertaste."

It screamed in pain and fury, a wounded animal on its dying breaths. It reared up to its full height, far taller than Hazel or the actress it had appeared as. As they had scuffled, its appearance had changed drastically. The limbs were bent at unnatural angles, seemingly more joints than before. It was more monster than human, its face barely retaining the visage of the actress it mimicked. Hazel pulled down on it with all her might to topple it. It gurgled, the heat from its burning throat palpable through the back of its neck as they fell backwards.

Hazel let go just as it hit the vanity, slamming its full, disjointed body into it. Already cracked from their tussle, it now shattered, tilting forward to cover the creature as the vanity rained shards of mirror-like crystal teardrops. A broken sob emanated from beneath the remains of the mirror as the creature burned away to nothing, and the actress known as Vee emerged from beneath, arms wrapped around herself as though she might fall apart. The director took a step into the room, eyes wide as he glanced between the duo and its star.

"Holy shit," he said, camera limp at his side. "That was *dope as fuck*."

Journal Entry

∽

Doppleganger

*T*he dark side/feelings of a person given form. Generally just 'the thoughts in your head', sometimes an idiot will dabble in shit they shouldn't and lets theirs grow a true form of its own. (See: the incident on set with Vee). They manifest differently depending on the feelings of the person—but can be known to grow in power as the person becomes more unhinged. For example, some are dark shadows, some are reflections, and some are whole-ass separate entities from their creator. In the case of Vee, the Doppelganger took over her reflection before trapping her in there with it, growing in its power.

Thoughts on why holy symbols worked on Vee's Doppelganger: potentially due to her own religious values, and headspace she was in when it was formed? The movie had a lot of evil versus good, and religious paraphernalia had an effect due to her own beliefs as a result?

CHAPTER TWO

❧

HAZEL

"**W**ere you aware that she was dabbling in occult practices at any time?"

Charlotte was spearheading the interrogation of the director as Vee sat to the side, wrapped in a fire blanket as she sniffled, cowering beneath the cover of the blanket. Hazel's friend had her no-nonsense face on as Jay vehemently denied having any knowledge.

They were in the dressing room of the male star of the film. Vee, once she had stopped wailing like a banshee, had begged them to take her out of her dressing room as they tried to question her. She was hysterical—*which, fair enough, but it was kinda her own fault*, Hazel thought—and no one was getting answers out of someone in the middle of a breakdown.

Charlotte kept pushing Jay. *Surely you knew something was up*, she argued. *That's the star of your film*. He kept shaking his head, hands raised in defeat, while Vee's sobs finally quieted down. Hazel watched her, eyes narrowed. Beautiful though Vee was, Hazel couldn't *not* see the evil that lurked under that soft, dewy skin. The actress's dark eyes glanced sideways at her, her chin dipping in acknowledgment.

"No one knew what was going on." Vee's voice was low, trembling. "I—I made a stupid mistake. I was just trying to get into character, to understand my role. I didn't... I didn't know any of it was real. I was just following what the notes said." She buried her head in her hands, weeping. Hazel raised a brow, unable to tell if the tears were genuine, or those of a well-trained actress. Either way, she was out of her wheelhouse, and definitely out of comfortable territory. She'd leave this to Charlotte.

Jay turned to Charlotte, eyes sparkling. "Should we be recording this? This is like some modern-day Warren stuff. Super fucked up what happened to you, hey," he clarified to Vee, "but fucking cool nonetheless, y'know?" His accent thickened as excitement laced his words, to the point that Hazel was struggling to understand him. Charlotte shook her head, cocking her head toward Vee; a silent gesture that said, *Can't you see how fucked up she is right now, dude?* He rolled his eyes, his shoulders slumping a smidge. He didn't pull the camera back out, though.

"Can you tell us about these notes?" Charlotte asked gently, placing a hand on Vee's shaking arm. The actress glanced up, mascara and eyeliner smudged. She looked wild, half-feral, as she sobbed again. Her slim shoulders shook as she took a deep breath, attempting to compose herself. She wiped at the corners of her eyes, smudging her makeup further.

"I found them in my dressing room one day, under my latest script. As if someone had just... left them there for me. I assumed Jay gave them to me, to really help me get into the role. They didn't make much sense at all—it wasn't a printout." She hiccupped. "They were handwritten. I tried looking for information online, but all that came up were some forums about demonology. So, I figured I'd act out how I thought my character would read them. I really wanted to dig into her psyche, to understand her.

"But it went badly." She lowered her head. "There was this... ugliness formed inside of me. Maybe it was always there. But the more I studied these phrases, these ideologies on the page, the more it grew. It was hungry and I was feeding it. All my insecurities, all my envy, all of my doubts—they grew while that monster inside of me fed on them, fed *into* them. Then it took over."

Hazel tilted her head. "I don't get understand why you'd fuck around with something you don't know shit about." Charlotte shot her a warning glance as

Vee flinched, as though hit. She knew that look on Lottie's face—it meant, *Shut up, and shut up* now.

Jumping down from the table she'd been perched upon, Hazel jerked her head at the door. "I'm gonna go do some recon, see if anything interesting was left behind. Have fun." She ducked from the room before Charlotte could shoot her a protesting look. Hazel was a hands-on sorta gal. Better she left before saying something that got her in trouble, after all.

Hazel slipped back into Vee's dressing room—now taped off by the crew, but that wasn't going to stop her—and clicked the door shut behind her, wincing as it latched. Hazel was certain no one else would come in here after what happened, but you couldn't be too sure. She pressed her back to the closed door and gazed about the room, wondering where to start, what to look for.

The room was in absolute mayhem. The havoc they had wreaked while fighting off the Doppelganger had spread further than she figured. She hadn't looked behind her after hobbling out earlier, her back in agony, but now she felt a twinge of guilt. Most of the furniture was shattered beyond use, Vee's belongings strewn across the space with disregard, holes now dotting the walls like Morse code. The room was still salvageable, but Hazel doubted anything within it was. If Vee hadn't been the reason it had all happened, she might have been able to argue with the studio for an upgrade.

Treading carefully, Hazel wove her way through the room. Vee had said something about following notes, and she had latched onto that. Notes to do what, exactly? If this is where she had done it, then surely, those would remain in here. They would need them to follow up on the case and do clean up, to make sure no one else got the same dumb idea. To see if anyone else *did* have the same dumb idea. Notes implied she got them somewhere—Vee was no occultist, after all.

That meant someone with knowledge was doling this shit out like schoolyard trinkets.

As she crept through the room, her boots crunching on shards of broken mirror like bones in a crypt, Hazel turned over bits of paper and folders, searching for anything that might provide a clue. She paused every so often to glance over something, accidentally spoiling herself for the new movie in the process. Charlotte would have told her she didn't need to flip to the back of the script and read the last few pages, though. And she'd probably be right.

She placed the notes down on the remnants of the broken coffee table. As she went to stand back up, a page that had floated to the floor caught her eye. Snaking a hand forward, she yanked it free from the corner of the settee it was trapped under. Her hand shook as she brought it closer to her face than necessary. For a moment, she thought she had imagined it. But there it was, clear as day.

Atticus.

Blood roared in her ears as she stared at the name, unseeing, unfocused. They had seen neither hide nor hair of the demon child since the night The Order had been vanquished. Since the night Wade had disappeared. Her hand trembled as she scanned the paper that contained the demon's name. It was one page of many, it seemed. His name was scrawled in ink with a question mark beside it, sloppily added, like an afterthought.

Who had written this and why?

She wanted to go interrogate Vee, to shake her down. Had she somehow spoken to the demon? Was there a way to? The cogs in her head began turning as she scrambled under the settee, hunting for the other pages. She grabbed a handful, about to scour them, when a knock came at the door.

"Hazel? You in there? It's time to go."

Fuck. She didn't want Charlotte to see these papers, to see the glimmer of hope they provided. "Coming, babes! Just, uh, making sure I didn't drop anything in that fight. It'd be real fuckin' stupid to leave weaponry lying around, y'know?"

She scrunched up the pile of papers and crammed them into the front of her leather jacket, zipping it with a grunt. It wouldn't close past her stomach. No wonder Lottie carried her dorky little satchel around. Hazel swept a panicked glance around the room. There had to be something she could hide the papers in until she could read over them properly.

There. One of Vee's dressing gowns lay abandoned at the side of the vanity, dangling over the cracked edge. Hazel vaulted over the debris, snatching it up. With one fluid motion she it slipped on and was tying it into place, papers stashed neatly away near her breast, when Charlotte opened the door. She stared at the Hunter, who flashed a grin.

"What are you doing?" Charlotte sighed. Hazel merely winked as she sauntered past the other girl.

"Just taking a souvenir, babes."

"This has been exhausting."

Hazel glanced towards Charlotte as the other girl leaned her forehead against the steering wheel of the RV, eyes closed. The clock on the dashboard flashed. 4:24AM. They'd been in there for an entire work day trying to figure out what was going on. They'd also been up for almost an entire twenty-four hours now, too.

"Babes, we physically cannot drive back to Boston tonight. That's like, a twelve-hour drive if we don't stop. Not happening. We can go stop in a Walmart parking lot or something, we need to crash for a bit. Scoot over, I'll drive." She didn't wait for Lottie's response before climbing over, waving her into the passenger seat. Charlotte didn't so much as whisper a protest as they traded places. Once her seatbelt was buckled, she kept her eyes closed, trusting Hazel to take over.

So Hazel put them into gear and drove away from the studio as her friend began dozing. Hazel kept the music off; both to let Charlotte sleep, but also to mull over what she had seen. There was no way in hell there was another demon going by Atticus. It had to be him.

And she was gonna find out why his name was on those papers.

Charlotte snored lightly away on the bed next to her, an arm flung out, wisps of hair loosed from her braid. Hazel was still used to sleeping alone, despite these trips together. Unfortunately for Hazel, Charlotte's heavy breathing had woken her from with had been a light, tumultuous sleep. Judging from the angle of her pillow and the sheets wrapped between her legs, it had been a night of tossing and turning. She stifled a yawn as flashes of nightmares burned their image into her mind: of a twilight sky; towering stone buildings; of dark winged creatures stalking the sky. She suppressed a shiver and rolled onto her side, propping her head on her elbow as she turned to watch her friend sleep.

Streaks of sunlight managed to sneak in through the edges of the curtains, bathing Charlotte's face in a warm glow, a smile on her face as she dreamed. *Was she dreaming about him?* Hazel wondered about what had happened in this very RV a year ago, when it was just Charlotte and Wade together. Hazel had gone separately to the Witch and the ghost, had a separate journey and travels that converged again only after a bond had been formed between the two. One, she was ashamed to admit, that had stoked fires of jealously within her.

What had been said in this very room? She only knew bits and pieces of the weird and unconventional relationship between them. Sure, they had been *obviously* infatuated with one another, stealing glances when they thought she and Gran weren't looking. But what *had* they been to each other?

She recalled the cold, early winter day they had said goodbye to Wade properly. They'd held a wake of sorts, and a small dam had broken within Lottie. One that

Gran said had needed to break for a while. There had been a festering wound in her friend's heart for a long time, and it wouldn't heal properly without a fresh cut. Afterwards, the pair had talked long into the night, about everything and nothing. They had curled up in front of a roaring fire, with cups of tea and a blanket wrapped around their shoulders, bringing them close together. And Lottie had cried.

She cried for her parents, for their absence. She cried for the years she had spent holding her grandmother at arm's length. And she cried for Wade and his loss.

Even at the end, Hazel hadn't quite understood Wade van Baird. An Edwardian ghost, his family one of the highest esteemed families in The Society, one day vanished. Then a hundred and ten years passed, and he was suddenly seen for the first time since he disappeared by none other than Charlotte, at the scene of a massacre. The pieces of his story were fleshed out into a narrative greater than Hazel could have ever imagined. Evil cults, a fascist seeking to overturn The Society from within, necromancy, and demon contracts. All these things were nonsensical to her even now, and she literally hunted down the supernatural.

Her thoughts drifted back to the notes she found in Vee's dressing room. How Atticus' name was scrawled across a sheet of paper. They hadn't had much to do with the demon child, beyond summoning him once for information. Not that he was much help. He had some sort of pact with Wade, and the Order of The New Dawn, but other than that—what was he, and why was his name involved in something that had so little to do with the events of last fall?

She'd ask Charlotte about the conversation she and the director had with Vee after Hazel left. In the morning, after some rest. Maybe Vee had dropped some hints; maybe she'd made contact with Atticus. Whoever had given her these notes knew of the demon, and that told her that maybe, just maybe, someone had reached him recently. And that meant maybe she could too. And then maybe she could reach Wade.

Smiling softly at her sleeping friend, Hazel laid her head back down on the pillow. Charlotte deserved happiness. Hazel wanted to do whatever she could to make sure that happened.

JOURNAL ENTRY

WHO IS ATTICUS

- *How did Vee's notes have his name?*

- *Must be a high-ranking demon??*

- *What would the sassy child want in exchange for info on Wade? <u>don't make deals dumbass</u>*

- *Winterbourne: any research available there?*

- *How <u>do</u> you summon a demon?*

- *Where would I find his <u>real</u> name?*

Chapter Three

Atticus

"Ah, I was wondering when you would awaken, my dear friend."

His heart skipped a beat as the words slipped from his mouth, heavy upon his tongue. His breath hitched slightly as his friend stirred from the slumber that had transported them there.

Wade's eyes snapped open, his mouth a tight slash across his face. His tousled auburn locks fell across his brow, a sheen of sweat glistening across it. He grunted, an indistinct sound, as he struggled into a sitting position, bewilderment etched across his face like an open book. But he *was* an open book, wasn't he? There was something about Wade that cracked opened something in the daemon's chest, a yearning of sorts. A desire of some kind.

"Atticus?" Wade's low tenor was raspy, as though he hadn't used it in some time. Atticus supposed his friend hadn't; time moved differently here, after all. Even he was unsure how long had passed since the battle of Umbra Hollow and their arrival in this place.

Atticus had woken sometime before in what could only be described as a cell. Rough, stone-hewn walls surrounded them. A spelled firefly provided illumination, grayish light from above. There were no windows here and the iron door stung when he touched it earlier. He had already scoped out the cell—about ten-by-ten feet, a cube that wasn't designed for two people to be comfortable inside. Well, it was not designed for *people*, he had conceded. Daemons didn't need any of the quaint comforts humans did. And who had expected a human to be imprisoned in the Mountain of the Daemon Realm?

He had only realized they were trapped within the Mountain after the sting of the door on his flesh. Also, the fact that he was contained in the form of a mortal teenager still, his power only available in low ebbs. He was confident it was merely a formality, due to Wade being bound to him. Once someone in his family came to sort this out, he could begin to find a way for him and Wade to return to the land of the mortals.

"Yes, dearest." Atticus crouched beside Wade, reaching out a hand. His friend flinched, and that stung worse than the door. The daemon sighed and withdrew his hand, but still remained on the balls of his feet, rocking slightly. "It is me. You're safe, Wade. I can promise you that."

"Where am I? Where are *we*? I—" Wade paused, a choked cry slipping from his throat. "*Lottie.* My beloved Lottie. Where is she? Is she safe? I... I cannot seem to recollect. Everything is a haze."

Atticus suppressed the urge to roll his eyes, if only for sake of his dear friend. Humans in love were sickening. "Fine, last I saw of her. Well on her way to reclaiming The Society from Dirk and the Order. I am certain she continues to fare well."

Wade buried his face in his hands and let out a low moan. Whatever magic had been affecting him, only the tether between the two remained. And that pesky red thread to the Blythe girl, Atticus supposed. Wade had returned to the evening wear that had adorned him for the last century within the phylactery. It was rumpled in places from his sleep in a way that it never had when he was a shadow of himself, a ghost. This meant he had returned to his preferred form though, Atticus was pleased to see.

"Where are we, Atticus?" Wade's gloved hands didn't move from his face as his shoulders shook from the unburden of unshed tears. "You must... you must tell me everything."

The daemon frowned, but who was he to deny his friend?

Unfortunately for them both, Atticus didn't have any of the details, but he had an idea of what was going on.

"We are in the Daemon Realm," he explained to his perplexed friend. "There are several layers; your mortal realm, the Veil in which spirits reside, the Beyond where souls are reborn, and here, the Realm of Daemons."

"Hell?" Wade interrupted, his voice a timid whisper. Atticus had stopped himself from laughing, pausing to consider.

"Not in the sense that your fanatics have painted, but similar. Powerful beings reside over the land. Some of the other families have inspired mortals in their imagery of demons and angels, but honestly, none of us are all too invested in what goes on in your world." *Most of them.*

"Am I truly dead now, then?" Wade stared somberly at his gloves, brows drawn together. The heir to the Van Baird family wore his heart on his sleeve, easy to snatch—and even easier to break. Resignation was scrawled across the pages of his broken heart.

"Of course not." Atticus reached over to pet his shoulder comfortingly, but Wade jerked away from him once more. He huffed, a sharp little exhale from his nose—the closest he'd probably ever shown to being frustrated with Wade. Why was his friend acting like this, after everything he'd done for him? He remembered how complicated and broken humans were and decided to let him be for now. He could continue to be the more forgiving one, the bigger person, so to speak. "Your soul was tied to me. Of course you weren't going to *die.*"

"But how? Lottie stabbed me after my soul jar was broken, and I was no longer tied to it by dark magic," Wade argued. "Humans die, Atticus. They pass on once that time comes. And I, through some curse of existence, have done so twice."

Atticus shrugged. "We had a deal. You made a pact to be my friend forever, and I would loan you my power. And part of that power is my own immortality. Don't you remember?"

Wade's slate-gray eyes locked onto Atticus, widening with horror. "You never said I would become immortal," he whispered.

"You never *asked.*" Atticus shrugged again. "I thought you would have figured it out from context."

"But I aged! How can I be immortal if I age?"

"I never said I gave you eternal youth, Wade. Don't be ridiculous."

Wade lowered his gaze again, staring at his palms. Atticus' chest tightened once more. He wanted to comfort him, to reach out again and breach the divide between them.

"My family will work this all out for us, and get us out of here," the daemon assured the mortal. "And when they do, I promise I will find a way to get us back home, dear friend."

"How long have we been here, Atticus?"

Wade finally broke the silence between them. After their talk, he had retreated to a stony corner, knees pulled up to his chest as he stared silently ahead, apparently lost deep in thought. Atticus had been scrutinizing the door for any weaknesses, testing the reach of his limited powers, when Wade's voice jolted him from his examination. His head snapped up, audibly cracking as he turned to Wade.

"Oh? You've deigned to speak to me, then?"

Wade's gaze remained fixated on the wall before him. He did not acknowledge Atticus' snide remark as he repeated, "How long have we been here?"

Atticus loosed a sigh. "I cannot say. Time doesn't work the way you know it to, not here. And I cannot say how long we were suspended in the in-between before they allocated us to this cell."

Wade's eyes shifted in a sideways glance. "What about your magic?"

"Unfortunately, rather limited. That's the whole thing about cells in our world. Splendidly crafted to work against magical beings, myself included."

"So you're not good for anything." Wade lowered his head to his knees. *Ouch.*

"I wouldn't say that." Atticus folded his arms across his chest. He wouldn't let Wade see that his words were getting to him. "I have connections, you know. From our time together, I thought you would know that I am not some lower-level underling. I am an heir to a Family. That might not mean something to you, but it does here."

They fell into silence once more, the air thick with tension. Atticus returned his attention to the door, an excuse to ruminate on their exchange. He trailed a hand lightly over the door, the spelled iron scalding his fingertips as he welcomed the discomfort. A distraction from the thoughts that were threatening to crash over him like a tidal wave. He wouldn't acknowledge them, acknowledge the distress they caused him. Not in front of Wade.

It was better they didn't speak on it any further, Atticus reasoned. Wade was too emotional, after all. His friend would go back to normal and they'd put this all behind them, eventually. He'd remind Wade of the summer days they spent together, sharing secrets in the shades of the trees, the midnight whispers as they lay on their backs, the backs of their hands brushing against one another as they giggled through the long, dark hours.

He will care again, Atticus told himself. *We are Wade and Atticus. We are destined to be best friends forever.*

Wade promised.

"Asterius."

Atticus jolted awake, the wisps of his blond locks sticking to the side of his face as he brushed them and sleep away. He had sat in the corner opposite Wade, determined to watch over his friend as he slept, like he had many times before. He hadn't meant to fall asleep too. He wasn't accustomed to it, didn't normally need it. Had it been that long since he fed? How little energy remained within him?

He recognized the voice as he grasped the stone wall and scrambled to his feet. His usual composure had slipped. He cursed silently as he straightened himself, forced himself to slip into the usual charm he wore like a shield. Atticus brushed his sleeve with all the nonchalance he could muster.

"Nox. How lovely of you to come visit us. Alas, I am deeply regretful and humbled to inform you I am unable to provide much hospitality in these quaint lodgings."

Atticus' older brother filled the doorway to the room. Atticus glanced behind Nox, a slight tug in his stomach to see that it was closed firmly behind him. The sounds of Wade rousing filled the space as he took his brother in.

Asterius and Nox, the two sons of House Lyra. He supposed mortals might have mistaken them for kin in their human masks. Atticus favored the form of a slighter, younger boy. Nox towered over Asterius, but they had similar coloring; blond, blue-eyed. Where Asterius was lean, his brother was bulky. It was almost comical—if it weren't for those few features they had alike, they may as well be night and day.

Nox's deep voice filled the room as his eyes slid over to Wade. Only the slight flicker in them betrayed any surprise, any emotion. "I'm sure you've realized this by now, Asterius, but you are to be put on trial for binding a human to you and bringing them here. You know that this was forbidden of you, and yet, you did it."

"I'm sure I'm neither the first nor the last, dear brother."

Nox ignored Atticus. "We will tend to your human companion soon. We realize that they have different needs than we do."

"Perhaps some better accommodations would suit his frail humanity better, then?"

A chill ran down Atticus' spine as his brother looked him deep in the eyes and said, "You aren't just in here to keep your magic at bay. It's keeping him safe. Do you not think his light would be devoured should he leave this room?"

Wade audibly gulped, and Atticus could feel him shifting, getting behind him. That relieved him somewhat. "Could we at least get the poor creature some mortal comforts brought to him then, if we are to be kept like animals?"

With a nod, Nox grimaced at his brother and left with a sweeping motion, the iron door clanking behind him. Atticus' heart raced as they were left alone once more. He was on trial. He'd never been before—he had always skirted the lines of what was allowed. But surely his family would intervene. There couldn't be any true consequences for a son of a Family. He would be fine.

"I forgot that was your real name," Wade said softly. "I... forgot a lot, it seems." Atticus turned to find Wade visibly shaking. "What did he mean about going on trial? Like in court?"

"Something akin to that. But it's just a formality, I am sure."

Wade looked doubtful, but said no more.

CHAPTER FOUR

∞

HAZEL

"**G**randmother! I can't find new my coat, have you seen it?"

Charlotte's voice floated down the staircase of Winterbourne, interrupting the sounds of a house awake and already in the thick of the day. Hazel lounged against the bottom of the banister, lazily biting an apple as her friend scurried around on the floor above, calling out again. Hazel had been ready for hours now; Charlotte, despite months of growth, still lacked time management skills.

"I thought she would be ready by now," Edith huffed as she hurried through a door down the hall towards the stairs, Charlotte's coat draped over her arm. Hazel shot her a grin as the older woman passed. Edith paused on the bottom step, brow furrowed. She leaned forward and wiped Hazel's cheek.

"Gran! I'm not a baby!"

Edith tittered and gave her a look. "I'm not treating you like a child, Hazel. Grandmothers can't help themselves."

Hazel rolled her eyes, but a glow of happiness filled her. It was nice to be considered one of the kids so readily by Edith. She had transitioned into being a member of the Blythe family so easily that sometimes the Williams family almost forgot that Hazel was one of them. It wasn't a bad thing; Hazel loved having two families.

"Come, chat and walk," Edith beckoned as she climbed the stairs. Hazel pushed off the banister and bounded after Gran, apple in hand. "I want to know how you're feeling about today."

"Breezy," Hazel quipped. "It's no big thing."

In reality, it *was* a big thing, and Hazel's stomach was knotted so hard her intestines could earn Boy Scout badges. In the past, meetings in The Society had taken place behind closed doors, in the homes of the bigger families. After the events of Umbra Hollow, there had been a shift, both in power and direction. With Dirk Ashgarde's death, and Charlotte's impressive—almost downright intimidating—display of power, the dynamics shifted. Without meaning to, as her friend took her place at the head of the Blythe family, Charlotte had taken over as the unspoken head of the community. And she'd immediately dragged Hazel along with her. *We are the generation of change*, she'd told Hazel late one night. *And we will make sure of it.*

And she'd been true to her word. After months of planning, of recovering after the traumatic events of last summer, they'd made leaps and bounds. Today was their first ever official open conference, open to the entire supernatural and occult adjacent community. Held in Boston Park Plaza for their opening year—covered entirely by the affluent families, thanks to Charlotte, who had argued it was only fair they paved the way for others in the community who hadn't had a voice before now—there were to be delegates from all across America. Hazel was going to be there to represent the small town she'd grown up in. Lottie made her hopeful for a better future.

She trailed after Edith to Charlotte's room. She was sure today was the start of a new future.

Hazel clutched a mimosa in one hand, the other thrust in her jacket pocket, fingernails pressed into her palm as she kept a smile plastered on her face.

They were in one of the more opulent, open rooms that the Plaza had to offer. A giant stage filled one end, decked and ready for discussions. Round tables were dispersed amongst the space, name cards on tables. Hazel hadn't seen sashes on chairs before, except one time at wedding—they were way too bougie for regular use. Along with the white stained walls and the gilt everywhere, she felt extraordinarily out of place.

Charlotte looked like she belonged there, though. Hazel trailed behind her friend, self-conscious about wearing her favorite leather jacket. She knew it was a mistake when she saw the high-waisted designer jeans and fashionable blazer her friend had opted for. *Her* outfit screamed authority, whereas Hazel's screamed, 'I don't like authority.'

They'd arrived as the catering was finishing set up, right before the doors opened for the meeting. They were mingling first thing, Charlotte told her as soon as they'd arrived. They had to set the tone for the day, to make those changes. Many of the Society families that hadn't been wiped out by the Order had chosen to send younger delegates at Charlotte's urging. It was their chance for a completely fresh slate.

And so they'd spent the last hour introducing themselves, sipping their drinks, and getting to know people. Hazel had shaken so many hands, she was sure she'd have to bathe in sanitizer to avoid getting a cold. But she'd done it. She'd worn her little stick-on name tag, and she'd listened, and she'd watched Charlotte act like a completely different person to the walled-off brat she'd first met. This Charlotte was confident, open, relaxed.

She wasn't faking her bravado anymore. She *was* brave. It made Hazel warm inside to consider.

"I heard those shadows that Dirk was using against us have been seen again."

Hazel's head whipped around, searching for the owner of the voice. She and Lottie had been engaged in conversation with some representatives from the west coast when she heard it. Charlotte was unfazed; she mustn't have heard anything. Hazel spotted the speaker: a younger rich girl, gathered in a small group of similar socialites. She returned her attention to the group she was in, but strained her ears, listening in.

"You've got to be joking. Ashgarde is *dead*. I saw him with my own two eyes after Charlotte Blythe went *at* him."

One of them gasped. "Are you for real?" The others tittered nervously. Hazel smiled blandly at her group. Maybe she could wander closer to listen in. She shuffled a step backward, but Charlotte was fast. Her hand snaked out, gripping Hazel's wrist. Not tight, but enough to know that she couldn't leave. All without her so much as breaking conversation or eye contact. Hazel resigned herself to listening from where she was. Was Charlotte also ignoring them, too?

The socialite that had gotten Hazel's attention continued now that the low 'oh my gods' had stopped. "He might be dead, but that doesn't mean his cause is. Someone else could be doing it. It's just a rumor, anyway. It's not like it's actually happening."

They murmured low agreements that Hazel couldn't quite hear. Is that really all they had?

"Maybe someone in their family is doing it?" Now *that* caught her interest.

"Nah, no way. They all died besides Bradley, and he's been super into this transparency thing that the Blythe's have been doing since the *thing*. Which, y'know, valid? It's a bit too goody-two-shoes, but it's way better than what we had."

"Yeah, no way Bradley is going to do that," one of them agreed. "I heard he ratted out his granddaddy pretty hardcore. So the Ashgardes' wouldn't have the people to make a coup happen again. There's only *one* of them left and they need to make kids happen." She giggled obnoxiously. Hazel was going to vomit up her mimosa at this rate.

"At least Bradley is super hot. That won't be hard for him to do. I'm surprised he hasn't been snatched up yet, given that, y'know, he's in charge of his family now."

One of them snickered. "Looks like Lots is going to be going after that particular title, if you know what I mean."

Hazel resisted the urge to roll her eyes. She was done listening to them now. They had no actual useful information. Like Charlotte was going to go after the grandson of the dude that fucked her and Wade over.

"Hey, have you even been listening?" Charlotte hissed at her as their own group broke up. Hazel smiled blithely.

"Of course, babes. That's what I'm here to do, right?"

Charlotte gave her a dubious look. "What are you thinking? You've got that look again."

Hazel was saved from answering by a little old woman toddling up to Charlotte, who immediately launched into a tirade about some hell-hounds that had been barking late at night and keeping her awake. Charlotte shot her a desperate look before turning her full attention to the problem. Hazel sighed in relief, taking advantage of the moment to slip away for a reprieve.

Hazel's drink was empty, but she didn't want to draw attention to herself, and flagging down a server for another would definitely do it. She had wriggled her way over to the side of the room and was now hiding by a pillar next to a long buffet table. She'd been slowly picking at the shrimp, and estimated she'd had at least three shrimp cocktails. Hazel figured that she wasn't paying for it, so she might as well enjoy herself.

She leaned against the pillar, one leg bent, foot planted against it as she picked at the remains of her fourth glass of food. She'd been watching Charlotte from a distance, keeping an eye on her. Should she have been more involved with things? Yeah, probably. It was nice to finally have her people, the underdogs of the world, included. But Hazel wasn't exactly a planner. She worked best *doing* stuff. If they needed her to take down some monsters, she was all over it. But as her family used to tell her, she wasn't the most *diplomatic* person. Not the way Lottie was. Her temper would flare easily and she struggled to communicate what she wanted.

Hell, even the first time she met Charlotte, she composed herself in the crowd and went over what she was going to say in her head beforehand so she didn't make a total ass of herself.

She couldn't talk the way Lottie did. She couldn't handle people as well as her friend. There was something to her, an aura that sucked people in, even when she wasn't actively trying to, like she was now. Hazel had felt it even when she was just watching Charlotte's videos. At first, she used her for information, but she'd been drawn in by her. They'd felt like friends before they'd ever even met. Even when Charlotte was being a melodramatic bitch, Hazel still loved her fiercely.

She placed her glass down on the edge of the table and stretched, dropping her leg back to the ground. It was probably time to wander back over. Lottie was going to be grumpy with her for hiding so long, but the surrounding crowd had thinned and her attention would be less divided now. As Hazel took a step toward Lottie, so did someone else.

A tall, dark-haired man approached Charlotte, hands in his pockets, walking in away that Hazel could only describe as *swaggering*. He was lean, and confident in a way that rich boys were raised to be. She knew exactly who he was—Bradley Ashgarde.

She clenched her fists as he crossed the distance to Charlotte, touching her forearm, bringing her attention to him. His hand lingered on Charlotte's arm as the two broke out in animated conversation. A horrid knot formed in Hazel's stomach, like she was going to be sick. The casualness of his touch, and the way Lottie didn't draw away from it—what was going on?

Hazel had resolved to stride over and break it up when a voice interrupted her thoughts of snapping Bradley in half.

"It's nice to see someone else deciding to hang out in the corner near the food for once, too."

Hazel's curls bounced around her face as she turned in surprise. It was a familiar, sweet, almost honeyed voice. Where had she heard it before?

The owner of the voice was a cute girl in trendy street wear, her long, silky black hair in a high side-ponytail. Her dark brown eyes sparkled as she gave Hazel a soft smile, and Hazel knew *exactly* where she recognized this girl from.

It was Cherry Pop, a famous Japanese idol. Hazel had dragged Lottie with her to the New York show just the other weekend. Hazel's eyes widened.

"You're Cherry Pop," she blurted out. She immediately felt her cheeks heat up. "I mean, you know you are, I, well—what are you doing *here*?"

It was Hazel's second celebrity crush up close in a matter of weeks, and she was blowing it. Thankfully, the idol let out a gentle, tinkling laugh and waved a hand. "That's just my stage name. My actual name is Rini Sakamoto. But you can call me Rini." Cherry Pop—*Rini*—had the slightest, softest accent punctuating her words. The idol winked at Hazel, whose throat closed up just a little. "And what can I call you?"

Hazel stared at her dumbly for a moment. Hazel was a ladies' lady and was usually instigating her flings. This was new, weird. Was Rini *flirting* with her? The idol cocked her head to the side, a smile still on her soft, lip-glossed lips as she waited.

"Hazel," she finally blurted out, stunned. "Hazel Williams. I'm, uh, here with Charlotte. Charlotte Blythe. She's running this conference."

"I'm aware of Miss Blythe." That laugh again. Hazel's stomach knotted further, a queer fluttering. "She was the one that extended me an invitation, after all."

"You were invited? To like, sing?"

Another laugh. "No, Hazel. I'm here on business. I'm a Slayer. Being an idol is just my day job."

Hazel's entire world was tilting. One of her favourite singers was not only here, but was also part of her secret, supernatural world? And a Slayer? What was that? Did that mean she was a Supernatural Hunter, too? Hazel asked her.

"Yeah, I guess that's what you would call it here." Her slight accent dotted her words, which honestly made her even cutesier to Hazel. "I hunt down the bad things, like Oni and Yurei, to keep people safe. There's a whole group of us that work together."

"How do you manage to do all of it? How do you have any time for yourself?" Hazel's curiosity was overriding those other feelings now. She relaxed her stance, crossing her arms, not wanting to seem too eager. Rini shrugged her slender shoulders, her blocky, zip-up hoodie doing little to hide her slim frame.

"It's life. You have to learn to balance things. I'm old enough now that I've worked out my priorities. It means some things I don't get to do, but that's okay. The things that don't make the cut into my schedule are the things that don't matter." She gave a grimace. "I wish some of them I could get rid of. I would love to not do workouts at five in the morning, but it's too important to two of the big things I love."

Hazel nodded. "I get that, babes. Like, ugh, I hate stretching and doing it for an hour a day, but if I don't limber up, something might get me."

"You're so right! Dancing has actually been so useful for fighting. I've used some of my choreography to get out of the way of things before."

Hazel's mouth opened in a silent 'oh.' "Aw man, I'd love to see that in action."

Rini smiled coyly. "I'd be happy to give you a personal demonstration sometime."

Hazel blinked. "Yeah, I mean, there are always things to beat up around here."

Rini reached into her pocket and drew out her phone. "Perhaps it'd be easier to show you if we weren't in the middle of fighting. Maybe, like, one-on-one sometime?" She stretched the phone out to Hazel. "Follow your insta for me so I can DM you. I'll be here for a while. I've just wrapped up my tour and wanted to have a little holiday while I'm in America."

In a daze, Hazel reached over for the idol's phone and searched for her profile on autopilot. She clicked the button and went to Rini's page. Followers: over three million. Following: eight-six, now eighty-seven. And Hazel knew most of those accounts were cute planner and bunny owner profiles. She'd stalked Rini's profile enough. She handed the phone back wordlessly.

"Cool." Rini giggled to herself. "It'll be nice to hang out with a cute girl while I'm here."

Hazel was trying to process what the idol said when Jay, the director they'd helped the other day, pushed through the crowd nearby and called out Rini's stage name, waving to her. Rini waved back as he hurried over.

"Cherry, girl, how are you? Glad to have caught you here. I have a project for you that would be sick as hell. I have a rough storyboard on my phone if you wanna look over it..."

Hazel nodded to the two and slipped away as Jay caught Rini's attention. She said a quick goodbye and said she needed to find Charlotte before the presentation started. Really, she needed to go gossip with her friend. Her mind was reeling as she headed into the crowd where she last saw Lottie.

Hazel sat behind Charlotte as her friend stood at the podium, answering questions and concerns from the crowd. The event had been going better than Hazel could have imagined, and her bestie was handling it like a champ. Hazel did wish some things were different, however.

She covertly eyed the seat beside her, currently occupied by none other than Bradley Ashgarde. Hazel grimaced. She couldn't believe he'd been given a space up there, after everything his ass-hat of a grandfather had done. Though she had cackled internally when he'd gone up at Lottie's behest, to apologize for everything that had happened last fall, and all the efforts he had personally put in to make up for it. Charlotte had pinched her when she leaned over and suggested she find some newspaper to make him a dunce hat to go with it, because he looked fucking stupid.

But it wasn't just Bradley and his grandfather, though. It was the betrayal of others in this community, fragile as it was. The way that people were happy to turn on each other so easily. It made Hazel think of Wade, and the harm that had been done to him.

Besides all of that, they were actually doing it. The Foundation—their re-brand and new management from the Society—was taking off. Everyone watched Charlotte as she outlined their plans to engage every aspect of their community: rich and poor, isolated and populated, trusting and untrusting. Hazel's heart bloomed as she explicitly stated her expectations for those in positions of privilege to share that privilege, that it would no longer be abused. So that they were doing their best to not repeat the actions of The Order of the New Dawn or the Society.

She was stupidly proud of her friend.

Journal Entry

~~Should I DM her? Oh my God I liked one of her old comments from three years ago. I can never let Charlotte know.~~

The notes I found in Vee's dressing room are a mess: I can barely make out anything about the demon summonings. How the fuck did she read these?

Chapter Five

Hazel

"How do you do it, babes?"

Charlotte frowned at the pile of papers in front of her, twisting an errant lock of hair around her finger. "Hmm? Do what?"

For the last hour since they'd gone into Charlotte's office, Hazel had been lounging on the chaise, occasionally offering commentary while scrolling through social media on her phone. There had been an overcast, miserable vibe to the day—the kind that left her feeling fatigued. All she wanted to do was laze about and do nothing. Yet Charlotte was plowing through an Everest-sized to-do list without so much as flinching.

"All of this," Hazel said, sitting up to gesture at the other woman. Charlotte glanced up, brow furrowed and head cocked quizzically.

"You do all of this, too," Charlotte pointed out. "At least, you should be. Hey, why *aren't* you working today? Why am I doing everything alone?"

Hazel waved a lazy hand. "Today is not the day for it, babes."

Charlotte paused, finger still wrapped with hair, to look at Hazel. "It's the job we signed up for, Hazel, whether we like it or not. The world keeps going, despite what we want."

"Taking time to rest is important too, y'know."

"We don't need to rest. We just had the weekend off." Charlotte dropped her hair to stretch. "You used to work a job with normal hours. You don't get to be slack now, just because you don't have a different place to be for work."

Charlotte was right. Working at the museum back home, as well as her responsibilities with the Foundation, had proved too difficult. So she'd quit her job as an archivist—despite how much she loved it—because this work, creating an equilibrium, was far more important. She'd made a commitment, one that she really should focus on. However, as she told Charlotte with a grin, "The urge to nap is just way too strong today. Maybe you should try having a break, too."

Charlotte sighed. "Are you going to be useful at all today, or are you going to just harass me and keep me from *my* mountain of work?"

Hazel grinned. "I think I'll go with the latter, thanks."

With a roll of her eyes, Charlotte returned to her work, muttering under her breath, the only sound being the scratch of her pen as she made notes. Hazel's attention returned to her phone. She bit her lip as she scrolled through Rini's profile again, watching videos of her singing and dancing with the volume off; she wasn't *that* much of a jerk to Lottie.

Man, she is insanely fucking cool, Hazel thought, her stomach flipping as she watched a reel of her latest concert. The one she and Charlotte had been at. Had this idol really approached *her*? To Hazel, there was such a distinct and hard line between their worlds. For one, Rini was a fucking celebrity. Two, while Hazel was confident in her game, there was something about the Japanese woman that had her feeling nervous; out of the other's league.

"Whatcha doin'?"

Hazel let out a shriek as Charlotte loomed over her, her braid whacking Hazel in the face as the Witch snatched the phone out of her hand. Though Hazel was quick to launch to her feet, her friend was used to her by now. Charlotte's lips curled into a feline smile as she held the phone above her head, out of the shorter woman's reach.

"What's this?" she crowed. "Cherry Pop's Instagram again, hey? Don't you think you're going to wear your screen out with how much you've been on it?"

Hazel scowled and snatched for the phone again. "Bitch, do not make me throw you, because I will."

The girls tussled playfully as Hazel tried to be gentle with Charlotte. It was difficult to ignore her instincts, to ignore her training, to not fight to win. Charlotte may have been taller than Hazel, but she was light as a feather, and about as durable. In the end, she flipped the Witch onto the chaise and snatched the phone back.

"Wow, I've never seen you so tense about a hookup." Charlotte waggled her eyebrows at Hazel, who snorted.

"We haven't hooked up."

Charlotte shot up in her seat. "Wait, seriously? That doesn't sound right. Weren't you going to message her for drinks last week?"

Indeed, Hazel had said that was her plan. In fact, that was what she had been contemplating once more as she stared at the idol's handle for the sixtieth time. There was something stopping her, though. She felt off her game, weirdly flustered. *Intimidated.* So Hazel had chickened out at every chance.

Her face heated as she jammed her phone in her pocket. "Yeah, well, I say a lot of things, don't I?"

Charlotte pursed her lips, but said nothing. Instead, she got back up to her feet and dragged Hazel over to the stately antique desk by the arched windows. "How about you look over what I've gotten done today?"

"Do I have to?" Hazel whined. Charlotte shot her a look.

"I'd like it if you would. Unless you want to tackle the list of things on your own agenda? Like getting that poltergeist out of the Michaelson's toilet?"

Hazel shrugged nonchalantly. "I'll get to it. The old nutters can deal with it for a bit. They were lowkey bitchy to me when I called them yesterday. Maybe," Hazel said, pointedly, "you shouldn't be throwing yourself so hard into the Foundation. Burnout is a bitch. You're allowed to be sad about him and focus on that, too."

Charlotte bristled at Hazel's words, returning her attention to her papers, but clearly wasn't focusing on the work. Instead, she was clearly pretending not to have heard Hazel. "It's okay to be lonely, you know, and to want to be around each other. I get lonely sometimes, and I know Grandmother does, too. You can hang out with me if that makes you feel better."

Hazel gazed up at the window frame, letting out a chuckle. "Me? Get lonely? Never have, babes. I can see why you'd miss my gorgeous mug, though. As well as someone else's." She picked up a paperweight on the desk and turned it over, examining it intently as she felt Charlotte's gaze burning into her. Hazel debated skittering out of the room, silently praising whatever benevolent being watching over them when Charlotte's phone rang. The Hunter dropped the paperweight and sauntered over to the windows while her friend answered the shrill cry of the phone.

"Yes, this is Charlotte Blythe. I'm sorry, what has happened? You're joking. Alright, I can organize someone to be out there pronto. Actually, never mind, I'll take care of it. I'll be there shortly."

Charlotte hung up, grabbing her satchel from where it was slung over the back of her chair. "A parent called up after catching their activism-inclined kids making alchemy bombs to throw at politicians. I have to go confiscate them and give them a chat about how we handle things around here. Hold tight, don't make a mess of the study. I'll be back soon."

Without another word, Charlotte had hurried from the room, leaving Hazel alone.

Hazel had never been particularly good at following instructions.

The front door of the grand Victorian manor had barely closed behind Charlotte when Hazel pushed to her feet, nervous energy crackling through her. Her friend had been so *weird* lately. *Well, she was always weird*, Hazel corrected herself internally. She'd been strange in a new way—a responsible, adult kind of way. And Hazel didn't appreciate that.

She sauntered over to Charlotte's immense desk. Gran and Charlotte had explained that it was some kind of family heirloom, passed along the female line. As she eyed it, Hazel thought it was more of a dick-measuring contest. It was intended to be intimidating, a show of power and money. She popped her hip up on the corner and wiggled onto the desk, leaning over to poke through the contents Charlotte had left sprawled across the green leather topper.

She wasn't usually a snoop—but Charlotte had been so secretive and closed off lately. Plus, she told her explicitly not to look. And how was Hazel meant to resist that?

There were multitude of papers scattered about; different reports on supernatural creatures, business contracts, accounting information for the newly formed Foundation. Boring, adult stuff. Charlotte's desk was cleaner than it had any right to be. She knew how gremlin-y her friend usually was. Hazel leaned across the desk, scattering some papers and pens as she brushed against them.

"Oops," she said nonchalantly, continuing her awkward lean across. She had spotted a little card attached to the daffodils that sat to the right of Charlotte's laptop. She'd thought the daffodils were weird when she came in earlier—Charlotte usually had fresh tulips from the atrium cut and placed on her desk. Reaching across, she gripped the little card between her fingers, flicking it open to read the contents. Hazel grimaced when she read over the little card, realizing who they were from.

Thanks for the dinner, Lots. Can't wait to see you on Friday. Bradley, xo.

Hazel gagged as she let go of the card and shuffled her way back across the desk. She should have figured it was him. Still, *ew*. She was about to jump off the desk and go back to her room, when she caught sight of the corner of a hard, faded-looking book. Curious, she grasped it, yanking it free from the pile.

It was dark and the cover was worn. It had to have been *old*. She hadn't seen it in Charlotte's research before. She flicked through, dust and ink washing over her, followed by the faintest whiff of leather and apple. Elegant, sloped script filled the pages. It took her a moment, but it clicked when she saw the dates. It must have been Wade's personal journal. She hesitated. Really, she should put it back. It was too intimate, too personal. Something he shared with Charlotte.

All of those thoughts flew out of the window the second she glimpsed Atticus' name.

Atticus, the demon. Atticus, who disappeared the same night as Wade. Atticus, who seemed to be at the center of a lot of their problems. She had considered trying to reach him somehow, since they laid Wade to 'rest'. But who knew how? Their last attempt, as he had so bitchily pointed out, had been a complete fluke.

She mulled over it as she skimmed a page, dated sometime in 1900, discussing some general japery between the two. Who knew boys were idiots even in old timey times? Hazel spotted the small blond's name often between the pages as she flicked through, wondering if something would jump out to her. Some sort of 'enjoy this secret code to find us, thanks!'.

Perhaps there *was* a code in there, though. It contained all of Wade's deepest secrets and thoughts. And clearly the youthful demon was prominent amongst the pages. Maybe there was something between the crinkled pages that housed a way to get in contact with them. The image of Bradley's arm around her best friend rose unbidden in her mind. Her lips twisted into a scowl. She'd pick the ghost over the Ashgarde kid any day. His Grandaddy might have been the one that was perpetuating evil, but Bradley was just as complicit for letting it happen and going along with it to save his own hide. She'd had this fight with Charlotte many times, including one time when Hazel had said that, "if it looks like a duck and quacks like a duck, maybe it's a fucking facist just like it's grandfather".

They hadn't talked for a few days after that particular fight.

Bradley might not have been Dirk Ashgarde, and he and Lottie might have had some sort of past, but he wasn't a healthy choice for her. Not the right one. And if the idiot took five minutes to sit there and let herself be sad, she'd see how much she missed the stupid ghost. How much happier she was with him. It was, and Hazel gagged to even think it, like the two belonged together. Despite being born a hundred years apart, there was something about them that just clicked. It would have been a lot creepier if he were a vampire or something, but their weird thing made sense in a way that didn't make sense to her.

Hazel just wanted her friend to be happy. Not this faux happy bullshit she had been pulling by burying herself in work, in what she thought people wanted from her. She wanted the *real* kind for her. The kind that made Hazel roll her eyes but secretly feel warm inside. The kind of happy that meant she got to live her life for herself, not for the others around her. And if Charlotte wasn't gonna try to do that for herself, well then, it was up to Hazel to figure it out. She was going to find a way to fix things and get them back to where they were supposed to be.

Journal Entry

Snippet from the diary of Wade van Baird

*F*ebruary 11th, 1906

Atticus has been frightfully excited about tomorrow. I'm not certain as to why, but I am not one to upset my curious little friend with my silly questions. He looks at me like I ought to know, ought to understand his jubilance. So I have been smiling and nodding, feigning excitement on his behalf. Perhaps it is the Saint Valentine ball we are to attend with the Emberly's that has him so riled up? He does quite enjoy dressing up. Perhaps he is excited to dance and be joyful. I cannot imagine that being a demon is all gaiety and happiness. And I would never be the one to deny him those joys.

I just wish that same feeling filled me, instead of this darkness that seems to be eating at my heart. I swear I can hear it in the still of night, its rhythmic thump as it consumes me. And I do not entirely believe that feeling is one that is all my own. It is like a beast that lurks in the shadows of my spirit, waiting to be unleashed.

I never want to admit it to anyone, but I do dread seeing Sarah Rochelle. There is something there lately, behind her eyes, that send disquiet into my soul. Like there is a void behind her eyes, soulless. I would never say this aloud about a lady, of course, as it is not done. But I cannot feel like something insidious lurks there, scrutinizing me. As if the day she fell through the ice took something from her.

Who is to say, truly? I must make peace with whatever feelings of discontent I may have, as this is the path laid forth for me. And I am a gentleman of his word. But I cannot shake the foreboding that seems to loom within me daily, a depression that has shrouded itself about me like a blanket, only to turn and wrap its tendrils about my throat. Regret lurks in my heart near constantly, despite my efforts to quash it.

I have felt hopeless far longer than I've care to admit, I think.

I should have been able to do things on my own, the day I saved her. When I saw her fall through the ice, I could have tried harder. Why wasn't I stronger, faster, able to do it without the assistance of a demon? While I do not regret the bond that has formed with him over all these years, there is a part of me that feels tethered to uncertainty. One foot in my own reality and fate, the other in another. But the moment he offered me a bargain, I was desperate to be more than merely Wade. I didn't just want to save Sarah Rochelle—I had to, to prove I was more than I am. I traded my friendship for his power without hesitation. And I think, despite how I feel, I would do it all again. Even if a little part of me, whispers a dreadful thing:

Why did I have to help her through the frozen pond that day? Why do I feel as though I am cursed in some way because of this?

Should I ask Gran about it? About this pact? He might not be my favorite but damn, poor Wade has had it rough.

CHAPTER SIX

HAZEL

"**Y**ou have to focus harder, Hazel!"

Hazel closed her eyes tight, squeezing them until they ached. Every part of her body and brain screamed at her, discomfort long ago turning into pain. What had originally been words of encouragement from Gran fast turned into a mantra of disappointment for Hazel. While Edith Blythe clearly meant what she said, urging Hazel on, there was a bitter edge for the young woman as she failed repeatedly.

"This is hopeless. Why can't I just give up already?"

Hazel panted as she opened her eyes, glancing longingly at the grass beneath her. She wanted to flop down on it, to not move for a century. It beckoned her in the cool breeze, taunting her. *Just take a little rest*, it seemed to say. *You're shit at magic anyway, so you might as well stop wasting yours and Gran's time.*

Edith stared Hazel down, as if she could hear the mocking words in her mind. "No grandchild of mine is going to give up that easily. Give it another go for me, then you've earned a break. But you will be continuing your training, whether you like it or not, young lady."

Hazel bit back a groan. She loved Gran and that she had accepted the girl without hesitation as one of her own. From the moment she had stepped over the threshold of Winterbourne, Hazel had been treated the same as any Blythe, despite being a Williams. Edith had told her that family is what you make of it—and that Hazel's family was their family. That had nearly brought her to tears. Her parents had died when she was young, and she had been raised by her aunt, alongside her younger cousin. Every day had been a struggle. And now, she had more family who cherished and supported her, both in Boston and back home—where Mama, Auntie Heather, and Ivy still lived.

So it was Gran's love for her that made her give it another begrudging go.

"Fine, she rolled her eyes. "I'll try once more, but that's it for the day, I swear to whatever alien entity that calls itself God. I am exhausted and desperately need a cheeseburger."

Edith nodded. "That's acceptable. Now, focus, one more push."

Hazel took a deep breath, ignoring the sheen of sweat across her forehead, the pitstains on her shirt. She had shucked her leather jacket hours ago, within literal minutes of starting. Despite the temperate day, she was burning up from her efforts. She was also starving and desperate for an iced latte. Though she'd never admit that last part to Charlotte. The coffee in Massachusetts just hit different.

Centering herself, Hazel spread her legs slightly, bending at the knees as she closed her eyes and stretched a hand out in front of her. She focused on the tightness in her core, the pit in her stomach, seeking. Gran was certain Hazel had magic in her, and that if she just focused, it would come. It was easier for witches like Charlotte, who had always been exposed to their gift; had been taught from such a young age that it was just an innate part of her. Hazel, clearly, did not have that same experience. She fought against her instincts, to let herself fall into herself and ignore her surroundings. It was so at contrary to how she operated as a Hunter, as someone who used their fists to vanquish the evil around her.

There. She felt a flicker. Like a pool of warmth that spread through her, a tingle. Like having pins and needles in a warm bath. Opening her eyes, Hazel nearly gasped at the small flame flickering in her palm, blue and sputtering. But it was *there*, she had done it. "Gran, look!"

"Well done, darling." Edith clapped her hands as the flame died in Hazel's cupped hand, as if the slight breeze had snuffed it. Hazel frowned at it, willing it to return, straining herself until dizziness threatened to wash over her. She dropped to the ground when she finally relinquished any notion of the flame returning.

"Why am I so shit at this? Lottie is like some insanely powerful witch, and I can't even make a flame big enough to light a fucking cigarette." Edith cocked a brow at Hazel, a silent reprimand for her language. "Ugh, I'm sorry to curse. But it's bullshit—I mean, it's ridiculous how hard it is for me, and none of you even have to think about it."

"That's comparing apples and oranges, and you know it, my dear." Edith crossed her arms as she peered down at where Hazel now lay sprawled out on the lawn. The older woman, layered in shawls and gossamer fabrics, had a whimsy and delicate vibe to her. Hazel knew better, and that despite her age and perceived fragility, that Edith Blythe could absolute *throw down*. "There are many skills you have that it would take us a lifetime to be even a fraction as good as yourself."

"Throwing things around isn't that complicated," Hazel grumbled. "I'm just the heavy, the sidekick. I get called in when things need to be slapped around a bit."

Edith sighed gently, a wistful expression etched across her lightly wrinkled face. "You're a hero in your own story, Hazel, and I wish you would see that, my darling girl."

Hazel's stomach clenched as she fought a wave of emotion—the kind that threatened to crush a person before they cried. There was something about Gran's words, that mothering tone, that almost broke her. Thankfully, they were interrupted by the arrival of Jacob, the silver platter he carried Edith's afternoon tea on clattering lightly as he treaded down the stone stairs to the lawns. Edith gave him a soft smile as he approached.

"Your afternoon tea, madam." Jacob bowed his head in greeting as Edith leaned in to kiss him gently on the lips in thanks. Hazel squirmed on the grass uncomfortably as the two—much like grandparents to her now—shared an intimate moment. Though Hazel was ecstatic that the two had worked out they were made for each other, it still felt weirdly perverse despite their wholesomeness.

Hazel let out a groan. "I'm right here guys, get a *room*, oh my God. I am basically a child."

Edith and Jacob shared a wistful glance, chuckling softly. Jacob placed a gentle peck on Edith's cheek before bowing to the two women and returning towards the manor. Sipping her tea, the older woman watched his retreating back, a slight flush creeping into her cheeks.

"Are you *blushing*, Gran?"

She scowled at Hazel, before breaking back into a smile. "Even us oldies are allowed to feel the flutters of early love blossoming, young lady. Perhaps we should return our attention to your magic practice?"

Letting out another groan, Hazel threw an arm across her eyes, shielding them from the afternoon sun. She was waning on energy, her stomach contorting as it growled in hunger. "Or we can stop and eat something. It's been *hours*, you monster. A gal has to eat sometimes." She moved her arm up slightly, peeking a glance at Edith, who was nodding to herself in agreement.

"Of course. I shouldn't be pushing you so hard. You need energy to reach the magic nestled deep within you. Come now, Jacob will surely have sandwiches and the rest of this delectable tea ready." She smiled again as she said his name, her eyes softening.

Edith cocked her head ever so slightly, her silver braid glinting in the afternoon sunshine, gesturing for Hazel to get up. The Hunter scrambled to her feet, brushing grass from her clothes, snatching up her jacket and bag as she fell in step with Edith. They followed the same path Jacob had taken moments before, the scents of afternoon tea and scones with jam and coffee wafting on the breeze as they closed the distance to the house.

"I truly hope you girls find love someday, Hazel." Edith's words, seemingly out of nowhere, slammed into her like a tidal wave. "I had it once with my husband, Edgar. And now I get to have it again with Jacob. I hear a particular young lady has caught your attention?"

Charlotte was a fucking tattle-tale.

"I guess." Hazel shrugged nonchalantly. "I mean, it's nothing yet. We haven't gone out or anything, no biggie. So, there isn't really anything to feel yet." She paused, a question heavy on her tongue. "Is Lottie gonna marry Bradley or something? Is that even what she wants?"

They had just reached the patio leading to the doors of Winterbourne. Edith stopped and turned to face Hazel, a sigh loosening from her lips.

"Charlotte is an adult. We have to let her make the choices she thinks is best for herself."

"But is she *really* making that choice for herself, or because she thinks she *has* to, to uphold some dumb generational baby-making plan?" Hazel argued. "It's like an ancestral ponzi scheme she's being sucked into."

"It's not our place to tell her or judge her for those decisions, lovely. We don't get to comment on it."

"But what about Wade?"

Edith placed her hands on Hazel's shoulders, squeezing gently. "Whatever she and that boy had, however odd it was, was special, yes. However, he's gone now, and there isn't anything any of us can do about that. If she's chosen to move on now, then all we can do is smile and encourage her to make healthy choices for herself."

"He isn't healthy for her! He enabled his piece of shit grandaddy! *Gran*! He's just hiding his toxicity behind those stupid baby blues."

Edith looked Hazel in the eye. "We cannot fault someone for the mistakes of their family. Yes, he was a scared young man. But he has always doted on Lottie and wanted the best for our girl, you can believe me. So we will be accepting of what she wants to do."

"But she wants Wade!"

"And *he* isn't here, lovely."

"What if he could be? What if we could get him back?" Hazel furrowed her brow, biting the inside of her cheek. Edith sighed again.

"You need to let this go, Hazel." Edith's tone was still gentle, but decidedly firmer now. "She already went through this with Stephenie and Jackson, she can't torment herself like that again. And you won't be encouraging it. He's no longer tethered to this plane, and we have to make peace with that."

"But we have his journal, Gran. I've been reading it. Atticus and Wade made a pact once before, right? That's how he became a lich. Isn't that what we all ended up agreeing on? So, what if we get Atticus to come here and make him bring Wade back."

"That is a dark and dangerous way to think." Edith's tone sharpened, her fingers squeezing Hazel's shoulders lightly. "We must never resort to making deals and messing with things beyond our comprehension."

"But she hasn't stopped to grieve for him! She's been throwing herself at work and Bradley and stupid traditions. I *know* she wants him back! And we haven't even tried for her."

Edith leveled her gaze on Hazel, her chocolate eyes—so like Lottie's—sparkling fiercely. "If you think she truly isn't processing what happened, then we can arrange something. Talk therapy. Together, as a family. We will do it together, be there for her. The *healthy* option. We cannot entertain wishful fancies that will break her heart again. We cannot do that to her, if we love her."

Pulling Hazel into a hug, she whispered into the Hunter's ear, "Maybe it isn't Lottie who is struggling to move on, dear." As she pulled away, the scent of her perfume, lavender and freesia, lingered in the air. "I'm going to go enjoy afternoon tea, lovely. Go clean up and I'll see you in there."

"Yeah, see you in there in a bit, Gran. I just need a minute," Hazel mumbled. Edith nodded once before trailing across to the back doors of the grandiose house. As soon as the doors clicked shut behind Edith, Hazel plunked herself on the top step of the patio. Dropping her bag and jacket beside her, she dug inside said bag, until she fished out a familiar worn book. She begun flicking through the pages of Wade's journal, intent to find any secrets that may be hidden within.

Journal Entry

Snippet from the diary of Wade van Baird

July 1st, 1893

Atticus is a strange little fellow. It's almost like he wants to be a human and not the elegant, refined creature that books have shown himself to be. He's not even terrifying like the ones in the Bible. He's almost colloquial, casual. He feels like my friend, not a monster. Mother and Father aren't the most certain about him, but that is okay. For we are going to become fast friends, Atticus says. And friends never leave one another behind.

I believe that.

He is much more jolly than Loren, who is basically a baby still. I like having him around. He even has a bedroom next to mine now, and we can tap secret messages through the wall at night when I am supposed to be sleeping.

It's like I finally get to have a brother. Again, I do love Loren, but there is something so different about the boisterous nature of boys. I hope he stays with us forever and that I never have to be lonely.

CHAPTER SEVEN

HAZEL

Breakfast with the Blythe family was never a frugal affair.

On this particular morning, it was a sweet filled, with waffles, creams, and many types of fruits to laden their plates with on the sideboard. Hazel had loaded her own plate with about three times the amount that Charlotte and Gran had, but she was never one to be conservative about good food. Especially when Jacob had gone to such lengths to prepare it, and all that.

Hazel adjusted her glasses as she chewed, listening to Gran and Charlotte. Specter sat on the seat beside her, purring in the morning sun. Their family portrait stared down at her, a soft, happy greeting.

"I wish I had more time to assist you both." Charlotte frowned at her fork, smearing her banana and waffle in a bit of syrup. "But it's been a real pain in my ass—sorry, in my rear—to get on top of everything for The Foundation. We've been making some real progress but Christ, it's not easy."

Charlotte flinched as Edith gave her a look. Hazel bit back a laugh. It was nice to see someone else get in trouble for their language for once.

"She'll get there in no time. I am confident that Hazel's efforts are seeing progress."

Hazel was glad Gran had the decency to say as much, even if she didn't actually think it. Hazel was still as garbage as ever and hadn't gotten any further than her wispy flame for a few days previous. "It's fine, babes. It's no biggie. I can still throw down with the best of them, and that's what matters. I could throw your ass any day."

"Language!" Edith admonished as Charlotte said, "And I'll set *your* ass on fire."

The two girls laughed as Edith shook her head reproachfully. "I will never understand you two, I swear."

"I wouldn't want to if I were you, Grandmother." Charlotte turned her attention to Hazel again. "I have a bit of time around things today, if you want me to show you anything?"

"Nah." Hazel brushed her offer off. She didn't need to see how good Charlotte was, how naturally magic came to her. She felt bad enough.

"It's really fine, I don't mind at all. Now that I can use my magic again fully, it's really fun—"

"I said not to worry about it, didn't I?" Hazel interjected. Shame flooded her, red hot and angry. She desperately wanted the attention to be off her. "Why don't we stop focusing on my useless magic progress and instead have a nice little chat about you and Bradley. I saw he sent you even more tasteless flowers. Petunias, really? That's something an auntie would send, not a *boyfriend*."

Lottie was silent as Hazel's words fell on her tongue like ash. She instantly regretted them, wished she could take them back. It didn't matter how angry she was about her failures, or Bradley. Charlotte continued cutting her waffles, but Hazel could see her ears reddening, her tell. Oh, she was *pissed* at Hazel. But what right did she have to be mad? Charlotte was the one dating the enemy, the grandson of a murderous twat who wanted to ruin all their lives, who played a hand in murdering Charlotte's parents.

So she dug in, despite herself.

"So? Why are you dating him, huh?"

"What does it matter, Hazel?" Lottie's voice was low, quiet. There was an edge to it that Hazel hadn't heard before.

Edith's brow creased with worry. "I think it's time we ended this conversation, girls—"

"Because I thought you love Wade!"

Charlotte was silent for a long moment, her hands gripping her cutlery tightly. "Of course I love Wade, you know that. But he isn't here, is he? He's gone, last I checked."

"Yeah, but—"

"I'm done with breakfast. Thank you for the food, Grandmother. I'll see you tonight. I have an appointment to get to now." Charlotte pushed away from the table, avoiding eye contact with Hazel as she stormed out.

Hazel's blood boiled. They weren't done, and she didn't mean it, couldn't help it, when she called out after Lottie, "Fucking Bradley isn't an appointment!"

"*Young lady,*" Edith snapped, aghast. Specter shot Hazel a reproachful look, jumping off his seat to dart after his master.

"Fuck, I know," Hazel moaned, dropping her head to her hands. Why did she say that? Of all the times to keep her massive mouth shut, that would have been a good one, but no. She didn't.

Edith got up from her chair, sweeping over to Hazel. She gathered her skirts and settled gracefully onto the seat that Specter had occupied moments before. Hazel glanced under her lashes as Edith. "I've messed up big time, haven't I?"

"I don't know what's come over you." A pause, a sigh. "You girls have never fought before and now you're hurling insults across the table? What is under your skin? Why are you so resentful?"

Hazel flinched, as if Edith's words had laid a physical blow on her. The truth was, she *was* resentful. For a multitude of reasons. And they all began to flood out of her, a garbled stream of word vomit.

"It's like she's forgotten Wade even existed, you know? Like she's gotten over it so fast, like we didn't all go through some insane, hella deep stuff together. They were in love, you could see it, and they saw it. But now it's like she doesn't matter because *Bradley* is there all the fucking time."

Edith stared at Hazel for a long moment before speaking. "Is it Wade you fear she's leaving behind, or you?"

Gran was way too sharp for Hazel's liking, sometimes. Hazel squirmed.

"Tell me she doesn't spend a lot of time with the pretentious dillweed, Gran."

"She will never replace you, Hazel," Edith said softly. "Whether you girls say it aloud or not, you're best friends, the closest to sisters I think that either of you will ever see. She won't replace you, ever, and she certainly isn't replacing young Wade. She's dealing with her grief the way she thinks she should, instead of wallowing. She doesn't want to repeat how she became after Stephenie and Jackson, I can see that. She misses her parents dearly. Perhaps it's in your best interest to spend some time with some company of your own. Have you messaged that sweet young lady back yet?"

A groan slipped from between Hazel's lips. "No, I haven't."

"Then perhaps that's what you should do then. Message her, invite her for tea. Our home is welcome to her at any time. That may help you with your mixed feelings about Charlotte spending time with someone else."

"Maybe," Hazel muttered, the pit in her stomach growing, as she thought about a future that didn't have her in the old house with her friend.

She knew she shouldn't have been doing it, but that never stopped Hazel.

After the disaster that was breakfast, Gran had excused herself to have a cute flower shopping date with Jacob. Hazel had searched for Lottie, to apologize to her friend. The other girl was long gone, though, leaving a sleeping Specter behind on her made bed. Hazel's stomach had tugged again, the pit from earlier growing.

She had taken Gran's advice after wandering back downstairs, and slid back into Rini's DM's, inviting her to Winterbourne that day for tea. She had cringed afterwards. It was like they were seven years old and she was inviting her over for a tea party. God, she'd hoped it hadn't come across like that.

Afterwards, though, that had left her alone in the big house. Even the staff seemed weirdly absent. Snatching up Wade's journal—where it lived in her duffel bag at night now—she strolled the property, looking for somewhere to read, to research. As though guided by an invisible string, she found herself at the little chapel by the family mausoleum.

Hazel knew the bear she'd liberated from the Van Baird summer home still sat within, a silent reminder of the chill winter day they had said their goodbyes some months ago. She thought maybe sitting by it would somehow influence the pages of the journal, that she would stumble on the magic formula to bring Wade back by sheer closeness to something of his. She sat in the chapel, on the floor against the wall, as the Blythe's didn't believe in having pews in such a small space. And she found nothing in the journal.

Not nothing, she corrected herself. She learned an awful lot about how Wade felt about the manners of other people, though that was something he hadn't necessarily been quiet about to her.

A smile tugged at her lips at the memory. What a weird ghost. She slapped the journal shut, her butt numb from sitting on the stone floor. Maybe she should go back to the computer and find out the easier way—by Googling it and hoping some individual out there on Reddit was right, or that someone else had stumbled across a queer little demon boy by the name of Atticus.

She climbed to her feet, sliding the journal into her inner jacket pocket. She waltzed up to the teddy bear, intent on paying her respects to Wade and his poor sister Loren, when her eye caught the candles sitting beside the bear. A thought crossed her mind in that moment; if their half-assed summoning circle had worked last time, who has to say it wouldn't work again?

So she'd snatched them up and found herself on the small slab of concrete outside the chapel, rigging up the world's worst summoning circle. She laid the candles out the same way as last time, attempting to summon a meager flame to light them, before resorting to her lighter.

Sitting cross-legged in the middle of them, the journal out on her lap, she started speaking.

"I know I shouldn't be in the middle of this, but I don't have a lot of people and I figure if you turn up, I have a decent chance of kicking your ass." She felt stupid speaking aloud to herself, but she plowed on. "But if you can hear me, Atticus, we need to talk. I... I need to talk to you. To find a way to get Wade back. I know if anyone can help me manage that, it'll be you."

Hazel's words were met with the rustle of leaves and the whistle of the breeze, nothing more. She waited silently, patiently, for several minutes. She clutched the journal, her link to Wade, tightly. Surely, if he were able to listen last time, he could this time?

"Well, I tried," Hazel muttered. She scrambled to her feet. "So much for summoning a demon, hey? Guess I'm just a big sucky failure at all this magical shit."

She blew out the candles, gathering them up to dump beside the bear once more. She gave it a gentle pat before leaving, wishing she could do more, do better.

Her attempt at summoning a demon had been a bust and now she needed a stress relief.

She had promised Gran months ago that she would quit smoking, but it was a process. She couldn't just go cold turkey, after all. And in moments of great stress, it hit the spot unlike anything else. So sometimes she found herself at the side of the atrium, nestled on the brick of a garden bed. Lottie had gotten some tall, leafy plants put in shortly after Christmas, and it had turned into Hazel's unofficial chill out spot. The plants hid her from view as she'd indulge in the occasional cigarette.

She puffed on one now, scrolling on her phone. She wondered if she should tell Gran about her shitty summoning circle, or to drop it completely. At some point, Hazel was gonna have to find Lottie and apologize. If she ever got a moment to speak to her, that was.

Hazel took a long drag, slipping her phone back in her pocket as the cigarette dwindled down to little more than the butt. As she reached for the old coffee can she kept hidden behind the plants as an ashtray, she heard a startled cry nearby and the rush of footsteps on cement. Throwing the butt into the can, she peered around the corner of the atrium, sticking her head between the leaves of the plants, her eyes widening as she beheld the scene before her.

Servants hurried down the stairs to the lawns of Winterbourne, their hands moving in intricate patterns, casting spells, as they barreled down the lawns. Hazel's stomach pooled with dread as her gaze shifted to the source of their panic. Black, flittering shadow demons, so like the ones that had tugged and pulled at them last year, snarled and raced across the grass towards the manor.

"Uh oh," Hazel intoned quietly.

"Uh oh, indeed."

She didn't know how or when the Witch got behind her, but Hazel yelped as Lottie yanked on her jacket, pulling her back through the leaves. She spun in Lottie's grip. "Babes, I swear I didn't mean to—"

"It doesn't matter what you meant." Charlotte was stern, her brow furrowed. "What matters is what you *did*. We have to go clean this up, and then we'll talk about the why and what you *meant* to achieve."

Charlotte dragged Hazel out from behind the plants, yanking her towards the lawn where the servants now pulverized demons with magic, setting them aflame. She caught a glimpse of Bradley, dark haired and lean, as he assisted. She considered using the chaos of the lesser demons as a chance to get a sucker punch in, but the dark look on Lottie's face implied that the other girl knew what she was thinking—and that she would be watching Hazel.

At least Charlotte had the decency to leave Bradley downstairs as she dragged Hazel to the study to ream her.

"I don't know what you were thinking, or what the shit is going on with you right now dude, but this is a colossal fuck up." Charlotte paced as she ranted. She wore her long hair down today, and was twisting the ends in her hands, yanking. "It's like you've turned your brain off. Have you hit your head too hard or something? Do I need to get you a CT scan?"

"I didn't mean for it to go this way, babes! How the fuck did I know that my shitty little circle worked?"

"You know you're meant to close these things, to say goodbye, right? You learned that after the séance last month, I thought, when you threatened to kill the ghost twice. Remember that? You let go of our hands and fucked the séance up."

Hazel flinched. Well, *now* she remembered that...

"Okay, so I fucked it up! Shit happens, alright, it wasn't like I was trying to do evil or something."

"And what *were* you trying to do?"

Hazel stared down at her palms, forearms splayed on her legs. She sat in the chair facing the desk as Lottie paced. Her friend stopped by her, sighing. "I don't want to be mad, Hazel. I just... if there's something I can do to help, you have to tell me. You've been weird lately. Like, weird even for us."

"I thought you were the one being weird," Hazel mumbled. "Everything has changed and it keeps changing and I just—I was looking for a way to make things go back to how they were."

Charlotte told Hazel to scoot over and slipped into the chair with her friend. She draped her legs over Hazel's, wrapping an arm around her friend's shoulder as she pressed their cheeks together. Charlotte squeezed her, hugging Hazel. "What do you mean by that? How did that end up with you summoning a tiny horde of evil?"

"I was trying to talk to Atticus." Hazel couldn't help the rawness in her throat, the threat of tears that loomed. She had hurt her bestie. "I thought... I thought, if I could find a way to talk to the sassy little demon kid, I'd find a way to talk to *him* for you." Wade's name hung between them, heavy and unspoken.

Lottie let out a sigh and squeezed her friend tightly, placing a kiss to her temple.

"I'm glad you care so much about me, Hazel. I truly do. But it's not safe for you to do these sorts of things. You saw what happened today, and it could have been so much worse."

That bitter tang, that feeling of insignificance, began to claw at Hazel again. She was useless.

"I'm sorry, babes," she mumbled. Charlotte squeezed her shoulder again.

"I feel like if he was still near the Veil, he would have let himself be known to me," Charlotte said softly. "But he hasn't. So, I have to be content, hoping that he's finally somewhere where he can be resting."

Hazel didn't say anything. Charlotte continued, "Maybe you need to focus less on me and more on yourself. I'm worried you're falling in a pit and not even noticing. I'll always be there to pull you out, but it'd be super helpful if you didn't fall in to begin with, y'know? Maybe focus on your love life instead of worrying about what might be happening in mine."

Charlotte hugged her friend again, urging Haze to follow her downstairs to apologize for the chaos of earlier. Hazel followed her, meek, quite unlike herself.

Hazel was sick of apologizing and craved another smoke by the time she was done. She was sneaking off to her planter hiding spot—less secret now that Charlotte had busted her—when Jacob interrupted her on the way out.

"Miss Hazel, your guest is here."

"Guest?" she cocked her head quizzically. She never had guests here. It was too far for her auntie and cousin to travel.

"A young lady by the name of Miss Sakamato is waiting in the formal sitting room for you. I believe she has an appointment with you."

Hazel's stomach began to flip and twist, curling into a tight ball that threatened to shred itself. She forgot that she had invited her over, like Gran had suggested.

It had slipped from her mind amongst all the drama of the day. She should have remembered to message her, to reschedule, to cancel.

She couldn't go on a date after everything had happened.

"Perhaps," Jacob interrupted her thoughts as he leaned toward her, conspiratorially, "seeing the young lady will soothe Edith and Miss Lottie after recent events."

Hazel sighed. He was right. And it wasn't fair to put her shit on other people. She forced a smile to her face, her usual buoyant charm and nonchalance. "Guess it's time for me to spend time with a popstar, then."

Journal Entry

Shadow Demons

Wisps of shadow and smoke. These are easily killed with magic, or a good old fashioned beating. Annoying little shits that are more effort than they're worth, and not the prettiest to look at.

CHAPTER EIGHT

HAZEL

April showers bring May flowers. At least, that's what Gran had told Hazel that next afternoon, having caught up on the events of the day before. She pet Hazel's cheek, telling her to leave the past behind with the changing month. And Hazel promised she would try. So that first day of May, Hazel found herself curled up in her room—once a guest room, now her own permanent space in the manor—her notes a jumbled mess on the massive, king-sized bed.

The waning rains of spring clattered gently against the window panes, a soothing melody. A last hurrah of sorts, as the days became longer, before the vibrant greens began to yellow and the cicadas sang long into the night. It wasn't nice enough to be out practicing. So, they had all retreated to their little bubbles in the home, wrapped up in their own worlds for the day. Hazel sought to spend it delving into Wade's journal, into unraveling more of his secrets.

She sat cross-legged in a pair of shorts and a sweater. On the bed side table sat an iced coffee, half drunk. To her left on her bed, her laptop had roughly two dozen tabs open. In front of her and to the right were Wade's journal and her own scribbled notes and thoughts. Thrown into a chaotic disarray underneath those were the notes she had stolen from Vee's dressing room. Clearly, Vee had known of Atticus, somehow, but had failed in her attempts to summon him. Hazel had filled in her journal notes on Doppelgangers further after reading through the papers.

She had spent her morning, coffee in hand, perusing the pages of Wade's journal, back at the beginning from when he first received it. The inside cover was dated May twelve, 1891. There was a note under it, written in a sloping hand.

Dearest Wade; happiest tenth birthday to our treasure. Love, Mother and Father.

That was a little something she hadn't know about the ghost and it made her feel oddly closer. It had humanized him to her more than anything they'd experienced as a group, honestly.

Her note taking hadn't let her know a lot about how to find Atticus, however. His journal entries weren't the longest, or the most often. She couldn't begrudge him that. He had been a dude, even if a weird old timey one. Hazel had made some notes, little bits about him that she thought Charlotte would appreciate later. There wasn't anything truly useful, though.

She stopped flicking through the pages, leaning back against the mountain of pillows littering her bed. Her eyes needed a break. She set her glasses down and reached for a sip of iced coffee before closing her eyes. Just a minute to rest, she told herself. It was a lot of information to take in, especially after the long night she'd had.

She smoothed the silk coverlet beneath her, her toes curling as she remembered the evening before.

Hazel had slouched in after Jacob into the sitting room, unsure of what to do with herself. There was a formality, an awkwardness in the air, that she wasn't used to. As Jacob announced her, a glint in his eye and the slightest devilish smirk upon his lips, Hazel leaned against the door frame, her hands jammed into the back pockets of her black skinny jeans.

"Ladies, please excuse me, I must attend to some important errands for Mistress Edith." Hazel shot the elderly man a look as he brushed past her with a wink. She glanced down at the ground as Rini cocked her head expectantly.

"So uh... I'm glad you came."

Hazel's head shot up as Rini let out a laugh, something between a giggle and a snort. "Really? That's how you're gonna say hi? That's pretty uncool."

Yanking it from her pocket, Hazel raised a hand to cup her neck, fingertips pressing into her skin as she rubbed. She could feel the heat rising in her face. "I'm a little thrown off my game, if we're being for real. It's been a rough one."

"Wanna tell me about it?" Rini shifted on the sofa, patting the seat next to her. Hazel's breath caught in her throat as her brain screamed at her to go, but her body froze up. Like some sort of prepubescent teen.

Come on, Williams, you're better than this. Fucking move, you look like an idiot, she scolded herself internally. *You've been doing this for almost two decades, you got this, fam*. It took her a moment, but she forced her limbs to cooperate and somewhat stiffly approached the sofa, like a robot imitating a person. She slumped down next to Rini, the barest whisper of their thighs pressing together. She gulped, flicking a tongue over her dry lips as she glanced at the idol.

"I'm so sorry, I totally blanked on our—on our catch up." Hazel caught herself before she dropped the word 'date'. She didn't want to scare the idol off. "Some drama happened and things have only just sort of cooled off. I still feel off, not gonna lie."

Rini wore her sleek dark hair down, falling around her shoulders and face like a sheet. Her dark eyes were accentuated by a thin, winged liner she wore, a dusting of blush on her cheeks, and the faintest tint of cherry-scented gloss on her lips, plumping them up. Hazel hadn't meant to, but she gulped again when her eyes landed on that crooked smile, that knowing look.

The idol giggled at Hazel's reaction. She wore high waisted, white baggy cargo pants and a green stretchy tank top with a bold print slashed across it. She was effortlessly cool in a way that Hazel would never, could never be. Japanese fashion was already a decade ahead of America, and Hazel didn't care to keep up.

"How about we just... chill out?" The slender woman suggested, nudging Hazel's shoulder with her own. Hazel was reminded of how close their bodies were, the heat between them.

"I guess," Hazel croaked. The scent of cherries and what appeared to be jasmine wafted over her, intoxicating in a way that no drink or drug had ever been to Hazel. As the temptation to lean in, to close the distance between them, grew, she became keenly aware of the fact that they were in Gran's house. Winterbourne might have been a second home to her, but there was a weirdness to doing something naughty near your grandmother's favorite chair. "Do you wanna uh, go outside?"

The other woman acquiesced with a nod of her head. Somewhat in a daze, Hazel led her through the manor, rambling as they drifted down the patio stairs, past where just an hour ago they'd fought demons, to the giant tree that she and Lottie liked to sit under and talk shit.

So Rini had sat with her under the shade of the tree as they chatted long into the afternoon. There had been an ease, a familiarity, that had surprised Hazel. She was far from prickly, but there was just something about the other girl that had felt right, had clicked.

"Your home is huge," Rini commented at one point. "I have a two-bedroom apartment back in Tokyo, with a living room just big enough to cram a couch and small table in, and that's considered big. America is such a weird place."

Hazel cheeks burned. "It's not... well, it's home, but it hasn't always been. I actually grew up in a tiny three-bedroom down in North Carolina, with my auntie and cousin. I've only had a space here for what, almost a year?"

She hadn't meant to, but she filled Rini in on her life growing up, on training to be a Hunter. About coming from a gifted family that wrenched her parent from her when she was young. How she had watched Charlotte's channel, and some instinct had told her she had to get to know the witch. *That, and her Auntie and Mama had told her.*

She regaled Rini with the drama from last summer and fall, how Charlotte had rediscovered her powers. How they had taken down The Society and had started building The Foundation from its ashes. They talked until their fingers went numb from the brisk air as the day settled into twilight. Neither had wanted it to end, it seemed, but even Hazel had felt the chill of the evening in her leather jacket.

When she'd offered a Rini a hand up, electricity sparked between them as she pulled the idol up. A little too forcefully, it seemed, as Rini had slammed into Hazel's chest. Hazel had good reflexes though, catching the slip of a woman easily.

"How clumsy," the idol had breathed against Hazel's exposed collarbone. "Thank you for catching me, though."

As Rini twisted and placed a delicate, fluttering kiss against Hazel's neck, it dawned on her that Rini's reflexes would have, *should* have, been as good as her own. She hadn't slipped—it had been intentional. Rini had caught her offguard, which never happened. Hazel was the one that flitted into town, picking up one-night stands with suave overconfidence.

And then somehow her hands had woven their way into Rini's hair as their mouths clashed together, hot breath and teeth tugging at lips. Their bodies moved together, two dancers that knew the choreography without rehearsing. Hints of cherry and soda tantalized Hazel as her tongue darted between Rini's lips, teasing her, urging. Hazel pushed the idol up against the tree, bodies pressed tight against one another. Fabric pulled at fabric, tugging clothes up to expose smooth skin beneath. The world fell away, the sounds of their pants and the scraping of bark filling the space around them as the women tangled together.

"We should go somewhere more private." Hazel was breathy, head spinning, as she pulled away for a moment. "Like... like upstairs. To my room."

"That's awful presumptuous," Rini purred. "But not a bad idea."

They had giggled as Hazel tugged Rini up the stairs behind her, shushing one another, like two teenagers sneaking behind their parents' backs. The door to

Hazel's room had barely clicked shut before they fell together, bumping against bed posts as they hastily pawed at each other's clothes, falling together on the bed.

She snapped out of the memory, shaking her head. Her curls bounced, their coils slapping gently against her cheeks, now warm. She had to focus. As good as the night before had been... she'd actually felt a little lost when the idol crept out afterwards. Hazel was *not* an overnight gal, but she hadn't wanted to let go of Rini's warm body. A pang had shot through her as she watched Rini slip from the sheets, kissing Hazel softly between tugging clothes back on. She debated messaging Rini, setting up a real date, like she deserved.

"Later, girl, goddamn," she told herself, slapping her cheeks. "We have investigating to do."

As she pulled Wade's journal back towards herself, a little voice began worrying in the back of her mind. Why *was* she so obsessed with finding a way to contact him? She loved Charlotte and wanted her best friend to be happy—could she maybe actually be happy with Bradley?

Hazel glared down at the journal. There were some perks to Bradley, she guessed. He was handsome—for a dude, she supposed—and had a history with Charlotte. And he had left her breadcrumbs to the truth. Maybe he *did* care about her, even if he would never be good enough for Lottie. Though his grandfather being a murdering psycho did still detract away from any potential positives he may have had.

And he didn't look at Charlotte the way Wade had. With a reverence, awestruck. Like he couldn't believe he got to exist near her. It was the same look Jacob gave Gran. Like daddy had given her mom.

Like they would go through hell itself if it meant they could be together for a moment longer.

She knew at least, that Bradley and Charlotte might have worked on paper, but they weren't destined to be together. That they weren't pieces of the same weird, broken puzzle like Lottie and Wade had been.

She wondered what it felt like to love the way they did, wondered if she ever would. Maybe, it might be possible. She thought of Rini and an ache spread deep inside of her. Every instinct screamed at her, told her that she had to get Wade back. It wasn't a fantasy, a fleeting thought. It was something she had to do. She could feel it in her bones, in her very soul.

Energy coursed through her, invigorating her as though she had been zapped. She was going to find a way to fix everything, to get everything to the way she knew it was meant to be. Snatching up Wade's journal, she began flicking through it again. No precision, no meticulous reading like she had been. She had a weird, unfounded faith that she was going to be shown what she needed to see.

Hazel let her eyes skim the words, unseeing, waiting, going off her gut. She knew she had a good instinct, an uncanny sense for stumbling across things that had paid off for her immensely in the past. And she told herself it was going to now.

Time felt like it slowed to a crawl when she flicked open to a page, somewhere near the second half of the thick journal. It was an innocuous entry, a day regaling about a picnic with the family and the Emberly's. Wade made a crucial error though when describing their company; Mother, Father, Loren, Mister and Madam Emberly, Sarah Rochelle, and Atticus. Though he hadn't used Atticus' preferred name.

Her lips formed around the single word, eyes widening. There was a single note in Wade's journal, in his stupidly perfect, looped handwriting.

Asterius.

CHAPTER NINE

ATTICUS

The minutes had turned into the hours, and the hours, into days.

And in those days, Wade had refused to speak to him. Not once.

Atticus prowled the cell once more, but he was certain there was nothing he could do to aid them in this room. He had asked several times when the meals arrived—the finest of human foods for Wade, surprisingly, and an energy elixir of sorts for himself—if he could speak to his brother, his parents, anyone. No answer. The iron door had clanged shut inches from his nose every time. They had, however, acquiesced to his demands for more suitable accommodations, at least for Wade; mortal, breakable, Wade. Two cots with scratchy bedding had been brought down for them, as well as other items for other *mortal* needs, that first day. He had been able to relax minimally, now no longer terrified his friend would succumb to illness, or some other such nonsense.

"Have I truly been brought here, merely to die for a third time?"

Wade's usual tenor tone had a rasp to it, his throat scratchy from misuse, apparently. Atticus resisted the urge to make a comment about how he had finally deigned to speak again. Instead, he sought to comfort his friend.

"No, my friend. You will not die here. I will promise you as much. I will scorch the ground they walk upon before I allow anyone to harm you."

"I feel I am going insane in here," Wade whispered. "Surely... surely they could allow us to leave these walls, if just for a moment? I do not think I can take it any longer."

The daemon shuffled, unable to provide the solace Wade sought. What was he meant to say, meant to do? Even he could not get that demand met. He was at the mercy of the Families, of everyone else. And honestly, it filled him with rancor. How dare they leave them so long without information, without any hints or even promises to come? They knew who he was, how *dare* they. So what if he had messed up, just the teeniest bit? Oh no, heaven forbid a human be in their realm. Not when they constantly made bonds with them, not when daemon's walked the earth all the time without true consequences.

Besides, Wade wasn't like other humans, anyway.

Atticus continued prowling along the walls, hands feeling along the hewn walls for any sort of weakness. He had done this many times now but had found nothing so far.

"Why don't you try things? Are you not filled with magic?"

"And what do you propose I try?"

Wade pushed off from the cot, where he had been sitting, head in hands, not unlike a statue. He stood now, towering over the daemon boy, setting Atticus' heart aflutter. Stubble lined his cheeks, a smattering of dark auburn. Dark hollows had begun to form under his stormy eyes. "You could try literally anything, demon."

Atticus straightened up to his full height—nearly an entire foot shorter than his companion. He stared up at Wade, his blond locks of hair brushing his shoulders. Atticus raised his hands in defeat.

"If you insist, I will try."

Atticus raised his left hand and snapped his fingers. Nothing happened. He then drew it back, as he would to hurl power, but nothing appeared, nothing happened. He shrugged, dropping his hand. "As you can see, I can't access my power in here. The iron-and-magic-infused walls and doors are designed to prevent my kind from having power, my dear friend."

"What are we to do then? What is our fate to be?"

"As I've reassured you," Atticus begun, "it won't be anything too dire. My family will sort it out. A trial means nothing. It's merely a formality, then I'm sure we'll be on our way. I will ensure our safe passage to the mortal realm again." While he might have mastered the air of casual nonchalance, a seed of doubt grew in him, a slight irk. He hated that he didn't know, couldn't know.

Wade didn't respond. A few moments passed before he spoke again.

"Is she alright?"

Atticus leaned back against the wall, crossing his arms. He looked away from his friend. "I believe so. She's strong, and not just her magic. Emotionally, physically. She'll be fine."

Wade stared ahead, unseeing. "I wonder if I will ever see my darling Lottie again."

"I will do my best to make it so," Atticus answered softly.

⚘

Nox sent someone to see them later that day, a cousin, a lower-level family member. They had never really gotten along, though, so he couldn't fathom as to why they had sent someone he could only describe as a hell beast. It was Caleo; a weaker daemon, more succubus than anything. At least, according to Atticus. He was a Princeling and an affable delight. She, however, was a raging bitch.

The two of them couldn't be more different, couldn't approach their existence in such opposite spectrums. Caleo fed in a vile, animalistic manner, and her chosen features were designed to ensure her prey came willingly to her. Tall, buxom, with honey-coloured hair, she was every generic *lady* a human man could find at a bar in any two-bit town.

Of course, that was her modus operandi, after all.

Caleo was expressionless as she let herself into the cell. Beautiful, but *such* a bitch. Atticus' lips tugged into an involuntary smile as he imagined Wade's *other* companions saying that. They would be right. She was intense, like a flame fluttering in a breeze, but she would burn you if you got too near.

"Caleo, I haven't seen you in a few centuries now. How does this fine day find you? I assume it's fine, given my lack of access to the outside world." Atticus gestured around the room. "Perhaps we should really put a word in with the Council. A window or two would really liven the soul down here."

Caleo fixed him with a stare. "Good to know that your time wasted, frolicking around the mortal realm, has not made you any less mouthy, Asterius." Her gaze shifted to Wade, eyes sparkling as they took him in, her tongue flicking over her lips. "I see why they had to lock your *little friend* away."

Atticus let out a low growl, jumping between Caleo and Wade. She let out a low laugh, a humorless bark. "Oh, Asterius, you need to hide how you feel much, *much* better, little cousin." She winked at Wade, a threat and a promise. Atticus growled. He would make sure she never got near Wade, the succubus.

"Tell us why you're here and then you can return to your duties as a soul sucking monster."

The coldness didn't leave her eyes as Caleo snapped, "They sent me here to tell you something. They don't want your brother spending so much time with you—not when you're such a bad *influence*. You're to go on trial tomorrow and this nonsense will be sorted out." Her eyes slid to Wade again. "I hope we have the pleasure of being better... *acquainted*, before your sentencing. I'll come seek you out, handsome."

Her cackle echoed as the door slammed shut behind her, leaving Atticus filled witha red-hot rage that consumed his very being.

Atticus awoke to the sound of iron grating on iron. He pushed up onto his elbows, head cocked as he listened. Wade remained silent on his cot, back turned to Atticus, the bits of his exposed suit rumpled. While he may have been afforded the luxury to clean himself, they hadn't been as kind to his clothing. Or Atticus'. His own billowing shirt was beginning to stain and the perfumes they offered did not cover that slightly stale scent that clung to the cloth.

The scraping grew louder, forceful. Something inside of the daemon screamed at him, a warning. This was not right, not usual. He had to prepare himself and Wade for whatever was ahead.

"Wade, awaken," he hissed. He pushed himself up fully, slipping from the cot to the one where his friend lay. It must have been the middle of the sleeping hours; even his kind required rest. He reached his friend, gently shaking his shoulder. "You must awaken now."

Wade huffed and sighed in his sleep as he stirred. Atticus shook him a little harder. "Something is happening. I need you to be prepared now." Atticus tore the blanket loose from Wade's body, keeping an eye focused on the door.

"What is happening?" Wade slurred. He rolled onto his side, digging the heel of his palm into his eye, rubbing at it as he yawned. "Why are you disturbing me?"

"Something is coming, this isn't right. You must be alert, for the worst might be coming."

That snapped Wade awake. He scrambled into a seated position, swinging his legs over the side of the cot. It took him only a minute to be back in his shoes and standing. "What are we to do, Atticus?"

The cell, as Atticus had gone over many times, did not provide much in the way of shelter or crevices. The optimal, and worst, solution for them would be to hide on the sides of the door. It swung outward, but perhaps, maybe, they could get a jump on whoever was coming. Atticus grimaced. If only he were in his true form, and not his preferred...

"Get in the corner, so I can at least cover you," Atticus ordered. Wade scrambled over as Atticus searched for the dregs of magic inside him, the ebbs that remained still. He knew his efforts were a waste; that unless he could push out of their cell, then he was powerless. The sounds grew in volume as he pushed Wade against the wall, his back to his companion, lowering into a half crouch. Atticus would literally throw himself in the path of danger before letting anything befall his friend.

They waited with bated breath as the locks on the iron door began to click, urgent, clumsily. Atticus' breath caught in his throat, his usual cocky demeanor vanishing as his slight frame trembled. There had never been consequences for his actions before, on this realm or the mortal one. Even with the whole Order and starting a cult accidentally—and the death that had gone along with it. Atticus winced; he felt what he *assumed* was guilt about his role in everything. It was a queer, tugging sensation, a heavy feeling of displeasure that washed over him.

"Leave us be!" Atticus roared as the door swung out, swathes of light spilling into the gray, drab, room.

"It's me," a voice hissed. Atticus dropped his hands, dumbfounded.

"Caleo? Why are you here? I swore, I told you, if you touch Wade—"

Caleo swept into the room, glancing nervously behind her. Her azure eyes sparkled, a hint of worry to them. No, that couldn't have been right. She never felt anything akin to worry or fear. Everything was wrong, upside down.

"You have to follow me," Caleo urged, glancing over her shoulder again. "I don't know how much time we have."

"What do you mean? Are we not going to trial? Does the Council realize what you're doing here? Are you trying to make sure we are erased?"

"I'm trying to help you, at the bequest of your family," Caleo snapped in hushed tones. "Nox sent me messages as things fell apart above."

Atticus froze. He could feel Wade's entire being vibrate behind him. "What are you suggesting?'

"House Lyra has fallen, along with other Families. There will be no trial, you will not get out unless you leave with me *now*."

Dread pooled deep in Atticus' stomach. "Surely you jest. I will not fall for your ruse, you vile witch."

"Why would I—no, I'm not arguing. I'm doing this for your mother and father, not for you, you little monster Princeling. Grab your friend now. I can explain as we go but we must make haste."

Without pause, Caleo turned on her heel and vanished around the door. Atticus glanced back at Wade. He didn't need to be told again. This might be their only chance for freedom. And if Caleo was lying—he was happy to throw her to the wolves.

"Follow, dear friend. We must keep up with her."

Reaching back, he took Wade's hand firmly in his own, and tugged, leading his friend away. He hesitated for the briefest second at the threshold of the doorway, before stepping over with determination. His entire being tingled as his magic returned, like warmth returning to a chilled body.

"Haste now, Wade." Atticus pulled Wade's hand, urging him along behind the daemon. Caleo clipped along the stone hallway, her heeled shoes clicking lightly as she hurried along, glancing back behind her.

"Can you two move it? Before anyone comes here, looking for your heads!"

Atticus' entire being thrummed as his magic pulsed through him, like blood through veins. Those tendrils, that beginning ebb of power. He would be able to keep them safe now and not rely on Caleo. He dragged Wade along behind him, his friend light on his feet as Atticus tugged. They caught up to Caleo at the end of the corridor, at the bottom of the twisting staircase. "Care to elaborate further, kind cousin?"

"Unrest has been brewing as you have been gallivanting about with humans like an insipid fool. For eons. Whispers have been spreading now for a while, rumors on the wind." Caleo's long legs took the stairs two at a time. Atticus' pressed hard, moving faster to compensate for the distance. Wade's hand grew cold and moist in his own. "Mutiny between Daemons and those Houses that refer to themselves as Gods. Wanting control, balance no longer. They have been meeting in secret, waiting for a moment to strike out against the Families. And they took your indiscretions as a chance to create an uproar and launch their little coup."

"In my defense, I could never have predicted such a thing."

Caleo scoffed. "I hope this has all been worth it for you, Asterius."

The mountain was a mess, a labyrinth designed to confuse those who were detained within its walls. Caleo led them astray multiple times as they scurried along, searching for the way out. They had several near run-ins with shadow servants as they flitted along the corridor paths, silent messengers searching for them.

"What horror have you caught me up in now?" Wade whispered as they pressed against a cool wall, waiting with bated breath as a group of harried, yelling Council members hurried through a corridor adjacent to them. They were so caught up in their argument, their voices reaching a crescendo, that they didn't notice the trio pressed in the darkness.

"Again, I must press that I wasn't aware this would happen, dear friend."

"We're almost at an exit, I know we're close. So keep your bickering to yourselves. I need you out of here so I can go check on my parents." Caleo's face was wan in the low light, and that dreadful pressure in Atticus' chest returned. Of course she would be worried about her parents, her own siblings. She was risking life and limb to free them. He opened his mouth, a freely given apology resting on the end of his tongue.

A resounding boom shook them, slamming them into the rough-hewn wall behind them. Atticus squeezed Wade's hand right as their bodies rag-dolled, catching them off guard. Panicking, he felt around for Wade, calling his friend's name.

"I am... unharmed. Bruised, I am certain. It has been quite some time since I felt pain like this." Wade winced as they pulled themselves to their feet. "What on Earth was that?"

"Someone getting extremely angry, I daresay." Caleo let out a soft sigh. "If this isn't a sign of what's to come, I don't know what is."

They pressed on, weaving through empty halls and winding staircases, until they found themselves face to face with an imposing set of doors. The phrase 'pereantintus' was carved into the granite archway above them.

Let them perish within.

Caleo and Atticus shared a glance, before stepping forward to push them open. The doors grated against the stone brick floor beneath them, a scraping noise that seemed to fill the entire space. The scene that beheld them was unimaginable to Atticus.

The twilit sky of Terra Doerum was streaked with ash. Fire raged in the distance, plumes of smoke reaching for the heavens above. Screams filled the cobblestone streets of the city beneath the mountain as the home he had once known descended into chaos.

Atticus turned to Wade, wincing. "Well, this is rather unfortunate."

CHAPTER TEN

HAZEL

H azel had spent the rest of the day formulating a scheme. She had to act
before she lost momentum, something in her screamed. That instinct in
her was her sounding board, her guiding point. The way that she supposed magic
was *meant* to feel. So she listened to it, followed her half-baked plan before she
could question it—or get caught. She had to move before she anyone caught onto
her.

She packed her hunting duffel bag that night, shoving anything she thought
she might need, including Wade's journal. Before shoving it in, she paused, gently
wrapped it in her freshly laundered sleep shirt. Charlotte would kill her if it got
damaged and she wouldn't blame her. In went stakes, salt, holy water in a squirt
gun—you name it, she had it locked and loaded. Lottie always kept her satchel
prepped too, so they'd be ready to go. Last second, before she zipped it all up, she
shoved in a pack of LED tea-light candles—more fire wouldn't be a smart idea,
given their last jaunt.

Hazel paused as she caught sight of herself in the mirror. Her curls were
beginning to frizz from the storm rolling in, the light drizzle from earlier turning
into an unseasonably warm downpour. The electricity in the air was palpable,
skittering across her skin when she threw the windows open before, embracing
the chaotic energy. There was a frantic glint in her eyes, framed by her large black
frames. She touched a hand to her face, feeling the rush of heat in her cheeks, a
fervor coursing through her. She would shower tonight, calm down, before she
asked Charlotte out with her the next day. Hazel could keep it cool; she *would*

keep it cool. Because in the morning, she was going to take Lottie to Umbra Hollow, the place that started and ended everything, and together they were going to go for round two—even if her bestie wasn't aware of any of it.

Hazel whistled as she slammed her bag into the trunk of the beat-up Camry. Charlotte watched her, a dubious expression on her face. Dressed in an over-sized, soft cream sweater and jeans, her hair held in place with her favourite ribbon, Lottie was all set for a cute lunch date—like Hazel had promised her. She felt a twinge of guilt as she slammed the lid shut, patting it as if in praise.

"Why are you dressed like a gremlin if we're meant to be on a girl's day today?" Charlotte demanded as Hazel turned to face her friend. Arms crossed, a playful breeze tugged at the loose tendrils of Charlotte's waist length chestnut hair. Sometimes it occurred to Hazel just how beautiful her friend was—that was, until she opened her mouth, anyway. "You haven't even tried to put any effort in!"

Hazel glanced down. She was in her usual battle attire—combat boots, skinny jeans, her favorite leather jacket. Though she *had* put on the emerald, cable knit sweater Charlotte had bought her for her birthday. Partly to dress up, partly as a peace offering for the summoning shadow demons incident. "I think I look alright, babes." Hazel swept a hand across her torso, pointing out the sweater.

Charlotte gave a small nod. "Yeah, I guess it's not plaid, at least."

"Wait, what's wrong with plaid?"

"And do we have to take your car? It's so small. We could take the family car. Also, didn't Grandmother agree to buy you a car made in this century? I'm always scared we're going to catch on fire in this thing."

Hazel grinned again, crossing her arms as she leaned against the trunk. "Babes, today is my surprise, I get to drive whatever I want. Besides, I have my seat the way I like in here."

With a roll of her eyes, Charlotte took a step forward. "And why does it have to be a surprise?"

"Well, because, uh, we haven't had time lately, between work and other... *commitments*." Hazel emphasized the end of her sentence, waggling her brows. Ah, there it was. Lottie's pallid face flushed pink and splotchy across her cheeks. "So I figured, as the greatest friend you'll ever have, that I should make it cute and exciting for you, babes."

"Your idea of cute and *exciting* will probably end up with us in trouble with the authorities somehow," Charlotte mumbled. However, she did make her way to the passenger door, sliding in. "Well, hurry up, then."

Butterflies twisted Hazel's stomach as she followed suit and hoped that her friend would forgive her. If not any time soon, eventually.

"What the actual fuck are you thinking? Actually, scratch that. *Are* you thinking? Have you lost the capability to filter your thoughts and consider them before acting on them?"

Hazel winced as Charlotte berated her, yelling as Hazel pulled along the overgrown drive. Crime tape fluttered in the breeze, the remnants from the year before, as the half-burnt remains of Umbra Hollow loomed over them. Wade's ancestral family home and the resting place of his spirit. Of where Charlotte last saw him, at any rate. She knew he had a strong connection to this house, they all did. Hazel, Charlotte, and Wade had all met there that fateful September day.

"Why are you doing this, Hazel?" the bite from a moment before was gone, Charlotte's words tinged with sorrow. "Why did you bring me here? I—I trusted you. You said we were gonna..." she trailed off, lip quivering as she slumped in the passenger seat, eyes wet with unshed tears as she gazed up at the remains of Wade's home.

All she was good at was kicking ass and fucking things up, apparently. Guilt twisted her stomach, knotting it and pulling tightly. Maybe Charlotte wasn't going to understand her idea—fuck, she wasn't sure if she would ever even forgive her. Hazel gripped the steering wheel tightly, the engine still idling.

"Babes, I promise you, I'm not—I'm not trying to be malicious. I might be stupid, but never cruel." She began to choke on her words, fighting the urge to cry as she caught sight of Charlotte's own tears beginning to fall. "I would... I would have told you, if I thought you'd still come. I'm the absolute fucking worst for tricking you."

"Told me what?" the Witch's voice was hoarse, the burden of her grief already overtaking her.

Hazel took a deep breath, wringing her grip on the wheel. "I found Atticus' true name, in Wade's journal. *Yes*, I never should have taken it," she rushed, as Charlotte twisted to stare at her, mouth agape, "and that is an absolute shit move on my part. And I'm sorry babes, but I figured it was worth asking for forgiveness rather than permission. If you just try this, I'll drop it, fuck, I'll even give Bradley my blessing and all that misogynistic bullshit or whatever."

Charlotte opened and shut her mouth a few times, as if trying to remember how to form words. Finally, she said slowly, "You found his true name? As in his demon name? What made you even think to—"

"Gran loaned me some books after it all happened. I read a bit, went hunting through the library and found some other family's old ass grimoires that talked about demon summoning's and stuff. And Atticus wasn't exactly quiet about wanting to make deals, y'know."

"And you're certain that's his true name?"

"If Wade is to be believed. Not that he'd have a reason to lie to his journal." Hazel didn't want to remind Lottie that he'd been perfectly capable of hiding the truth last year, however. "And I figured... well, this is where they had the most connection to—at least, we *think* so, right? So it would make sense—"

"To try and contact him here," Charlotte finished her sentence, her gaze shifting back to the Queen Anne mansion. Hazel nodded, a lump forming in her throat. Without looking away, she asked Hazel, "Did... did it make him seem real, reading his journal? I... I haven't been able to touch it. I can't bring myself to. I almost wonder if he was a dream, a beautiful dream I don't want to wake up from; don't want to forget."

"Oh, they were both real as hell, babes. Even ten-year-old Wade wrote like a two hundred something old man." Hazel mimicked how Wade comported himself. "June sixteenth. I fear that I have not had enough time to be a big old know it all."

Hazel nearly melted with relief when Charlotte giggled, snorting. "That does sound like him."

"If I have it my way, you won't need a stinky old book to hear his voice. Though I suspect I could do a one-man comedy act as him."

Charlotte was pensive, slow to respond to Hazel. She spoke slowly, brow furrowed. "And how exactly do you expect us to speak to him? What's your grand plan?"

"I figured we'd try summoning Atticus here, try and get him to talk to us. See if we... if I can't make a deal, to find a way to get to Wade."

Charlotte was silent for a long moment. Hazel began to fidget, itching all over as discomfort began to creep in. How hard had she fucked up by doing this? She wanted to speak, to ask Charlotte what she was thinking. She couldn't stomach silence, the way time and space seemed to create a gaping chasm between them.

"Is this what you were trying the other day, when the shadow demons were across the estate?" Hazel flinched, but nodded. "You were trying to find a way to speak to Atticus?"

"Yeah, but I didn't exactly know his name so I was just throwing shit to see what would stick."

Again, silence filled the space. She debated just putting the car into gear, she could *actually* drive them to brunch and treat Lottie to apologize for being such an inconsiderate dick—

"If this means you'll allow me to finish grieving, fine, I'll do it." Charlotte was blunt. "I'll go along with whatever you want today but after this is all done, we put the past behind us and look forward."

It was the Hunter's turn to be silent. She hadn't realized her friend had yet to grieve, hadn't finished. She'd figured that Charlotte had begun to move on. But she was throwing herself into Bradley and work to forget, instead, maybe.

"I've been an insensitive jerk," Hazel said quietly.

"To be fair, you generally are at any given moment." Charlotte gave a half-hearted chuckle. Hazel thought it was meant to be a joke, but it seemed a little bitter, sending a stab of shame through her. Charlotte sighed.

"I won't ever stop grieving Wade, not really. There was a future of 'could have been' that were never going to be. I was lucky we even go to meet. The sheer insanity of our situation; we never should have met, Hazel. He should have been dead long before I existed on the same plane of existence. And I'm lucky, grateful, that I got to spend the time with him that I did, truly.

"But life is life, and you gotta get on with it. Me wallowing and not living my life isn't going to give him his back, like with my parents. Look how long I wasted, being sad and angry, instead of living my life. I don't think they, or Wade, would want me wasting the time I have left on this Earth. You exist whether you're ready for it or not, but it's up to you as to how you handle it."

Hazel was silent as Charlotte finished up. Her friend made many excellent points, and at any other time, that might have aggravated her. Today, though, it just left her feeling hollow, pathetic. She was being unnecessarily selfish, as much as she argued her actions were for Charlotte. But...

"You shouldn't just accept things without fighting for them first," Hazel argued. "Yeah, sure, accept things when it's time to, but it's not time yet. We haven't even tried anything, that's not fair for you."

"Life isn't about being fair, Hazel. You need to learn to be okay with that."

Hazel let go of the steering wheel, thumping back against her seat. Why did she have to be alright with that, though? Who made that nonsense rule? "Bullshit, I don't have to be okay with it unless you are. And I know deep down, you aren't, you're just trying to do what you think you're meant to. 'Cause you're a good egg and want to not show your pain."

Charlotte stared up at the once grand home for a long moment, seemingly deep in thought. Hazel had to fight every urge in her not to fidget. When Charlotte finally spoke, there was a tinge of resignation to her tone. "If it helps you feel some sort of control, or whatever it is you need right now, then fine. Let's go summon a shitty demon and see if he's less of a dick than the last time."

Hazel fought the triumphant cheer that bubbled up inside of her as they crawled out of her well-worn car. They slammed the door shut, and Hazel sauntered to the trunk, her mood bolstered. She could feel success in the air, the way the sun warmed the skin of her forearms as she pushed her sleeves back, the chirp of a starling in the distance. She shot Lottie a grin as she went to grab her duffel bag. Charlotte gave her awkward thumbs up as she tapped away on her phone. Hazel hoped she wasn't texting Bradley.

Charlotte's discomfort was palpable as they crossed the lawns towards Umbra Hollow.

They'd met here almost a year ago; how things had changed in such a short period of time. The beautiful home-turned-museum still had a grandiose air to it. The wildflowers that surrounded it were beginning to grow back, despite Charlotte's magic singeing them, turning so much to ash. Hazel shuddered as she remembered the terrible day. The day Ashgarde snatched Charlotte. The insane memory of finding out he was the leader of a cult that had taken over the secret supernatural society that governed them. It felt made up, like something you would read in a book or watch in a movie.

Surprisingly, the foundation of the house appeared relatively intact. Police tape— some from before Lottie had even set it on fire—wrapped around the porch poles, blowing loosely in the wind, some parts ripped, or near so.

"I can't believe we're here," Charlotte said softly. She had stopped short of the stairs, a wistful expression on her face as she stared up. It made her look far younger than her twenty-nine years of age, almost cherubic in how her eyes and mouth softened. Her brows—usually so severe—furrowed gently, her thin shoulders slumping as she let out a sigh.

Hazel kicked at the grass beneath her. She vividly remembered that first day, when she had finally caught up with Charlotte, after months on the road following the girl. After her auntie told her she they were destined to meet, to be friends. There was a day she'd had that weird gut instinct, telling her she *had* to find Charlotte then. It wouldn't stop pulling at her, an itch that she could never reach, unless she found her. And she knew the moment she had. It was like her gravity had shifted as she spied that ribboned braid, and she knew she had found where she needed to be, and that the next steps would come.

That was how she felt now as she gazed up at the imposing mansion. All roads led back to Umbra Hollow, back to Wade, she just knew it. Swinging the duffel bag over her shoulder, she asked quietly, as not to spook Charlotte, "Do you wanna go up first, or me, babes?"

Charlotte shook her head. "I... I think I should be first. I can do this. It's just a house, right?"

"It sure is, babes." She smiled encouragingly as her friend furrowed her brow further.

"Never let anyone take me again," Charlotte demanded abruptly, her voice low but serious. Hazel's stomach flipped. "I know this is childish, because we won, and they didn't... they didn't truly get to hurt me. Well, that's fucking untrue, they beat the shit out of me. But I've had nightmares about this place, about being chained down, about.... about him coming to get me. And it's this stupid mixture of fear and relief. Sometimes I wonder if I wanted him to kill me, so we could be together."

"*Fuck, babes!*"

"I'm not in that place anymore." Charlotte shook her head. "I don't think I ever really was that low. I was ambivalent, if anything. Like if I died, I died. I'd never make active efforts. But you have to promise to go through literal hell if anyone takes me again." Lottie reached her hand over to where Hazel knew her scar still ached, despite the many years that had passed.

Hazel dropped the bag to the grass, swooping her friend into a crushing hug. She pressed her cheek close to Charlotte's, her throat catching as she whispered, "I'll burn the world down before I ever let anyone hurt you again, babes."

Ushering a sigh, Charlotte wrapped her arms around Hazel, and the girls stood embracing each other for several long moments, lost in each other's companionship. After some time, Charlotte pulled away, patting Hazel on the back. "We better get on with this insane plan. It's getting late enough."

Grasping her bag in one hand and Charlotte's hand in the other, Hazel tugged them up the stairs, dodging around wood that looked worse for wear. The heritage society that oversaw the home hadn't locked it back up. In fact, a condemned sign hung on the door. Hazel made a mental note to ask Gran if they could buy it, see what they could salvage. She cringed a little. What a privileged notion, to buy a museum home. Perhaps she could be its archivist—wishful thinking.

The inside of the large home was much like she remembered; the blurs of it, anyway. She hadn't spent a lot of time within, only racing in to try to find Charlotte after everything had fallen to pieces. Scorch marks singed wood, had lapped at the edges of frayed carpet. It *seemed* safe enough within—Hazel had been to much sketchier places. She took the first few steps in, keeping her friend behind her. If anyone could take the brunt of a falling roof or beam, it would be her, not Lottie. Using her duffel bag as some sort of battering ram, she used it to push through doors. Glimpses of a study, with beautiful books lining its cases, relatively undisturbed. A drink cart, full of half-finished scotch. Flowers so decomposed in their vases they seemed to disintegrate in the green-tinged water as they passed.

Eventually, they pushed into the room she'd been hunting for. The ballroom that had found Charlotte chained to the floors. It was in disarray. Furniture remained crammed against the walls, the deep, jagged etchings a startling reminder of what happened. She could feel Lottie tense up behind her, heard her ragged short breaths. Hazel squeezed her hand, turning back to face her friend.

"Babes, you okay? I've got you, baby girl, shh, it's okay." Hazel placated Lottie with soothing words, much like her auntie would when she'd cry out in the night as a child. "I... fuck. They aren't going to get you, I'm here with you. I will legit bust heads if anyone comes near you."

"I can't believe we're in here, that it happened," Charlotte whispered. Her eyes were wide as she took the room in, an edge of fear to her, a stiffness. God, Hazel felt like an asshole dragging her there. She could have done it herself, alone. What the fuck had she been thinking?

"Babes, we can leave—"

"No," Charlotte interrupted. "We're here now. I'm not a baby or a little bitch." She shot Hazel a weak grin. "I'm a goddamn ghost hunter. I can handle a few spicy memories."

Hazel squeezed the other woman's hand tightly. "You say the word and we bail."

They crept across the floor of the ballroom, using the light of Lottie's phone to cast a glow. While streaks of light managed to wriggle their way in through the cracks in the curtains, it wasn't enough to stop them tripping on splintered wood. Hazel cursed as the tip of her boot got lodged in a particularly nasty groove. "What the fuck were they doing in here, exactly? Did anyone ever tell you?"

Charlotte helped tug her free. "I'm not really certain. Some sort of necromancy soul magic stuff, like they did to..." She trailed off, gulping, as though unable to say his name. *Wade.* "I guess we could ask Bradley sometime, see what he has to say."

"I guess he was in their inner circle, wasn't he?" Hazel said brightly, a pointed jab. Charlotte shot her a look.

"Didn't you say something about backing off?'

"Au contraire, I did nothing of the sort. Giving a blessing doesn't mean not making snarky comments."

Lottie mumbled something under her breath that Hazel couldn't quite hear. Crouching down, she slid her leather satchel off her shoulder, plopping it onto the floor to flip open. She let out an otherworldly shriek as she unbuckled it. Hazel dropped into attack mode, sliding knives from the sheaths on her belt, ready to throw one.

"Specter, you naughty boy, how on earth did you get in there? How didn't I notice the whole trip?" Charlotte scolded. Specter Blythe, resident cat and troublemaker, popped his little dark head out of the satchel, mewing. Then his ocher eyes flicked to Hazel. He was a judgmental little void. Hazel relaxed, shifting back to a standing position, twirling her knives before returning them to their sheaths.

"That fucking cat is gonna give me a heart attack one day." She slid her box of cigarettes from the inside pocket of her jacket, lighting one up. She cursed again as Lottie clicked her fingers and the end went out, a little magic trick that the Hunter hated.

"No, those fucking *cigarettes* are going to give you one," Charlotte admonished. She let the cat out, and he slinked over to Hazel, brushing his tail against her legs as she fought to relight her cigarette. Letting out a sigh, she crammed it and the lighter back in her jacket pocket for later.

"I have stuff." Hazel kicked her duffle bag over where she'd dropped it before, when her foot got stuck. "Candles and all that." She crouched down, giving the Witch a crooked grin. "You ready for round two of summoning a demon?"

They sat crossed legged in the middle of the circle. They'd made a circle of LED tea lights and salt, sitting on the grooves in the wood. They held hands, forearms across their knees as Specter weaved between them. Hazel took several deep breaths, calming her nerves. Last time they had summoned Atticus, they'd been outside of the circle, fearful. This time, she planned to tackle that little sucker and make him give her what she was after.

"Are you ready?" she asked Charlotte. In the low light, the head of the Blythe family looked like she was about to projectile vomit as she nodded. Hazel wriggled a bit. She could do this. Sucking in a deep breath, she said, "If you can hear us, show yourself to us. Come on out, *Asterius*."

They waited with bated breath, muscles taut as they gripped each other's hands. Even Specter paused, still as night as they listened, waited. A minute passed, then two. Nothing happened. Charlotte let out a sigh and they dropped hands.

"It was worth a try, Hazel. Come on, let's pack up. We still have time to go do that cute girl's day if we hustle. Goodbye, spirits, it was fun."

Dejected, Hazel said, "Yeah, I guess so, babes. Let me turn these little lights off and cram them in my bag." Reaching over, her hand closed around the first light. She flipped it to toggle the little switch underneath, when the ground beneath them rumbled. "Earthquake?"

"It must be. Come on, we better get out before this old house decides to come down on us. Forget the candles." As Charlotte reached down to offer Hazel a hand up, she let out a gasp and slipped, tumbling into Hazel. The ground shook fiercely, the candles dancing across the floor as Specter jumped onto where they clung to one another.

"Babes, I think we need to start crawling out—"

Hazel's words were cut off as the ground beneath them crumbled, opening up into a hole. The two girls screamed as they tumbled into the earth, down into a hole that looked like the night sky.

CHAPTER ELEVEN

ATTICUS

"What do we do now, Atticus?"

The urgency in Wade's voice cut through the ringing in the daemons' ears as he stared out at the scene unfolding around them. The urban sprawl of Terra Doerum was alive with flame and light; with the howls of its inhabitants. He stared, dumbfounded, as Wade grasped his arm and Caleo fidgeted beside them.

"I think, for the first time in his existence, cousin is lost for words." Caleo rubbed her arms, goosebumps breaking out across the flesh of her form, despite the pleasant warmth to the air. "This isn't the moment for you to try new things, Princeling. Think," she snarled.

The dull ringing began to fade away as he snapped back to the reality of their situation. He glanced from the drawn expression on his dear friend's face, to the terror that lurked in his cousin's eyes. They were relying on him, expecting him to navigate this uncertainty for them. He pet Wade's gloved hand—he could make this up, like he'd done time and time again.

He had fumbled through too many failings before to let this stop him.

"Well, we have to make our way to House Lyra, that is for certain. Once we do that, we can convene with my parents and brother, and they'll fill us in on what we don't know and direct us."

Wade visibly relaxed while Caleo gave him a look that clearly said, 'is that seriously all you have?'. He shot her a dark look before turning to smile broadly at Wade. "Come along, dearest. We will march our way through this catastrophe and to safety."

While he kept a smile on his lips, his insides screamed at him. This was beyond the unprecedented. Atticus had never been one to curse like the mortals did, but this was one of those moments where he felt like it may have been appropriate. Like that vulgar Hazel girl, who Wade's *lover* had been so attached to. He stared out at the city he had once known as home, unable to fathom what was unfolding before him, despite his cool demeanor.

Terra Doerum had been around longer than the concept of time itself—or so he had been told. It had influenced every aspect of mortal life, a world that became a poor imitation of the original. Their religion, their conspiracies, their wonders, their monarchies, their architecture—daemons and gods alike had whispered in the ears of men, directing them, leading them to create in their image. Gothic architecture studded the skyline of the great city, wrapping itself around the mountain that lay at the heart of the city, the urban sprawl beneath spreading out towards the great lakes and the forests beyond. Perpetual twilight cast it in shadows, the pinks and purples never quite fading into total indigo. Stars and moons lit the sky up, normally casting a soft glow across his home. Now, the sky filled with plumes of acrid smoke and the hard edges of flame.

Someone, something, had wanted this, and had set it in motion.

When he was here and not in the land of mortals, he only knew of his life as a Prince, small and isolated. He was kept in line, kept to his duties, as much as his family could manage to get him to. Part of Atticus was aware of more outside, past that all, but it had never occurred to him to care. The Houses kept whatever lurked beyond in line, safely away from them. Besides, his interests laid beyond the realm he'd called home. Earth, the human world, had been his home; would remain his true home.

"Atticus?"

Wade's voice snapped him out of his reverie. "I'm sorry, dear friend, did you say something?"

"You need to get him out of here before someone snatches him out," Caleo snarled, swooping in, inches away from Atticus' face. "He is a beacon, Asterius. You can smell the *differentness* on him. Lesser daemons are running rampant down there and he cannot protect himself here. You need to get out of here. And I need to return to my family."

If Atticus could believe it, he almost thought there was a touch of fear to Caleo's Aphrodite-like face. He wasn't about to give her sympathy, however. "Perhaps you should hurry on ahead then, *dear*."

Caleo shot him a look of disgust.

"As petulant and pathetic as ever, Princeling." She slipped back into the shadows, fading away until only the bright sparkle of her eyes remained. As they too began to fade, her voice drifted across the breeze, caressing him. "Perhaps you will do us all a favor and finally perish and stop entwining us in your stupidity."

Rage filled Atticus as he spun to face where her form had been a second before, but it was too late. The succubus had slipped into the shadows, making her way home, he presumed. He dearly wished he could do the same, but it was impossible with Wade at his side. They would have to do things the human way, it seemed. When he saw Caleo again, however...

"Atticus?"

There was an edge of fear to Wade's voice. The rage filling Atticus began to dim, the shadows that pulsated around him retreating inward. He smoothed a smile over his face before turning to face his friend once more. "My apologies, dearest friend. I understand your familial relationships were never as tumultuous as my own."

Wade eyed him, caution rife in the way he held himself. "So, what are we to do now that your... family... is not here?"

Atticus took a step forward to grip the stone railing. They'd exited onto a landing, an observation platform of sorts that protruded out of the side of the mountain. Stairs, carved into the mountain themselves, winded their way down its steep slope. Chaos reigned below, smoke billowing, setting the twilit sky ablaze.

He'd never taken the stairs down—had never needed to, with his abilities. In fact, he hadn't truly ever really needed to *be* at the Mountain.

He stared out into the world below. How long had it been now since he had returned home? Centuries? Well before he had met Wade, or the Emberly's, or The Order, surely.

Yet, he remembered the winding streets and paths as if it were yesterday. Even as the city loomed with violence and chaos, its beauty and majesty blended into the flames. Though his heart belonged elsewhere, he was compelled by duty and pride. He would find their way through and lead them to safety.

Asterius, son of Nova, was a Prince, and a daemon to be reckoned with. He had magic and charisma that had guided him through many obstacles over his existence.

And he would not be defeated by some mere *stairs*.

He was not built fragile and breakable like humans. He could rend the night itself apart, if he truly desired. So why did his thighs ache and his lungs feel ready to burst? And he was going *down* the horrendous stairs, for goodness sakes! He debated momentarily, as they reached a landing partway down, of letting himself bleed with the shadows, and meet Wade at the bottom. But he knew he couldn't do that; they would eat him alive.

He sucked in a deep breath, leaning against the metal-wrought rail with what he hoped was casual nonchalance. Staring out at the unfolding scene below, he said to Wade, without looking to his companion, "We can rest here, if we must. I know that your mortal body must be aching with these exertions—"

"I'm fine. I feel limber, actually. Moving after being confined to that room for so long is invigorating. Besides, do we not need to reach your family?"

Atticus' pale brow twitched in annoyance. How could Wade, a human—and an older one now, at that—not need to rest? Perhaps he was running on adrenaline. Atticus had seen that before. It was quite common for humans who felt as though their lives were in peril or that danger would befall them in some way. Atticus wished that would work on him now. It should have. As he looked across the cityscape, he could see homes burning, could hear the feral snarls and screams of discord.

Normally, he thrived on this sort of division. He fed on emotion—that was the terms in his deals. He wanted to consume those feelings, to experience every single one as a delicacy. After spending so long yearning to feel emotions the way the humans did, it was so tantalizingly close. And discord and chaos were some of his favorites.

There was something so overwhelming, so fearful, about seeing his home at the center of it, however. He had seen cities crumbled, empires shattered, lives ruined and conquered. But this was different. Terra Doerum was meant to be the pinnacle of existence, the thing that all was modeled after. So how did it seem so dangerously close to falling, so dangerously *human*?

"Are you quite alright, Atticus?"

Wade's soft timbre shook the daemon from his thoughts once more. Atticus gave the slightest shake of his head, flashing a dazzling smile to his friend, his lips split wide in a grin. "Of course, why would I not be?"

Wade didn't seem so convinced. They had been companions for some time. Not as long as some of the lives Atticus had seen lived out, admittedly. But Atticus had seen Wade grow from a boy to a man. Had watched him grow even further, even after his life had been claimed. There was something in his soul that had drawn Atticus in. The auburn-haired gentleman with the sombre expression and scarred jaw merely stared at the daemon, his large gray eyes drawn together in consternation.

A spark of a true, earnest friendship. And it was that friendship that Atticus knew meant that Wade could see through his facade, even if only through the smallest cracks in his armor.

"You can speak to me freely, you know this." Wade's gentle voice sent shivers down Atticus' spine. "I know that we have had our difficulties. But I wish you would speak openly with me, old friend."

Like a knife in the heart. Wade didn't need to say what he was thinking—*despite your betrayals, I am still here for you. I am better than you.* Atticus knew his mortal friend was better than he could ever hope to be. Of course Wade was; he was kind, clever, thoughtful, so full of compassion that, at times, it had made Atticus recoil.

"Now is not the time to dwell on thoughts and feelings," Atticus murmured in response. "We have more pressing concerns."

"Like literal Hell being on fire, I presume?" Wade's lip cocked with the faintest smile. Atticus shook his head ruefully.

"I see that the Blythe girl has influenced *that* particular aspect of you."

Wade shrugged, a half-hearted effort. But Atticus knew. He could feel the thrum of Wade's now beating heart from where he stood, the way his pulse quickened and his breath caught at the mention of the girl's name. How woefully and pathetically he was in love with her, yearned for her. Jealousy was an ugly knife, carving out Atticus piece by piece as he pushed away from the railing.

Wade was meant to be *his* friend, *his* dearest companion.

Sauntering over to Wade, Atticus grabbed his friend by the hand, much like they used to when Wade was a boy still. When they would spend long nights awake, whispering, sharing secrets. Sharing their dreams of the world. That felt like an eternity ago, even to him. Wade, thankfully, did not resist as Atticus tugged him towards the steps. They had a long way to go still, and there would be no changing the past without looking toward the future.

"I *will* keep you safe," Atticus whispered, his words laced with conviction.

"This is magnificent."

The awe that filled Wade's voice filled Atticus with unearned pride as the daemon beamed at his companion. It had taken some time—a lot more than the Princeling would like to admit—to reach the bottom of the winding stairs that carved their way down the mountain and onto the first cobblestone path of Terra Doerum. It had been worth every valiant effort to keep his exhaustion hidden to see the look on Wade's face as he took in Atticus' home properly.

The streets of Terra Doerum wrapped themselves down the gentle slope of the bottom of the mountain, stretching out into their own suburbs. Large, ornate lamps that had inspired the gas lanterns that had been so popular in Wade's youth lined the fronts of colorful row houses, beautiful creeping vines wrapping around balconies and windows. Large, winding trees filled with lavender foliage climbed up the sides of the houses and across the eaves, their perfumed petals mixing with the ash and smoke in the distance. The houses were like mini, colorful cathedrals, stained glass in every window reflecting the light of the lamps. The were dazzling, Atticus knew. That's why the humans were so obsessed with it to this day. Even if they made everything so *dark* and melancholy. Not everything had to be dreary punishment.

"This is nothing on my family's home." He couldn't help that tinge of ego in his words. "Yes, the Rows are beautiful, but my home is one of the Family manors, and quite resplendent. So if you like these, you'll love our home." *If it still stands. No.* He had to shake those thoughts away. They would all be fine, everything would be fine. They would work this out.

"Is that so?" Wade murmured. He was staring around, spinning in place like a child in a candy store for the first time. "It's so breathtaking, though."

"I used to tell you all the time that your world was a pale imitation of my own, dearest. I wouldn't lie to you." *Not about that.*

"I suppose you did." Wade wandered away from Atticus, reaching a hand out to touch the building. He pulled it back though, as if thinking, before silently removing his glove and laying it upon the smooth stone. A gasp slipped between Wade's lips as his fingers brushed the stone, reaching for the flowers. He snapped one off, mesmerized. His chest rose as he inhaled deeply, followed by a sharp exhale. "I never thought I would feel anything beneath my fingers again."

Wade's words were filled with unspoken emotion—sorrow, joy, nostalgia. A pang of guilt shot through Atticus. His beloved friend had spent so long tucked away, unable to feel, to experience. *He* had taken that away from Wade, he knew. Even if he had worked so hard to right it once more.

"I hope you experience many more pleasures from here on out," Atticus whispered. The longing in Atticus was palpable, he was certain. Wade either didn't notice or didn't want to acknowledge it, as he kept his gaze fixed on their surroundings, soaking in every detail. It was as if Wade had been living in black and white and was finally experiencing the nuances of color again.

Reaching out a hand to his friend, he wanted to comfort him, to say something. To hold his dear companion close and make things right. What was this feeling that was overcoming him? This tightness to his chest, the aching in his heart as it thundered beneath his flesh. So... *human.* He drew rapid breaths, tight-lipped.

A nearby explosion snapped Wade out of his reverie at last. Atticus melded into the shadows, appearing before his friend, pushing him against the wall of the house they stood by. His eyes narrowed, darting about, taking it all in. Where had that explosion come from? How close was it to them?

Finally, he spotted a plume of dark smoke in the distance—up the mountain. His shoulders loosened, but not entirely, as tension gripped his body. That wasn't a good sign.

"What on Earth?" Wade choked out. Smoke was filling the twilit sky, sending a cascade of ash upon them, filling Wade's mortal lungs. Catastrophe seeped around them, thicker than any smog. It filled every nook, every crevice, weaving around them unbidden, like a dark entity waiting to suffocate them.

"We have to make our way home."

CHAPTER TWELVE

ATTICUS

T he time before Wade had been dark for Atticus. He had no fond memories of then. The times he spent in the human realm were splotches of light in an otherwise bleak existence. There were only two sides to him, with no nuance, it seemed. In the human world, he was Atticus. A chaotic being that slipped in and out of the shadows to sow discord and delight. Back home, he was someone else.

Asterius, second son of House Lyra—Prince, and menace. He knew how the others, daemons and gods alike, viewed him. He was aware of their snickers and whispers in Court, the way they commented. *Good thing he is the second child*, or, *how do they cope with such a spoiled princeling?* How his mother and father argued for him, defended him. Despite how he embarrassed them. *What sort of daemon spends more time in the human realm than their own?*

One that hated home, he wanted to tell them. He wished he could tell them how much it irritated him that nothing changed, that he could live an eternity at home and it meant nothing compared to a short, vibrant life amongst the humans. He hated the return between, the wait between one contract and another. It didn't matter how he left his name scattered; whether whispered between the mouths of mortals or scrawled between the pages of a journal. He was always waiting for the next to be brave enough to summon him, to bind him to the world he so desperately desired to be back in.

His most recent contract had passed. They didn't last nearly long enough. This idiot had gotten his head chopped off, only a few mere human years after binding

Asterius to him. Their family had taken turns binding themselves to him before they died, passing him along, keeping him tethered to their realm for several centuries. The daemon sighed. He'd been enjoying France and all the oddity that was emerging amongst the humans. The delicious, biblical art and sculptures, the cherubic children. He'd been proud of how many master artists had approached him, begged him to be their muse. He missed the taste of their excitement, their fears, the anguish he caused others.

The Princeling lounged on his throne, nestled slightly behind and to the left of his mother's. Nox's was to the right of Father's throne, his heir. Court hadn't met that day, so the room was empty of everyone, including the servants. He dangled his legs over the edge of the stone armrest, swinging them with a petulance only he could muster. Candles flickered along the walls, perpetual light that never needed replacing, casting the vast room with shadows. A refuge, for now.

Atticus the demon, as the mortals knew him, was feeling sorry for himself. If that idiot had handed the daemon off to someone before they took him to the guillotine, he could still be roaming the palace. Instead, he was confined to home, the last place he wanted to be. He sighed, melancholy, letting himself get lost in memories of the springtime, of cut grass and roses, the scent of promise and hope that humans embodied.

His thoughts were interrupted by the groan of the heavy wooden doors pushing open. "So, that's where you've been hiding, Asterius."

Lolling his head to the side, the young Princeling gave a lazy smile. "Dearest brother. To what do I owe the pleasure?"

Nox strode across the marble floor of the grandiose room. He was straight backed, rigid as he walked, the good little soldier his father had trained him to be. "Mother and Father have been looking for you. I see you've been sulking like a child still."

Atticus sniffed. "I wouldn't call it sulking. Taking stock of my life and its prospects, perhaps."

Nox grimaced as he reached his younger brother. He towered over the daemon, casting the younger in shadows. His blond locks were pulled back, secured with a dark ribbon. "Father wants you to meet with him, to discuss you joining us for training."

Atticus let out a moan. "Unfortunately, I will have to decline at the present moment. I have a bit too much on my plate currently."

Nox let out a laugh, a harsh bark. "Asterius, brooding like a child is not work, as much as you put effort into doing so. You have a duty to attend to. It's an honor to commit to House Lyra and ensure its prosperity."

"Atticus," he corrected. All childish whimsy and sulking disappeared, replaced with a more serious tone. "Asterius is not a name I prefer to be known by." He swung his legs over the side of the throne, planting his heeled boots on the platform their seats resided on. He propped his elbow up on the armrest, pressed his cheek against his fist. "And just because your Father's obedient shadow, does not mean I wish to be the same, dearest brother."

"Asterius is the name you are known as here. We do not care for what you do amongst the mortals. It is time for you to clean up for your slovenly ways and be of assistance to your House, to your family. You are a *Prince* and you need to begin acting like it."

Atticus shot to his feet. His brother towered over him as he glared up. "And who says that? Father's royal decree? What does it matter what I do? I'm the spare, not the heir. I should be allowed to frolic and roam amongst the humans as I please. At least they respect me, treat me with the grandeur and fear I deserve."

"You're being a child."

"So what if I am!" Atticus threw up his hands, his velvet coat rustling. "I have a right to grieve my losses. Perhaps I shall never be of use to you, or Father. But I have a use there, to them!"

Nox let out a low chuckle. "Are you done with your rant, or do you wish to stomp your feet, perhaps?"

Atticus could not resist, could not bite his tongue. He rose to the bait. "Oh, you and Father would like that immensely, wouldn't you? You would love for me to be miserable in this accursed place, the perpetual child, the forgotten son." A small part of him *did* want to stop as his brother stared at him, his face blank, revealing no emotion. Atticus shuffled uncomfortably under that gaze. He hadn't won the argument, but he desperately wanted to. Several beats of silence passed between them, and when Atticus couldn't stand it any longer, he threw himself back onto his throne.

"I shall weep here and not move until my fractured heart is mended once more."

A noise slipped from Nox's lips—one that Atticus was not used to. One of sympathy.

"Asterius. Atticus," he corrected himself. His younger brother pretended not to be intrigued. Nox knelt down at the throne by his brother, looking up through the sheet of blond hair to the small, child-like face beneath. "I know that I sound cruel and like a tyrant. I know that's what you think of Father and think that I am the same. And my words may hurt, but know that is not my intention.

"But this obsession with humans is the thing that hurts you, that fills you with such angst. They are fragile, breakable things, much like that heart of yours. They are doomed from the moment they breathe, but that is what makes their lives so precious, so meaningful. Like flowers in the meadow, they have their moment sprung from the earth, before returning to it once more."

Nox finished, reaching a hand for his brother, who ignored it. Atticus was silent as his brother waited patiently for a minute, before retracting it.

"No one can say I haven't tried," he muttered. Nox swiftly rose back to his feet. "You're a Prince, Asterius. Perhaps you should think about that and what it means for you."

Sometime later, Atticus still remained alone in the great throne room. He hadn't left out of spite—at least, that's what he told himself. Perhaps, deep down, he was a little fearful of his next steps. He couldn't remain in the Daemon Realm. Because even surrounded by family, even his role as a Prince, he was so lonely, and it scared him. Therewas no place for him in the world he called home. It was a prison, a place that he had no choice but to return to when he was no longer soul bound.

Was he Asterius the daemon prince, or Atticus, the lonely boy?

He knew he was different from the mortals he so longed to be amongst. He would never age, would never die of mortal illness like them. Even the emotions they felt—so tender, so raw, so fragile—he couldn't really understand. He was resentful, envious. He wanted to experience the full spectrum of human emotions, good and bad. His soul ached for it.

His thoughts went dark, quiet. Did he have a soul, like the humans he loved so did? Or was he an empty shell, a husk? A mere vessel for some greater thing? He had always been taught that the daemons and gods were superior to humans, that they were a higher form of being.

But were they, or were they merely different?

It bothered him. He stared out in the darkness, at the vast emptiness of the throne room. A room that humans had modeled their own world after over the span of their existence, from the influence of his own family, and others like it. There was a coldness to the corners, a lack of that spark that humans had, that they gave their items and the things that they cared about. They breathed life into everything—objects, moments. Newborn babes, that were one moment inside their mother wombs, the next they were in the world, their own separate being.

It astounded him.

And he envied it all.

Chapter Thirteen

Hazel

The world was a swirling, chaotic void around her. There was no up, no down. Like Alice falling down the rabbit hole, there was no rhyme nor reason. Worse than any alcoholic drink, worse than any drug she had ever consumed. Time was meaningless as they fell.

Light and color danced around them, random patterns that seemed to make no sense, bright bursts of light and hues in the darkness. At some point, she screamed for Lottie, searched for her, but she was weightless, limbless, bodiless. Unable to seek purchase.

So she kept falling.

Pain bloomed at the back of her skull, like she'd slammed into a wall with a hangover. Hazel groaned, mouth gritty, colors dancing behind the lids of her closed eyes. Everything ached, like a full body work out. She wriggled her toes, her fingers, fighting through nausea and discomfort to ensure nothing was broken. Negative. She breathed a sigh of relief as vomit crept up her throat, swallowing it again. *Nasty.* She fluttered her eyelids, moaning, barely able to rasp a single word. "Babes?"

"Mmm," came a weak response. Oh, thank God, she was there. Hazel would get up, would check on her, make sure they'd survived the house collapsing.

Fuck. Umbra Hollow had collapsed beneath them. They must have hit their heads. She strained against the ache in her head, desperate to remember what happened. Lottie, Specter, herself—they were in the summoning circle, closing it up, when the floor gave out. Then lights and colors. She must have had a dream while passed out. She had to wake up properly, to get them out, before they were buried under rubble and killed.

Mustering every bit of strength remaining, her body screamed at her as she flopped about, forcing herself into a plank as her eyes opened. They were blurred—she must have lost her glasses. Shadows danced before her limited vision. Of course it would be dark. She stretched out an arm, searching for them as her left arm wobbled, bearing the brunt of her weight. She felt for her glasses, praying she hadn't landed on them. She recoiled as her hand brushed up against something furry, something warm and swishing—

Thud. "Mew?"

"Thank fuck that's you, cat," she croaked, coughing. She could barely make out the yellow pinpricks of his eyes in the dim light. He brushed up against her again, purring, pushing her hand. She fumbled, grasping, dewy grass beneath her fingertips. Hold the fuck up, *grass*? How did grass get under them? Her fingers grasped something cool and metal. Her glasses, thank fucking Christ. Using one hand, she awkwardly flipped the arms out, sliding them onto her face. They were a little smudged, but now everything was relatively high definition, and she could see again.

They were in fact, on grass, the world setting and fading into twilight around them. Specter mewled at her as he slunk past, making his way to where Lottie lay face down against the grass, sprawled out haphazardly. Hazel army crawled across to her friend, the aches and pains subsiding as she pushed through. She'd had worse—and probably would again, at some point. A little bit of bruising and a headache wasn't gonna stop her.

"Babes, you alive?" she hissed as she pulled up beside Charlotte. She reached a hand over, shaking the waif of a girl's shoulder. Charlotte stirred, groaning. She kept shaking until the witch began to move, to raise her head.

"Let me die, I feel like a fucking bus hit me."

"Me too, but we gotta get up, moving, work out where we are. I don't think we're at Umbra Hollow. I don't even know if we're in Salem."

"We're probably in Hell, given how I feel," Charlotte moaned, visibly wincing as she tried to roll onto her side.

Sucking in a deep breath, Hazel mentally counted down from three before pushing herself onto her knees, staggering to her feet. Steadying herself, Hazel shook her head, taking a beat before she took in the scene around her.

Forest surrounded them on all sides. They were in some sort of clearing, a small one, littered with white flowers that seemed to glow in the moonlight. A small pond sat near them, its surface still. She peered over it. If she didn't know better, she would have said it was made of liquid starlight. It didn't look like any pond she had seen before, dark as onyx, silver sparkles glittering within it.

"Come on babes, we gotta get up, work out what happened. Here, gimme your hand, I got you." Hazel tugged Charlotte to her feet, the slighter woman leaning against the Hunter, protesting the entire time. "We gotta work out what happened."

"I know exactly what happened. You tried to summon Atticus, failed, and we fell into the floor—" Charlotte froze as she finally opened her eyes properly, widening them as she took stock of the woods around them. "What the fuck is this?"

"I'm not sure. Nowhere I've seen. I guess we're not in Kansas, huh?" she joked weakly. Charlotte twisted her head to look at Hazel so fast that it audibly cracked.

"What did you open?" Charlotte hissed. "This is clearly not our home. There are *three fucking moons in the sky.*"

Hazel glanced up, a pit forming in her stomach. "Well, shit, you're right babes."

With a snarl, Charlotte pushed away from Hazel. "Of course I'm right!" she staggered slightly, as if she were drunk. "We're not home anymore. This isn't our... this isn't where we come from, clearly. You've taken us somewhere, you opened up something, and it's yanked us here. Oh my God, we are so absolutely fucked."

Charlotte continued to curse, drawing in sharp, whistling breaths, hyperventilating. Hazel stretched out a hand to comfort her, but Charlotte smacked it away. "Don't touch me right now or I *will* kick your ass."

"Okay, cute jokes aside, we gotta work together—"

Hazel didn't see the punch coming. Her jaw cracked as Charlotte's fist connect with her cheek, sending her staggering. The Hunter straightened up, snapping, "The fuck is that about?" as another fist slammed into her. She danced back, out of reach, her hands coming up to protect her from more blows. "Wanna fucking tell me why you're wailing on me?"

"I told you I'd kick your ass if you touched me," Charlotte puffed, her fists raised. Hazel let out a bark of a laugh.

"Kick my ass? Babes, I love you, and you're all of a hundred pounds—can you *stop that?*"

Charlotte had launched at Hazel again, kicking while she pelted the Hunter with her fists. Charlotte let loose anguished sobs as she pummeled Hazel. Hazel braced herself, letting the other woman rain her fury down on her. She would wear out soon enough, surely. It took a minute before Charlotte's blows had slowed, stopping. "Are you done yet?"

Huffing, Charlotte backed away. Her pale cheeks were flushed a blotchy pink, her eyes sparkling, brows knitted together. She raised her hands, started weaving them in the air. Hazel's eyes widened as she began to ask, "*Now* what are you doing?"

Before the words left her lips, however, she felt herself being slammed backward by a gust of wind, an invisible punch to the gut. She kept her footing, digging her heels into the muddy grass beneath her as she was shoved along. Charlotte had never, *ever* used magic against her—not even when she'd broken the fancy new coffee machine.

"Okay, that's enough." There was an edge to Hazel's words as she straightened her glasses. "I don't think it's fair to use magic, especially after I let you get a few decent hits on me. So why don't you calm down—"

"*No.*" There was a crazed undercurrent, a frenzy, to Charlotte's tone. "I've had it with keeping my shit together, with being the one to be calm. Maybe I'm done with being calm. Maybe I deserve to throw some punches, and maybe you deserve to take one." Charlotte's breaths came out ragged, her chest heaving as she planted her feet apart, ready to fight.

So, she wanted to fight, then? Hazel rolled her shoulders, limbering up. If that's what she wanted, fine, then she'd give it to her.

As Charlotte drew symbols in the air, drawing her arms back to fling another spell, the Hunter darted forward, keeping low to the ground. It grazed the top of her buoyant curls, a loud whistle that filled her ears. Lottie was fast, weaving her hands again, readying another one. This one clipped her in the shoulder as she zigged wrong, the invisible wind sending her rolling across the dewy grass. *Fuck.* She hissed internally as she covered her face with her forearms. She was up again as soon as she stopped rolling, crouching into a sprinter's start position.

Charlotte was maybe twenty yards from her. The other woman's rage still hadn't subsided, it seemed. Well, she was going to have to come off the defensive, then. She began sprinting towards Lottie, keeping low to the ground, ready to throw herself to either side if she had to. The other woman might have been taller, but Hazel was a ball of muscle and had a nice, low center of gravity. Lottie wouldn't be able to fight back as long as Hazel got her arms around her. Fifteen yards. Ten. Charlotte hadn't made a move yet. At seven odd yards, she saw the blue flame that Charlotte was summoning in her hand. She dropped lower, but she still felt its scorching heat as it soared past her head.

Three yards. Charlotte let out a yelp as she realized she wouldn't be able to get out of the way in time. Hazel slammed into her, arms wrapping around her friend's waist as they surged forward. They slammed into the ground, rolling as they grappled, pulling hair and name calling as they tumbled. They scratched and cursed, slapping at one another like angry children. Eventually, they rolled to a stop at the edge of the small pond. Hazel had landed on top of Lottie and had her grasp around the girl's shoulders, dangling her over the water.

"I swear I will dunk you in there and give you the baptism you need, because you're acting like an unholy *bitch.*" Charlotte's braid skimmed the water as she squirmed in Hazel's hold.

"I'm not a bitch, *you're* a bitch! You're trying to water board me!"

"You literally just tried to set me on fucking fire, babes!"

"Then call it even." Charlotte gasped as the top of her head skimmed the water. "Pull me up, truce, truce!"

Begrudgingly, Hazel tugged Lottie back up, away from the water. The two girls sprawled out on the earth, blades of grass scratching at bits of their exposed skin as they panted, spread out like snow angels. The howls of animals and the chirps of insects filled the dusk air. They were silent for a long moment, their ragged breaths joining the melody of sounds around them.

"I'm sorry." Hazel was the first to break the silence. "I didn't mean for this, babes."

"I know."

"But you're mad at me."

Charlotte was silent for some time before answering. "I think I've been mad for a while and not really acknowledging it. Not just about this—about everything. Obviously, you being an ass is getting to me. But there's everything. The Foundation, Bradley and being in charge.... Wade..." Her voice cracked on his name. She took a deep breath, rolling her head to the side on the grass so that she and Hazel were gazing at one another.

"Sometimes, I feel like I'm drowning, and I'm doing everything to keep my head above water. And your attempts to help are just you grabbing onto my shoulders, dragging me beneath the waterline." There was a resolve, an edge, to her words. "And I love you dude, but you have to let me sink or swim, y'know?"

"I know." Hazel's reply was soft, repentant. She reached a hand across to squeeze Charlotte's. "I'll try harder, I promise, babes."

Their moment of peaceful truce was broken by Specter's hiss cutting through the air, and a familiar shrill chitter as talons raked across Hazel's thigh.

Pain like hot needle pricks danced up her thigh as Hazel surged into action. Rolling onto her stomach, she pushed onto her feet, spinning to face the thing that had scratched up the length of her jeans. Blood welled on the exposed skin where the talons had torn the fabric. She cursed to herself—she'd just bought this pair. She sprang to her feet, casting an eye over to Charlotte. Her friend appeared unscathed as she also scrambled to her feet.

One of the shadow demons that had worked with the Order of the New Dawn—like those Hazel had summoned accidentally to Winterbourne during her failed first attempt to talk to Atticus—snarled and gnashed its teeth at them. She hadn't seen one so fully realized before, always less than flitting shadows; here, they were more formed, more corporeal. This one stood tall, towering over them. Its veined wings were like smoke at the edges, swirling and wispy. It wasn't unlike a gargoyle made of darkness and miasma as its snout twisted, eliciting another snarl. It was bigger than what she was used to; less malnourished, she supposed.

Charlotte called out to her as it hurtled forward towards her, gray veins protruding from its toned arms. Hands splayed and claws extended, it was clearly going to slash at her again with its talons. She waited until it had closed most of the distance between them before side-stepping it easily. Her body ached from her tussle with Charlotte and her hard landing earlier, despite the ease of her movements. She felt her hips for a weapon, ready to take out the creature on its next pass by. Horrified, she patted down her hips, her inner pockets. Only her small knives remained in her holster and her smokes tin in her pocket. Cursing, Hazel ducked, narrowly avoiding a body slam as the demon launched at her again.

She caught a glimpse of Charlotte's hands weaving in the air, concentration etched across her face as the barest flicker of a flame appeared before her. Her friend must have been just as drained from their fight as she was. Hazel was distracted by Charlotte and unfortunately, she didn't see the shadow demon in time as it launched at her once more, finally connecting with her body. It slammed into her, solid and heavy. A gasp slipped from between her lips as she landed on her back, chest aching as it winded her.

"Help," she wheezed as it pinned her down, talons grasping her shoulders as it bared down on her, a dark crimson tongue lolling between its jagged teeth as it sniffed her, a mere few inches away from her face. Warm, putrid breath washed over her, the scent of decay and rotten flesh. She gagged, stomach roiling as she worked her left arm free, slamming her forearm into its throat as it chomped its teeth, eager to take a bite from her.

It snarled, shaking its head as a small burst of flames bashed into the back of its head. Its grip didn't loosen on Hazel, however. The talons that gripped her tightened, the tips pinching her through the leather of her jacket. She thrashed beneath it, kicking her legs, desperately seeking purchase. As Hazel contemplated what to do, a sickening crack resounded as its neck bent, a branch connecting with the side of the demon's face as Lottie swung and screamed.

"Keep going babes," Hazel cried as its talons pierced the leather, scrapping and stabbing into the tops of her shoulders. Her vision blurred as tears welled in her eyes. Hazel struggled beneath the creature as crack after sickening crack sounded out, its body pushing down against hers as Charlotte laid out whack after whack. She knew her friend was faltering, that her Victorian, waif-like sensibilities did not make her a strong fighter. She would have also been worn the hell down from their tussle before. Hazel gritted her teeth, tears pricking at the corner of her eyes as she wracked her brain for a solution, a way out, before her face was mauled.

The pants and snarls of the creature were interrupted by Specter's familiar caterwauling as a blur of darkness streaked across her periphery. The cat had launched himself at the demon, claws sinking into its face as his teeth—were they sharper than normal?—sunk into its face, biting and tearing, ripping. A preternatural scream shattered the night as it was yanked from Hazel's body. She lay there, stunned, as the twelve pound ball of muscle somehow wrestled with the demon.

"Holy shit. Um, okay, here, let's get you up."

Hazel winced as Charlotte appeared beside her, wrapping an arm around the Hazel's shoulders. The talons hadn't gone too deep, just enough to draw a bit of blood and leave as light puncture wound behind. It was going to sting like a bitch for a while, she suspected. But she'd had worse.

Specter's snarls filled the dusk-hued woods as the demon shrieked, a dying animal. She had never seen the cat so much as engage before, and here it was, shredding this monster like he was a jungle cat, not a house cat. Her arm slung around Charlotte's slender shoulders, Hazel's free hand pushed her glasses back up her nose as she watched in amazement as Specter's teeth gnashed and tore through sinewy limbs.

"Fuck me," she muttered as the creature's body went still. Specter bounced over to them, a jaunty spring to his steps as he moved, weaving around their legs and purring. She tilted her face towards Lottie's. "Have you seen him do *that* before?"

Charlotte shook her head, murmuring, "I'm not surprised, though. Silly kitty always finds ways to show off somehow. Are you hurt, Speckles?" He meowed at her, rubbing his face against Charlotte's skinny jeans. "Yeah? I'll take that as a no then, mister. Seeing as you're safe"—she turned her face towards Hazel's—"let me check this big idiot's cuts, then."

Hazel begrudgingly let Lottie examine the flesh the shadow demon had pierced with its talons. The Witch murmured to herself as she poked Hazel's thigh, digging into her satchel that had been dropped beside them when they'd landed. She yanked out a packet of tissues, dabbing at the scratches.

"It's superficial, barely even broke the skin. It'll sting more than anything as it heals. I'm not getting anything bad off of it." Hazel winced as Charlotte poked one of the scrapes. "Oh, don't be a baby. It didn't get anything bad in there. Grandmother and Jacob can look at it for you when we get home, if you don't trust me."

The smudges under Charlotte's eyes were looking dark again, more than they had in months. Her braid was still held in place, but leaves littered her hair. Hazel stretched a hand out, tugging them free with a gentle, tender touch. Streaks of dirt stained Charlotte's cream sweater. Hazel would take it to the dry cleaner when they were home, she promised herself.

"Now what?"

Charlotte closed her eyes. Her skin glowed in the moonlight under the trio of moons, her usual wan, washed-out coloring beautiful in the low light. The sharp cut of her jaw softened in the twilight glow, the faint freckles that dusted her nose deepening in colour. The urge to reach out, to tuck that loose tendril behind Lottie's ear, overcame her.

Hazel's gut twinged and she quashed the odd yearning that nagged at her. Lottie was her best friend. No misplaced feelings of affection would do anything to ruin that. She would do anything to not lose that friendship; that love that felt so desperately like home.

"We work out where we are and how to get home. We're smart. If anyone can manage their way out of this, it's us." Charlotte drew in a deep breath, opening her eyes. "We might be sore and injured, but we aren't dead yet, and I intend on keeping us that way. So, let's work it out."

Chapter Fourteen

Hazel

*W**hack.*

Hazel drew a breath as she dispatched another shadow demon. It was the third they'd encountered as they groped their way through the forest they'd found themselves in. She'd fashioned a club out of a branch that had fallen, using it as a sort of makeshift baseball bat. Charlotte's energy was still coming back to her, small feats of magic available to her only. Specter, their surprise muscle, was more than happy to help Hazel finish off the stray enemies they encountered on the way.

So Hazel and Specter led the way, the blind leading the blind, as they stumbled through the unfamiliar woods and unknown world. Every step had them pausing, holding their breath as they listened for the snarl of evil. Occasionally they had been caught off guard, trying to avoid the demons on their home turf.

She found, after a while, it was best to just follow the cat. He seemed to have an uncanny sense of direction, a weird familiarity with the unknown terrain. An intuition that had the Hunter side-eyeing him as he plucked his way through thigh-high grass. How did he have such a confidence to where he wandered? Was it his superior cat senses, or was it something else? Who was to say?

Either way, she was suspicious as hell.

The wooded area that surrounded them seemed unending. Clearings of wildflowers that the Hunter had never encountered spiked her allergies. She tried her best to contain her sneezes and sniffles, but they escaped anyway. Even Specter didn't seem immune to the pollens of this strange place, and his little kitty sneezes had Charlotte cooing over him.

The three moons hung low in the sky above them, a terrifying visage of a reality that wasn't their own. The trees—not quite pines, but close enough—swayed in a breeze that Hazel didn't feel against her skin. There was an eeriness, an off-quality, that she couldn't quite place. It was so similar to home, to the world she knew, but the tiniest details were threaded with a silent message: *this isn't your home*. A beat of danger and discomfort, her intuition. The thing that kept her alive.

One of the other things that had Hazel on edge was the lack of *sound*. She didn't hear the expected usual scuffles and scurries of woodland creatures underfoot. No chirps or hoots of birds, no rustle of their feathers as they danced along the tree branches. There was an absence that hung heavy and thick in the air, the lack of life that left a hollowness behind.

Like a picturesque, apocalyptic landscape.

The only interruption that came from their unrelenting trudge through the woods was that of the shadow demons. They hungered, a primal rage bolstering them on as they attacked the trio in a frenzy, disregarding their lives and limb as they let out an unhinged flurry of blows. It was this sloppiness that made it so Hazel could counter them effortlessly. Their sloppiness was the only thing that stood between them and potential death as exhaustion began to loom over Hazel like a darkened rain cloud.

"What the hell do these things want?"

Charlotte's voice snapped Hazel out of her thoughts as they bashed down another one, a sickening crunch as the makeshift bat slammed it into the ground beneath. The Witch leaned over, hands on her thighs, drawing in desperate gasps of air. She had just lunged out of the way of demon—and bat—as the most recent one aimed right for her face.

"No clue." Hazel didn't want to admit that she was equally puffed out by the efforts. She was also desperately craving a cigarette. Did she have any on her?

She didn't remember if she filled her cigarette tin. "Maybe you're just that tasty, babes."

Lottie let out a scoff, but didn't say anything in response. Instead, she plopped down onto the grass beneath. It was slightly yellow and crunchy, that feeling when the summer's relentless heat eased and it began to soften with autumn rains. Her pants scrapped against the grass, a symphony of scratching and rustling. Her cat plopped down beside her, nuzzling against the Witch, letting out a soft mewl.

"Can we just rest for a bit?"

Hazel conceded. They *had* been trekking through the woods for a while, with no plan, and no clue as to where they were going. She threw herself onto the ground beside them, pulling her metal cigarette case from her jacket pocket. Yes, she had some left! Lottie gave her a nasty look, but Hazel didn't care. It was well earned; after the day they'd been having, it was worth it. Lighting it up, she took a deep drag of it. The hit of nicotine hit the back of her throat, like a warm breeze welcoming her home as she melted into the familiar peppering, tingling feeling. She leaned her head back in bliss, cigarette ash flaking away from the tip. The ash floated away on a phantom breeze.

Doubt began to fill her, a rising balloon in her chest that threatened to overwhelm her. Normally, she would be able to suppress that fear, to make the dread and anxiety become little more than a worrying at the back of her mind. But right now, even she knew how deeply she'd fucked up.

"I'm sorry," Hazel murmured.

"Huh? Did you say something?"

"I said I'm sorry. I didn't mean for any of this. And I promise, I'll make this better. I'll stop fucking up so hard, babes. I'm sorry. I've been a mess." Hazel took another long drag, looking up into the purple-indigo twilight above. The stars hadn't seemed to have moved a fraction since they'd begun their journey.

Charlotte pulled Specter into her lap. "It's okay. I understand, you know. I get frustrated all the time too. I get how you feel. You were just being Hazel, trying to take care of me the way you knew how. I forgive you for that."

Breathing a sigh of relief, Hazel stubbed out the remains of her cigarette on the grassy woods floor. She debated leaving the filtered end behind, but shoved it back into the case. Who knew what could come out of littering in a strange world? Something about the Butterfly Effect, she was sure.

"Alright, babes. That's enough resting on our laurels." Hazel got to her feet, extending a hand to her best friend. "Let's follow the cat and find our way home."

"You know, we don't often get a lot of time to just chat like this. Like, time that isn't taken up with other things, y'know?"

Hazel's tone and words were nonchalant, but she felt anything but it. Despite their conversation before, there were many words that hung heavy between them. Months of dancing around certain topics, of avoiding grief and heartache. Charlotte had a strong dam inside her, but Hazel knew all too well that one day, those cracks were going to break once more. And she wanted to be there for her friend before it all happened.

"I guess we're just always busy doing work for the Foundation right now. We took over; of course we're going to get busy." Charlotte plucked at imaginary lint as they strolled after the cat. Hazel knew all too well that whatever she wanted to talk about, Charlotte didn't. *Well, too bad. You're my hostage right now.*

"Yeah, true." Hazel willed casualness into her voice, relying on her usual sense of ego. "But that doesn't mean that we can't make time for some girlie talk."

"Girlie talk?" Charlotte arched a brow. "Oh boy, I'm really excited to see where this is going to go."

Letting out a sigh, Hazel continued on. She wasn't about to let some sarcasm deter her. "Look, I know that there's been a lot going on, but I'm here to talk about Wade—"

"There's nothing to talk about; I already told you as much." There was a sharp edge to Charlotte's tone, and that wall that came up so little those days was teetering, threatening to erect itself.

"Yeah, but come on, no one gets over their grief that fast."

"I never said I had, Hazel. In fact, I recall saying the opposite." Charlotte's tone was icy now. "I just don't have the luxury to dwell on it, okay? I have a life I need to get on with. I already told you as much. I don't know why you're choose to hash over this *again.*"

"Because I care about you, you stupid muppet!"

Hazel couldn't help the anger that laced her words, the bursting feeling of rage and incompetence that threatened to swallow her; what had been the ebb and flow of a tide now turned into a tsunami of repressed feelings that were looking to drown her, to yank her away from the shore.

Charlotte bit her lip, but continued marching after Specter. Silence hung thick and heavy between them, cloying. It was inescapable. She would wait, though, however long it took. Their friendship was precious but not fragile. They could weather this storm and find themselves on the other side. Eventually. Her best friend was proving to be more resolute than she could have anticipated.

"Forget it," Hazel finally muttered. They would pursue it later. For now, they would follow the cat, and make their way through this unknown landscape, together at least.

Hazel was grateful they had Specter to rely on.

They traversed through the thick woods, winding their way through trees, rather than any set path. They encountered more pools of starlit water like they had earlier, the night sky seemingly trapped within their inky depths. Hazel's parched throat tempted her close to them, eager to quench her thirst. A scolding

Charlotte told her that drinking water in an unknown world was the height of dumbassery.

She liked to think she had done much dumber things, and proudly told Charlotte as much, who had rolled her eyes and strolled after the cat in response. Hazel followed Charlotte, persisting with her comments, asking why it would be so bad if she were to quench herself. Charlotte's only retort was to tell her that if the Fae offered her drink and food, that Hazel wouldn't hesitate.

They continued following Specter, his sure-footed pattering silent as he wove a path forward for them.

Eventually, the trees began to lessen; the branches began to become less dense, the leaves let in more light from above. And as they did so, another source of light began to illuminate them, like the Star of Bethlehem guiding them forward. They shared a look as Specter began to speed up into a trot, eagerly making his way towards the light. They raced behind him, breaking into a light sprint as the cat began to race like some sort of jungle cat, racing out of the woods and into the world beyond.

Both girls let out a gasp as they broke free of the treeline. Hazel skidded to a stop, the heel of her boot sending mud and grass flying as she lurched in place. There were no words to describe what they had arrived upon—at least, none in her vocabulary. Before them lay more fields of flowers, and the triple moons were still heavy in the sky. But the world around them was no longer the dimly lit forest full of demons and silence. Instead, an immense cityscape wrapped around a towering mountain; it loomed over them, a surreal, fantastical sight.

Towers and spires littered the view above, many pinpricks of light illuminating the stone-hewn buildings. Atop the mountain rested what Hazel could only describe as a castle, lording over the buildings below. Daunted wasn't a word that she used often, but this was one of the few times in her life where it seemed appropriate. Hazel gulped, turning toward her friend. Lottie's deep brown eyes were wide as she took in the view before them, sucking in a small, sharp breath as she gazed with both wonder and horror on her face.

"What the hell is this?" Lottie whispered. Hazel reached out a hand to her friend, who gripped it without looking. Hazel gave it a tight squeeze, her attention returning to the scene before them.

"I don't know babes, but I guess we're about to find out."

Chapter Fifteen

Hazel

One demon. Two demons. Then too many demons to count. Hazel's limbs began to tire as they crossed the sprawling meadow that lay between the woods and the winding cityscape. She continued smacking them down with her makeshift weapon, undeterred, unwilling to let Charlotte see how drained she was.

What a fucking nightmare of a day.

Their determined march turned into a trudge by about halfway across the field. The tall grass swished gently against their calves as they marched, iridescent flower petals swaying with their movements. They'd stopped and stared a few times, breath taken. What kind of world was this? Sweet florals filled the evening air, intoxicating Hazel as she kept stopping, bending to inhale their fragrant aroma. Specter's tail was raised and twitched in annoyance, side eying them as he let out a growl as if to say, 'hurry along'.

But she wanted so desperately to stop and rest. She was tired. Being the brawn was *hard*. She constantly had to be one step ahead, had to have the stamina to continue fighting even when she was pushed beyond exhaustion. What was the cat's hurry, anyway? They were fucked. They were in a strange world, with no idea where they were, or how to get home.

Hazel's stomach sank. How *were* they going to get home? Could they even? How badly had she fucked up this time?

"Lottie." She rarely used Charlotte's name, let alone her nickname. The other woman stopped sniffing the flower she had plucked and stared over at Hazel, wide-eyed. "I fucked up hard. I've fucked up so fucking hard."

"It's... it's okay. We all make mistakes."

Hazel shook her head, tears pricking at the corners of her eyes, burning. She shoved her glasses aside, hastily rubbing at them with the back of her hand, grateful she didn't wear makeup. She wasn't going to cry, she wasn't going to break. "This wasn't just a mistake. This was a colossal fuck up."

"Well, yeah." Charlotte wasn't one to pull punches, and Hazel was grateful for that. "You fucked up. But there's no changing that. All we can do is try to fix it. No different than when we're at work." Hazel grimaced. She didn't like fucking up at work, either. Charlotte caught her expression and sighed. "It's okay to make mistakes, as long as those mistakes don't end the world, Hazel."

Specter let out a low hiss, just in time for Hazel to swing around, her weapon in hand. A wispy, dark shadow had leaped at her, and she caught it just in time with her bat. It connected with a thud, and she swung down hard, slamming it into the grass with a sickening crunch. It began to howl, an otherworldly shriek. With a grimace, she raised her bat, slamming it down repeatedly on the demon's head. Vile smelling black fluid began to leak from its skull as she kept bringing down her weapon, long after it had stopped twitching. She was done, she was so fucking *done*. Done with this place, done with these creatures, done *ruining* everything she touched.

Why was she such a fuck up?

"You can stop, Hazel."

Charlotte's voice snapped her out of her thoughts, out of her trance. She looked down at the mess she had made, horrified. Blood, sticky residue now covered her hands, covered the length of her bat. The creature's wings stuck out at an odd angle, its body bent in an unnatural position. Its head—the remains of it, anyway—was splattered across the grass, unrecognizable. Specter trotted over and gave a sniff. Before either of the women could process it, he began lapping up the dark, sticky ichor.

"Specter, *no*," they yelled in unison as the cat licked up the remains, as if enjoying a refreshing quench from his water fountain. He ignored them, though, gingerly stepping his paws around the remains of the creature to get to the crater that was its skull. Hazel's stomach twisted as Specter began to drink in earnest, the putrid scent wafting over them, like a several day-old corpse on a warm summer's eve.

Charlotte, clearly, couldn't take it. She bent over and heaved onto the beautiful wildflowers. *What a horrifying juxtaposition*, Hazel thought, the triple moon highlighting Charlotte's delicate, convulsing frame in the background, with Specter in the foreground supping down the creature's lifeblood like it was the wine of Christ at the last supper.

Stepping around the mess she had made, Hazel tip-toped to her friend, dropping her bat beside her bestie. She turned Charlotte's body away with a gentle nudge, so they were facing away from Specter's desecration. Rubbing slow, soothing circles on the Witch's back, she murmured placating words, reassuring her.

"This is so fucked up," Charlotte sobbed between heaves. Her hands were to her stomach, holding it as she wept. Nothing was coming out of her at this point, but she still braced her body. "How the fuck did we get here?"

A pang of guilt shot through Hazel like a hot knife. *She* was how they'd gotten there. She was the reason for this all. And she had to fix it.

"I'll be right back," she told Charlotte gently, before pulling away. Pacing a few steps towards Specter, she faced him and the demon corpse, hands on her hips. "Alright, cat. That's enough demon soup for one day. There's something fucked up and weird about you, but you seem to know where you're going. So you're in charge. We're gonna follow you and find our way out of here. So step up, and take care of your mama, and show us how to get home."

The cat blinked lazily at her, his large eyes endless pools of topaz starlight. But he listened; at least, he seemed to, because he stopped slurping at the demon liquid and slunk over to Charlotte. He wove his way around her legs several times, nuzzling up against her, his purr a loud vibration that filled the critter-less night air. She had finished heaving, her hands to her thighs as she bent over, her pallid complexion somehow leeched of more life than usual.

"Sorry, kitty," Charlotte murmured, sucking in a deep breath. "I'm just having a bit of a time."

He mewed, as if in understanding. He nuzzled her again as she exhaled and pushed upright. Charlotte's face was drawn, her chocolate-brown eyes puffy and red from tears and exhaustion. More white-hot guilt burned a path through Hazel's chest, a dance of distress. She hadn't seen her friend this run down in a long time—or had she just not been paying attention? Hazel went to open her mouth, but no words came out. No jokes, no banter, no apologies. No nothing.

"Come on, we have a long way ahead of us, I assume. So, lead on," Charlotte told her cat. She brushed her long hair aside, shot Hazel a glance, and began trekking across the meadow once more. Hazel followed in contemplative silence, wondering what she could do to make it all better.

It took them a while to reach the end of the meadow, but in the end, it was worth it.

The winding mountain city they had seen from the forest edge was unfathomable up close. The light that had reminded Hazel of a big city didn't seem electric at all; as they approached the outer edges, there were sprawling houses and buildings that followed narrow cobblestone paths, lined with gas lamps. It was as if a rainbow had thrown up on Europe somewhere. At least, that's the best way she could describe it.

Before them were colorful houses of all manner of sizes. Despite their differences, they all had long, pointed arches, spires, and stain glass windows depicting different things. Some had beautiful flora she had never seen, others stars and moons—and a few had what could only be described as battle scenes of some kind. The ones closest to them, closest to the meadow, were cottage sized, with small, fenced in yards that contained multitudes of interesting plants that wove up the sides of the houses and across lush, damp tilled soil. Spread out from one another, the cobblestone paths were sparser, more dirt filling in the space between the stones. If Hazel were to hazard a guess, the poorer denizens of this world probably lived in these humble little cottages on the outskirts of the ineffable city.

Still better than where she lived in college.

Curiosity got the better of her as they approached the first house. With a feline grace, she quietly crept to the window of the house, despite hissed protests from Charlotte. Hazel waved a lazy, dismissive hand. She was a Hunter. Recon was part of the job. Know the enemy, and all that. Her boots padded against soft, loamy dirt, a heavy imprint left behind despite the lightness of her tread. She would brush them away after.

Motioning for Charlotte to follow, she crept around the side of the house, looking for clues, for information. Eventually, she found a large window around the side, only the center images stained. The rest was completely, and thankfully, transparent.

There was something so familiar about the scene that she gazed upon within. Despite the eclectic outside of the cottage, the inside was reminiscent of a homestead. A long, heavy wood table sat in the middle of a tiled kitchen, small cabinets hanging over benches full of knickknacks and utensils. Herbs hung from wooden drying racks, a fire burning on the back most wall in a gigantic fireplace that took up most of the brick wall. A cast iron pot —not unlike a cauldron—hung over the open flame, something bubbling within.

"Oh, that's fucking *cozy.*"

"Hazel Julia Williams, *get the fuck away from that stranger's window!*"

She rolled her eyes as she turned to glare at Charlotte. She knew what she was doing. She was a professional. She was born into, raised into, this life. Her friend was dithering on the outside of the small, crooked fence surrounding the property. Hazel was *fine*. There was no one in the room; the one door leading to it had been closed, and she would have heard it open and ducked away if she had. With another roll of her eyes, she turned back to the window, and came face-to-face with a small creature.

It was childlike in size and features, with gray-tone skin, narrow dark eyes, a shock of red hair, and a curious expression. It had the same dumb look most kids had, at least Hazel thought so. They stared at one another in complete silence, unblinking, unmoving. Time seemed to slow down for Hazel as they engaged in a staring contest, as she waited for it to blink, to react. It was like they were in their own bubble, separate from the rest of the universe, until the being opened its mouth wide and let out an ear-piercing howl.

She didn't mean for what happened next—she acted on instinct. A terrible, nonsensical instinct. One moment, her makeshift bat was leaning against the side of the house where she had placed it before peering inside. The next, she had it in hand and was slamming into the window like she was going for a home run.

Glass shattered around her as the creature's high-pitched wail became a low, animosity filled rumble full of snarls and hissing. Its face contorted from the serene expression of a child to a horror-fueled monster. Its forehead extended, those dark narrow eyes flattening into slits as its nose widened and flattened like a pig snout. Darkness seemed to creep around it, like a cloak settling upon its shoulders.

Dread filled her, a cold unease that spread from her stomach outward, tendril-like vines that wrapped through her very veins. There was something deeply wrong with the creature—worse than the shadow demons. Her heart slowed as they stared once more, time slowing, as the remains of the broken window swung forward on its hinge.

And then it launched itself at her.

Charlotte's scream cut through the haze as Hazel launched into action, pure instinct and adrenaline driving her forward. Hazel ducked, and the creature narrowly missed her face. However, it did manage to snarl its dirty talons in her curls, and yanked, pulling her to the ground in a fit of rage and screams. She thrashed blindly as it knocked her glasses from her face, sending them tumbling where she couldn't see.

Cursing loudly, Hazel dropped her makeshift bat and clutched at her hair, desperate to remove the vile little creature from her curls. She yelled out to her friend. "Some help would be really fucking nice, babes."

Hazel had to rely on instincts over her sight as it hid behind her, using her own body as a shield. Inhaling deeply, centering herself, Hazel launched into action. She could feel the demon child on her back, snarling as its taloned fingers dug into her scalp, scraping at the flesh. As it let out a feral screech, Hazel twisted her body and fell back against the brick wall of the cottage, slamming the demonic child and herself against it. Then she did it again, slamming as hard as she could against the wall as it let out a horrific, squealing grunt, not unlike a pig being slaughtered.

"Let go, you grotesque little fucker," she rasped as it crawled up higher, wrapping its stocky little legs around her neck, squeezing. Coarse fabric scratched against her skin. *Charlotte, do something, babes.*

"Stay still so I can try, then!"

One moment, the small creature was wrapped around her firmly, choking the air out of her lungs. The next, she was loose and light once more. She let out a groan as her curls were yanked hard, and the creature was released from her hair. Tears blurred the corners of her eyes, unbidden. *Holy fuck, that stings.* Reaching a shaking hand up, Hazel felt her scalp, making sure no hair or skin had been pulled away. It seemed intact enough. Charlotte wrestled the creature, its arms pinned between hers, its back against her chest as she hauled it away from Hazel.

"Be careful of your glasses, they're near your foot."

Hazel wasn't as blind as Charlotte made her out to be, as much as the other woman teased her. She could wear contacts or get by without the glasses. She just liked things being clear. With a roll of her eyes, she snatched up her glasses with a single, swift motion. Rubbing the smudges off on her shirt—which honestly, wasn't much cleaner than the glasses, despite her sweater protecting it—she returned her attention to Charlotte and the demonic beastly child she was handling. Charlotte didn't have the best grip or upper body strength on a good day; today, she was floundering harder than ever. The small creature was unharmed by its tussle with Hazel, but it was shrieking and spitting like a cat thrown in water. Which she knew what it sounded like, cause she'd done it to Specter when he snatched her lunch once. It slammed its small body against Charlotte, who's arms quivered with the effort of restraining it. Cracking her knuckles, Hazel strode over and grabbed the demon, pinching its wrists together.

"Let go, babes." Charlotte did as Hazel requested and left the child dangling in the air as Hazel held it aloft. It stared back at her with black, matte eyes, a haunting visage. Its body was almost cherubic—it was chubby and dressed like a Victorian porcelain doll. Sharp, fanged little teeth gnashed together as it snarled at her. Its skin was the color of when formaldehyde was used in embalming—the grayish tinge of the dead—its wrists twisting where they were encircled in her grip. It was thrashing wildly, trying to loosen her grip. "And what about you, lil' guy? Feel up for a chat?"

It hissed at her again, a nasally, low sound. She grimaced at it, staring it down. She could get anything to talk with enough pressure—even if it wasn't in words. Everything could communicate fear in one way or another. And she was a maestro of fear and discomfort.

"How about we make you comfortable for our conversation, then?"

Charlotte looked like she was going to vomit again as she pressed her back against the kitchen counter. Which wasn't unusual for her—for a witch who got into ghost hunting, she was a squeamish girl. Even if Charlotte could push through the worst of things, the after always got her.

Maybe Hazel was just desensitized.

They wriggled in through the window, much to her friend's dismay. Specter had leaped through without a second thought. Hazel had crawled in after them, wrestling the Fae-like child—it reminded her of a Changeling—in with her as it squirmed in her grip, trying to bite her. She was grateful for her leather jacket; she'd had worse things try to nip at her before and not break through the fabric to her skin.

They'd found spare rope meant for the drying racks and tied the creature to the chair. It had bellowed and wailed fiercely as she did so, and Charlotte had panicked. What if something heard them? They didn't know what this place was, what this creature was. What if something worse came out for them?

Hazel had argued back and told Lottie if something worse was going to come get them, then it would have already. The Witch had closed her mouth then, unable to retort. Hazel had sent Specter off through the cottage to scout, though, as she began her interrogation.

"Now, listen here." She knelt before it. It was secured to the chair at its legs, its arms tied behind so it couldn't scratch or attack her. Its flame red hair fell in its eyes, the distorted, ugly features smooth once more, staring at her with widened eyes. She knew better, though. It was trying to trick her, pretend to be more like something it wasn't. "I don't have time for you to be a little shit. I know you might not understand the exact words I'm saying, but you know context, or you wouldn't have jumped out at me like a fucking possessed animatronic. So, one way or another, you're gonna tell me what you are and *where* we are."

The creature remained silent, its bottom lip trembling as it glanced to Charlotte. She heard Charlotte take a step forward hesitantly. Hazel put a hand up to stop her. "Babes, don't give into it. It's trying to mess with you. You should know better, goddamn."

The creature scoffed then. Hazel's eyes narrowed as it tilted its head inquisitively, a grin splitting across its face. A gasp slipped from Charlotte as a low cackle rumbled from the child-like being, deep and sonorous. Hazel furrowed her brow, staring down at it. "Well, if you can laugh, I assume you can speak. So speak up."

Head remaining cocked, its grin split open wider, baring a maw of sharp teeth. Based on its nibble on her jacket earlier, the Hunter knew its mouth would be no joke if it latched on. She waited for it to speak, giving it a chance to crack before she applied pressure. Every creature knew the universal language of pain, and she suspected this monster was no different. She could tell it was threatening her, its composure an attempt to scare her, make her falter.

She'd fuck it up before it had a chance to get under her skin.

Leaning back against the counter, she waited, wondering if it could free itself from its restraints but chose not to, just to mess with them. Maybe it would. Maybe it wouldn't talk. Maybe she wasn't good at her job. Maybe she couldn't keep Charlotte safe.

Self-doubt crept into her, a tugging, gnawing discomfort. It winded its way through her body like a ribbon of darkness, through her veins, across her bones, tying up her up and pinning her in place. Everything she ever did, ever tried to do, she seemed to fuck up. Even the things she thought she could do well. Maybe she'd just been lying to herself; perhaps everyone else had been lying to her, too. People did that, when they didn't want to hurt someone. Lied to protect them. Like how Charlotte lied to her to protect her, like her parents had before they died—

"Stop it!"

Charlotte's voice, loud and commanding, cut through Hazel's thoughts. She snapped back to the kitchen in the cottage, head spinning, as she took in the scene before her. Charlotte had darted forward and was face-to-face with the entity, mere inches away. And she was *pissed*. Hands twitching at her sides, flexing, Charlotte whispered loudly, "Cut that out right this minute."

It tilted its head back in the chair and roared with laughter, a deep, booming chortle of derision. Heat flooded through Hazel as realization dawned on her; it was laughing at them, laughing at *her*. It kicked its legs—as much as it could with the rope ties—like a little kid who had just told the most hilarious joke.

She was the joke.

"Your kind is all too easy to mess with," it mocked. Its voice was not unlike its laugh, deep and obnoxious. Fury clouded her head, clouded her judgment, as it trained its eyes on Hazel. "Far too easy to manipulate indeed, aren't you?"

She opened her mouth to retort, but nothing came out. No witty banter, no snide comments, no deflection. That tightness in her chest, that insecurity from before, was like an icy grip around her heart, refusing to let go. The work of the monster in front of her, she was sure.

"How did you get in our heads? Spill it, or I'll make you."

Rarely did Charlotte take over as bad cop, if ever. More shame flooded through her; she was meant to be the strong one, be the one that took care of her friend. Yet here she stood, pathetic, limp. Unable to move, unable to speak. The creature's eyes were trained on Hazel still as it grinned once more.

"Oh, it's just a fun little game we like to play. So easy to tamper with. You make yourself wide open to it when you wear your feelings on your sleeve."

The way it spoke, the cadence and the condescension, reminded Hazel of someone. It was there, niggling at her mind. The attitude, the sheer audacity—

"Demon." The word slipped from her lips unbidden. This thing, this creature, reminded her of Atticus. The petulant, nasty, little brat. Its dark eyes flashed at her as Charlotte took several hurried steps back.

"That's a name that we are known as to your kind, yes," it conceded. "Though you mortals have a limited grasp and understanding of our reach, our power."

"Can't have that much power if I managed to tie you to a chair."

It shot her a withering look as the words slipped out of her, her confidence returning as its power receded. It was as if it was beginning to fear her now, its tendrils slipping free of her mind as she pushed back. It emboldened Hazel. "And if you could get out, I assume you would have already. Which probably means you're not top shit around here, are you?"

It scowled, its face contorting into the same ugly expression as earlier. *Bingo.* She was right on the mark. "I'm going to take a wild stab and say that you can't change your features much then, either. Though I suspect others of your kind can do so. You wouldn't be very good at tricking humans at all, would ya, babes?" Its dark eyes were mere slits as it pressed its lips together tightly. She'd continue taunting it, then, trying to get information.

However, as she went to question it, the creature spoke first. "Stupid human. You talk a lot for such a dumb animal."

"It's just trying to provoke you, Hazel. Don't listen to it."

"Don't listen to it," it mocked, repeated Charlotte. It let out a laugh. "You should have run while you could."

Hazel snorted. "You can't do much, strapped to that chair. Didn't I already tell you that?"

It merely chortled again. As it laughed, Specter returned, hissing, his yellow eyes wide with concern. Hazel's eyes darted to him, to the doorway where he stood, the warmth draining from her body as she saw a massive shadow fall across the entryway. The small creature hadn't been alone, and the horrendous cackle it let loose confirmed as much.

Staring in horror, Hazel watched as the shadow became a gargantuan creature that filled the doorway. It wasn't unlike a gargoyle, with fangs and a snout like the creature tied to the chair. Its hulking frame squeezed through the door, an angry rumble emanating from it.

"Run," Hazel whispered to Charlotte, while Specter lunged for the door to the cottage as the creature made a dive for them.

They dashed from the cottage after Specter, the monsters hot on their heels as they slipped in mud and sprinted their way up the slope into the city beyond. The creature let out a roar, and a chorus of others swelled in the distance, a warning call, a siren.

They were absolutely fucked.

They ran.

Hazel prayed that Charlotte could keep up with her as they raced after Specter through narrow streets. Smoke permeated the air the further into the city they ran, tendrils of acrid air burning their lungs.

"Run faster, babes."

"I'm running as fast as I can! I'm not an athlete!"

Specter let out a loud mew, as if in encouragement, before he skidded to a stop. Hazel nearly tripped over him, heart stopping as she saw why he'd stopped. Terrible, slate-skinned creatures with veined wings towered over them at the end of the path, blocking off their escape. She glanced around, running on pure instinct. She could smash a window, shove Charlotte through. But then what? Could the Witch use magic again yet? Hazel was about to call out to her friend, when she glimpsed Charlotte collapsing in her peripheral vision. It was as if time was moving in slow motion as the world went silent as she felt herself be tackled from behind, and her head hit the path beneath her.

Chapter Sixteen

Atticus

His power seeped through him now, magic that had waned mere days ago. It crackled like a pulse, like blood flowing through his veins. Being without it in that cell was like being without air, without sustenance. He was still weak; he needed to feed soon. He would find a lesser daemon, take their energy. But he was whole and hale enough.

Atticus breezed through the narrow alleys of his home, like a bird catching the wind, harmonious and at peace. They ran into their fair share of lesser daemons, worthless underlings that he could shatter with a single strike of magic. He carved his arms through the air—once, twice, a dozen times—sending out blades of air that were sharp enough to decapitate, soaring at his enemies.

Wade had been his silent companion, watching with unblinking eyes as Atticus led the way to safety. His confidence escalated as he kept his dearest friend out of harm's way. He could do this; he was competent, he was able. Atticus pounced, sending a wave of air at another lesser daemon. It sliced through the creature, turning it to ashes mid-lunge. The Princeling puffed out his chest in pride as he turned back toward Wade.

"See, dearest? I told you that I would be able to manage anything that stepped within our path!"

His friend's eyes were downcast, a forlorn tug at the corner of his mouth. Why was his friend looking this way, feeling this way? It made no sense to him. Atticus was taking care of him, getting him to safety. Everything was falling into place, everything was going to go back to the way it was, before the Emberly girl got involved. So why was he making that damned face?

"What is it?"

"I cannot help." Wade stared down at his gloved hands, clenching them together. "I have never been of help, in this life or the past. I am beyond useless, beyond despair."

Atticus cocked his head. "Whatever do you mean by this?"

Wade's shoulders slumped delicately, a wistful sigh slipping from his lips. His auburn hair was mussed from their trek through the back streets of Terra Doreum, but it only made him all the more handsome. The moon lit sky and the low light of the street lamps had his vicious jaw scar glistening as he raised his head once more to the sky. "I wish to be of use."

"Of course you're of use. Your existence is plenty."

A grimace, Wade's beautiful mouth twisting. It was a sin, a mockery—how something so radiant could become so sorrowful and disconsolate? Why was his soul so fragmented, still?

"Is it about the girl?"

Atticus' breath hitched in his throat even as the words spilled out of him. Why had he asked about *her* when they were fixing things? Wade's alabaster brow furrowed. He towered over Atticus, a tall, slender being made of perfection. Humans modeled many things from daemons and gods, but he knew that Wade was the closest thing they had to an angel.

Wade shook his head, a soft, delicate motion. "No. I merely wish to be of service. I am a burden here, unable to procure even a modicum of my talents. How am I meant to keep you or myself safe?"

He wants to protect me, too. Heat flooded Atticus' cheeks. "I can take care of you."

"But what if something was to happen to you and I was to be left there to watch?"

Atticus knew what Wade meant as his dear companion's gaze strayed back to his hands once more. He'd wanted to protect the girl, to take care of her, and had been unable. Atticus knew that, knew how it ate at Wade. His stomach filled with a gnawing, fluttering sensation, an almost queasiness. He stilled his desire to reach out a hand in comfort. What could he do to make this better for him, to give him that sense of hope, to feel as though he could be of service?

It hit Atticus like a punch to the gut as he gazed at his companion, his heart twisting and snarling like a thorn bush had encased it and was slowly squeezing it tight. Despite it all, despite all the suffering, Wade still wanted to push on, push forward, to be alive once more. And he needed everything he could to make that happen.

"You need your power. You can't use your magic here." Realization dawned on the daemon as Wade clenched his hands.

"Yes. But I cannot feel it, cannot access it. It is as if it were drained wholly from my body, leaving me bereft of its song." His words were tinged with melancholy longing, a sadness that weighted him down like a current in a raging sea.

"What... what if I were to be of assistance?"

Wade scowled, a beautiful, haunting mar across his face. "You already are, Atticus. What more can you offer me than protection?"

"I can offer you power."

Wade stilled, the angry line that etched his face like a master painter's brush frozen in place. He did not appear to so much as breathe. Long, agonizing moments passed before Atticus saw him draw a fraught, rattling breath between his pink, soft lips.

"What do you mean, you can offer me power?"

Had Atticus not been waiting to hear Wade's response, he may have missed his companion's words. They were tender, fragile, yearning and soft, as the world around them filled with the crackle of flame and screams of agony. Wade was one who wore his heart on his sleeve, his emotion on his face. He could not hide how he felt, and Atticus knew fearful hope flooded his friend. A chance to have power again also meant a chance for almost certain doom once more.

"It is not without its risks." Atticus was quiet, demure. "But it is the best option we have."

"What if things were to go awry once more?"

Wade's whisper was heart-achingly soft, despair tinging them. Atticus would not let his worries weigh him down, though. For now, they had a singular goal, and they would worry about the rest when the time came.

"It is not the time to fret about that, dear one. We have to keep our sights trained on getting you out of this safely. The rest can come later." Those smoky, gray eyes raised from the ground, training themselves on Atticus as Wade took the daemon in, as if contemplating him fully for the first time. Atticus' skin prickled, the flesh facade he wore dancing with delight and nerves, as if Wade's gaze were a touch upon his skin.

"You're right, Atticus. We have to make our way to your family home, and 'wing' it, I suppose." A smile lifted the corner of Wade's mouth, a ray of glee shining through his sombre expression.

"Yes, like the mouthy girl *would* say. Pretend you are her, dearest. What would she do right now?"

Wade let out a huff, a mix between a laugh and a snort of derision. "She would merely barge ahead and expect the rest of us to catch up, lest we be left behind."

"Then, that is exactly what we must do now."

Atticus remembered the day he met Wade; a boy no older than twelve, barely more than a child, as he yelled for help. The Emberly girl—Atticus had not cared for her and protecting her was not in his contract—had fallen through the ice. Atticus had been watching from the shadows, his own tasks to accomplish, when fate had intervened for him on that day. No one else had been around; the child had run off from her nanny. Perhaps they expected him to keep an eye over her. It wouldn't have surprised him if that were true. He'd lazily been watching her, curious. Human children were so fraught with mortal peril, after all. Why show interest in something so breakable?

It was a cold Victorian winter, and the small pond was frozen over as the girl had made her way to it, climbing over piles of snow. It seemed she had tired of snow angels and instead sought something more exciting. She had hesitantly stepped on the ice, bending her knees to skate across. Then a short, sharp scream had punctuated the frigid air. One moment, her honey, curled hair was flapping in the wind; the next, it was gone from the horizon. Atticus had noticed the young boy who had been passing by. Dark red hair and a slash of pale features blurred past Atticus, who was now fully paying attention as he witnessed the stupidest and more heartfelt display of empathy in his time in the mortal realm.

Wade van Baird had raced after her upon seeing it, careless for his own safety as he threw himself onto the ice and hauled her to safety. She hadn't been breathing when he brought her to the surface, his wool coat soaked up the armpits in deathly cold water. Somehow, his fragile, boyish body had summoned the strength to haul up the water-laden girl, much heavier than she should have been. He had dragged her—her face tinged a deathly blue—toward the snowbank and began sporadically breathing into her while compressing her chest. It was clear the boy had no idea what he was doing, or that he couldn't sense that she was no longer with them.

That wouldn't stop the boy, though. He was obstinate to a fault as he tried to breathe life into her, pausing to slap her small, chubby cheeks. Atticus watched, slipping through the shadows, as the boy reached into his pocket, yanking a vial of black liquid from it. He uncorked it with trembling hands, cushioning her head with his arm as the other tipped the concoction down her throat. The liquid wouldn't go down voluntarily; the boy had to massage her throat, urging it down. Atticus smelled the magic on him, the tinge of daemonic energy in the vial. Ah, that made sense. The boy had access to power like his own.

Magic users were not unheard of this world. They were the reason daemons like him were able to come and strike deals, to come and feed on this world. Power in exchange for energy. Too many humans were eager to make that deal, to give that up. This boy was too young, his soul too clean, to have made his own pact. The energy coming off him was irresistible, an invisible thread that pulled Atticus closer, an unseen and unstoppable force.

"She's dead."

Atticus had stopped behind the boy, hadn't realized he had gotten so close or spoken until the stranger had jumped. The auburn-haired angel had looked over his shoulder at Atticus, eyes red and face wan as he observed the daemon.

"You can't know she's dead," the child had insisted, voice cracking. "I just... I just need to get the water out of her lungs..."

With a shake of his head, Atticus had placed a hand on the boy's shoulder. "Feel her skin, her pulse; no heart beats within her chest, child. You aren't going to be far off behind her if you do not get out of your wet clothing and somewhere dry soon."

He'd shuddered at Atticus' words, as if finally realizing he was, indeed, cold. His slender body had trembled, his hair mussed from the wind and his exertions. "I can't just give up. There has to be something I can do. She's just a little kid; she's just like Loren! Please help me."

Atticus had no clue who this Loren was, and hadn't cared. But the ferocity in the boy's words, that shining, gleaming white aura, mesmerized him, entranced him. That energy pulled Atticus in again, threatening to swallow him whole as he stared into those wide gray eyes, sparkling with tears.

"I'll help you. But only if you make a deal with me."

The words tumbled out of Atticus' mouth. Normally he was sly, cornered his favorite humans as though they were play things for his amusement. They were accessories, as much as he could enjoy their companionship. This boy was different, though. From the second they locked eyes, Atticus knew that his destiny was tied up with this boy. He didn't want to be around him—he *needed* to be. There was a compulsion that was greater than anything he had experienced before.

"You will? And what deal do you want?" The boy eyed him with suspicion, shivering, the dead child tenderly wrapped up in his arms. A pang shot through Atticus. He swallowed, dry and harsh.

"If you be my friend, I will help the girl and keep you safe as long as you and I are bound."

Atticus had never made such a deal before. He knew in his core what those words meant. And as he locked eyes with the boy, he nodded once, before whispering, "Yes."

Atticus dropped to the ground beside the boy. "I need you to know my true name and that you swear you will never reveal it. You must make your deal in blood, or it will not be bound, and I will not be able to maintain my end of the deal."

A tinge of terror flickered in the boy's eyes. He clenched his jaw, resolute as he nodded once more. "I understand the terms of your bargain, demon."

So, the boy knew what he was, then. That would make this easier for him. "Give me your true name and I will give you mine."

"Wade Enoch James van Baird." There was no hesitation as Wade gazed into Atticus eyes, stretching out his palm, removing his wool glove, exposing his blue-tinged fingers beneath. Wade was a goner without Atticus. The boy shivered violently, but did not break eye contact. With a nod, Atticus slashed his palm with a taloned finger then Wade's, faster than the boy could blink, clasping their hands together.

"You may call me Asterius."

He did not falter as he gifted the child his true name and the bond between them formed like the blood vessels in a newly born heart. Warmth washed over Atticus like a summer breeze as the boy drew his hand back, mouth wide as his palm healed over under his gaze. Atticus' daemonic energy, his power, now pulsated through Wade's very blood. And for the first time, Atticus's heart skipped a beat, a hollowness in his chest bursting like a water drop hitting the ground. A gasp slipped from the daemon's lips. He stared in wonderment, perplexed. What was this feeling that threatened to consume him?

"How do I save her?"

Wade's words broke Atticus from his reverie. Ah, yes, the child. His magic would tether her to the world, but Atticus did not dare tell the boy that when she came back, she would be broken, never whole again. It might not even be the original girl that took up residence in the corpse; but that wasn't what Wade had asked for. He had just asked for her to be saved.

She would come back wrong, no matter what Atticus did.

Still, he helped Wade use his magic to bring her back. They each placed a hand to her small, unmoving chest as their magic intermingled and breathed life back into her, a golden thread that wended its way inside her. Color returned to her cheeks as she spluttered, her eyes dim and hazy as part of her returned to the mortal world. Wade had stared down at her, and despite his pact with Atticus, his white aura shone brightly.

In the narrow alleyway, with the sounds of the city in peril filling the wind around them, a daemon and a man faced one another. The energy between them was much different than the first time they had made a contract with one another. A level of desperate desire emanated from Wade still, but there was as stronger resolve. He wasn't a child who wanted to help from the goodness of his small heart; he was a man who was determined to use whatever means to get to his ends.

Wade stared at Atticus like Lucifer in Alexandre Cabanel's *L'Ange déchu*, his dark eyes a swirling storm, his beautiful lips a hard-pressed line. His Edwardian sensibilities were prominent as he stood tall and resolute, resolve emanating from him. His once fine evening suit had begun to see the effects of time and wear, but he wore them still as though they were freshly laundered coattails. He was every bit the proud gentleman as he waited for Atticus to speak.

"If we are to make a deal, it will bind us together once more." The wind around them began to whip up, as if it sensed the enormity of the moment. "Are you prepared for that?"

His tormented friend grimaced then, his mouth twisting into a bitter, downward curve. He nodded, despite this. "I now understand the ramifications of our deal."

Atticus winced, his heart pounding at Wade's words, the implication that a young Wade had not realized what he was getting into with his bargain. Atticus had never meant to hurt or deceive, despite his nature. He had only ever been filled with love for Wade, even if he hadn't understood what that meant. Even if he had been misguided in learning what that was.

"If you are willing, then, Wade Enoch James van Baird, then I, Asterius, will bequeath you my magic. I make this in exchange for your assistance and compassion in rectifying your circumstances."

Wade stared at him in disbelief. "Is that all you want?"

Atticus nodded, a hard lump in his throat. "This is all I request."

The dark tempest in Wade's eyes quelled somewhat as he regarded Atticus differently now; less cautious and more curious. That meant he had made the right choice. It had been a gamble. There was every chance that when they got out of this that Wade would not wish to know him any longer; that the fragile tether that was their bond would snap completely. But if he were to attempt to repair that, it had to be delicate, careful. There was a human saying he had heard once: if you love something, set it free. If it comes back, it's yours. If not, it was never meant to be.

He had to be okay with letting Wade go, if he ever wanted a chance for him to come back.

"I agree to the terms of your deal, demon."

Much like the day on the ice, Wade removed the glove from his hand and extended it, willing and waiting. Hesitation flickered in Atticus, a moment of pause and doubt as his heart thudded. Would everything go okay, or was he doomed to make another error? No. He could not hesitate. There could be no room for doubt in him.

He slashed at Wade's palm and then his own as he had done once before, their hands clasping together as human and daemon blood mixed together. Atticus' palm tingled as Wade let out a low gasp, no doubt the same sensation working its way up his arm into his core at the same moment. Golden light wrapped around their enclosed fists, sealing their deal into a contract as the world and time slowed down around them.

Wade finally broke eye contact when the golden light dimmed, averting his gaze to their entwined hands. Wade slipped his hand free of Atticus' as the skin began repairing itself, tugging his glove on once more. "I suppose that is it, then."

"Yes, I suppose so."

Wade flexed his fingers, sparks crackling between them. An immense sigh of relief slipped from his lips as he saw the dark energy, muttering a low, "Thank goodness."

"We must make haste now, dearest. You no longer need to rely on me, so there is no longer a need to be so cautious. The sooner we are out of the streets and home, the sooner we can find out what is amiss."

No sooner had he spoken, when Atticus picked up the lightest of trails on the breeze. It was so faint, he wasn't even sure he had; perhaps it was mere imagination. Wade opened his mouth to speak, but Atticus raised a single finger to silence his companion before delicately sniffing the air. His nose crinkled, distinguishing the different scents; the sweet scent of Wade's sweat mingled with his mortal stench, smoky ash, the slight saltiness of the ocean in the far distance. But there, under it all, he got the briefest of whiffs.

He knew that smell, slightly acrid and feline. It was the one they called Specter. His scent marked the buildings in the alley they were in, as if he had rubbed himself up against everything. Darkness was like petrichor, permeated with under-tones of honey and sunshine. And underneath that, what truly gave him pause, were the scents of Charlotte Blythe and Hazel Williams. Wildflowers and woods, then pumpkin and cinnamon mixed with the unmistakable tang of cigarette smoke.

"It cannot be," he murmured to himself.

Wade cocked his head slightly in question. "What do you mean, Atticus?"

"They cannot be here. How did they make their way here? This is impossible. And yet, that is their scent."

"What do you mean, Atticus? Speak plainly." Concern etched itself across Wade's alabaster brow as he peered down at the daemon.

"They're here, Wade. I am certain of it."

"*Who is here, Atticus?*"

"The angry one, Hazel, as well as the cat, seem to have found their way here with your Charlotte."

Wade's brows knitted in confusion, before realization dawned on him. His brow relaxed and a gentle 'oh' slipped from him as he stared, wide-eyed, at Atticus.

CHAPTER SEVENTEEN

HAZEL

Pain seared through her scalp, disjointed aches along the back of her head. Hazel let out a low hiss, groggily reaching a hand to the back of her head. Her eyes remained closed, but she was familiar with the feeling of cold, hard concrete beneath her body, and something soft under her head. She groaned, pulling away her hand, rubbing her fingers together. Tender, but no blood. She would have felt it.

Hazel's eyes fluttered open, and the world slowly came into view. She still had her glasses on as the world, dimly lit, slowly came into view. The first thing she saw was Charlotte a few feet away from her, upright, surprisingly, hands wrapped around her knees. Her friend was sitting against a similarly concrete wall, forehead pressed against the top of her knees.

"You alright, babes?" her words came out as a slight slur, as though she was just waking up from a twelve-hour sleep. She swallowed, mouth dry and metallic, desperate for a drink—water, coffee, a beer, *anything*. Charlotte's head shot up at her words, and her friend scrambled across to her.

"Oh, thank God, you're alright. I've never seen you knocked out like that before, that was horrific. Are you feeling okay?"

With Charlotte's help, Hazel pulled herself into a sitting position and finally took in their surroundings. They were in a dimly lit concrete room, no larger than one hundred and sixteen square feet. Shelves were pushed against walls, blankets piled to the side. She realized that the softness beneath her head was one of the blankets. A wash tub of sorts sat nearby, and boxes were strewn around the small space. A small, shitty staircase made of rotting wood led to a heavy, wooden door. Rubbing at her head once more, Hazel winced.

"How many times today am I going to have to endure being knocked out like a heroine in a romantasy novel?"

Charlotte let out a huff, something between a sigh and a laugh. "I don't know, but it's starting to become more tiresome than comical, if you ask me."

Soft light emanated from behind Charlotte like a halo as she stood back up. Only then did Hazel register the sparse candles mounted to the walls and the meager light they cast. There was something so weirdly Victorian about them, such a stark contrast to the almost contemporary vibes of the basement room.

Hazel gave a curt nod and climbed to her feet. She swayed slightly—she wasn't having the best day—and began to survey the space around them more thoroughly. Running her fingers over the walls, she tried to look for anything; a lock, a catch, something to see if the door up the terrifyingly bad steps was the only way out. Rough-hewn stone caught at her fingers as she dragged them over the walls. Charlotte watched her, a brow raised, as Hazel made her way around the room.

"You don't think I already looked?"

"Yeah, but I bet you had an ADHD look."

Lottie glowered at Hazel from where she stood. "I'm sorry, but I had nothing better to do while you were having your beauty sleep."

"What fucking beauty sleep? Did you not see me on the floor just then?"

The two bickered as Hazel continued her surveillance, eventually coming to the foot of the stairs. There were no discernible weaknesses, nowhere to hide, nothing really of note in the small, cement coffin of a basement. That left only the stairs. Hazel stared up at them, heart thundering in her chest as she grabbed the rotting railing and hoisted herself up them, one by one. They creaked and moaned under her, the warped wood threatening to give way under her. She should have sent Charlotte up them—that girl was light enough that she would blow away in a stiff enough breeze.

Finally, after a perilous moment when one of her boot-clad feet broke a step and slipped through, she made it to the top. It was a narrow staircase—more akin to a ladder than stairs, really—and left barely enough room for her to stand at the top of the squat landing. She'd made it, though. Turning back, she shot a thumbs up to Charlotte. Then she did what she did best and slammed her body into the door. Well, as best as she could. She couldn't exactly gain purchase on a small landing while feeling like she had the worst hangover of her life.

Over and over, despite the aching, dull pain in her body, Hazel rammed her shoulder against the door. It didn't so much as flinch under her body weight. She cursed under her breath, more loudly with each attempt, until she was almost yelling.

"Open. The. Fuck. *Up*." Hazel grunted, sweat beading at her hairline, each word punctuated with the thud of her shoulder on the door. If the staircase was so fucking neglected, why did this door hold like the final line of defense to a medieval throne room? "I said *open*, you absolute shit lord."

"Hazel, back up."

She hadn't heard Charlotte approach her and nearly knocked her friend out as she paused mid-shoulder ram. "Holy fuck babes, warn a girl, would you?"

"I tried to, but you were too busy swearing enough to make a sailor blush!"

Hazel scowled, but turned to face her friend. "Okay, alright. What's going on, what's up?"

Charlotte ducked around Hazel, delicately stepping onto the landing with her. It groaned under their combined weight. At some point, the Witch had commandeered a candle from the wall, which she now held to the door. "Oh, are we going to set it on fire? That'll work."

Scowling, Charlotte shook her head. "Didn't you see the marks here?"

Hazel, in fact, hadn't looked at the door that closely. Like she was going to admit that to Charlotte, however. Instead, she leaned forward at Charlotte's beckoning. Lo and behold, there were indeed deep, scar like marks on the doorframe, with runes not unlike the ones she saw on the papers from Vee's dressing room. "*Oh.*"

"They definitely seem demonic..." Charlotte trailed off, brow furrowed as she became lost in thought.

Hazel gulped, thinking back on the papers she had swiped and read under the cover of night as Charlotte slept beside her. How Atticus' name had appeared, how it had spurred her onto making the choices she had. The choices that had led them here.

"Yeah," Hazel muttered.

Hazel lost track of how long Charlotte stood at the top of the stairs, poring over the runes. The Hunter had long retired to the bottom of the basement, poking over the room once more half-heartedly. This room was not designed for humans to break out of, apparently. Resigning herself to their fate, Hazel threw herself on the floor, stretching out on her back to stare at the concrete of the ceiling above.

Eventually, the sounds of Charlotte's boots thundering back down the rickety staircase reverberated throughout the basement. "Anything?" Hazel queried. Charlotte's sigh was answer enough.

"I can't recognize a thing! And my magic doesn't do a thing on it," Charlotte grumbled as she collapsed on the ground beside Hazel. "I have no fucking clue."

"I guess we're dying down here."

Charlotte shot a scathing look at Hazel and her cheerful tone. "Do you need to joke like that?"

"Is it really a joke, though?"

Silence filled the space between them as Hazel's words settled over them like a heavy blanket. They probably would die down in that basement, in another world, with no one knowing where they went. And it was all her fault.

"I hope Specter is okay and finds a way home," Charlotte whispered, dropping her head to her knees. Her shoulders began to shake slightly, and a tell-tale sniff had Hazel bolting upright to wrap her arms around her friend.

"Hey babes, hey, don't cry. It's okay, I'm sure he's okay. He's a plucky cat, after all. I'm sure he'll outlive all of us." *Especially if we die in here...* Charlotte pulled her knees up to her chest, squeezing tighter as her body became rigid under Hazel's embrace. Hazel wasn't going to be deterred, however. Instead, she squeezed her friend tighter. "I've got you, babes. I promise you. I will do anything for you. I'll throw myself in the way of a million demons if I gotta, okay? I'll die for you."

"I don't *want* you to die, you fucking idiot." Charlotte's words came out in gulps between her sobs. "I love you, you're my best friend. *I don't want you to get hurt.*"

"Well, yeah, I don't wanna get hurt either, babes, but I would if I had to, y'know?"

Charlotte had dissolved into proper tears at that point. Hazel held her friend, the bond between them her last bastion of hope.

Hazel's mouth was gritty and dry. She swallowed, eyes fluttering open as a pain shot through her neck. With a grunt, Hazel reached a hand to rub the aching pull in her neck. Charlotte let out a soft, sleepy sigh from her lap.

At some point, Hazel had tugged them over to the wall, pulling Charlotte into her lap as she let her friend weep. So Charlotte cried, her slender body racked with all the tears she had spent months shoving down as Hazel smoothed tendrils of hair from her friend's face, shushing her softly like a mother would to her child. They must have fallen asleep as Hazel rocked her friend gently, tending to her bestie.

Hazel straightened up as best as she could, stiffness radiating throughout her body, cold concrete pressed against her back. How long had passed? Her bladder twinged in discomfort as a sleeping Charlotte nuzzled against her abdomen. Was she really going to have to relieve herself in this concrete box? Thank God it was just a piss. For now.

As Hazel debated waking up Charlotte—the discomfort in her bladder growing by the second, it seemed—Hazel was roused by sounds from the other side of the door. If she was gonna fight, well...

She slipped her sleeping friend from her lap, tucking the blanket that had been under her own head earlier underneath Charlotte's. she winced as she crept over to the weird woven laundry basket, piled with linens. At least she had someone's laundry to pee on as she squatted. She bundled some blankets beneath herself, tugging one aside for wipe up, before unzipping. She'd pissed in enough woods to not be too fazed. She felt a vindictive sense of victory as she peed on their soft, white blankets. They should have at least left them a bucket. Served their captors fucking right.

Hazel groaned in relief as the pressure from her bladder subsided somewhat. She rubbed at her aching abdomen while trying not to look at her sleeping friend. When she was done, she kicked them aside, wrinkling her nose. Oh yeah, it was gonna smell like piss. However, the sounds above were getting louder. Wiping her hands on her pants, Hazel scurried over and shook her friend's shoulder. "Charlotte, someone's up there. Wake up, babes," she hissed.

Charlotte shot up from her sleep, launching to her feet. "Who's up there?"

"I'm not sure." Hazel pulled herself up, albeit much slower. Pins and needles radiated down her thighs and ass. She winced, moving from foot to foot as she used the wall for leverage. "I just heard movement; I'm not sure who or what it is."

"I guess we gotta be ready, then." Charlotte stretched, limbering herself up. Hazel frowned. It wasn't a bad idea. They had been sitting awkwardly for who only knew how long. She watched her friend stretch with all the grace of a newborn fawn. And by that, she meant with zero grace.

"Copy me, Charlotte. You're gonna hurt yourself," Hazel chided. Charlotte shot her a glare. "Yeah, yeah. You can shoot me as many daggers as you want, but this is why things slam into you. Get over here. We're gonna stretch properly if we want a chance in hell at dodging anything."

With an eye trained on the door, Hazel ran Charlotte through some of the basic warm up stretches she would do before ballet. Inner thigh stretch, quads, and hamstrings. She needed their legs limber, because as soon as that door opened, they were bolting for it. Was it her best plan? Hell no. Was it a plan? Probably.

Soon, they were as limbered up as they were going to be, and Hazel's attention had shifted to the sounds drifting down from above. Though muted and muffled, she picked up the occasional word; 'human', 'captive', 'plan'. Sometimes she caught other words, but they were spoken in a gruff, coarse language she didn't recognize. They spoke in an excited tone that she *did* understand, however—the kind that monsters used when they were about to have fun hurting something, or someone.

"Okay, babes, I need you to be ready." Hazel cracked her back, eyes narrowed at the landing.

"I'm always ready," Charlotte muttered, flexing her hands, readying her weapons. Hazel had scoured the basement for something usable; a pipe, a pole, a fucking broom even, and had turned up empty handed. So, she'd be relying on pure strength and strategy. A part of her twinged, knowing it might not be enough to keep Charlotte safe this time.

"Hey, babes?"

"Hmm?"

"I'm sorry again for fucking up. I didn't know this would happen. But I'll do my best to protect you. I promise."

Charlotte dropped her hands to her side, turning to face Hazel. The din above them lessened. Her chocolate eyes were wide, sincere, her countenance soft and gentle. "Hazel. I know that. I get that we're in a shit situation. But apologizing endlessly isn't going to fix it. We just have to do our best, okay?"

Reaching out a hand, Charlotte beckoned the Hunter over to her. Hazel's boots scuffed against the floor as she closed the space between them. Charlotte yanked Hazel into an embrace, and the Hunter found herself melting against the familiar warmth of her friend.

"I'm glad I have you as a friend." Charlotte muttered against Hazel's shoulder, breath warm against the Hunter's neck.

"I'm glad I have you too, babes."

As the duo embraced, the world above them came back to life with a cacophony of crashes.

CHAPTER EIGHTEEN

ATTICUS

Wade was hot on Atticus' heels as they raced through the winding back streets of Terra Dorreum. Cobblestone streets and colorful houses bled together as Atticus' heeled boots slapped against the ground below, their feet echoing in tandem as he followed the scent of flowers and whiskey.

"Are you certain?"

Wade's words were laced with the same tentative hopefulness as the last ten times he had asked the daemon. "Yes, I am certain, dear one. As I have plainly reassured you. Their stench is undeniable."

"My Lottie does not have a stench," Wade muttered under his breath as they ran.

"I can assure you that she most definitely does, but you are blind to it, as a human and her lover. Your senses are far from refined, after all."

They rounded a corner, cresting over a slight hill. The path diverged there, branching into several different streets. Some led back into Terra Dorreum, and one of them made its way down the mountain, towards the fields. Atticus paused, dithering at the way point between the paths. While their scents hung thick in the air, a cross wind swirled up around them, blowing in tendrils of smoky ash that masked the direction of their scents. He sniffed, turning on the spot, his shirt sleeves catching on the window and billowing around his slender arms.

"Atticus? What is the matter?"

Auburn curls lay stuck to Wade's forehead, slick with a sheen of sweat. Poor Wade was looking more bedraggled by the minute, but his gray eyes were blazing with focus and determination. Despite the obvious discomfort from running in his dress shoes, Wade was as poised as ever as he came to a stop beside his friend. How could he look ever the gentleman, despite his innate humanness, his mortalness? Once again, Atticus was confounded. How could angels have been modeled on Atticus' kind, when one like Wade existed?

"I... I cannot seem to discern which path the scent leads." The admittance was like acid on his tongue, burning its way down his throat as he choked back his failure. "I have let you down."

Atticus almost sprung out of his skin as a hesitant, gloved hand found its way onto his shoulder. "You are trying your best, that is plain to see. And I thank you for that."

Though Wade's grip was brief before he retracted his hand, the weight of it remained still there even after, his warmth burning through to the flesh. Wade stepped back, making sure to keep a pace between them.

Forever at arm's length.

He pretended it didn't sting, even though Wade's words had been soothing, comforting. Instead, he acted like a Prince of House Lyra. He straightened up, and took stock of the situation. "We just need to come up with a plan, then. I suggest we backtrack into the city, down these paths here, and see if we can pick up the trail. If not, we know we can return here, and find a different approach."

Atticus wasn't used to taking charge, to actually doing what needed to be done. Yes, he fulfilled his deals and bargains, but he never went out of his way to comfort, to make sure others benefited. Not the way he did with Wade; not the way he wanted to now.

"I can do this," Atticus muttered to himself. He stopped, closing his eyes, taking in several deep breaths, centering himself. With his eyes closed, the colors of magic ignited around him; while his eyes were blind, his other senses were wide open. Ribbons of dancing lights swirled in front of his closed eyes, magic threads that no mortal could perceive. Though they used that same magic, they did not understand it; humans did not realize that it was the energy that made up everything around them. But he understood it.

Energy surged through him like electricity coursing in his very veins, igniting him. It set him ablaze, rivulets of power washing over him like the sea breaking against a cliffs edge. It was coarse and soft all at once, a desperate desire that threatened to drown him. He sought out that thread of magic, the source of all power, of all life, and urged it to come to him—

"Atticus?"

"Not now," Atticus muttered, eyes still clamped shut. He'd been so close. Inhaling deeply once more, Atticus sought to refocus himself. He could find them, he could prove himself to Wade—

"*Atticus.*" Wade's tone was more urgent now, louder, an edge of excitement to the way he said the daemon's name. Atticus' eyes snapped open, a tinge of anger blooming inside him like the first petals opening on the spring flowers. He raised a brow as he looked to Wade, who pointed in front of them, bouncing on the balls of his feet. Following Wade's gesture, Atticus' stomach lurched. Sitting on the path in front of them, licking a paw, was none other than Specter Blythe.

Atticus locked eyes with Specter, one set blue, one set topaz. A silent conversation transpired between them in looks, as Wade stared at them, before finally breaking the silence by asking, "That *is* Lottie's cat, am I correct?"

The daemon would recognize that sweet, honey and rain scent anywhere. The cat was, truthfully, more than he appeared. There was a darkness in him that called out to Atticus, a sameness that drew him towards the feline. Though he remained in the form he showed to Charlotte Blythe, the edges of the creature showed the dormant monster within.

"Yes, dearest one, this is Specter." Atticus crouched down, extending a hand to the feline. Specter pattered forward, rubbing against the daemon's palm, purring.

Atticus stroked the silky fur of the cat, marveling at how soft the creature was, how warm. He saw why Charlotte liked to sleep with the animal, now. "It is unmistakable."

"She's really here." Wade drew in a breath, staring at the cat in wonderment, like he could not believe what he was seeing. Crouching down beside Atticus, he reached out for the cat, a mirror image of Atticus. Specter purred as he rubbed up against Wade's suit, burrowing his head against the gentleman's legs. Wade scooped the cat up, hugging him tightly. "You're really here, you most formidable feline!"

Specter's eyes narrowed, but he allowed Wade to hold him close, shoulders shaking as tears began to gather at the corners of his eyes, gentle sobs wracking his body. Atticus reached a hand out once more, confident this time, as he placed it on Wade's shoulder. And this time, his dear friend didn't flinch. Emboldened, Atticus shifted his hand and instead wrapped his arms gingerly around Wade's neck, pressing their foreheads together, Specter nestled between them, like some odd, broken family.

"He's here, she's here," Wade sobbed, resting his head against Atticus. The daemon's heart swelled as he held his friend close. "My beloved Lottie is so close, Atticus."

"I know, my dear sweet one," he murmured against Wade's hair. Wade smelt of cedar and apple soap, despite how long they had been in the cell, of sweat and saltiness. He brushed his lips against Wade's temple, planting the softest, tenderest of kisses. Wade did not pull back from his touch, did not startle at the display of affection. He merely held Specter closer as he continued to sob.

"I am the most fortunate of souls to have found you, you minx of a cat! I cannot believe in a world of demons, you have managed to find me."

"And now, he shall lead us to your love." Bitterness coated Atticus' tongue as he spoke, a vile taste that he had to swallow back. He pulled away from Wade, wrapping his arms around himself. His companion was either too preoccupied to notice or didn't want to draw attention to it. "If you would allow me to ask him, that is."

"Surely we are just going to follow him and see where he leads us?" There was an incredulous edge to Wade's words. "You cannot ask a *cat* questions."

"I most assuredly can; it just depends on if he deigns to respond, is all."

Wade's stormy eyes narrowed, but he didn't press further as he loosed his grip on the cat. Specter jumped from the man's arms, trotting a few feet away from them. Specter turned to face them, sitting on his haunches, an intense, knowing looking in his ocher eyes.

"It's as if he can see into my soul," Wade murmured. Atticus dropped to his knees, thighs aching from crouching. He leveled a stare at the cat, who's large, unblinking eyes bore into his own.

"Hello, Specter." Atticus spoke aloud to the cat, probing the air between them with thin fragments of magic, like spun yarn. Shimmering, golden light, imperceptible to mortals, coiled between Atticus and Specter, forging a bridge between them. Atticus relaxed, keeping himself wide open. Specter's head bowed ever so slightly.

Hello.

To Wade, it would have seemed like nothing but a purr. To Atticus, the word was spoken directly into his mind, a velvety, smooth baritone that surprised him. The daemon's face remained smooth, however, as he began to question the cat. "I smelled your master, and her friend, the loud one. They are here with you, are they not?"

Specter bowed his head again. *Yes.*

"Ah, perfect, that's good to know. I suppose we must find them, then, before we continue on. Where did you leave them? Why are they not here with you now?"

Specter mewed. *Trapped. Taken by strangers. I searched for you.*

"They were taken? What do you mean, taken? And trapped?"

Wade tumbled to his knees, hands sprawling out on the ground in front of him as he shuffled towards the cat. "What is he saying, what does he mean? How do you understand him?"

"Hush, dearest," Atticus said to Wade, returning his attention to the cat. He nodded, urging the creature on.

House. Fields. Flowers. Monsters. Ransom.

"Ah. Well, at least they haven't been consumed thus far, that's good to know. What else do you know?"

Basement, hidden away. Angry. Magic weak. Need your help.

Atticus nodded. Alright, that all seemed to make enough sense. "So it's a jail break, is it? I can assist with such."

Specter mewled and Wade glanced to Atticus. "They are being held captive? Where?"

Atticus shrugged. "In a basement somewhere. I'm sure he can lead us to them." Atticus raised his brows at the cat. "You *can* lead us to them, right?"

Specter let out a hiss. *Of course. Can't you smell them?*

Low blow. He'd done pretty good tracking them as far as he had, he thought. He wouldn't let the cat see that his words had stung. It was undignified. "Yes, I can. But there are a lot of scents, and the city is burning. I am also not as attuned to the scent of your mortal companions." Did the cat just roll its eyes at him? Atticus bristled. He was a *Prince*, did this feline not comprehend that? He urged himself to quell his rage, drawing in a deep breath.

Fine. I will lead you there. Bring the human man.

Atticus rose back to his feet, gesturing to Wade to follow. "We're going to follow Specter. He can lead us to them."

Visible relief washed over Wade's features. "Truly?"

Atticus nodded, tugging the sleeves of his shirts. "Yes. Now let us make haste."

They raced after Specter, hot on the cat's heels as he led them down the mountain, down to the lower levels of Terra Doerum. Not once did Wade complain of fatigue, of his mortal body aching though it must have. Atticus was impressed that he was able to push through.

Eventually, Specter led them to a series of slightly more run-down houses. The slums. Atticus had never ventured this low into the rainbow city—there had never been a need to travel amongst the lesser daemons. Most of his time had been spent in the mortal realm, the rest on his duties. The colors on the houses were more faded, here, their structures smaller, a little more unkempt and well loved. Crooked shutters and planter boxes with herbs decorated windowsills with peeling paint. The vibrancy that he associated so dearly with home was muted here, lesser. Duller.

Specter paused in front of a shuttered house. Narrow fences separated the houses here, small paths leading down to small yards. It was a two-story house, cramped, with two windows above, and one downstairs. The azure door had a chipped gold knocker on it. Atticus crept up to the window, attempting to pry the window open to look inside. He could hear the rustling of movement inside, but could not gain purchase. Muttering, he dropped down from the windowsill and returned to where Wade and Specter waited on the worn out path in front of the house. "You are certain this is the one?"

The cat mewed once more. *Yes.*

Atticus sniffed the air. Fragments of flowers and smoke. And the undeniable stench of the lower denizens of Terra Doreum, of sulfur and wet dog. Ah, the cat was correct, after all. Atticus turned to Wade. "They're in here, we are certain."

"Let us make haste, then! We cannot delay their safety any longer." Wade's stormy eyes flickered as he straightened, self-assured poise in his movements. The

Alchemist drew a deep breath, readying himself. "We must break down this door and rescue them."

Atticus grinned. Chaos was where he thrived. Drama and destruction, this was a language he knew well. And Wade knew that. While the daemon could handle things with finesse, breaking them was so much more fun. "I assume this means I have permission, then?"

Wade nodded. In the past, in Wade's youth, he had been the responsible one, teaching Atticus to do things 'the proper way', to stop and think before acting out. The Princeling had never really done so before then, preferring action to thought. But Wade had cautioned him, taught him patience.

Fuck patience, as that Hunter girl would say.

Atticus cracked his knuckles and twisted his hands together, murmuring a slight incantation, before sending a stream of emerald-green fire at the door. Did he feel a twinge of remorse? Yes. Could he have knocked on the door? Also yes. But they had kidnapped the humans, and he wouldn't stand for it. Shouting arose from within the building as Atticus focused his magic, keeping it contained to just the door.

He didn't want to set their entire house ablaze, after all. Just enough to teach them a lesson. His magic melted the door away completely, until nothing stood between the threshold and inside.

Several burly daemons came into view, in their normal form, no disguise. These creatures were the basis for the gargoyle design that humans used for their grand Cathedrals. Olive-gray with veined wings, hunched backs, snout-like noses, and furrowed brows, they were repugnant in both appearance and smell. Their taloned feet clipped the hardwood of the floors as they scrambled to the exit, bursting out into the street. Wade stumbled back a few feet as Specter raised his hackles and hissed at the approaching daemons.

Atticus, however, did not flinch, even as they ran out of the house, snarling at him, ready to 'throw down. What were some common, lesser daemons going to do to someone like *him*? He could destroy them with a single glare, if he wanted. And he would, if the nasty beasts got any closer.

"Stop," Atticus said coolly, gaze leveled on them as they swiped talons in his direction, fangs gnashing. "Is this how you treat a Prince?"

The one in front skidded to a stop—and if it could pale, it would have. The other two were either stupid, or hadn't heard him, for they lunged out behind their friend for Atticus. The daemon Princeling raised an arm and sliced it through the air. One second, the two daemons had charged him; the next, they lay crumpled on the ground. The first one froze, fear flicking in its onyx eyes.

"My lord," the daemon rasped in the Old Tongue, frozen in place. "Please, spare my brothers."

Atticus had not spoken in the Old Tongue in a long time, preferring the rustic language the humans used. Still, he would converse with the creature the way it desired. "They are not dead. But they will be if they try that again."

Wade's brows shot up at Atticus' words. The Princeling tried not to stumble over the sluggish, heavy dialect, keeping his focus on the miscreant in front of him. "You have something of mine in your possession."

The creature fell to its knees, groveling, his brother's chests rising and falling heavily beside him. "I do not know what you mean, sire. We have not stolen from any of the Houses."

Tutting, Atticus dropped into a squat. "Look up at me, wretched creature."

The lesser daemon, trembling, raised its head, gaze averted. A smile twitched the corner of Atticus' mouth. Good. He was pleased he could still inflict this kind of fear, even after all this time away from home. "I am sorry, my lord."

"I do not wish for you to waste your words on apologies. I merely wish for what is mine to be returned." Atticus' throat ached from the raspy language. "The mortal girls that you hold captive."

The daemon froze. "They are yours, sire?"

"Indeed. And if I find they have been harmed..."

"No, sire, they have not been touched, I beg of you." The lesser daemon stumbled over his words. "We were merely going to trade them for favors, I promise."

"Here's a favor." Atticus lowered his voice, dark and menacing. "I will not *end you* for taking what is not yours, as long it is returned to me *now*."

The daemon, though three times Atticus' size, backed away, head still lowered. "Yes, my lord. Immediately, my lord. Please." The creature turned, still on its hands and knees, and scrambled into the house.

Atticus turned to Wade, shooting him a smile, fluttering his lashes. "Let us go greet the girls, shall we?"

Atticus led the way into the house, Wade and Specter on his heels. It was not unlike the human world homes that he had seen, albeit a little cramped. The narrow hallway had several doors coming off it, and the lesser daemon barely fit through the hallway as he crawled toward the back of the house.

"Why don't you just use your disguised form?" Atticus asked in disgust, the Old Tongue heavy in his mouth. "Surely you do to make your way in your home?"

"Apologies, my lord," the creature mumbled pathetically. "I was ready for an attack, as we didn't know what was burning down our door." A twinge of guilt flickered in Atticus, but he waved it off. They could replace a door easily enough.

"Yes, well," Atticus mumbled in English. "That's no excuse for kidnapping."

"What did he say, Atticus?"

"It's nothing, dear one." Atticus waved Wade off, shooting a smile over his shoulder. The Princeling returned his attention to the creature crawling down the unlit hallway. At the very back of the house, a heavy door sat shut, carved and bloodied runes covering the door frame. Crude, rudimentary holdings. He was a little shocked that it managed to contain the Hunter and the Witch.

"Unlock the wards," Atticus kept his voice bored, petulant. The facade of a Prince.

The lesser daemon scrambled, hastily muttering over the wards as he drew a taloned hand over them. They glowed a soft vermilion before fading back to dark wood. The creature stumbled backward, bowing low, making space for Atticus. "It is done, my lord."

Atticus eyed off the lesser daemon. He was over this cramped hallway, this cramped house, this entire ordeal. He wanted to be back in the mortal realm with his beloved friend, gallivanting about. Still, he straightened himself, brushing off imaginary lint. "Alright, you may open the door, then."

The lesser daemon scurried back to the door, pulling the bolt out that secured the door physically. The opening door groaned under its own weight, swinging out slowly. As it did so, thunderous pounding shook the stairs leading down into the darkness, and none other than the wretched Hunter, Hazel Williams, burst out into the hallway, yelling and swinging.

"Do you wanna fucking *go*?" Hazel launched herself at the daemon, who had not removed itself from the doorway yet. She grappled it, sending him and herself into the wall as she slammed against it, wrapping her arms around its thick neck in a choke hold. "I'm gonna splatter whatever you call brains all against this wall with my bare fucking hands, I swear to all that is holy."

She tore at it with her nails, true to her words, as she tried to press her fingers into the creature's eye sockets. Atticus watched on, brow raised, mirth twinging his lips into a smile; Wade's mouth was agape, as if he couldn't believe what he was seeing. The Hunter, caught in the throes of battle, clearly hadn't noticed them. The lesser daemon slammed her back into the wall, trying to dislodge her as it let out a horrid roar of a cry. Atticus winced as she managed to get one of her thumbs to press down on its eyeball. It started cursing at her in the Old Tongue, threatening to shred her to pieces, amongst other things. Atticus winced as the lesser daemon started going into gory detail about her entrails.

"That's enough." Atticus finally interrupted the squabble. He raised a hand, cutting it through the air. The lesser daemon crumpled beneath Hazel, falling to the ground in slow motion. She fell on top of it, an 'oof' escaping her as she slammed against the creature. "Hazel, get off."

Hazel froze on her hands and knees as Atticus spoke, in shock. "No way," she breathed. "It can't be."

"It can, and most assuredly is." Atticus approached the Hunter, extending a hand. She looked up at him, glasses frames askew, her eyes wide. "Would you like to get off the floor now, then?"

As Hazel stared at him, rustling came from the stairs. Tentative steps, like someone walking on the tips of their toes, hesitant. Atticus glanced up from where he was bent down, hand reached out to Hazel. There Charlotte was in the doorway, hair disheveled, purple smudges under the hollows of her eyes. And she had locked her gaze onto Wade. Atticus' stomach plummeted.

"Is that really you?" Charlotte Blythe's voice cracked, her words a rasp, as if unshed tears rubbed her throat raw. Her body shook, a tremble, a shiver. The waif of a girl was like a newborn fawn, uncertain as she took a step forward.

"Truly." Wade's dress shoes scuffed against the wooden floors as he took a step forward. "Is that you, my Lottie?" His voice quavered on her name, as if he couldn't believe he was saying it. As he said it, it was like something broke within her, too. Charlotte raced past Hazel, Atticus, and the daemon sprawled on the floor, sobbing as she threw herself into Wade's awaiting arms.

Atticus straightened, turning to face the pair as they embraced. Hot pain coiled in his stomach as Wade reached his hands up, cupping her face between them, stroking Charlotte's cheeks, eyes full of wonder as he repeated, "My Lottie, *my Lottie*," before brushing his mouth reverently against her lips. That heavy, hot pain in Atticus' expanded, burning him alive from the inside, as he watched her arms wrap around his beloved companion, as they melded into a singular being, uncaring and unaware of the world around them.

"How are you whole again?" Charlotte whispered against his lips.

Pulling away just enough to speak, he murmured, "It is a long story that I will fill you in on later. For now, it is enough that we are safe and reunited."

"Ahem." A voice behind Atticus caught his attention, tearing his gaze away from the scene in front of him. Hazel had crawled off the lesser daemon, and now stood behind Atticus, arms crossed and brows raised.

"What?"

"It's nice to see you too again, little demon," she scoffed. She looked like absolute hell; her curls were in a disarray, her jacket had tears, while she had bruises forming on her neck and cheeks. "Now that we've found you, and Wade, you're gonna help us get the hell out of here."

Atticus scowled. "It's not that simple."

"Yeah? Well, I don't care for excuses. We'll just have to work it out."

Atticus stewed over Hazel's words as he listened to the soft murmurings of Wade and Charlotte behind him.

"I missed you," Wade whispered against her mouth.

"I never thought I'd see you again," she breathed against him.

And a part of Atticus wished the two had never seen one another again.

It was one of the most awkward moments of Atticus' long existence.

They had all gathered in the kitchen of the house; a small, utilitarian space, with minimal decoration. It was limestone and bare, with no table, just counters and a small, squat hearth. Even so, it was a cramped space; three giant lesser daemons, three humans, a cat, and a daemon Prince took up every square inch of space.

They had crammed themselves in to fill each other in on what happened; the lesser daemons had followed, apologizing profusely. Both Charlotte and Hazel had gestured at them with pointed fingers. The daemons hadn't understood what it meant, but had understood the intent. They had, at least, the sense to appear contrite, chagrin.

"How did you two get here?" Atticus was the first to break the silence as they gathered in the room. *How* and *why* were they here? Had someone stronger, more nefarious than himself, dragged them there? It was truly an astounding feat that they stood before them, alive, no less.

Hazel and Charlotte shared a look, Wade's arm wrapped around the latter, before the Hunter took a deep breath. "Well, it's a bit of a long story..."

Atticus and Wade listened on in fascination and horror as Hazel detailed the months that had passed since they saw each other last. How the mortal world, and their lives, had changed. How Hazel had been searching for ways to contact *him*, to find a way to bring Wade back. How they eventually opened a portal and found themselves flung into the daemon realm.

Honestly, Atticus was impressed. How had this mortal girl managed that? He had to interrogate her later, find out all the ins and outs, all the details. This could open up a whole slew of possibilities to him in the future.

"I cannot believe you would meddle in something so serious, Miss Williams. Think of the terrible things that could have happened!" Wade, as ever, was aghast. Hazel merely shrugged.

"It coulda been worse."

"It could have been a *lot* worse, yes!"

The two began bickering, interrupted by an exhausted sounding Charlotte raising her voice. "That's *enough*. I get it, dumb ideas, dumb mistakes; that's in the past now, and we have to focus on our current predicament. Namely, what is going on, and how do we get home. Also." She stopped, turning her gaze towards the trio of daemons, her voice turning icy cold. "I think we are owed some apologies, are we not?"

"They're lucky I don't finish them off right now," Hazel murmured beside her. The daemons murmured something; it could have been an apology, it could have not been. Atticus, even with his phenomenal hearing, couldn't tell.

"We smelt the magic on you, and thought we could barter you for a better life, for more magic of our own." The lesser daemon who had let the girls out was at least somewhat remorseful as he lowered his head. "We did not realize you were allies to a Prince and a Family. We just want to survive the Reckoning."

Atticus furrowed his brow. "What do you mean, 'the Reckoning'?"

All three lesser daemons turned their focus to Atticus. "Sire," the leader of the trio rasped in the Old Tongue. "Have you not seen the smoke, the sulfur? The Reckoning that was foretold, when the Houses would fight one another for control, is coming to past. Where have you been that you have not known that our world is in chaos and peril?"

Locked in a cell in the Mountain, was what he wanted to say. Instead, he merely shrugged, the movement as nonchalant as he could muster as he kept a neutral expression plastered across his face. The lesser daemon shook his head, switching back to English.

"The powers at play have decided that ruling side by side is not enough. House is fighting against House, seeking dominance over Terra Doerum and the rest of us. Someone wanted an army, a way to invade the mortal realm, and seek more power."

Even Atticus struggled to remain calm as the humans with him let out a collective gasp. A hand flew to Charlotte's mouth. "No, they couldn't possibly. How would they manage such a thing?"

The lesser daemon cocked its head, staring at Charlotte with curiosity. "How are you not frightened being here, mortal? I thought your kind are frightened of our kind in your world."

Hazel scowled and answered for Charlotte. "Because we can kick your ass. Not all humans can, and its fucked what your lot is cooking up!" Cracking her knuckles, the Hunter looked ready to fight, to back up her words.

The same lesser daemon scowled. "It is no fault of mine or my brothers; perhaps you should be asking Nova of House Lyra why this is happening."

Atticus was a young daemon again, his stomach fluttering, small and unsure, at the mention of his father's name. Clamminess made his hands slick, and he felt ready to keel over with light-headedness. "Are you certain you mean Nova?"

The daemon scowled. "I know which Lord I mean. There was a convening several moon sets ago. There was a fight, and arguing, and the Houses could not agree. Several wanted to take more power, and Nova pigheadedly fought against them. He wanted to maintain order, even as the others vouched for *us*, sought more for all of daemon kind. Nova is archaic, trying to hold us back, trying to put our food before us. It is unfathomable."

Atticus could see the rage on the faces of his mortal companions. Specter let out a hiss, a nasty, angry noise. The daemon continued on, oblivious. "House Lyra had gotten away with too much for too long, and apparently one of the heirs was on trial, which was believed to be a farce of a trial anyway. So, some of the Houses staged an attack against them, before it could happen."

Icy dread washed over Atticus.

CHAPTER NINETEEN

HAZEL

The vibes in the kitchen were tense.

Hazel leaned back against the counter, the dingy space rife with sweat, sulfur, and smoke. Couldn't they at least crack the window? She scrunched her nose up and shot a glare at the demons. They filled up a lot of fucking space, for sure. She swung her makeshift bat menacingly, having retrieved it on her way back upstairs from the basement.

"Are you certain you mean Nova?"

Hazel and Charlotte—mostly Hazel, as Charlotte was attached to Wade like a barnacle currently—had filled them in on their exploits and adventures. Hazel had tried to leave out some of the finer details about how they had gotten to the daemon realm, but that's when Charlotte had remembered she could speak again and decided to interject. Finally, though, they'd told their tale. Hazel was suspicious as Atticus' eyes had lit up with pride.

Now, Atticus seemed to be fighting with the other demons, heated urgency in his words. Who was Nova? What was going on? Hazel glanced between the small demon child and the thickset demons who towered over him but cowered under his gaze. Interesting dynamic. She zoned back in on their conversation as Specter launched onto the small table shoved to the side, an angry black shadow.

"So, it is a coup?" Atticus spat. "Nothing is ever enough for your kind, is it? Are you not well taken? Are you not satisfied?"

"Are scraps something to be satisfied with?" hurled back the main demon who had been speaking. "If Nova—"

"What has become of them? What has become *of my family*?"

An icy chill settled across the room like the first blanket of snow in winter. Hazel shivered, eyes widening. Atticus' shadow seemed to lengthen behind him, flickering, as he set his azure gaze upon the three demons. Though he had not raised his voice, the venomous edge to his words were enough for her to take a step back, bumping into the canoodling couple beside her.

The three demons cowered as Atticus stepped toward them, hands clenched at his sides. Atticus wore billowing, cream sleeves, a green velvet vest open over it, and black trousers. There was something oddly Victorian about his dress and energy. Though he looked like a small child, his energy was ancient and foreboding. "I am going to ask you one more time. What has become of my family?"

"We did not know that you were of House Lyra, my lord!" the main demon groveled, the others mumbled in reproachful response with him. "Please, forgive us. But we do not know what state they are in."

Hazel almost felt sorry for Atticus as she watched his small body quiver with rage and sadness. His emotions were palpable, seeping into the very air in the room, making them breath in his raw feelings. From the corner of her eye, she saw Wade disentangle himself from Charlotte and make his way toward the demon child. The ghost—sorry, *former* ghost, as she reminded herself—approached Atticus, placing a gloved hand on their shoulder. Side by side, they looked like father and son.

"It is okay, Atticus. We are here with you. We will come with you and ensure the safety of your family, I promise you."

The demon seemed to instantly calm down with Wade's soft placations. "You are right, as always, dearest. I appreciate your sentiments, but if the words of these degenerates are true, I must go alone. I cannot risk harm to you or your tender, mortal friends."

Wade scowled, turning Atticus to face him. He gripped both of the demon's shoulders, bending down so they were eye to eye. "Atticus. Despite, and because of all we've been through, I am not leaving you in your hour of need. I will stand by you, as you have tried to do for me."

Hazel glanced at Charlotte, awkwardly trying to keep her gaze from the sappy, sentimental moment occurring in front of her. She wasn't the greatest with heavy emotions at the best of times, and this felt like a tense build-up of them being let out. Charlotte, however, watched the two intently, tears brimming in her eyes.

"I need to send you home, while you're all together." Atticus' voice was low and tender, full of love and reverence. "It is the safest bet."

"But what of you?"

Atticus let out a low laugh, placing a hand gently on Wade's arm. "I will be fine, dear one. I can fend for myself much better than any of you can. No offense, that is." Atticus glanced to Hazel before looking back to Wade. "I need to send you home now."

"I suppose so," Wade breathed softly, his gray eyes downcast and somber as ever.

"It'll be alright," the demon placated him. As she listened on, Hazel felt oddly voyeuristic, uncomfortable, watching these old friends comfort each other with tender intimacy. She wondered how Charlotte felt, knowing she loved Wade, and the weird connection her lover had with the demon boy.

It was all a little too much for Hazel, if she were to be honest.

"I get this is a touching moment for everyone," Hazel pushed away from the wall, her mask of casual bravado slipping over her like a second skin, "but we have bigger fish to fry right now, right? Sounds like everything is going to shit, and we need to make tracks pronto, right?"

"Something like that." Atticus shook back his pale blond hair, turning his attention to the lesser demons, who trembled under his gaze. "You three. I don't care about your opinions or what you've done. Terra Doerum is under attack, and you can and will find those that need safeguarding and get them out of firing range. Lift your jaws from the floor," Atticus snapped. "This is an order from a

Prince, and you *will obey me*. I care not for your quarrels. Do as I ask, or I will ensure to return and eviscerate you."

The trio slammed into the door frame as they hurried to leave, pushing past each other with snarls and growls. Once the door to their home slammed shut behind them, Atticus returned his attention to Hazel and the others. A charming smile lit up his face as he bowed mockingly. "Shall we, then?"

It seemed like Hazel and Charlotte hadn't been moved that far from where they'd run into the gray demon child. Leaving the other demons behind—after Atticus had a brief conversation with them in a gruff, foreign language that sounded threatening—Atticus led them down the sloping, winding streets, towards the fields that Charlotte and herself had trekked over what seemed like a lifetime ago.

The city—Terra Doerum, as Atticus had explained to them—was alight with flames and screams as they hurried down the broken streets. Shattering glass and howls filled the twilit air as Atticus told them to ignore it, to focus on the task at hand. Hazel couldn't help but wonder what was happening, though Atticus' explanations had been hurried, brief. This was his world, his home. His family were in danger. He needed to get them out so he could focus on that, instead of worrying about them.

Could a demon really care? Have true feelings? Or was it just the monster using whatever means he could to get what he was truly after? Hazel was skeptical, but it didn't matter. They'd gotten Wade, the reason they were here, and they could return safely home now.

As if sensing the unsaid tension between the demon boy and the lich, Charlotte trailed behind them, her footfalls in step with Hazel's as the women watched the backs of the duo ahead. The two were speaking quietly, voices low. She couldn't quite make out what they were saying. She wanted to know, nosy as she was, but she supposed that when you were best friends with a demon, there would be secrets and summonings between you.

She knew there was between her and Charlotte, after all.

Specter, curled up on Charlotte's shoulders as they walked, mewled at her, as if to berate her.

Eventually, they were past that first cottage, and out into the open mud and field of wildflowers once more. Nostalgia stirred in the air, a sense of relief, a sense of home. They were near the end of their journey. If this was a television episode, this was the wrap up component, the climax. Hazel and Charlotte hung back awkwardly as Atticus stopped suddenly amongst the flowers, turning his attention to Wade.

"I cannot say where either of our futures will lead us, dear one. But I can only hope this is a temporary goodbye, and not a forever one, and take solace in the fact that you are able to have a future now. One that you are owed; that you are deserved. I would ask for forgiveness for the sins of the past, but..." The demon paused, glancing away. "But I understand that atonement is not offered freely or lightly."

"I forgive you." Wade's words were said with no hesitation, carrying over on the breeze to the two women. "For all friendships have their highs and lulls. That doesn't make those friendships any lesser. And I could not have it on my heart, knowing we may not get to speak again. Heavy is the heart with such a burden."

"Agreed," Atticus replied softly.

The two gazed at one another, a lifetime of communication transpiring without words, it seemed. Hazel bounced from one foot to another. Strong emotions were not her forte, she knew. And there had been a *lot* of them today.

"It is time, then," Atticus said, as if overhearing her thoughts. Maybe he could. She didn't know how demons operated. She was a little disappointed she wouldn't be able to ask him more. It was a bit hard when his world was literally on fire. As though her thoughts summoned it, a thunderous roar shook the world around them. The ground quaked beneath them as Charlotte slapped her hands over her ears.

"What *is* that?" the Witch cried out. The fivesome turned back towards the mountain city of lights, watching in horror as they flickered and waned.

"That is very, very bad news." Atticus' mouth was set in a hard line as he beckoned for them to come to him. "We have to get a move on, now."

Hazel didn't hesitate. She grabbed Charlotte under her arm and started tugging her friend towards the demon. "Alright, little buddy, let's get this show on the road, then."

Atticus narrowed his eyes at her, but nodded curtly. "Yes, indeed. Alright, gather together and stand back. I need to access my full energy for this. Creating a portal without a contract or a summon is no easy feat."

Hazel could believe it wasn't an easy task. But she had seen this demon in action. She knew, in her gut, if anyone could handle it, it was him.

CHAPTER TWENTY

ATTICUS

A tticus could do this.

Wade bowed away too, heading back towards the girls. The three moons that Atticus had come to know so dearly from the window of his bed chambers waned beneath the shroud of smoke that covered them. He longed for the clear twilight, longed to see the expanse of sky and stars without the ceiling of haze between them. But, one step at a time. He had to make things right with Wade and the others before he could fix his home.

Staring out into the field of purple flowers and tall, swaying grass, a sense of relief washed over Atticus. The urgency and fear that'd had a chokehold on him leading up to this moment slowly dissipated, like flakes of ash fading on the wind. He wrapped his arms around himself for a moment, drawing in a deep breath. He was a Prince. He could, and would, handle things.

He let himself go, feeling the magic pulsate in the air and earth that centered him. Even the blades of grass that swished against his legs in the soft breeze had magic in them. It was all around. Drawing in another deep breath, Atticus exhaled, focused. Raising his hands in front of him, Atticus wove intricate patterns in the air, spelling out runes in the Old Tongue, calling upon the magic around him for assistance.

It coursed through his body, magic akin to blood in his veins. He visualized the portal, the pool of starlight that would take them home, take them away from his world. And he expelled his energy, let the tingle along his arms and palms send it out into the world, manifesting the unseen into the known.

Atticus' magic—his source, as his father would call it—had always come out an emerald-green, distinct to him, even when others' dealt primarily in dark, shadowy wisps, magic that slunk and hid in the darkness. His was loud—violent, even. Different to the others. Just like he had always been.

Except now, that was. Nothing came out, even as he felt the magic dance like lightning between his fingertips, emerald sparks flicking in the perpetual evening. He shook his hands, a frown curving the corners of his lips. Perhaps it was merely a falter, a moment of anxiety. Drawing in one more deep breath, he readied himself, and tried again.

Yet nothing came.

"What's wrong?"

Hazel's voice cut across the field to him, ringing in the openness. His mouth tugged further downward as he redrew the runes he knew would open a link between Terra Doerum and the mortal realm. And yet—nothing appeared. Frustration hollowed his chest out, spilling his feelings out of him. In a rage, he sent an arc carving through the air. Wind sliced through the field, crackling green sparks dancing in the air as the tops of the grass in the wind's path were sliced off. Cold, prickling dread fluttered across the nape of his neck. So it wasn't his magic that was the issue. It was something else. Something greater.

"I don't understand," Atticus murmured to himself, to the world. "Why can't I access you?"

As if in response, a cacophonous roar shook the city once more, reverberating the meadow beneath their feet. His companions let out started yelps and gasps, holding onto one another. Atticus whipped his head around, staring up at the great city he knew as home.

All magic was connected, and someone was using it all up.

"I can't send you home." He was pragmatic, matter of fact, as he glanced back to their worried faces. "Something is blocking me, stopping me. I don't know who or what, but we have to find out if we have any chance of getting you returned home safely."

He crossed the field to them, his boots pattering against the soft earth. Coming to a stop, he looked up at Wade, falling to his knees like a sinner seeking forgiveness. "Can you trust me?" he asked his dearest companion softly. Wade hesitated for a moment, glancing to the two women beside him, before looking back to the daemon.

"Of course I trust you," came his soft, earnest reply.

That was enough for Atticus. He rose back to his feet. "War is brewing," he said softly, staring back up at the Mountain. It was so high up, looming over them. It reminded him of his father's shadow cast over him. "And we are caught in the middle of it."

Clasping Charlotte's hand tightly, Wade asked, "And what is it that we can do to assist?"

"We need to find my family, as before. And we may need to fight. It is the unfortunate circumstance we find ourselves in."

Hazel cracked her knuckles. "I'm always down for a fight."

"I bet," Atticus replied dryly. "And I'm sure you're going to add immeasurable amounts of chaos to that which we will encounter."

Hazel paused for a beat, her dark brown eyes narrowing as she assessed Atticus. "I will throw you down in a heartbeat, no hesitation, if you do anything to fuck us over, demon."

"I expect nothing else," he quipped. "We can 'throw hands' if you wish, Hunter."

"Don't talk like that. It's like seeing a boomer use social media. It's cringe, babes."

Atticus felt a surge of giddiness. While she might have using a tone that didn't denote happiness, there was a casual familiarity in the way she spoke to him. Like they could be friends, one day.

"Is it a truce then, at least for now?" He did his best to hide the excited edge to his words, that surge of happiness that fluttered in his stomach like butterflies. The others nodded. "Alright, then follow me."

The cityscape had changed so much in the time that had passed since they escaped their cell in the Mountain. The smoke and ashes from earlier were no longer just floating to them on the breeze. Houses were actively burning around them as they jogged up the path back into the city. Lesser daemons were fleeing their homes in fear, stumbling past them to head to the fields and starlight ponds beyond. Some carried their children in their arms, others carried their most personal belongings. A shocking number of them were masked, in their mortal world glamor's.

Atticus' stomach knotted as they pushed past them. They were all so focused they didn't even notice the humans in their midst. Instead, they just shouldered past them, unfocused.

"Watch it!" Hazel snarled as one of them slammed into her. The lesser demon didn't even pay attention. They just kept running past. "What the fuck is going on here?"

"I've never seen anything like it." Atticus shuddered, cold, icy fingers tapping down his spine, taunting him. "This is... unprecedented."

He had seen smaller coup attempts in his years. When one had been around along as he had, one was bound to come across scuffles and scraps. None had been remotely successful, and the power had always lain with the Houses, as it should. They took care of the denizens, made sure that Terra Doerum functioned and that the Veil between the worlds stayed tidy. Without them in charge, the magic wouldn't be balanced.

And who knew what would happen.

CHAPTER TWENTY-ONE

HAZEL

Hazel had seen a whole lot of fuckery in her life, but this definitely took the cake.

This city—no, this entire *world*—was unlike anything she had ever experienced before; demons running, screaming, the world plunging into fire and chaos. Magic crackling in the air like electricity in a storm.

Atticus at a loss for words.

She was the first to admit she didn't know a lot about the child-like demon. However, she did know he was smug, arrogant, condescending. She suspected a lot of his attitude was a ruse. She'd seen herself, Charlotte, and a lot of other people use bravado to cover their insecurities over the years. He might have been a demon, but from what she could tell, he wasn't that emotionally different to herself or any other human.

And right now, he was shitting himself.

Hazel narrowed her eyes as Atticus gulped, his eyes flicking over the scene before them, assessing.

"We just need to get to House Lyra," Atticus muttered, taking a hesitant step forward. He seemed so unsure, so uncertain of himself. The demon flinched as a roof started collapsing near them, smog thick in the air. Atticus jumped as Wade began to cough.

Hazel took a step toward him. "Well, no matter what, we can't stay here, can we? The world is on fire, and we're just going to burn with it. We need you to take us to this place, if you're so confident that's the answer."

The look on his face told her wasn't all that confident. She wondered how he had managed this far, had gotten Wade here—how he'd managed a literal fucking cult for so long. A meow yanked her from her thoughts. Specter stood at her feet, yellow eyes looking up at her expectantly. "What's up, little buddy?"

He meowed again, eyes locked with her a moment longer, before stalking off toward the path that Atticus dithered at. He bounced past the demon, confidence emanating from his movements as he began to journey up into the strange, demonic city. Without thinking, she began to follow him.

"Where are you going?" Atticus demanded as she walked past him. She stopped, glancing back over her should at the demon child.

"You're sure as fuck not making a decision, and that cat has never led us astray so far. So, I'm going to trust him. You have a better plan?"

The demon worried his lip as Wade and Charlotte hurried behind to catch up. Wade placed a hand on the demon's arm. "That cat is something else, and he can lead us to safety, I'm sure."

"I know," the demon mumbled, brow furrowed. He let out a sigh. "Fine, feline. Lead us away."

She was really fucking sick of walking. Her boots rubbed against the back of her heels, her socks gross from stepping through the fields earlier. And everything was so uphill in this awful place. Who designed a city like this? These creatures might have been masters of contracts and negotiating for their own selfish will, but city planners they were *not*.

She could see the discomfort in her companions as they jogged behind Specter, trying not to lose his shadowy form in the dust and smoke. Everything smelled of sulfur and ash, of despair. But they couldn't give up. Though everything ached from running, from being thrown around, from being beaten—she had to get Charlotte home safe.

This was her mistake, and she had to fix it. She didn't get to complain.

Hazel almost tripped as Specter came to a stop and let out an otherworldly hiss. She stumbled, coming to a stop. Charlotte slammed into her back, almost sending her flying. That's when she saw the issue.

They had come across a bridge. A river of starlight ran beneath, its gentle flow breaking against the sides of the canal that contained it. It was a beautiful stone arch bridge, curving gently on the river. On the other side of the water, she could see ostentatious mansions lining the streets, purple flowering trees dotting the path, their petals scattered. Between them, however, lay a problem.

A small army of black, shadowy figures huddled together, blocking the path to the bridge. Her stomach recoiled, remembering the night in Umbra Hollow, when they almost lost Lottie. Her palms were slick with sweat as she clenched them together.

"Back up," Atticus hissed. "We'll find another way."

"But surely you can take them out with ease?" Wade's face was hopeful, naive.

"I don't want to draw attention to us, dear one. In case you've forgotten, you're all human. And the city is in shambles. I can't fight *and* protect you. So, we'll back track, find another path—"

Atticus was cut off by terrifying shrieks and howls as the shadows began to move erratically, flooding the bridge. What was happening *now*? She turned back to the group. "Can't we zip past them? They're distracted," Hazel argued, raising her voice to be heard over the din. Atticus shook his head.

"See how they're moving? One could attack us at any moment. I don't understand why they're behaving this way, it's almost like they're—"

"—being attacked," Charlotte breathed, cutting him off, eyes widening. She pointed at the bridge, grabbing Hazel's jacket with her other hand. "Holy fuck, isn't that Cherry Pop?"

Hazel's head whipped toward the bridge, back toward the fighting. Heart racing, she scanned the scene before them, stumbling forward to get a better look.

Charlotte was right. There, in the middle of the group, stood Rini Sakamato, blade in hand as she deftly wielded her katana, slicing through the shadows before her. She was dressed in cargo pants and a cropped tank, not unlike the last time Hazel had seen the other Hunter. Her long, silky black hair was tied in a long ponytail, swishing behind her as she ducked and yielded, parrying her enemies.

"We have to help her." Hazel was dimly aware of Charlotte's words as she raced forward, unthinking, focused only on the woman in front of her. It didn't matter. She just had to get there. The world went quiet around her, the sounds of her breath ringing in her ears as her boots slammed against the cobblestone beneath.

Rini's time as a pop idol was evident in her movements, in the way she fell into her routine. Dance, slice, and slip away. Dance forward again, blade slicing upward. Slip back to safety. Any other day, any other circumstance, and Hazel would have been in awe. Right then, though, terror gripped Hazel as the shadows seemed to multiple, intent on consuming Rini, on hurting her. There was a grin on Rini's face as she sliced and banished away shadows.

Even the best of Hunters got caught unaware sometimes, though. Hazel knew that all too well. It was as if time slowed down as Hazel saw one of the shadows rise up from behind, unbeknownst to the pop idol. A scream rose in Hazel's throat as a creature, larger than the others, slammed into Rini, grabbing her from behind around the throat. The Hunter struggled in the demon's grip, slashing wildly with her katana as it held her high in the air. Too late, Hazel realized this one was not just shadow and smoke, but had a form—was more creature than darkness.

Every bit of rage in her came hurtling out in a throat-tearing screech as the monster held Rini aloft, her katana clattering to the ground, struggling body over the edge of the bridge, a sardonic grin over his face as her body dangled over the starlit water.

Hazel saw red, and nothing else.

Time stopped as she raced forward toward the bridge, her bat in hand as she surged into danger. She didn't care how many of those demons there were, how powerful they were, or how absolutely destroyed her body was from all the fighting and scrapes. It didn't matter. She had to save Rini.

Hazel swung her bat with disregard as she narrowed the distance between the demons and herself. She was going to take them all out. She was fueled with anger, with humiliation. Since they'd been thrown into this place, the Hunter had felt wildly incompetent and ineffective. Not now, though. Not with Rini's life on the line.

How and why was the idol even *here*? How badly had she fucked up that the other Hunter had been dragged in? And who else was here, too? What had happened? It didn't matter. She just had to fix it. Her thoughts were a mess as she charged in, hitting demons with all her might. Some vanished or slipped away with her furious swings. She heard footsteps behind her; the others must have followed. Good. She'd make a path for them, and together, they'd make these demons *suffer*.

She swung her bat upwards, slamming into the contorted face of a shadowy demon. Then she saw them. The demon that held Rini over the water by the throat, a dark rumble of a laugh washing over them like a thundercloud. Hazel whistled, fingers in her mouth, drawing its attention away from Rini.

This demon was different to the others. He was taller, his limbs bent oddly, knees inverted, his skin a dark, scaly gray with onyx veins protruding beneath. Tendrils of darkness swirled around the monster, like a cloak upon its shoulders. There was something so lizard-like about the being, his long, forked tongue hissing between a lipless mouth around spurts of laughter.

That wasn't going to stop her. The creature turned to face her, wide, deep set crimson eyes flickering as it took her in. "Oh, another meal?"

"Yeah, and I'd be your fucking last. Hand her over," Hazel snarled, bat raised.

The creature whipped its head back, letting out a roar of laughter. "You, a mortal, think you can fight me, Hasmondus, Servant of the House Cygnus? I have power that you couldn't comprehend, you fleshy little wench."

Fuck it. She went in swinging, aiming for behind its legs. She'd break its legs, its arms, its fucking face. Whatever she had to. Before her bat could connect with limbs, though, the creature swiftly raised a hand and cut a symbol into the air. The bat splintered in her hands, shards raining down on the bridge beneath her. The demon let out another rumble of laughter, filling the air around her. "You're pathetic," it sneered.

Hazel dropped the remains of her bat, hands raw and aching from gripping it so tightly. Though she knew in most aspects of life, you could solve a lot of problems by throwing a punch, she knew when she had to change tactics. This was one of those times. She sucked in a deep breath, recalling the advice Gran had been giving her about learning magic. She could do it. Hazel was going to use magic and send this sucker plummeting to the depths.

She twisted her hands, copying the moves that Gran had shown her, searching for that energy that she *knew* was inside, somewhere. And then she sent that sputter out.

And a sputter it was. A slight ignition of fire, a pulse of energy. Like a lit match dying in a downpour. The creature, Hasmondus, laughed harder. "Is that the best you have to offer, mortal? That was pathetic, even for one of your kind!"

Rini let out a gasp as the creature tightened its grip around her throat. Panic seized Hazel, a tightness in her chest, choking her from the inside as Rini struggled for air, her body growing heavy as she stopped struggling, going limp in the demon's grip. *Fuck. It.* Hazel let out a vicious cry and raced for the demon, throwing herself at it with all her force. She would knock the fucker down, and pummel its face in, the old-fashioned way.

As she lunged for Hasmondus, he drew an arm back and back handed her with its giant, webbed hand. It caught her cheek, sending her flying to the side. She landed against the stone of the bridge, her body scraping across the ground as she slid along. A cry slipped from her as her jacket and shirt rode up, exposing skin that grazed along the ground.

Hazel wheezed, the air escaping her lungs as the demon took a step toward her, bringing Rini back over the ground. Good. She was safer, even if she was still in the demon's clutches. She blinked back tears as pain radiated through her body.

"Hasmondus, was it?" Atticus' voice cut through the air, a bored nonchalance to his tone. The demon snapped its head up, looking behind where Hazel lay. "House Cygnus is your master, you say? Well, I am Asterius, Prince of House Lyra. And you fucked up."

Hazel pulled herself upright as two arcs of green light lit up the world in front of her. Hasmondus' eyes were trained on Atticus as a second passed, then dark green blood began to drip from the demon's throat. Another few seconds, and Hasmondus' head slid from his shoulders, and his grip slackened. Rini fell to the ground in a gasping heap as the lesser demon collapsed, slipping over the edge of the bridge and plummeting soundless into the water below.

Using every ounce of her energy, Hazel pushed past the pain and crawled over to Rini. The idol was spluttering, eyes wide as she took in breaths. Hazel could already see the purple bruising on the idol's neck. Hazel pulled Rini into her arms, cradling her, a hand gently caressing the idol's cheek. She was hurt, and it was all Hazel's fault. Guilt and shame ate at her as the others fought around her, dealing with the remaining lesser demons. This was all her fuck up, all of it.

"I'm sorry," Hazel whispered. "I'm sorry."

"It's okay." Rini's voice was bruised and battered, raspy.

But it wasn't.

Hazel let the others clear out the demons. It was too late for Atticus' plan to not be seen—not with what had happened. So she'd cradled Rini while they dispersed the shadow demons and sent them on their way. Eventually, the world was silent again, save for the screaming and fire in the background that was engulfing the city. She had to make things right, make them better.

"We have to move. Can you get her up?"

Atticus' voice cut into Hazel's thoughts. The demon hovered over her, his face contorted with anxiety.

"We're both hurt," Hazel said dully. Atticus sighed.

"I can see that. We don't have a choice, though." He gestured broadly around them. "It is as if the end of days has come. And it waits for no man, no demon, no Hunter. We have to press on."

Hazel was about to argue when Rini interrupted. "He's right. We can't wait here. We have to move."

Gritting her teeth, Hazel nodded. "Fine. We move on."

Charlotte and Wade hurried over, pulling Hazel and Rini to their feet as Atticus scanned the horizon. Specter mewled, butting their legs as if he were trying to help. Slipping an arm under Rini's shoulders, Hazel introduced her.

"Rini Sakamato, this is Wade, and the little blondie is Atticus the demon."

"A *demon*?"

"It's a long story," Charlotte sighed. "But... how are you here, Rini?"

"I followed you two." The idol—and Slayer—didn't even try to deny it. "I saw you guys fall into the floor. I wasn't going to leave you two alone. I turned up for our date and Charlotte's Grandmother told me how to find you. She said she had a feeling where you'd be. Well, your car was there, I followed you in, and you can fill in the rest. I've been looking for you, Hazel." Rini said Hazel's name softly, with affection. Hazel gulped in response.

She'd forgotten she'd planned a date with Rini the same day. Oops.

"This is a nice little reunion, but can we talk and walk, ladies?" Atticus clapped his hands together, and if Hazel hadn't been supporting Rini, she might have slapped him.

"We really should get moving, before worse things happen," Wade chimed in, hovering anxiously behind Atticus.

"Can you guys tell me what's going on and where we're going?" Rini asked as they began hobbling across the bridge.

"Well, it's been a day..."

CHAPTER TWENTY-TWO

ATTICUS

Atticus hovered to the side, watching the emotional reunion. This girl that Hazel held protectively, she was new, different. She changed the dynamic, and Atticus wasn't sure how to process it.

"That's fine, just take it from the beginning," Rini answered.

As Atticus ushered them along, Specter trotting beside him as he led the march, the daemon listened in on the jumbled, tangle of narratives. The Blythe girl and the angry one filled the dark haired, dark eyed girl with the blade, who he felt eying him suspiciously from behind. Wade interrupted occasionally, filling in details of his journey with Atticus. Every time his companion mentioned the daemon's name, the new girl gave an odd little 'hmph'.

Atticus didn't know what her deal was, and he didn't care to know. The others may have known her, cared for her, but she was not his burden. And he was more than happy to cut any dead weight.

"Can we move it along? We have places to be. You can have a tea party and gossip all you want after this is done." Though he tried to keep his voice neutral, an irritated note woven through his words.

The new girl, not subtly at all, asked, "And what's up his butt, then?"

"We're going to his family, I think. I'm going to be honest, I'm not entirely following what's going on here." Atticus looked over his shoulder for a moment as Hazel spoke, her arm under the new girl, dragging her along. Everyone looked ragged, worn. Their clothes were disheveled, dried blood and bruises forming on skin, the murky blood of lesser daemons splashed across their attire.

Charlotte made a sympathetic noise. "It sounds like we're caught in the start of a war. Definitely looks and feels like it, anyway. We've done nothing but fight and get kidnapped since getting here. And now, well, we have to work out the why. And Atticus is our best guess."

"Have you considered that it's a good thing if the daemons fight amongst each other? They might wipe one another out, and we won't have to clean them up or have them interfere with our world anymore. We might even get a break from wiping out monsters." The new girl's voice was soft and sweet, but there was a malicious edge to her words.

That was it. Atticus didn't care if the world was on fire, that dread clawed at him like a hungry beast in the wilderness. He spun around, facing them. The foursome stopped abruptly, barely avoiding colliding into him and the cat. Wade was wide eyed, puzzled. Charlotte and Hazel looked confused. But the new girl. There was a glint in her eye—like she wanted to provoke him, wanted a fight. Fine. He would. He had no allegiance to this insufferable wretch.

"Say it to my face," he growled. Anger bit at him, burning hot. "Tell me what you think of me. Of my family. That we're monsters."

"Didn't I just say that?" Rini replied coolly.

Hazel, arm still wrapped around the newcomer, laughed nervously. "Maybe now isn't the time for this, babes."

Atticus raised a hand. "No, Hazel. Your... friend, here. She wanted to comment. She wants to disrespect me, here, in *my* home. After we saved her, after all." He wanted to unleash his fury, but he fought to keep his voice steady. "You chose to come here. No one made you. And yet, you insult me. Wish harm on those around me—"

"Do your kind not harm people all the time?" Rini interrupted, voice rising in volume. She pushed away from Hazel, a dark, plum-colored bruise forming on her left cheek. Her throat was turning a similar shade where she had been choked, and the louder she spoke, the scratchier her voice became. "You feed off us, make your sneaky little deals."

"Do your people not benefit from those deals?" Atticus snapped back, wind rustling his hair. "Do they not get something out of that bargain?"

"You use them!"

"If it weren't for those deals, people like Wade wouldn't be around still," Atticus snarled. "Do you want that for Charlotte? To be without her soul mate? They wouldn't have even met if he and I hadn't made a deal, as he died eighty years before she was even *born*. So go ahead, call me a monster, a daemon, whatever you wish. But know that if it weren't for me and my kind, that your lives would be worse off. The symbiotic relationship we have with humans its beneficial both ways. And yes, sometimes things that happen *are* cruel or horrid. But you don't consider that it's other humans weaponizing us and our skills. It's not something I just *do*. This is a choice your kind makes to hurt one another, and if you didn't have us to use as a tool, you'd use one of the many evil ones you've invented yourselves."

The newcomer blinked at him, as if lost for words. Charlotte slid her hand into Wade's before speaking. "And I'm grateful for you, Atticus. For bringing him to me. For keeping him safe. I... I know we have had our differences. That I don't agree with everything you've done, and never will. But that doesn't mean I can't appreciate what you *have* done." She looked up at Wade, her chocolate brown eyes filled with love. Another pang of jealousy shot through him, but at the same time, he was flooded with warmth. He was appreciative of her, he realized.

"Thank you," Atticus mumbled, his anger beginning to dissipate. "That... that means a lot to me. I am not cruel, or wicked, or unkind. I am merely... different to you. But I still have family, and those I care for, just the same as you. And right now, they could be hurting. And I need to make sure they're alright so I can find away to send you all back to your homes." He waited for the new girl to say something, to continue her fight. Instead, she shuffled uncomfortably, the fabric of her ridiculous attire rustled together with her movements.

"I—I'm sorry," Rini muttered, eyes downcast. "When you spend your free time fighting, you don't consider that there is another perspective. That perhaps we can be similar. I don't really understand your kind. I've never spoken to one of you before."

"Yes, well, now you have." They stared at one another in silence as the sounds of war surrounding them, a rising cacophony. "And I am begging you to please just trust me."

Rini stared at him for a few beats, before nodding once. Firm, decisive. "Fine, demon. Keep leading the way, then."

Good.

The wind gained momentum as they stumbled along, harsh breezes covering the city he knew as home in soot and ash, smoke billowing across the great city of Terra Doerum. Ash filled their lungs as they hiked up the winding streets, following the familiar path home. The rest of the trek was done in complete silence, not a word spoken between them. The tension was palpable, thick enough to cut with a knife. Atticus was rife with anxiety as he ushered them between alleyways, past broken windows and fragmented howls. Magic blasted in the distance, not unlike human bombs going off. Wade would flinch every so often, but the girls were stoic, used to the sounds of chaos and suffering, it seemed.

Atticus was used to it in their world, but not his own. His world didn't behave like that. They didn't have war. They didn't make each other suffer the way humans liked to inflict on one another. And he was impatient to find out why this was happening, what had caused it all. Why, after all this time, there would be fighting between the great Houses.

How had his family had gotten caught so in the middle of it all? He knew his father as a hard man, one that expected perfection—or, at least, near enough from his sons. But he wasn't a cruel daemon. He was just, wise beyond measure. And it had taken Atticus this time away, this time seeing the depths of human sorrow and misery, to understand how fortunate he was to have a father like Nova.

Atticus shook away his thoughts, focusing on now, on the present. So he spurred them on, their shoes clacking on the paths past the grandiose homes as they reached the quadrant of Terra Doerum where his family home resided. Finally, though, they crested the home where the great House Lyra Manor awaited.

The scene before him was both familiar, and completely unrecognizable. The heavy steel gates that separated his family home from the rest of the mountain city were wide open, swinging on their hinges. The garden lay dormant, silent, the hedges and flower beds weirdly muted from the blackened soot of fire and ash that fell across them like a blanket of snow. The main doors, heavy double doors with carved images of flowers and art nouveau styled decorations—many of which he knew inspired the great ocean liners of the previous century—lay as open as the main gates. The wide windows were darkened, no light showing from within.

Atticus' stomach plummeted as he stopped right within the gates. The manor house was imposing, a formidable foe that stared down at him like a child paralyzed by the dark. His heart raced in his chest, an overwhelming urge to run away cascading over him. The lamps that usually lit the gardens lay dark for the first time in his existence.

"Oh no," Charlotte breathed beside him.

Oh no, indeed. She was certainly putting it mildly. Numbness seeped over him like ink spilling on parchment as he began stumbling towards the open doors. Everything felt too loud in the silence around the manor, too much. His boots clattered with every step, and each step brought him closer to the truth.

"Hello?" Atticus called out, stepping over the threshold to his manor home. The foyer was dimly lit; candles guttered in their holders, barely able to cast a shadow. Debris littered the floor—papers scattered everywhere, swathes of ripped fabric, and chunks of wood from ornamental pieces. His footsteps scuffed across them as he stepped inside, a cold chill running down his spine.

The wide pocket doors to the main living area remained open, and as he ducked through the foyer, the grandiose staircase—centered in the middle of the room, splitting off to a balcony above—was dark and ominously quiet. He was used to the sounds of servants and members of the house tending to tasks. Not often was this staircase quiet, even during the lulls of sleep. A coil tightened in his stomach as he called out, "Mother? Father? Nox?"

No response. He glanced around the room, at the severe portraits of House Lyra members from millennia past, judging him. Maybe if he had been here when things went down, it wouldn't be so bad.

He was small, smaller than the others. He always knew that. His mother said he had been the runt of the litter. He was her baby, her precious gift. And it didn't matter if he was smaller, weaker—for she loved him fiercely.

He had come some several hundred years after Nox had been born. They had said that Aurora Lyra just might not be able to produce a second heir. Some of their kind couldn't, wouldn't. At night, when he was small, she would lie down beside him in his bed and tell the little Princeling that she had beseeched some power greater than her for him. How she had offered her magic in exchange for him. He remembered her holding him, stroking the short fuzz of his pale blond hair as they stared out the window at the moons, and she would whisper all the wonderful things she wanted for her Asterius. How he was born for greatness, how he was her little star.

She had been his safe space in a world full of anxiety and unknowns. He was the spare, and thus, Father didn't pay him as much heed as Nox. His father, tall and imposing, had looked down at a young Atticus like a mighty God might. It had spurred the young Prince on, had encouraged him to try his best. Atticus had tried to keep up with his brother as he grew—oh, how he had tried. But he was smaller than everyone else. Smaller than Nox, smaller than his cousins, smaller than all of them. Even the true him couldn't keep up.

He remembered trailing in the shadows of their home, watching everyone with jealously from the darkness, where they couldn't see him—or they chose not to. This angry, hot ball would form in his stomach, watching them laugh together, work together.

Why did no one want to do that with him?

He learned to withdraw into the dark and learned that he would always be on the outskirts, the baby holding his mother's hand, to them. So he gave up trying to fit in, to be like the others, like Nox and Caleo. They called him the selfish Princeling, when he chose not to interact with them. That he thought he was better than them. And the more they said it, the lonelier he became.

So the day he got his first contract, he was out of there and didn't look back.

Atticus floated through the manor like he was in a dream.

It had been upended throughout. Like vultures had come to scavenge through the history of his family. Furniture was strewn about, heirlooms shattered on the floor. With some relief, the crystal that stored power and managed the house was still in one piece, merely knocked from the device that allowed it to power things. The crystal was a magical conduit that fed on the energy of the world, through wires—much like tree roots feeding into the ground. The dark oak wood panel throughout was stained with darkness—he shuddered to consider what it was. He didn't pause to think.

He called out as he wandered through, his voice hoarse. He wondered, for a moment, how Nox would feel about the humans knowing his true name. They could bind him, if they chose, make a deal with him he might not want. *Maybe there won't be a Nox to make a deal with.*

He gulped hard, stopping on the second-floor landing. The doors to their rooms were wide open. In front of him was his own. He could smell his perfumes, the scent of Mother and his childhood. He glanced a peek at his dark, carved bed, the plush velvet of the sitting chair Mother would sit in him when he took to the bed, unable to shake the dread that would wrap him in a vice grip.

"Mother," he said softly, placing a hand to the door as he looked into the darkened room. The curtains were drawn, same as when he last left his room. A rustling from within the room had him jumping back, the quintet behind him yelping. Atticus didn't hesitate as he readied a ball of fire, calling out authoritatively, "Show yourself!"

"Asterius? Brother?"

Atticus nearly loosed the fireball in shock. Nox's voice was hollow, with a hopeful edge to it as he called out for the Princeling. With a shaking hand, Atticus held the flame aloft and took a step into his childhood room.

It was much the same as he remembered. There was a portrait of the family hanging on one side of the dark armoire, a portrait of him alone on the other. He knew the clothes he had collected over the years from the mortal realm sat within. A small writing desk was shoved beneath the drawn curtains.

And under his bed crawled out Nox, heir to the Lyra family.

"Brother?"

Atticus stared at his brother, as though in a stupor. The great heir, the great Prince, was hidden beneath his baby brother's bed, his face bruised and battered. He had begun crawling out, stomach to the floor—slithering out like a worm—when Atticus entered the room.

"Your *brother?* What the hell is going on int his place. What the fuck is happening, Atticus?" Hazel hissed behind him. He ignored the vulgar girl.

"Nox, what happened? Why are you on the floor?" he demanded. He leaned down and offered Nox a hand. His brother's was more calloused than his own, having seen hard work and toil. Nox crawled out the rest of the way, breathing heavily as he stumbled to his feet.

"They came in, an attack. They're waging a war, seeking dominion over Terra Doerum and the other realms. Several of the Houses have banded together and staged an uprising. They came for Mother and Father."

"They got Mother and Father?" Icy dread pooled in Atticus' stomach. His brother shook his head.

"No, the servants got them out. I remained behind to ensure their safety, to fight off the rest. I hid in here after, hoping you would get out, come home. I sent Caleo for you, because we needed you home."

"You... needed me?" His heart pounded in his chest. Nox nodded once, staring down at his little brother.

Atticus exhaled. Mother and Father were safe; that was something. Atticus placed his hands on his hips. "Right, then, we need to go help and stop this uprising then. I can handle this."

With a twist of his hands, Atticus sent a blinding light over the group, healing their scrapes and cuts. It hadn't occurred often to use his magic to heal; the last time had been when Wade had sliced his throat.

Hazel threw her hands up in the air. "You could have done that *this whole time*?"

Atticus let a laugh, not making eye contact with anyone. He was a Daemon Prince, and he could handle this.

"Alright. We need to think of a plan, and fast. We need to team up, for all our sakes, or there won't be a home for you to return to."

There was a wary chorus of agreement amongst the group as Atticus faced his brother. "We must take care of the humans and find a way to stop this. We must... work together." He stuck out a hand then. Atticus liked to make deals, but had never done so with someone of his own kind. Nox eyed him off, before nodding once, clasping Atticus' hand.

CHAPTER TWENTY-THREE

HAZEL

C alamity had struck, and the fires throughout Terra Doerum had spread. Sulfur tinged the air, a mixture of magic and despair. Screeches and howls filled the twilight sky, a cacophony of sounds. It burned her nose and ears, singeing the back of her throat as she breathed in more ash than she would smoking a cigarette.

The fire had begun to spread up the mountain, toward where the fancy-ass bougie houses stood, including Atticus' parents' manor house. It rose in plumes, splashes of ink across the indigo and rose horizon. They stood together, gathered in the silent gardens, staring up at the sky.

"This is all really happening, isn't it? This isn't some sort of awful fucking fever dream?" Hazel's arms were heavy at her sides as she glanced down at the motley crew they had gathered. Atticus' brother towered over them, his golden skin gleaming in the low light, somehow. He looked so much like the bratty, snobbish demon she was used to, but they were so different too. Atticus was smaller, paler, more fragile. His brother looked like he could, and had, taken and dished out beatings. They were the sun and moon by one another—Nox the day, Atticus the night. The way they held themselves, though—that's where the similarities really shone through. That arrogant, entitled way they set their shoulders, as if they were used to being on top of the world.

Atticus frowned, brows furrowed. "What is your plan, brother dearest?"

Nox continued staring up at the sky as a flash of green spanned the horizon, not unlike a shooting star. "I am afraid to say this, but I am lost for words, for thoughts. We were just so blindsided by this." His brother loosed a breath, hands clenched at his sides. "This was unprecedented. Who suspected a coup, let alone one this successful?"

Hazel went to speak, when her thoughts were interrupted by a resounding explosion. Her ears rung as the ground beneath them tremored, like an earthquake was rolling the earth beneath them. Specter let out a snarl, fur standing on end, as he raced forward, away from the group.

"Speckles, no!" Charlotte cried, darting after her cat. Hazel leaped into action, hot on the heels of her friend and her dumb ass cat. She heard the others scramble after them as Charlotte continued calling after Specter as he raced from the manor grounds, past the obnoxious gates and back into the streets of the war-torn city.

"I can grab the creature!" Nox exclaimed. His legs were longer than Hazel's, and though she had endurance, her ass had been kicked a lot since they had found themselves there. Wade, who has been keeping stride with Hazel, surged forward too, ahead of the Hunter.

"Wait up!" Atticus yelled. Hazel threw a glance over her shoulder to see Atticus pattering along as fast as he could in his heeled boots, Rini right behind him, her vision fixed on him. Ah, she didn't trust him; Hazel supposed that was fair. Hazel slowed down to keep pace with Rini and Atticus. She could tell the demon wasn't used to physical labor; his outfit was definitely a sign of that. While everyone—save Wade in his coat tails, and Nox in what appeared to be some sort of family crested armor and leather daddy gear—dressed sensibly, Atticus was dolled up. Everything about how he dressed screamed, 'I can't tell if I'm a poor Victorian poet or a poor Victorian page boy'. His velvet vest, billowing sleeves, weirdly buttoned trousers and booty heels were not exactly the fashion of an athletic individual.

Time seemed to slow down as Hazel returned her attention ahead of her, and disaster struck once more. Hazel skid to a stop, almost caught completely off balance as what could only be described as a Lovecraftian monster erupted from one of the houses lining the street. Atticus let out a squeal as a mass of onyx, elongated limbs—larger than any being had a right to be, at least five times Hazel's size—came hurtling out into the street, slamming into the path as if it had been thrown. Stones were sent flying as the creature made a horrendous scraping sound, like rock-on-rock.

Hazel stared in horror as it lifted an arm—easily twice the length of her body—and sent a tidal wave of darkness toward the house that it had just been sent careening from. Hazel felt herself being flung backward, unable to brace herself from the force of the magic projectile. She slammed into the ground several feet back, groaning as her hip hit cobblestone. Raising her head in horror, she stared at the scene before her.

The black mass had begun to rise to its feet. Silvery slashes were indicative of eyes; a maw of sharp, crimson teeth gnashed in its wide, dislocated jaw. It let out a horrifying roar, high-pitched like a child's scream that reverberated around them. It slouched as it stood, towering over the manor houses in the street, its arms bent, fingers distended, like it had too many knuckles.

"What in the fuck is that?" she stuttered, throwing a glance over her shoulder at her companions. Rini looked as horrified as she felt, while Atticus was pale and frowning, but didn't seem shocked. She pointed an accusatory finger at Atticus. "You. Tell me. What the fuck is this thing?"

"That's a true form." His eyes were locked onto the creature as he answered her. "So, this is how dire things have become. It's true they're involved."

"*Who?*"

As the creature let out another roar, Atticus said hastily, "The creatures you know as angels and demons—they're just us, the Houses. We have the forms we present to you humans, and the ones that are our *true* forms. You see how I am indistinguishable to one of your kind? This is the main form we will take. That, what you see there, is magic unbound."

As Atticus finished up, a small woman with long, copper hair strode from the house that the creature had been sent flying from. She was petite, golden skinned with hazel eyes that were trained on her prey. Her pace increased as she closed the distance between herself and the roaring beast. It was gonna swallow her whole—it was easily five or six times her size. Her power walk became a full-blown sprint as she raced toward the creature. It began snapping at her, its movements slower but powerful as it raised an arm to swat her away. A scream rose in Hazel's throat—to warn her, in fear?—when everything went from terrifying to worse.

The girl leaped into the air. One moment, she was full human, no different to Hazel or any of the others. What was realistically mere seconds, but felt like an eternity, the world exploded. Her limbs began to extend, shadows erupting around them in a twisted, magical girl like fashion—like those Japanese cartoons her cousin liked. The girl grew in size, her body contorting and shaking the world around them as she exploded into a creature not unlike the one that was howling before them. Hazel stumbled back in horror. The girl was now like seven or so times the size of the average werewolf, and nastier looking than any she had seen. Red, bulging eyes swiveled on the sides of her head like a chameleon, fur as dark as onyx. Her face twisted into a long snout, yellow, drooling teeth snapping as she lunged at the other creature.

A terrifying shriek rose from the first creature as the werewolf-like monster clamped its massive jaw around the creature's neck. Thick, black fluid seeped down its neck as it lifted an arm, bringing a mangled fist up and sending it slamming into the once-a-girl's face. An otherworldly snarl emanated from her as they began to grapple one another. Debris was sent flying as they tackled each other, slamming into the ground as if in slow motion, their sheer size making their movements slower, more exaggerated than anything Hazel had seen before.

"We better get away, before they notice us." Hazel glanced over to Atticus, who was paling by the second. "We don't want to get involved with this. We can backtrack, find another way past."

Then she remembered that Charlotte was caught on the other side of that fight.

"They're going to get hurt," Hazel gasped.

"*You're* going to get hurt if we don't get out of the way," Atticus snapped. "Those are fully fledged demons and they will destroy you without hesitation.

Do you want to die, you silly mortal girl? Because I can most assuredly tell you that you will."

"What about Charlotte? What about Wade, and your brother? Don't you care about them?"

"Of course I care about them! But I also care about you not dying either, you absolute fool. Your friend would have my head if you were harmed, and Nox can take care of the others. So how about you learn to listen for a day in your life instead of being a spiteful brat?"

"Have *you* considered not being a spiteful brat yourself?"

"Can you *both* quit it?" Rini snapped, finally chiming in. She slammed her hands over her ears as one of the creatures screamed again, ear piercingly loud. "We have to *go*."

"Fine," Hazel snapped as the ground shook beneath them. Atticus let out a sigh of relief and turned, ready to scramble away. Hazel was about to follow when cold dread filled her spine as Charlotte wailed in the distance.

"Someone, please, help!"

Nope, fuck that. She had to go in. Hazel darted forward as Atticus yelled at her to stop, but she was flying through the air, running on pure adrenaline. That was her *bestie*. Debris from the wrestling monsters whizzed past her as she ducked and weaved, despite her body screaming out in protest. She was wracked with pain, despite Atticus' weird magic removing her superficial scrapes. Whatever she was suffering on the inside stayed there. It had merely been a bandage to stem the bleeding.

One moment, her boots were clattering against the cobblestone. The next step, they didn't reach the ground. Hazel yelped as she felt herself being dragged backward in the air, like she was on a horizontal bungee cord. The night air whipped past her, a cold sting on her cheeks, as she hurtled toward Atticus and Rini, away from her friend. She let out a gasp, the wind knocked from her, as Atticus dumped her unceremoniously on the ground beside him.

"Listen to me, you petulant mortal. I'm not telling you this for fun. You cannot fight a demon like that. You will not win. They will tear you to shreds if they notice you. You're immensely lucky that they didn't to begin with, or you'd be dead already. This is my realm, not yours, and you have to learn to *listen*." He'd raised his voice, a dark rumble beneath them. Like something lurked behind the veil of what he was showing them.

Hazel bit the inside of her cheek as hot tears pricked at the corners of her eyes. "But... Lottie..."

"I know." Atticus' voice softened, as did his expression. He was a gentle, unassuming boy again. "Please trust me."

She nodded once, a lump in her throat as she turned away from her best friend, following the demon and the idol.

They didn't make it far before things went from bad, to worse.

They'd barely made it around the corner onto another street when more horrible beings filled the horizon. Atticus had said these were demon true forms, and she was unsure she'd seen anything like it. They were some kind of eldritch horrors, gods from another time and place. Beings made of darkness and light so blinding that Hazel had to wince when her eyes fell upon them.

She was beginning to see why biblical angels were as horrifying as they were when a creature with many eyes, and feathery wings made of dazzling, iridescent light, emerged from behind a manor house. It let out a screech like a strangled parrot as it raised itself into the air, a dozen wings flapping at once. Dust and detritus created a mini cyclone beneath it as it hovered above them. Rini let out a gasp.

The monster floating in the air had thousands of eyes across its face, like a spider. It had to be at least twelve feet tall and double that across at least, accounting for the wingspan. Its body, though humanoid in shape, was decidedly devoid of anything human-like. It was sterile, millennial white with no discernible features—except for the thousands of blinking eyes and the light of its wings. Like a mannequin a toddler had stuck whatever they could find to, it was horrific and defied logic.

"Is that some sort of final boss?" Hazel joked uneasily.

"You could say something like that," Atticus muttered behind her, wringing his hands. "Let's backtrack—"

It was too late. It had spotted them. The monster screeched again from where it was hovering, all its arachnid eyes on them as it fluttered its wings. Hazel didn't have time to react as it sent out a beam of light at them with rapid speed. Hazel cringed, squeezing her eyes shut as the fairly tepid night became hotter than Arizona in the middle of a heatwave, washing over her like a tidal wave.

Reaching out a hand, she found Rini's, squeezing the other girl's hand. Was this how she was going to die? No one would know they were here, that they were dead. That they'd even gone missing.

A few seconds passed, then a few more as Hazel held her breath. She cracked an eye open to find Atticus in front of them, arms spread wide, bearing the brunt of the light and heat. He turned his head, looking over his shoulder at them. "Get behind cover," he said between gritted teeth. "*Now.*"

She didn't need to be told twice. Rini's hand still clasped in her own, she yanked the other girl behind her, barreling toward the closest brick wall. It was on the side of one of the giant houses, not unlike Atticus' family dwelling. A door hung on its hinges, swaying in the force of the wind caused by the giant floating demon. Hazel tugged Rini inside, using her free hand to grab the door and force it back into place.

"Help me," she grunted, struggling with the door. Rini dropped her hand, allowing Hazel to grab the doorknob with both hands as the idol wrestled with the lock. Eventually, though, it clicked, and both women breathed a sigh of relief. The door rattled still, but they were safely inside. There was a part of her that was dimly aware of the fact that they'd left Atticus to fend for himself.

"Now what?" Rini asked softly. Her face was smudged with dirt, her katana strapped to her back. Hazel desperately wanted to clean the idol up, to take care of her. Her stomach flipped, knots forming as she looked into Rini's warm, dark brown eyes. Hazel threw caution to the wind. Closing the space between them in two strides, Hazel cupped Rini's face gently between the palm of her hands.

"I want to kiss you," she breathed. "Can I kiss you?"

Rini reached a hand up, her fingertips tracing a pattern across the back of Hazel's hand. "I thought you'd never ask."

Hazel didn't need to be told twice. She leaned in, brushing her lips against the idol's. She tasted of cherry lip gloss, of warm summer nights and hopeful dreams. She tasted of a future that Hazel had never thought of, never dreamed of.

She tasted like a choice that Hazel had already made.

Hazel swept her tongue over Rini's lips, prodding and probing, a gentle question. As Rini parted her lips, she had her answer. She moved a hand from Rini's face to cup the idol's neck, slow and languorous licks exploring the idol's mouth.

They had done things, yes. She had done a lot with Rini that she had done with other women. Hazel was a 'bed 'em, not wed 'em' girlie. She liked her affairs light, sexual, and over as fast as they started. Rini, though, set a fire inside her. A fierce protectiveness. She was a need, not a want. Every kiss, every raspy breath between them, stoked the flames of her passion and longing.

Rini was more than a girl that Hazel would hook up with, and if they got out of this hell, she was going to let the idol know that. That for once, Hazel wanted more than a hook up, more than a promise to call. She wanted stability, security—the things she thought she would never be afforded.

She wanted to get out of this demon hell scape, no matter the cost to herself. She wanted to try her best, to let herself be vulnerable, to be more soft and feminine and scared; if Rini would let her, would have her. She'd be a better friend and ally to Charlotte, be kinder to Wade. Whatever she could. If only she could be given the chance.

Time seemed to slow down as Rini circled her arms around Hazel's waist, and the two locked in an embrace that was filled with a longing, a yearning, that Hazel couldn't articulate. It was one of those moments that she knew she wanted to last forever, though it couldn't. Reality came crashing down around them, pulling them apart with deep, broken gasps of breath as an explosion shook the manor.

Rini let out a shaky, breathless laugh. "I guess this isn't really the time for this, huh?"

"Is any time really the time for a make out session in a demonic, apocalyptic war?"

Another laugh. "I guess we gotta take all the moments we can get."

Hazel stared into Rini's eyes for several long moments. She was right. Any moment they could get. Like Charlotte had with Wade. Charlotte hadn't fixated on the past, on the could haves. She focused on the next step forward, on the things she could control. Hazel would have to learn to let things go.

Charlotte. Dread pooled in Hazel's stomach as her thumb stopped absentmindedly stroking Rini's cheek. Her friend was out there. Specter was out there. Wade and the weird, gothic Victorian demon child—they were all out there, in the midst of it all. And here she was, hiding. She wasn't a hider.

She was a fighter. A Hunter.

"We have to go back out there," she breathed. "And... it might not be pretty."

"I know," Rini answered softly. "But it's better than dying inside and hiding, right?" A pang shot through her heart. This woman understood her so well, somehow. Despite so little time together, they clicked, made sense.

"Yeah."

"Well, we aren't going out without a fight." Rini dropped her arms, stepping out of Hazel's embrace. The briefest flicker of doubt ignited in Hazel's stomach. It was quickly extinguished by Rini adding, "We need to find you something to fight with. You need all the chances you can get."

The demon home they had found themselves in wasn't unlike Atticus'. Rini and Hazel had hastened through the empty rooms, their footsteps echoing across stone floors, dodging partially collapsed ceilings, as they sought something for Hazel to use. She would have taken a lead pipe, if that was all she could get.

Hazel had seen a lot of opulent houses since meeting Charlotte. Rich society, she found, was unaware of the ridiculousness of their gaudiness. *New* rich, anyway. Charlotte had been quick to correct her on that one. Demon upper society, apparently, wasn't any less tacky than new rich, it seemed. At least, this one wasn't. Atticus' home reminded her more of Winterbourne. *This* place, though.

Loud colored wallpaper lined the walls, and gold fixtures dotted them. Ostentatious chandeliers hung in every room they raced through, crystals and candles swaying from the ruckus outside. Though they ran across plush, luscious carpets, the richness of it all felt spectacularly cheap and tacky thanks to the obnoxious decor. If she'd had the time, she would have loved to have used her camera to snap some shots.

Finally, though, they found what they had been looking for. In a small room off what appeared to be some sort of grand hall, there was a glass case, a weapon mounted within. Something like a scythe crossed with an ax, it had a snath that was about sixty-seven inches long. The head of the weapon was obscenely big—large enough to cut down even the burliest of men, should they get in the way.

It was perfect.

Hazel wrapped her jacket around her fist and smashed the glass with several forceful punches. It shattered, leaving giant shards of glass littering the ground surrounding it. Shucking her jacket back on, she grasped the weapon and tugged it free of its holder. It had a solid heft to it, heavier in her hands than she expected. She was already so sore. But she had to do what was needed, and push through.

Holding the weapon in front of her, Hazel turned to Rini. "Let's go save the others, babes."

Hazel was done hiding behind others, done not cleaning up her own messes. She had gotten them all stuck in the demon world, and she was going to do everything in her power to get them back out again.

With Rini hot on her heels, Hazel raced through the house, kicking in the door that they had locked behind them what felt like a lifetime ago. Her blood pumped through her, hot and angry, urging her onwards. She was Hazel Williams. She was a Hunter. She was smart, and brave, and strong. And she was going to kick some serious ass.

Hazel and Rini emerged out onto the same street they had been on before, but the scene was decidedly different. Atticus was to the side, throwing out blasts of magic as another dark being engaged in battle with the angelic monster from earlier. Taller than any of the others they had seen, this one was wisps of smoke, no concrete form, as it wrapped itself around the many eyed beast, ribbon-like shadows becoming manacles. A petite, soft-curled woman stood off to the side. She looked over her shoulder as they came bursting out, blue eyes wide. Hurrying over to them, the woman tried to usher them back.

"It's not safe out here." Her voice was soft and melodious, like a little chirping bird. She was clad in a soft, flowing gown, a pink sash around her waist. Extremely pale, her cheeks were the softest rose red. There was something about the way she held herself, the way she spoke, that Hazel couldn't put her finger on. She was delicate and poised, but something seemed too gentle about her, breakable almost. Like a porcelain doll. Was she another demon? Was this all a disguise? "Let Bee and your friend handle it. It's not safe for humans."

Hazel readjusted her weapon, narrowing her eyes. "Are you one of them, or one of us?"

The girl stared at her for a moment, her long dark lashes fluttering as she finally answered. "I was like you, once, a long time ago now. Now... I'm not sure. I'm different. But you can trust me. I know what it's like to be in your position. So please, believe me when I say it's not safe."

"It's a bit late, isn't it?" Rini gestured. "We have friends we need to help, though."

The girl nodded. "Then help, we shall."

CHAPTER TWENTY-FOUR

ATTICUS

A tticus had never been more grateful for his kind than after he had sent the two human girls running. Herstafont—the daemon who had blocked their passage—was cruel, unkind, and had locked her many eyes on Atticus. They had never seen eye-to-eye in the past, and he just knew that she was going to use this war as an excuse to commit as many atrocities as she could. She had gone at him, screaming, her full power unleashed without the container of her human-presenting form.

Her wings sent cyclonic gusts of wind whirling around him. He had to brace himself with all his might to remain standing against the onslaught as Herstafont came careening at him. A narrow beak opened between the eyes—so small that one wouldn't see it unless she was upon you—and a horrendous, bassy groan emitted from her as she swooped down at him.

He narrowly dodged her, using the shadows to transport him behind her. With a flick of his wrist, he sent out a flame at her. Though it hit, it didn't even singe her. It did, however, piss her off further. Another bassy, reverberating howl escaped her as she adjusted her flight, turning like an owl flying throught he night to face him.

She spoke in the Old Tongue, pulsing words that emitted like one of those music machines that humans used. The words were disjointed, incoherent slurs, but they got the message across enough—she had a chance to kill him, and she was going to take it. That was fine with him. She'd needed taking down a peg for a millenia or two, anyway.

The streets weren't as narrow as the hodgepodge paths of the slums, but they also weren't wide enough for a creature like Herstafont in her true form to navigate cleanly. He had the advantage over her. If he kept dodging, he could blind her, take her down that way. He had bought the other two time at least, while he handled this beast.

As he slipped into the shadows again, he spotted an old friend in the same pocket of darkness. Silvery eyes peered at him as he paused, suspended between places. Ribbons of darkness curled and beckoned as a deep, sonorous voice stated his name. "Asterius."

"Balkexet." He hadn't seen the daemon in so long; Balkexet of House Convallaria. They had been somewhat chummy in their youth. Truth be told, he was one of the few daemons that Atticus had stomached, had not hated being near in the mortal realm, when their paths did cross.

"Bee?" a light voice echoed in the darkness with them, feminine, soft. Atticus blanched at the humanness of it.

"He can be trusted." Balkexet's deep voice was smooth, soothing. "It is fine, Kitty."

Atticus didn't have the time to work out who or why this Kitty was here with Balkexet. He hadn't run into the daemon in at least a century and a half or so—at least since he'd met Wade. "What are you doing here?"

Mirthful laughter. "Never change, Asterius. So direct. We are here to fight, like you. Is that not what you are here for?"

"It's complicated."

"Is it not always?" More rumbling laughter. "I should like to hear more from you after the world is back in order."

Their chatter was ended by another echoing groan from Herstafont, who had started flinging herself at the building that Hazel and the Rini girl had run into. They had waited too long in the darkness, and the she-bitch had chosen another target. "Will you help me, Balkexet?"

They stepped from the shadows together. Balkexet's chosen form loomed over Atticus, all bronze skin and dark, long hair. The girl—Kitty—was smaller even than Atticus, with curly hair, a pallid complexion, and bright eyes. There was something about her, not quite human any longer, not quite like him. He could smell it all over her, floral perfumes and sulfur intertwined. *Interesting.*

Herstafont was going to regret picking this fight.

Balkexet did the bulk of the fighting.

Atticus had stepped forward, but Balkexet had put a hand in front of his chest. "Take care of Kitty for me. I'll handle Herstafont."

"I'm *not* a child, Bee," the young woman had complained. Still, she had complied and stayed to the side with Atticus, hovering by the doorway that he had seen Hazel and her friend dart into. He wondered if they were okay, if they could leave Balkexet alone for a moment to go search for them.

No. He had to help his friend. Atticus needed to prove that he could be helpful, could be trusted. That he was more than the Princeling who cried in the dark. He was more than someone who put on a mask.

Atticus darted to the side. Balkexet's true form, a wispy, elongated cloud of darkness, coiled around Herstafont, attempting to cut her off. He could help without hurting his friend, he was certain. So he started blasting, throwing out arcs of wind, intended to slice at her wings, immobilize her. She fought hard against the shackles that Balkexet created as he carved off her plumage. Things were going well.

"We're coming!"

Atticus stiffened. Oh no. He turned to bark at Hazel, to ask why she had left the house after he'd given her orders to get to safety. His eyes widened as she saw her, Rini in tow, carrying a Daemonic Blade—one of the few items that could kill one of their kind wholly and truly. One swoop of a Daemonic Blade would be enough to strike down anyone. Even someone like his father. He recognized it as Gilderon, the weapon that won the Timeless War. Somehow, Hazel had it in her hands. And she had a twinkle in her eyes that he knew meant one thing.

She was going to cause chaos.

He went to call out to her, to tell her to stop, but the words were swallowed up as Herstafont burst free of Balkexet's grip and sent a blast of air straight toward them. Unprepared, Atticus hurtled backward, slamming into the brick wall behind him. Pain radiated through him as he breathed through it. She hadn't damaged him, just knocked him a bit. And now he was angry.

Pushing himself upright, he flittered into the darkness again, looking for a shadow close to Herstafont so he could cut off Hazel. This stupid mortal girl had run in without care and was going to get herself killed at this rate. The one with the blade wasn't much smarter.

Time seemed to slow down as Atticus materialized from the darkness. It was over in a flash, but every second was excruciating to him. Balkexet was about to weave his shadows around Herstafont once more as Hazel and Rini came in, swinging their weapons. She was faster than the two mortal women, though, and swiped at them with one of her wings. It sent them careening backward, slamming them into the ground as their weapons clattered away from them.

Atticus froze as he watched them, their bodies rag dolling as they hit the ground, bodies limp on impact. As they hit the ground, Balkexet squeezed himself around Herstafont once more, and time sped back up again. He couldn't move, couldn't think. This was his fault, it was all his fault. They were hurt, and here he was, unable to move. Unable to do anything.

Maybe he *was* just a pathetic Princeling who ran away from his problems. Maybe he was destined to the be runt forever, the eternal disappointment. Maybe he would never be good enough for anyone.

"Atticus? *Atticus, move.*"

Wade's smooth tenor cut through his dark thoughts like a knife through soft-ened butter. Wade? Where had his dearest companion, his best of all friends, come from? Atticus jolted out of his dark reverie, glancing about wildly.

Looking a little more worse for wear, Nox, Wade, and Charlotte jogged towards him. His brother had a dark, oozing gash on his face—iron in his blood. Atticus grimaced. That was going to be a nasty wound to heal. Charlotte and Wade were covered in dark crimson and emerald smears—daemonic blood. Whatever had happened to them, they were victorious. And that was all that mattered to him.

"You're safe," he breathed, taking them in as they reached him. He stretched out a hand, not caring who he grasped. He just wanted to touch them, to know that they were, indeed, standing before him.

"This isn't the time for a reunion." The small woman who had been with Balkexet appeared at his side, her bright blue eyes wide with concern. "Your friends are in trouble."

Oh, the Hunters. He'd forgotten them in that moment of joy. Wincing, Atticus turned back to the scene from before. The two had not remained prone—they'd pulled themselves back up, using their weapons as crutches. They were struggling, pain clearly radiating through their bodies.

"Hazel?" Charlotte's voice was a whisper as she stared out at her friend. Her cat wove between her legs, brushing up against the girl, as though trying to comfort her. She took a hesitant step forward, then another, before breaking out into a sprint. Wade's dark gray eyes sparkled with fear as he hurried after her. Charlotte lunged for Hazel, wrapping her arms around the Hunter's waist, pulling her backward.

"You're going to get yourself killed if you go in there," Charlotte sobbed, pulling her friend back. The Hunter was stubborn and continued trying to make strides forward. The other Hunter dropped her blade and assisted Charlotte, tugging on the obstinate woman. "So just *listen* to us, please! You big fucking *moron*."

"Someone has to fight," Hazel snapped in return. "If we don't fight, we don't have a chance of making it out alive. None of you do." A small sob caught in the Hunter's throat as she doggedly pushed on.

Atticus' stomach plummeted. *He* should be fighting, not them. *He* should be risking himself, not the mortals. It was his home, and it was his fault they were there. But why did he feel this fear, this almost loathing toward himself?

Nox clasped a hand on his young brother's shoulder, looking down at Atticus. He couldn't remember the last time his brother had touched him, had given such a gesture. He peeked up through his bangs, like a child staring up at a parent. Nox had a grim slash across his face, but he squeezed Atticus' shoulder reassuringly.

"I don't understand you," Nox admitted. *Off to a great start.* "But I can see you care for you these fragile, mortal beings. Your contract told me a bit about your… relationship. We will keep them safe. For your sake."

Atticus' heart raced in his chest, blood coursing through his veins, hot and sharp, like a blade slicing him open. His brother, the Heir to House Lyra, was taking care of him and his friends—not just because of a truce, but because his brother cared enough to do it for Atticus' sake. The daemon reached a hand up to pat his brother's.

"Thank you, dearest."

Nox stared down at his brother for one long moment. "Then we shall fight."

He hadn't trained or fought with his brother since the before times. Before his father gave up on him, before his father realized that Atticus wasn't even good enough to be a spare. Those days, he would sweat out beside his brother, unable to move as fast, fight as fast, wield a blade as well, no matter how much he tried. He could use magic in a way his brother couldn't, could feast on emotion so unlike the other daemons, who preferred pacts and blood sacrifice. He was so different to them, and it was never something that Nova had appreciated about him.

But it was like slipping back in time as his brother lunged ahead of him, racing toward Herstafont and Balkexet. He was dimly aware of the mortals to the side, tending to one another, as he raced after his brother, dipping into the shadows as he stalked their prey.

Herstafont was still straining against the shadowy manacles that Balkexet had created, but it was obvious to anyone watching that he was faltering. His shadows flickered and waned, his true form consuming too much energy, even as Herstafont struggled against him. If he let go now, she would dive for a killing blow—there was no mistaking it.

Nox made the first move. His brother never relied on magic. Steel and iron were the ways to go. He was old fashioned, like his father. Magic was saved for the ritualistic, for the special. Though Atticus would argue that fighting a coup d'etat against their own kind was one of those times that was reserved for magic use.

His brother pulled the great sword that he kept buckled to his back free of its scabbard. Atticus paused when he saw it though. It wasn't the blade that his father had gotten made for Nox—a standard steel blade with the lightest coating of iron on it.

Nox wielded a heavier blade. It had intricate patterns and runes detailing the length of it—their summoning rites. It was made of dark iron, and the silver of the runes glinted in the light of evening. It was their family heirloom—it was a Daemonic Blade like Gilderon. Celestium was their family's most valued item.

When did Father give that to him?

His brother lunged at Herstafont, a cry tearing from his throat. His brother scraped the blade along the ground like a flint, sparks flying as he lifted it up in an arc. Herstafont didn't have time to react as Balkexet loosened his grip, slinking into the shadows with Atticus. She could barely flinch as Nox curved the blade upward. Iron and steel sang out as they connected with Herstafont.

It was, to put it mildly, disgusting. She let out a strangled, ear-piercing screech as the iron tip pierced through several of her eyes, dark blood oozing as Nox continued to yank the blade upward, gutting her like a fish. It made a horrid squelching noise. Nox let out a victorious roar as Celestium sought to finish off Hertsafont.

Nox's cry of victory was too soon, however. Atticus began morphing from the shadows, a cry on his lips as he saw her wrap her dozen monstrous wings around Nox and crush him in with her. Atticus gasped as Nox slipped, his grip on Celestium faltering. His brother fell against the edge of Celestium, slicing himself on its blade. *No.* Atticus felt himself flying through the air, his rage barely contained as he launched toward Herstafont.

Heat enveloped him, his magic a physical raging fire as he slammed into Herstafont's wings. She buckled slightly against him, but held tight onto his brother, her screams deafening. So, he pulled back and slammed into her again. And again. And again.

Herstafont and Nox's screams mingled together as Atticus set her ablaze, her feathers catching fire. She stumbled then, releasing her hold on Nox. She fluttered her wings weakly as she stumbled backward, unable to send herself heavensward. Celestium slipped from where it was lodged, clattering to the ground as Nox fell to the ground beside the ancient weapon.

She continued to scream as Atticus sent another blast at her, his slight form shaking with uncontrollable fury. He watched as she stumbled backward and fell, empty inside as Herstafont burned away to ash.

Nox lay prone on the ground.

And Atticus didn't know what to do anymore.

Chapter Twenty Five

Hazel

"**N**ox? Nox, you have to get up now."

Hazel watched on from beside Charlotte and the others as Atticus fell to his knees beside his brother, reaching a shaking hand out to brush his brother's hair from his face. Blood and dirt streaked across the face of the golden-skinned demon, his complexion wan from the loss of blood.

Small sobs escaped Atticus as he stroked his brother's face, begging softly as the last embers from the other demon burned away, cinders floating like confetti through the air over them—a veil of despair.

She should have been out there with them. Human or not—she should be fighting until she couldn't stand any more. That was her *job*, her role in society. And she had backed away like a coward when Atticus told her to.

And it had cost him.

It would cost them all, at this rate.

Wade was the first to leave the group. He stumbled across to Atticus, as though in a stupor, and knelt beside the demon boy. "Can you not use your magic to heal him, Atticus?"

Though Wade's words were soft and hopeful, Atticus sobbed harder. He reached down for his brother, drawing him close to his chest. "This isn't something I can fix by myself, the iron hit him."

Hazel took a step forward, unbidden. Charlotte let out a gasp as they saw the damage.

The blade had pierced through the armor that Nox wore. Hazel kept walking toward them in a trance as Wade reached over and clumsily unbuckled the sides of the chest plate armor. Dark blood seeped through the linen tunic, a large tear in the fabric. Hazel winced when she glimpsed the skin beneath. Though it was a small cut, it was the angriest she had ever seen. It was weepy and pus-filled already, angry red skin puckering at the edges. The veins lying underneath were beginning to push against the top of his skin as they turned an insidious black beneath. Like he was being poisoned.

"Why can't you? Your magic is strong. You cleaned us up before." Wade's voice was wavering as he helped his friend push aside the fabric, using the hem of the tunic to dab at the wound, to try and clean the edges. Wade ripped part of it off, pressing it against the cut, trying to staunch the flow of blood and pus.

Atticus' chest heaved as he spoke, his voice raw as though the very words were being torn from him. "Iron is deadly to us. Our magic can't be used against it. That's why they were able to lock us in the Mountain, dearest. Because our magic is nothing compared to it. And now it's in Nox's blood, and Father isn't here, and I am too weak and pathetic to fix it."

She had never seen the demon so... vulnerable. It made him almost sort of human. And she pitied him for it. Cause he was right. He *was* kind of weak and pathetic. He talked a big game, acted like a condescending know-it-all. But in a lot of ways, he was just like the little kid he presented to the world. Small, afraid, unknowing of everything.

"You can't die, Nox. What about Mother? How will she feel, not having you here? Her heart wouldn't be able to take it. You need to wake up for me, for her." His voice was lower, more fragile as it cracked on the words. "You can't leave me alone. You're my older brother, my *only* brother."

Charlotte hurried over to them. She brushed her pants as she squatted down, close to Wade, glancing nervously at the wound her ex-ghost-lover was trying to staunch. "What about my magic?"

"What do you mean, what about your magic?"

Charlotte tugged on the end of her hair. "Could I try to use it to heal it up?"

Atticus shot her a scathing look. "I mean this in the nicest possible way, dear mortal girl, but where do you think *your* power comes from?"

Charlotte blanched as though he had slapped her. "I... I guess I hadn't thought of that before," she murmured. "I just assumed it was... inherent."

"Inherently inherited from somewhere, foolish girl," Atticus growled, tugging his brother's head into his lap.

"You don't have to be such a bitch," Charlotte snapped back, sniffling. "I was trying to help you."

Wade placed his free hand on her arm. Blood was beginning to soak through the usually pristine ivory of his dinner gloves. "Lottie, my love. He doesn't mean it, truly. He's hurting."

Charlotte glowered at Atticus, reaching a shaky hand to cover Wade's, her mouth in a tight line. Rini, glamorous as ever despite the wear and tear of fighting, floated over, standing behind Charlotte, her blade in hand. "Your brother could have company if you really want," she threatened, a brow raised. The idol may have been petite, but the flex of her hands on her blade said that she was willing to put her money where her mouth was.

"Quit fighting, all of you! It is imperative that we work together to resolve this, lest Atticus' kin perish!"

The two women fell silent as Atticus slapped at his brother's cheeks gently, and Wade mopped up the blood, his efforts futile as it leaked and stained his own clothes. She felt like she was caught still in time, an unobservable bystander. It kept moving forward, yet there she was, standing still.

She had to reach out. She had to do something. She couldn't be the only bystander.

Her feet started moving on their own as she approached demon and ghost. It was as though a string tugged her forward, and she was merely moving at its mercy. It was funny. Dimly, she remembered her Mama and Auntie talking about fate and destiny, and all the different possible strings one could follow. Maybe this was one of them now, and she just didn't realize it.

Hazel dropped to her knees beside them, ignoring the sting of debris beneath her knees, poking her through her jeans. She had seen a lot of nasty wounds in her time—had even stitched a number of them up herself. This was unlike any gash she had seen before. It wasn't deep or long, and didn't seem to have it anything too severe about it. But it almost pulsated, thrummed, with something alive, something dangerous. She imagined Mama concocting a salve, or her Auntie consulting the spirits for guidance. There was no one here to turn to. Everyone that sat with her, they had all given their best shot. And each shot had fallen short. What would her shot be, then?

She wracked her brain on her knowledge of demons and iron. She knew it was lethal to them; Atticus had confirmed as much. Like when you staked a vampire or lycan with silver. It was basically their kryptonite.

But it was such a small amount, a surface level wound, really. It hadn't pierced through. So, was there a way to remove it from the blood, like venom from as nake bite? Could they flush it out with saline, or magic?

"What do you mean, flush it out?"

Hazel jolted, making eye contact with Atticus. His blue eyes were rimmed in red, snot leaking from his nose. *So human.* She hadn't realized she'd been speaking aloud. She shrugged. "I don't know. I was just thinking about like, when you get a nasty cut and you pour vodka on that bad boy to sterilize it and clean it up. Cause that's what you do to clean a wound, right?"

Atticus stared at her, face unreadable. The demon child was one thing, and that was emotive. To see him so impassive, so hollow, was almost frightening. Finally, he spoke. "Show me what you mean."

Hazelcocked a brow. "Uhhh, well, I can't really—"

"*Teach me*, human girl. I must do something, and fast."

She blew out a breath. She could do this. "Alright, ghost boy, out of the way," she commanded. Wade obliged, lifting his makeshift gauze and shuffling out of the way on his knees. That suit was definitely dumpster worthy after all of this.

Nox was beginning to worsen by the second, it seemed. The throbbing black veins—pulsing with the iron that seemed to be poisoning him—was beginning to decay, to actively rot. She was overwhelmed by the metallic scent of sickness, of looming death. She tried not to hurl as she peered at the wound. She was used to death and rotting things, things that were far gone, or supernatural.

She wasn't used to alive things dying.

Hazel peered at the wound, wondering how she could explain what she meant. Her Auntie, her Mama—her own mother, too—they were natural born healers, connected with the spirit world and the Earth. Even Ivy had shown promise of being able to connect. So surely, she could do this. She reached a hand out, poking at it. Despite his unconscious state, Nox blanched, skin paling.

"What are you *doing*?" Atticus snapped. Hazel shrugged her shoulders.

"Fucking around and finding out?"

Atticus shot her a scathing look through his tears, and she almost felt bad. Almost.

Hazel chose to refocus her efforts. She could do a little magic now; Gran had been teaching her, after all. And she was used to flushing out her own wounds with a bit of vodka after a particularly nasty tryst with a monster or two. So how hard could it be with magic? Gentler than when she had poked at it, Hazel reached over, placing light fingers on either side of the gash.

Hazel closed her eyes, trying to recall everything Gran told her. Magic was a thread, and you were the needle guiding it. Or something like that, anyway. Magic was definitely not her strong suit. Drawing in a deep breath, she felt for the magic in her. She imagined it, cold and soothing, like the cool blade of a knife against warm skin. There. There was a little glimmer of something in her, a tug in her gut. She spread her fingers out, blocking the world out and drawing in steady, even breaths. Was this meditation? Maybe she could try it sometime, like Lottie kept telling to do.

Her fingertips prickled, like pins and needles. There was the magic! She pushed down on it, gritting her teeth as she urged the magic to come to her. Sweat beaded her brow as she forced herself to pull at her energy reserves, to try and force it into him, to expunge the darkness permeating Nox's wound. It scraped against her brain, eliciting a gasp. It was like it was knocking at the door, asking to be let in. It was a poisoning wanting to infect her too, and there was no fucking way she was going to let it. So she pushed back, feeling for the source of the pain, feeling the pricks and scraps of darkness and iron as she urged her magic in to wash it away. It ebbed and flowed, teetering.

Nothing.

Hazel let out a grunt, squeezing her eyes shut harder. She felt for that spark of magic, but it was gone.

She was hollow inside again.

"I can't do it," she whispered, eyes snapping open. "I can't... I can't do this magic shit." Atticus stared at her. As if he expected nothing less. Heat burned her ears as she looked away. "Maybe Lottie and Wade should try. They have more magic."

Wade and Charlotte shared a glance, before nodding. Hazel scurried out of the way, defeat pricking at her cheeks, hot and angry. She pulled her knees up, wrapping her arms around them as Wade and Charlotte copied her pose. A few moments passed and they shook their heads sadly.

"We can't get through it. It's like there's a wall in the way," Charlotte explained. Wade nodded in agreement.

"More like an oil spill in an ocean," Hazel muttered. "I feel like I was trying to scoop it out with my hands and just... couldn't."

Charlotte eyed her off. "That's interesting that your magic could feel that. If only you were more practiced," Charlotte sighed, "then you'd be able to sieve through the iron, maybe?"

Atticus clutched his brother close, murmuring. Hazel leaned in, frowning. "What did you say?"

"I need your magic. My magic can't push past the iron, because of my demon blood. You can't harness your magic, as you are unskilled, unpractised. I need your magic to save him."

Hazel stared at the demon child as his fingers splayed tenderly against his brother's cheek. Dread pooled in her stomach, her spine tingling as though spiders danced up it. Was he saying what she thought he was saying?

"You want a deal with me."

"I told you before, together, we could do something great. Perhaps the great thing you could do with me would be something unselfish for the both of us."

She chewed the inside of her cheek. Never make deals with a devil. Never trust the super or preternatural. Never let them talk more than to get information out of them. These were things she was taught as a young Hunter, before her mother and father passed away. Evil liked the sound of its own voice, after all.

But... was Atticus truly evil? He was annoying, selfish, unapologetically weird. But here he was, holding his brother, begging for a chance for help. And he had taken care of Wade for a long time—in his own fucked up way, at any rate. She stared down at Nox. Did she want to save this demon? What would it mean to her to do so? To give up a part of herself, a part of her soul?

"What's in it for me, if I made a deal with you?" she whispered. "I know what you get—my magic. But what do I get for it? For giving up a piece of me?" *And what piece did he want to take?*

"What do you desire, mortal girl? What do you want of me?"

"I want your assurance that you'll get these guys home. No matter the cost to yourself." The words came unbidden, unthinking. "That you will do everything to ensure that it happens."

Atticus stared at her for a long moment. "You realize I would do that regardless of a deal, don't you?'

She shook her head. "I don't trust the words of a devil. A pact means you *have* to do it, right?" Atticus answered with a nod, and she breathed a sigh of relief.

"I want you to feed me your negative emotions to power me, to gift me your magic to save my brother. In exchange, I will ensure the safety of your companions and make sure they arrive back in the mortal realm as unscathed as is within my power."

That was going to have to be enough. She reached a trembling hand back to Rini, touching her index finger to the blade of the idol's katana. She didn't even feel it, it was so sharp. Blood welled on the tip of her finger as she stretched her hand over Nox's limp body to Atticus. "We have a deal, then, demon child. But if you fuck me babes, I will hunt you down to the ends of the fucking Earth. I'm warning you now."

"I, Asterius, promise to get your friends home."

So formal. So at odds with the moment they found themselves in. Hazel gulped. "I, Hazel Williams, accept."

"We have a deal." He nodded solemnly. Hazel fought against a yelp as the demon leaned over, licking the blood off the tip of her finger, instead of shaking it like she expected.

"What the fuck?"

"I needed your magic in me," he mumbled. With a gentleness that surprised her, Atticus placed his brother on the hard ground, tearing a bigger hole in the tunic. The wound was festering fast. It reminded her somewhat of a plague boil. It was alive, throbbing as the iron worked its poison deeper into the demon. His golden skin was slowly being leeched of color, a pallor washing over him. Like when someone was dying, and the light was fading from them.

Atticus leaned over his brother, placing his small, child-like hands to his brother's abdomen. "I know we haven't agreed at the best of times, but I know we can agree that this is going to hurt a little. It's better than the alternative though, my dear brother."

Hazel watched in fascination as Atticus pushed his fingers to the wound, physically digging them in. He flinched in pain as his flesh made contact with iron, but he bore down on it, face contorted in agony. Green magic pulsed at his fingertips, into the wound, a calming salve of light. The demon's fingers danced over the skin, poking and prodding at the gash like a surgeon.

Slowly, bit by bit, the black of the iron began to recede as Atticus pushed down. The pulsing slowed down as the darkness subsided. Atticus grunted, his arms shaking as he held them against the wound, pushing that light into them, his brow furrowed in concentration. They watched in awe as black became pink flesh once more until finally, the last dregs of darkness vanished completely. Atticus was wan as his hands shook and he brushed his hands over the remaining wound, sealing it with magic.

It was as if the cut had never been there as Atticus let out a sigh and collapsed against Nox. The color was returning to his skin within moments, as though nothing had happened.

"You are safe, brother," Atticus whispered against Nox, breathing heavily. "It's all over now."

Hazel realized something as she watched Atticus tend to his brother. It wasn't weak to be vulnerable. It was weak to not accept help.

CHAPTER TWENTY-SIX

HAZEL

"**N**ow what?"

Atticus' brother's breathing had stabilized, his wound healed and unmarred from the strange combination of her magic with Atticus' own. *Her magic*. What a weird realization. She had a power in her that the others did not. That they *needed*.

And now she had a deal with a devil.

It made her skin crawl to think about, even though it as a pact with a time limit on it. She remembered being a little girl, her mom and dad showing her how to defend herself about monsters—both supernatural and human. They had told her never to make a promise or a deal. Even if she was comfortable with the debt, some things weren't worth it.

Maybe they would still be here if they had been a little more flexible. Maybe they wouldn't have left her all alone in the world. Hazel wrapped her arms around herself, remembering the soft lavender of her mother's perfume, the leather of her daddy's holsters. She remembered sitting with them while they rubbed their gear with protective waxes.

She had made the right choice; that's what she told herself. If she hadn't, what would have happened to Lottie, her new family? Or Rini, a potential for a future? Or to Atticus, and his family?

Demon or not, he had the right to love them. Right?

Hazel was torn from her reverie as Atticus replied to Charlotte. "He's safe. You upheld your end of the bargain. I shall await for him to awaken, and we proceed from there." The golden-haired demon stared up at the night sky, head tilted back. His pin-drop straight hair fell back over his shoulders like a waterfall, his pale face illuminated in the light of the trio of moons.

He looked like a Raphaelite angel as the moon bathed him in a halo. Hazel's heart squeezed; she was beginning to understand how people were lured and charmed by him and his kind. How Wade had fallen victim to a deal him. Maybe she shouldn't have been so hard on the alchemist-turned-ghost-turned-lich. He'd made a deal to save someone he didn't even *know*.

Like she just had. Even though she'd vowed to herself to rid the world of demons when she lost her mom and dad. Hazel's stomach churned as she watched the slender demon, thinking about her parents. Normally, she'd push down those thoughts and feelings, but it was like a dam had broken in her when she'd made that deal.

They'd died almost twenty years ago. She still remembered the day it had happened, like it was yesterday.

Her parents had to leave for a mission that night, like most nights. She swore she spent more time in the spare bed in the sunroom at Mama's than she did in her own bed. They had worked all day at their normal jobs while she was at school. Mommy had met her at the bus stop like she did every day, a smile on her face, and a bag with a ham and cheese sandwich in her hand. She'd enveloped Hazel in a hug, sweat and lavender suffocating the eleven-year-old.

"Mom, I'm a big girl." She rolled her eyes as her mom held her tight. "I'm basically a teenager now. You're gonna embarrass me in front of the other kids!"

Her mom chuckled, releasing Hazel. "Alright, kiddo. I know it's not very cool or hip of me to cuddle my baby."

"Neither are those words, oh my God!"

She scrambled away from her mom, hoisting her backpack on her shoulders as she waved to her seat buddy, Monique. The girl pressed her face flat against the window, pushing her nose into a snout as she breathed heavily, hands pressed either side of her face. Hazel let out a snort of laughter, and her friend grinned. It was their goodbye ritual everyday for the last three months, and it hadn't gotten old.

As the bus pulled away, she took the paper bag from her mom and began devouring the sandwich, spilling the drama of the day between bites. How Mark and Jason had fought at lunch. Mrs. Waters was pregnant—again. How she had led the ultimate game of tag between all the fourth graders.

"You did good, baby." Her mom played with Hazel's curls as they walked home, chattering.

Her mom always told her she did good. Even when she hadn't. Hazel long suspected that moms were meant to say that, no matter what. But it was OK—she liked mom telling her it. It never got old. Dad was the same. He didn't say it as much, but it filled her with warmth, with happiness.

"So, baby, you're going to stay at Mama's tonight."

Hazel let out a groan. "Mom, I am big enough to stay at home alone now. Kimberly L gets to all the time."

Her mom snorted. "I'm not raising a latchkey kid. Mama loves having you stay over. And I know you love being there. She tells me you fall asleep cuddling her and Heather all the time."

Hazel tried not to blush, but her mom was right. She did like cuddling her auntie when she came home from college for the day. "Yeesh. Fine. But you better feel bad for me when everyone calls me a little kid."

"Darling, you are a little kid."

She had been restless when Mama and Heather tucked her into her little guest bed in the sunroom, a fan pointed at her. It hadn't been the heat making her skin hot,

though. It was fall, and the heat of summer had already died off. Her bones ached, all the way deep down inside. Normally, she would have fallen straight asleep, her hair braided by auntie, her tummy full of Mama's stew. They'd sing her to sleep, comforting her.

Not tonight, though. The air was thick, wrong. She peered over at the Hello Kitty clock Mama had set up beside her bed. Almost one in the morning. Her eyebrows had shot up. She had never been up this late before—not even for New Year's.

Slipping from beneath the sheets, she had padded to the door of the room, left ajar in case she needed the bathroom—or if Mama had wanted to check in on her. Hazel pushed the door open, expecting to see the hallway night light on, Mama and Heather's doors shut. But, no. The end of the hallway flooded with light from the kitchen. She could hear the low murmur of voices. More than just Mama and Auntie. With a frown, Hazel had tiptoed up the hallway, pressing herself against the wall to listen in.

"Sage, I don't know what to tell you."

Hazel's heart pounded in her chest. Not many people called Mama by her real name. They all called her Mama. She wanted to go in there. Who was this strange man talking?

"That's not good enough, Robert. You saw them last, correct?"

Mama's voice was quiet and even, but Hazel knew that tone. Mama was pissed. Who was Robert, and who did he see?

"The creature had a young girl, and Flora doesn't know a lost cause when she sees it. So she chased, and Marcus ran after. We tried to keep up, but... We don't know where they went."

Hazel couldn't help herself. She burst into the kitchen. "Where's Mom and Dad?"

"Baby, what are you doing out of bed?" Heather hurried over to Hazel, pushing her gently toward the door. "Why don't we get you back to bed—"

"No. I wanna know what's going on. Who is that? Where are Mom and Dad? I'm old enough, tell me what's going on," Hazel demanded.

Heather and Mama shared a look as the tall, wiry stranger dropped his head.

"Well, baby, I don't know how to tell you this..."

The days after had been a blur.

They found her mom and dad eventually. A vampire had gotten them, they said. She heard Heather break down in the kitchen when the stranger—Robert—had come back. She had felt her insides curl in on themselves, strangling her from within. Mama had come to find her in the living room, staring out into space as the sofa threatened to swallow her whole.

She wished it had swallowed her up.

"Baby, I have to tell you something." Mama had her scarf wrapped around her head as she sat beside Hazel, the first few fine lines beginning to show around her eyes. When did Mama start looking so tired? The other night, when Mom didn't make it home like she usually did?

"They're dead," Hazel said flatly, staring into Mama's eyes. "That monster killed them, didn't they?"

Mama let out a soft choked cry and pulled Hazel into an embrace. She wished she could have felt Mama's hug. She wished she didn't feel so far away from her own body.

They were dead, and no one could bring them back. That was forbidden magic. She knew that, cause Mama and Heather talked to the spirits. At night, as she slept in her bed in the sunroom, she heard Mama and Auntie try to reach them, her parents.

She also heard them fail.

The funeral came not long later. She didn't go to school that entire week. Monique must have missed her. But she couldn't leave the house, leave the bed. Auntie had dressed her in an itchy black dress and stockings, with little boots. It was so unlike the bright, colorful clothes Mommy had dressed her in. She hated them.

They had taken her to the little cemetery the rest of the family was buried in. It was a drab, overcast day. There wasn't a church service like Kayla's grandpa had when he died—she'd told them all about in class. They didn't believe in church. Instead, they'd had a lady come to Mama's house, where her mom and dad sat in some big wooden boxes—a casket, she was told—and people talked over them, spoke to them.

Hazel wasn't allowed to see them. Mama wouldn't let her. "You don't want that to be your last memory of them, baby."

But she did. She wanted to know. So when everyone had been chatting and giving condolences to Mama and Heather in the kitchen, she had sneaked back into Mama's living room. All the furniture had been pushed out the way to make room for the big, heavy boxes mom and dad were in, and she was too short to see into them. So she had dragged the ottoman over, climbing up, to look inside.

Hazel had never seen a dead person before. Only ever in cartoons and movies. They were always ghostly white and gross looking. Mom and Dad looked normal, though. Like they were sleeping. Their warm, brown skin looked paler than normal, and they were cold when Hazel reached a hand out to touch Mom's. She held her breath as she did, wondering if mom's hands would stop being folded over and snatch at her.

"Mommy, Daddy?" she breathed. "You gotta stop sleeping. You look stupid. You can wake up now."

That was how Mama and Heather found her when they and the other guests had come back in. Sobbing over her parents on tiptoes on the ottoman, asking them to wake up. Heather had picked her up as if she weighed nothing, wrapping Hazel around her like a baby. Hazel clung to her auntie like she was a lifebuoy, and she was drowning in the ocean.

Not long after that, they'd gotten in Mama's car and driven to the cemetery while a long, black hearse took Mom and Dad's bodies. Not them. Their bodies. They were bodies now. Not people. Everyone kept using that word earlier.

"Mama, Heather? Why did Mommy and Daddy leave me?"

She stared down at the two caskets being lowered side by side. On top of each sat a bouquet of tulips. Mama had said they were symbolic of love—of their love for each other, for Hazel, for family. Right now, she hated tulips. They got to be with her parents forever as dirt piled on them. I hate them, she thought with a rage she'd never experienced before.

"Oh, baby, you'll love tulips someday," they had whispered, but never answered her question.

Why had they left her?

The first day back at school, she got off bus looking for Mom, but she wasn't there, sandwich in hand. Hazel felt as though she had been kicked in the stomach. It hadn't been real until then. Even seeing their caskets go in the ground, it hadn't been real. There was still a chance they would come back, that it was all a prank. But for the first time ever, Mom hadn't been there to pick her up.

She was only going to wear black from then on, she told herself. The little girl that she was died the day her parents did. And she was going to be the Hunter that would rid the world of the monsters that took away her parents.

"Hazel? Are you okay?"

"Huh?" Hazel snapped out of her thoughts. Everyone was staring at her, and Charlotte had a hand on her arm. Shooting her a smile, Hazel let out a forced laugh. "I'm all good, babes. Sorry about that, it's been a bit of day, hasn't it?"

A cough made them all jump as Nox let out a groan. Atticus helped his brother sit upright as the towering demon coughed and moaned. "Are you alright, dear brother?"

"I am certain that I was about to die," Nox rasped. "I feel as though I've been run through. What happened to Herstafont?"

Hazel and Atticus shared a glance. "She is gone, dearest."

Nox grimaced. "I can't say I'm torn up about it."

Rini stood up then, brushing herself off. "Excellent, the demon man is alive. That means we can proceed and find a way out of here again, right?"

It was as if Rini had summoned the chaos. As soon as she spoke, the earth beneath them began to rumble and quake.

Hazel missed the days where she was the predator chasing down her prey. She'd had enough of being quarry, and it didn't seem like it would end any time soon.

Clouds of dark, acrid smoke billowed in the sky, obscuring the remaining bits of starlight above. Ash filled the air, raining down on them like snow flurries, coating their hair and shoulders. Then they saw the source of it.

When Hazel was little, she was obsessed with the Disney version of Hercules. Especially the titans, and the way they crawled up to Mount Olympus. To Hazel, this moment was kind of like that. Creatures as tall as skyscrapers stood up, towering over the city, over the houses, reaching for the sky like they could grab the very gods if they tried. And she wouldn't be surprised if they could.

Two creatures rose up, both made of blazing tendrils and burning rage. They were made up of flame whirls that danced in the breeze, sending a wave of heat over them even from a distance, sweeping over them like a blanket. They were like a roaring forest fire, threatening to consume everything in their path—including Hazel and present company.

"Fuck me," she whispered. "What are they?"

"They're the ones that launched the coup, I would hazard. It looks like they plan to destroy everything getting in their path." Atticus' voice was low, disconcerted. "We have to stop them."

Rini waved a hand. "Hello? They're literally raging balls of flame. What are we gonna do, go get a firetruck?"

Atticus shook his head. "I... Nox, we have to do it. We have to... use our true forms." The demon child looked almost sad as he glanced toward his brother, who nodded.

"I don't see what other choice remains."

"What's the big deal about changing into your... true form? Seems like everyone else around here is doing it." Hazel didn't see what the big deal was. Fight fire with fire, right?

Nox and Atticus shared a look, and Atticus sighed, looking visibly uncomfortable. "We can't... we can't get away if something happens, when we use our real forms. If we are injured..."

"We die," Nox finished.

Wade let out a gasp, turning to Atticus. He was almost as pale as when he was a ghost. "Surely you jest? You're a demon. Are you not immortal?"

"You saw what happened to Herstafont," Atticus said quietly. "We aren't impervious. And we will be much bigger targets."

Wade reached out and pulled the demon child into an embrace. "Then you mustn't risk it."

"I have to." Atticus' voice was muffled against Wade's waistcoat. He reached his arms up, wrapping them around Wade in kind. "Or you may not make it out of here."

"Then we must go, Atticus. We must end this war, end this foolishness." Nox stared out at the raging fire demons. They couldn't have been more than a few streets away. Surely, from that height, Hazel and the others were surely noticeable...

Hazel's heart leaped to her throat as Nox raced forward. Like something out of a movie, Nox transformed before them, shedding his human skin; it was jarring, horrific, mesmerizing. Rini and Charlotte let out a scream, stumbling back as he transformed. Wade seemed nonplussed, frozen as he stared in bewilderment. Hazel didn't know how to react. It was slow but also over in the blink of an eye as golden, tanned skin morphed into dark gray, streaks of white and black through his sleek, silky fur. He was taller than even Wade on all fours as he snarled and shook his head, turning an azure blue eye toward them. He let out a huff, inclining his gigantic wolf head toward Atticus.

"Yes, brother." Was Atticus shaking? "I... I will join you. Just a moment."

Atticus took a deep breath as he glanced toward Hazel. "Hazel," Atticus' voice was low and urgent. "May I ask—can I draw on your power? You can say no. I'd understand. But... I am too drained to do this alone. Nox is still so injured, too. I need you and Wade to help me."

Hazel cast a doubtful glance at Wade. The gentleman didn't even hesitate. "Whatever will get my Lottie home safe and sound."

Your Lottie? She's mine, too, you jerk. She wasn't going to let him make all the sacrifices. "Whatever you need, then." She pushed up the sleeves of her jacket, extending an arm toward Atticus. "Let's fucking rumble."

Atticus raised a brow, staring at her. "Why have you stuck your arm out?"

Hazel's cheeks warmed. "So you can, like... take blood?"

"What manner of monster do you consider me?"

"A, uh... demon?"

Atticus shook his head. "I don't want your blood, you silly mortal girl. I just want to feed off your negative emotions. And I know you've been brimming with them. I could feel them before. You're positively shrouded in darkness and angst. It's delectable to get even the smallest of morsels of, really."

Hazel grimaced. "That's... so much grosser, somehow."

"That doesn't answer my question."

Hazel shuffled uncomfortable, imagining what her parents, what Mama, what Heather—what they would they say if they saw her cavorting with a monster? Helping him?

One step at a time. You just gotta survive. They can't be disappointed with you unless you manage to make it home.

"Fine." Hazel drew in a deep breath. "Do what you've gotta do, demon child."

He was breathtaking in a haunting kind of way.

It was like the first time Hazel saw a ghost. They were mesmerizing, fascinating to look at, but little Hazel knew to be scared of them because they were different, other. They could look serene, calm, but you never knew what danger lurked beneath that harmless looking exterior.

Atticus' human form was designed to lure people in, to make people trust him. That much was evident with the gentle voice, the aura, the *clothes*. The fact that he chose to look like a kid, when so many other demons they had seen chose more adult forms. His true form, though...

He was radiant, hard to look at, but impossible to look away. Atticus shifted before them, growing in size and color. His body became pearlescent as his limbs elongated, his legs extending out as though they were stilts. Wings tore open his back in a shower of muddy white blood, the color of the first sleet of snow. His clothing remained, turning the same iridescent color as his skin as it transformed. His vest lengthened to follow the shape of his new, spindly body, his golden hair becoming white as fallen snow as his face distorted, rounding out as he grew. His blue eyes sunk back in his head, the pupils widening as the blue of his eyes deepened and became a thin ring of scarlet. His body twisted, morphing as he towered over them, body hunching over with his rapid size change. His mouth split into a wide, mocking grin, like a titan looming over them with razor sharp teeth. His skin glimmered like diamonds—like cold, hard, marble.

Hazel could have sworn she had read a monster like that in a book somewhere.

Her blood thrummed through her, hot and loud as it gushed through her veins. She swayed, lightheaded as she stared up at the towering Atticus monster.

CHAPTER TWENTY-SEVEN

ATTICUS

Power coursed through him like he had never tasted before. It was melodious on his tongue, a sweetness that he could never hope to replicate. Wade and Hazel's emotions swirled together on his tongue, a fragrant wine of sadness, remorse, guilt, and anger. It was intoxicating, a plethora of aromas and taste.

His wings fluttered behind him, stirring up the smoke and ash. How long had it been since he felt them be unleashed? Felt the wind ripple over his true form? He glanced down at his companions. They were so small—he was so used to them towering over him, and yet, they were like looking down at toddlers now. How peculiar. He watched Hazel sway, Wade turning a deathly pale beside her. Yes, he could feel their power in him, their magic. He felt a tug of guilt for their condition, but the power thrumming through him made it hard to care too deeply.

He was powerful, unstoppable.

Atticus raised his head, toward where he had seen the two daemons emerge earlier: Gulivior and Sporas. They were as high ranking as Father, heads of their respective houses. And they were destroying everything they had helped build in Terra Doerum. And it was up to him and Nox to stop them.

There was a distant scream from somewhere far below as he began to flap his wings, raising himself into the air. Nox was sprinting between the houses, making his way to them, closing in. He was going to go straight to the source. Atticus flew through the air, like a knife cutting through butter. He couldn't tell where the magic began and he ended. It was exhilarating. His grin widened as he soared.

Then he felt himself careening sideways.

He didn't have time to think as he landed into a rooftop, tiles flying around him as he hit it hard and fast. He felt nothing as the magic coursed through him, feeding him. Is this what being high felt to the humans? He had seen them before, with their drugs and concoctions, hadn't understood it. Never before had he truly felt so invincible as he did now. He didn't miss a beat as his head snapped up and looked for what had derailed him.

Gulivior had slammed a fist into his face, knocking him down as he approached. Atticus let out a mocking laugh, a deep, dark rumble like the beginning claps of thunder in a storm. He pushed himself upright, bringing back a fist to slam right back into Gulivior's molten face. It should have hurt—his form was made of flames. But he felt nothing, even as his own skin bubbled and blistered.

He pulled his hand back and punched the daemon lord again. And then again. Then again.

Atticus was dimly aware of his brother howling somewhere as he laid into the elder daemon over and over. Gulivior's son, Bastion, had been a relentless bully toward Atticus, picking on him for his smaller form, the way he shied behind his mother. Gulivior had been no better, making snide comments about Atticus to his father at Council, insinuating that all he did was hide behind his mother's skirts.

They called him a coward, weak. He would show them.

Asterius. You're burning.

Nox's voice cut through his mind. Atticus flinched as he realized his skin was bubbling and melting up his wrist and forearm. He didn't feel it at all. And he didn't care. He was ravenous for blood, for chaos. The emotions of the humans roiled through him, a cacophony of delights and pain. He could drown in their feelings, in their desires and inner demons—ironic.

Gulivior took advantage of Atticus' distraction to hurl himself into Atticus. Flames engulfed Atticus like chains as he was sent flying back into the same roof. The house began to collapse under their weight as the two daemons tussled with one another. The slammed through, stone and wood groaned as they splintered, shards flying everywhere as they fell, slamming into the ground below.

Furniture cracked beneath them as fire tried to burn Atticus up, flames lapping at his skin, his hair. Gulivior aimed for his eyes, but he managed to loll his head out of the way in time. Gulivior pulled his hand back again to aim for Atticus once more, but was stopped by a snarling Nox launching at him and ensnaring his wrist in a bite.

It must have burned his brother, but he didn't show any fear or pain as he pressed his jaw closed, tighter through the flames. Gulivior let out a haunting shriek as Nox bit through, the crunch of snapping bone reverberating through the air like a gunshot. The Lord fell over backward, away from Atticus, trying to scramble away as Nox remained clamped to his wrist. The house they fell on began to light up, flames licking at curtain drapes, the scraps of broken furniture kindling.

Atticus hauled himself upright, gesturing for his brother to let go. Nox dropped Gulivior's wrist as Atticus swooped into the air, above the rising flames. His body was healing through the burns, using up the magic the others had granted him. Nox bounded after him, streaking out of the house into the square beside it.

Gulivior and Sporas had picked Central to transform. This was where the High Houses convened for meetings, for all important events. They must have hijacked a meeting. Atticus' blood ran cold, imagining his mother and father sitting there as the Lords who had planned against them seized control. Had they harmed them? Who had they killed? Nox said mother and father had gotten away—had they run back to the house? Had Nox escorted them out?

Where were they now? Where were the others? Surely these two hadn't been working alone. His thoughts were interrupted by Sporas joining the fray, raining down on them like flaming hail drops as he loomed over them, skin spun of fire. His skin stung as they pricked at him, burrowing into his flesh. Atticus pushed past the feeling, stumbling out into the square. He wasn't used to his true form—when was the last time he had even used it, if ever?—and it made movement harder, sluggish, as he fought past searing pain. He was dimly aware of Nox scurrying away from Gulivior beside him as the night air became thicker, cloying, as the house they fell into burned. Smoggy ash rose into the air as paint fumes mixed with the ancient wood that burned now. Atticus furiously beathis wings, propelling himself skyward, away from the haze of smoke and flames. Millennia of history and lives, gone in moments, as the flames lapped up into the air, a surging bonfire.

The square was almost as old as the Mountain. It had been built some time not long after, allegedly. Tall buildings gilt with gold and ivory towered over thes quare, with a giant clock tower above the main building reserved for Council meetings piercing the sky. Paved stone wrapped around the ground in a circular fashion following the curve of the fountain, magic lit gas lamps illuminating the space. Ornate golden gates were hammered into delicate, intricate patterns. Motifs of faeries dancing amongst gentle leaves and petals made up the gates, stories in of themselves.

A grand fountain made of mtorolite sat in the center; indigo, starlit water filled its pool reserve that lapped gently against the emerald basin. It was mined from another world long ago, said to be calming, centering, and resilient against adversity. A spectacular sculpture of a man took up the focal point of the fountain. He was resplendent, a benevolent being standing on the toes of one delicate boot, the other bent behind him. He was dressed like a soldier, an ornate surcoat fitted to his lean frame, his hair tied back in a loose ponytail blowing in an invisible breeze behind him. From his epaulettes flowed a cloak of starlight water, a fantastic waterfall that cascaded behind him. He was a noble, elegant man, caught in time for in perpetuity. He gazed up longingly at the night sky, a wistful expression gracing his features, his gentle brow furrowed, his lips curled into a hopeful wisp of a smile. He was beautiful in all the ways that Atticus had wished he was.

He remembered sitting out here, staring up at this unnamed heroic figure while Father and Nox attended meetings. Mother would sometimes sit with him, and they would make up tales about the stranger in the fountain. They would tell stories about his epic journeys, his battles across the realms. Sometimes he would be the Founder of Terra Doerum. Sometimes he was as a mortal that found himself there from another time. Sometimes—all the time, whenever Mother told the story, truth be told—he was a Prince, just like Atticus, the savior of their House. She would weave stories of him fighting not with a blade, but with his words. A soldier of feelings and emotions, not just battle and punishment.

Atticus missed those times with his mother.

A howl broke through his thoughts, wrenching him back to reality. Atticus snapped his head up, looking for the source of the noise. It had come from behind him. He turned, as though in slow motion, eyes widening at the scene that folded out in front of him.

Nox hadn't been as fast as him, apparently. His brother was lower to the ground in his true form, and had to navigate the falling, burning debris of the manor as it collapsed in on itself, a microcosm of the chaos that was now unfolding across Terra Doerum. However, that had slowed him down, it seemed, and allowed the two daemon Lords the opportunity to grab him.

Sporas now gripped his brother between two hands. Heat beat down on Atticus as he lunged back for them, intent on knocking his brother free. Nox let out a yelp of pain as his fur caught alight and the flames lapped at him, threatening to consume the Prince. Nox's face contorted in pain as he howled and yipped, an unbearable whine of pain and sadness. Nox let out a shudder and collapsed in Sporas' grip, going limp as his fur ignited.

Nox towered over Asterius, looking down at the crying Princeling.

He always had, to be fair. He was the older one, the big brother. And he naturally grew bigger in his chosen form. Atticus supposed he could have to, but being small suited him fine. He would remain unnoticed more, hide away better.

That hadn't always worked for him, though. He was the little Princeling, the one the sons and daughters of the other Lords bullied, harassed. He was weak, effeminate. He wasn't strong and intimidating like Nox was. He wanted to be, wished he could be. Even Caleo was bigger than him, and she was a girl. The others were sure to remind him of that when they taunted him, beat him down.

He hadn't meant to hurt them. One day, a group of the other Lords sons had cornered him in the training grounds by the Mountain. Nox had still been at training, and Asterius was reading one of Mother's beloved books.

"It's Asterius, the Little Princeling," they had sneered. He tried to ignore them, like Mother told him to. Don't give them fuel to fight with, *she would warn him. But that didn't stop them. "Always so condescending, always thinks he's better than us."*

He used to argue back, tell them he didn't think that. He just liked to be quiet, be out of the way. It wasn't condescension—it was self-preservation. And that day, they had pushed too far. They had cornered him, laying fists into him, bruising the soft porcelain of his skin. Kicking and laughing as they taunted the little Princeling, the weak one, the unnecessary spare. They'd told him that his Father would be grateful if they got rid of him, would be doing House Lyra a favor. That his mother wouldn't have to waste her time fawning over a baby any longer.

He had let go, then. Let his emotions take over as his true form ripped through his skin, unable to be contained any longer. He had let the daemon out, and hurt them back for the first time ever.

It was the first time he had ever tasted fear, and he'd liked it.

He didn't remember a lot of what had happened. He knew he had hurt them, had burned his rage through until nothing but embers remained. He didn't remember becoming small little Asterius again, didn't remember his brother finding him. But he had. And that was how he had found himself on the ground once more, staring up at his older brother.

"I'll make sure Father doesn't get angry at you over this," Nox told him. "They had it coming."

"Why?" Asterius had asked through his sniffles.

His brother had smiled at him then, whispering, "Because you're my little brother, and it's my job to protect you."

The noise that came out of Atticus was unnatural, even for a daemon Princeling. As if centuries of fury and pent-up rage decided to unleash itself in a single, furious roar. His brother has going to die right before his eyes if he didn't do something. He sprang at Sporas, intent on knocking his brother free. Gulivior slammed into Atticus from the side as he reached for Nox, knocking him out of the way of his brother. He screamed as he wrestled with the daemon Lord, desperate to get to his brother.

They grappled, and Gulivior knocked Atticus down, climbing atop him. Flames lapped at the Princeling's skin, burning, melting, as the Lord wrapped his flaming hands around Atticus' throat, tightening. Stars bloomed across Atticus' vision as searing heat overwhelmed him, and the world felt like it was floating away.

It can't end like this. What about your friends?

Magic pulsed through his veins, alive and angry, like a rattlesnake about to retaliate. It coiled before launching out of him, consuming him wholly as he felt his skin alight with icy heat. His vision began to return, blurry, as Gulivior was sent flying from him. He landed against Sporas, and Atticus watched through his shoddy vision as Sporas released his grip on Nox at last, dropping the flaming giant wolf that was his brother.

The world exploded into suffering as he reached for Nox, weak from using his magic, weak from being attacked. He was lost in a void of chaos and pain, suffocating. Is this what it meant to die? Is this how Wade had felt? Isolated, hurt? He'd never asked, and now he regretted it.

He regretted a lot of things.

His vision blurred in sparks and stars, gold and silver lines and dots that exploded like fireworks before his darkening sight. What was he meant to do? Should he
be glad that the end was actually going to claim him, after all that he had done
over the years to make others suffer? Would there be a finality for him to accept,
a judgment to face?

"Specter, no!"

Atticus tried to move his head. That was the Blythe girl's voice. Foolish mortals
must have found the way there, instead of hiding. He wished he could help. But
the darkness was so overwhelming, so placating... he shut his eyes. It would be just
for a moment.

"You have to get up, dear friend."

Wade's soothing voice was in his ear, as syrupy and soft as ever. Ah, his friend.
His truest, first companion. He had made many deals, but none had treated
Atticus the way Wade had. A friend, a brother, a real confidant. Not just an
immortal servant with a debt.

Wade spoke again. "You have to do it, for them. They aren't able to do this
without you. None of us can, Atticus."

The daemon Princeling finally opened his eyes again. Though his vision was
full of static, he could make out his friend standing over him, concern softening
those storm gray eyes. He was beautiful, even though his styled hair had strands
sticking to his face, now streaked with dirt, his coattails in disarray and full of
tears. Atticus had never felt sore or tired like this before.

"Use my magic, my energy," Wade urged, low and desperate. "I do not care if
you must use every ounce of my remaining essence. Charlotte will not be trapped
here. She will not die here. As my friend, not a demon, I ask you to promise me
this, Atticus. Promise me you will get her home safely, for I love her, and I know
you love me."

Something stirred within Atticus. Warmth in his chest, an urge, something like
pride. He did love Wade, and therefore, he wanted to do what his dear friend and
companion needed. He had to get up, to help. So Atticus probed the connection

between them. Once upon a time, that thread used to be tighter, thicker. Back before all the things transpired between them. He could feel, could see, the knots that were in it now, trying to strengthen those weaknesses, though they could never be truly repaired. He reached for the magic on the other end.

Wade's light was a pure, soft white, like fresh snow. Just being near it felt like it could cleanse him, wash him free of his sins. He let himself bathe in it, a baptism of sorts, as he rejuvenated in the warmth of Wade's feelings and his magical essence. It replenished him, filling that well that he had fed from. Feelings of love and resentment and insecurity washed over him; Wade's emotions were fraught and complex, and normally all he would want to do would be to savor them, to taste and understand him.

Atticus pulled himself up, reaching for the sky once more. He wasn't better, but he could push forward as Wade's energy fed him. His friend looked tired, paler than before, fists curled tight as he nodded up at Atticus. It would have to be enough for now. Wade was a strong warlock in his own right, even without their pact. He would be able to withstand more than Atticus gave him credit for.

Sporas and Gulivior's attention had been turned away from Atticus and Nox. They now stomped across the square to where Hazel and the new girl waved their arms in the air, calling out things he couldn't make out over the sizzle and crack of their flaming skin. The girls were luring the daemons away, trying to make space for him, he realized. They were going to die, though. He wouldn't make it in time, couldn't intervene.

There was also the issue of his prone brother.

He had to make a choice. Go for him, or save the mortals.

He promised Wade. Wade had blessed him with that, for a specific purpose. He had to do what his dear friend asked. No matter the cost.

Time started to slow and warp as Atticus reached for the girls. He would throw himself at the two, do whatever it took, whatever he could. It didn't matter. None of it mattered, now. He had promises to keep. His wings tore through the air as he surged forward, the seconds drawn out. He wouldn't make it.

In the end, it didn't seem like he had to. As Sporas and Gulivior reached for the duo, a streak of darkness collided into them, and for a moment, Atticus saw Specter as a cat, hurtling through the air, until a visage of pure horror took his place.

He was a nightmare given shape, truly the definition of a monster.

Atticus knew there had been something curious, something special, about the being that Charlotte Blythe kept closest to her. He was no ordinary house cat—he was not even an ordinary witch's familiar. Atticus wasn't even sure he was a daemon. There was something that pulsed within the creature that was unfamiliar, alluring, *powerful.*

Specter contorted into the air, the several pound ball of fluff became the thing that haunted dreams, that stalked the shadows, that made humans believe in Heaven and Hell. He became silky darkness, veined wings exploding from him, six different leathery wings sweeping him into the air as his body warped into an almost serpentine frame. Long, curled horns protruded from Specter's forehead, his face extending into a snout as his golden ocher eyes blazed. He was a Leviathan, a calamity of silky onyx scales and crimson, blood-red membrane.

His new form was over a hundred feet long, his wingspans easily half of that. Smoke curled around his snout as he breathed, giant fangs gleaming in the light of the flames. He let out an almighty roar that shook the very earth they stood upon. A tail lashed out at the two daemon lords, razor sharp spikes swiping at them, as Specter blocked their access to the mortals.

Hazel let out a whoop. "I fuckin' *knew* it wasn't a cat, Lottie!"

Sporas and Gulivior were distracted. It was his turn to do something. Atticus slammed into them with a snarl. Gulivior shook but remained upright. Sporas fell, however, landing on the fountain. The handsome man cracked as Sporas landed upon him, breaking the statue at the base. With a sickening thud, the statue landed on the ground, spiderweb cracks lacing up the statue, fraught and delicate. The daemon Lord let out a shriek of pain as the starlit pool washed over him, extinguishing his flames. It was like the opposite of watching Nox and himself burn earlier. Steam rose from Sporas' body as the flames began to die, eating away at the burning flesh of his body. Atticus leaned over the Lord, and pushed him down into the water, submerging the daemon's head.

The statue crashed against the ground beside them as Atticus pushed his full weight onto Sporas, extinguishing the flames that lapped at his skin, letting the stark coolness of the starlit water wash over him like a soothing balm. Sporas' gurgled, dark eyes wide with panic as Atticus watched the light go out in those murky depths. It felt wrong to kill his own kind. It was the ultimate betrayal.

They left you no choice. It was you, or them. You have to do what you have to do.

Chapter Twenty-Eight

Hazel

"**I** fuckin' *knew* it wasn't a cat, Lottie!"

There was no way that cat, who seemingly melted from the shadows, was an actual cat. Hazel loved Specter, but he was *weird*. And now he was some kind of shadow dragon looming over them, keeping the demons away from them. What in the fuck was happening? Was this all some nightmare fever dream? Had she hit her head while she had been on set with Charlotte, investigating for Jay?

Fuck, was she dead already?

Specter roared again as Atticus held down one of the demon's under the water of the fountain, that twisted titan face still in a leering grin. No wonder he dressed like a little Victorian ghost—somehow, it was less creepy. She was going to make a note to ask him to never transform near her again. He was no magical girl, after all.

She was itching to fight. She hated being sidelined like some sort of damsel—or worse, a mediocre white guy. The magic she was feeding Atticus coursed through her, pumping through her veins, like adrenaline urging her on. Fuck it. When in Rome, right?

And in this Rome, you punched demons in the face.

She turned to her friends. Wade had his arms wrapped protectively around Charlotte as they watched the onslaught, the flames lighting up their pale, frightened faces. Hazel briefly wondered if she could even pry him loose from the Witch ever again. He'd probably die *again* before letting her go. Her stomach flipped watching them. She had done the thing she wanted—get them back together. And maybe they would die here together, because of her.

Man, she kind of sucked sometimes.

Then there was Rini who stood a little way from them, somehow still poised and beautiful and perfect, despite the attacks she had taken. Forever an idol, it seemed. How could someone as Goddess-like as Rini ever want anything to do with a gremlin like her? She was going to have to work hard to prove she was worthy of the other woman after they got out of this. *If* they got out of this.

A shooting pain ran up her arm. Wade grabbed for his left arm at the same time, letting go of Lottie. Hazel and Wade shared a look before looking over Specter's immense, swishing tail. Atticus, who had been drowning one of the fire demons, still held him under as the other now grabbed his left arm and yanked, the skin searing and hissing like meat on a grill. Atticus's terrifying teeth stayed close, his giant eyes wide as he continued pushing down on the other demon. Hazel felt herself grow dizzy as Atticus' flesh melted away, sloughing off the bone. She tried not to gag as a piece of flesh slid off.

"We have to do something, or your little buddy is going to die," she told Wade, trying not to dry retch. "And then we're all good as dead."

Wade grimaced as he clutched his arm. "I suppose you are correct."

Hazel glanced up at Specter, the terrifying shadow of a dragon. "Do... do you wanna help, kitty?" Plumes of smoke furled around Specter's snout as he bore his head down and rushed into the fray, trotting in. He even ran like a cat still. She let out a war cry as she began chasing after him. "Hell yeah, let's fuckin' *go.*"

She hurtled after him, gaining a second wind. Or was it like her sixth wind? Either way, she was *going*. She would fight with her bare fucking hands if she had to. She heard the others clatter behind her, chasing, the metal twang of Rini freeing her katana filling her ears. Specter raced ahead of them, slamming into the demon that gripped Atticus. He body slammed the creature, giant teeth snapping at the sentient flames.

Hazel and Wade stumbled in unison, tripping and falling to the ground. Hazel groaned as she hit her shoulder, thankful it wasn't her head. She felt weak, groggy, depleted. Like she'd gone on a three-day bender and had finally collapsed in bed. Atticus was waning. That was obvious to see. She groaned again as she lifted her head to see what was happening.

Specter's teeth had clamped down on the fiery demon's neck, and he was yanking at it as it unleashed cyclones of fire that began to whirl around the foursome, locked into the strangest dance as they grappled with one another. Atticus' grip held tight on the demon he was struggling against as the other howled and released him, swinging at Specter now. It clocked Specter in the face, causing Specter to drop his hold on the demon's throat.

Hazel let out a gasp as dizziness washed over her, energy coursing through her once more as the demon's grip on Atticus was relinquished at last. Hazel pushed to her feet again, swaying with the effort. They had to move. Mini tornadoes of fire whirled around them, a choreographed, silent dance. A dance that threatened to catch them all on fire and kill them all, if they didn't put out the flames. She flinched as they began to pirouette toward the buildings that surrounded the square. That would be really, *really* fucking bad.

"Well, babes, it's now or never," she yelled at the others. "We have to do something while they're distracted or else we're going to burn like cheap vodka down a sorority girl's throat."

Wade grimaced as Charlotte helped haul him to his feet. "How charming, as ever."

"It's not my job to be charming, ghost boy. It's my job to keep your asses alive."

"I'm not even a ghost anymore," he muttered as he brushed himself off. He flinched, grabbing Charlotte and yanking her out of the path of one of the mini cyclones. Things were too chaotic, too pressing, for them to waste time arguing.

"Specter and Atticus have to deal with them. We gotta stop these fires." Hazel stood before the others, taking charge. She needed to be in control of something, anything. "Charlotte, your magic isn't fucked up, right?"

Her friend nodded. "Yeah, I guess not? I feel okay enough." Charlotte flexed her hands, sparks dancing on her palms. "Yeah, seems to be in working order."

"Good. Wade and I are getting absolutely railed by Atticus leaning on us, so you and Rini are gonna have to take point for us. I need you to funnel that fucking water or something and put out as many of those fires as you can before they get bigger."

"And what are you going to do?" Charlotte frowned. Hazel shot her a grin.

"I'm gonna do what I do best. Cause havoc."

They divided into two teams. Rini's job was to watch Charlotte's back as the Witch used the last of her own energy to blanket the flames with the water from the fountain. Hazel knew they could handle themselves—they were big girls, after all. As for her and Wade...

It wasn't so much of a plan as it was the mishmash of some thoughts and vibes. Atticus needed their energy, to feed off them to fight, to survive. So, they had to be close to him. At least, she assumed so. She didn't understand how any of this shit worked. But she was good at causing trouble, and finding herself in it, so that was where she was going to start.

"I don't think getting so close to them is a good idea," Wade puffed as he jogged behind her. They had escorted Rini and Charlotte to a safe area—well, safe *enough*, a spot with a bit of broken wall from a house that had been part of the casualties before. It offered them a little protection, and a fairly good line of vision to the fountain. That was where they left the two women as lich and Hunter raced back into the path of destruction. "What if they harm us?"

"Babes, every fucking time they melt the skin off Atticus, they are harming us. What are you gonna do when he dies and we die with him 'cause we were dumb enough to make pacts with a little demon boy?"

Wade blanched. "I... I hadn't considered that."

"Yeah, I figured. So why don't we worry about getting our asses kicked later, and do whatever we can now?"

They were closing in on the fight again. Atticus had let go of the demon in the water, and now he and Specter closed in on the other one as it lashed out at them, sending blasts of fire at them. Atticus' brother, still an enormous wolf, lay to one side. "Actually, quick change of plan. Try and keep up!"

Hazel skidded to a stop and pivoted, turning on her heel and racing for the other Prince instead. Maybe they could help him with their magic like Atticus had done earlier. Wade was a Warlock or an Alchemist or something, wasn't he? Surely he could use his weird bond between them to do something. Anything to help. She darted around Specter's tail, parkouring over the end of it as it went to slam into the fire demon once more. She dashed straight for the giant wolf.

Nox was looking worse for wear. She wasn't even sure he was breathing. Parts of his fur were so singed that it revealed burned flesh beneath, sizzling and bubbling. Hazel felt a twinge of sympathy as she stood over him. What a majestic beast to lay in ruin. How did he look in his humanoid form? Was his beauty broken, scarred, marred perpetually now? Weren't demons meant to be so powerful? Yet, she had seen so many lay broken and beaten in such a short period of time.

Her own body screamed at her in agony as she glanced over him, not sure of what to do, where to even begin. She looked over to Wade, who looked as lost as she did. *Fuck.*

"Can... can you try and do what Atticus did earlier, to help?"

Wade closed his eyes, pinching the bridge of his nose. "As in, healing magic?"

Hazel nodded her head. "Yeah, he like, fully fixed everyone earlier. Can't we sneak a little of his magic back, just long enough to heal his brother? Surely that won't fuck him up." Wade looked doubtful. She tried again. "I'll go keep their attention off you, go keep an eye on your boy, whatever you need me to do. I'm good at being a menace."

"That, I can confirm to be true." *Snarky, much?* She could be the bigger person and ignore him, just this once. Instead, she took a deep breath.

"I'm going to leave him with you, okay? I'm going to help out however I can."

Wade glanced up at the fighting nearby, paler than usual. His jagged scar was illuminated in the moonlight, almost glowing, it seemed. She wondered if he felt it still, if the scar tissue beneath tugged and pulled ever. What it looked like raw, fresh. She looked away from him, heat creeping up her neck. What a morbid curiosity.

"Take care of the other demon dude, and I'll be back."

She jogged into the heart of chaos, into the heart of hell.

Hazel was dimly aware of the world around her as she made her way toward Atticus and Specter. Charlotte and Rini were doing their best to put out the whirling tornadoes in the distant corner of the square. Wade was knelt over Nox, hands over him as if in prayer, supplicant over the body of a God. There was a reverence to the way the lich-ghost-old-timey-gentleman held himself, his composure. It reminded Hazel of that girl in that video game she had played as a kid, the one who got stabbed while praying.

Hazel nearly whiffed it as she ran into the path of danger. She had unsure of how she was going to help as she raced forward. Specter and Atticus had moved in the moments she had left Wade to care for Nox, and they had gone skyward with the other fire demon. They danced in the area, teeth gnashing and flames lapping at skin as Atticus held the demon above the ground as Specter bit into the demon, tearing at searing flesh. And this is where Hazel almost whiffed it.

A chunk of flaming demon flesh fell right into her path, Specter dropping it from his dragon-like maw. She let out a yelp and threw herself to the side as it slammed into the ground. She tripped but didn't fall, catching herself like she was practicing for a recital, her feet giving out after long hours of dance. Her boots were beginning to rub and sting badly. When had they last rested, last stopped?

It didn't matter. She had to keep going.

The fire demon was struggling in their grip, igniting himself as he sent roaring flames along Atticus' arms. She gasped as the fire licked along his arms up to his wings, catching them ablaze. Atticus let out a roar from his horrifying, perpetually smiling mouth, and began to fall, the demon still in his arms.

Directly above her.

She scrambled as fast as she could as their shadow cut across her path.

One moment, she was running. The next, she was hurtling through the air, careening toward disaster. Time seemed to slow, though the wind ripped at her clothes, at her hair. Was this what dying felt like? Like everything was slowed down to a crawl as you watched that inevitable scythe of death lunge for you?

It all stopped as suddenly as it started as she felt herself colliding with something hard. She began to slip to the ground, slowly, head spinning. Whatever she had hit was velvety and weird to the touch as her vision wavered.

It was Specter. He must have dived for her, stopping her. She hadn't even gone that far—maybe several yards, at most. Everything was a blur as the ground shook, and she realized that the fire demon and Atticus had hit the ground. That must have been what had sent her flying.

Atticus was losing now. The fire demon was on top of him. Specter snarled behind her and leaped over her, racing for the demon and Atticus. That's when she spotted the giant demon scythe she had liberated earlier. She hadn't remembered dropping it in the chaos, but it was like it had summoned itself. Waiting for her.

She dragged herself to her feet once more, stumbling toward the giant blade. It was a demon weapon. It could hurt them. It sat by the edge of the fountain, near the statue of the man that had graced it earlier. His cape was gone, his fine sculpted uniform cracked and chipping. He lay in ruin, much like the rest of the square. Much like her friends. Gathering up the last of her strength, Hazel hoisted up the scythe, feeling its weight, the burden of it.

She was used to dealing with monsters, dispatching them, killing them. She wasn't used to helping them. But that was what she had to do.

The head of the scythe dragged across the ground, sparks flying from its head, agrating noise buzzing around her as she marched toward Atticus, Specter, and the demon Lord. He must have been strong, as he was still grappling with Atticus even as Specter swatted at him.

The demon child was burning up, and she could feel herself waning as he drew on her power. Could she even make it to him without collapsing?

Use my power.

She jumped as Atticus' voice filled her head, nearly dropping the scythe. Was he actually talking to her, or had she imagined it?

Use my power like I've used yours. I know you can feel the tether. Tug on it, so you can use Gilderon against Gulivior. I am too weak to fend him off. But that blade will rend him dead.

Fuck. Okay. She took a deep breath. She could do this. She thought back to Gran teaching her to access her magic in the back gardens of Winterbourne. Center yourself. Focus. Feel the knot in your tummy, like butterflies. She could do this.

There. There was a tug inside her, a weird feeling. Like when her intuition pulled at her. She latched onto that feeling, following that thread, and tugged on it back. The sensation was almost indescribable, surreal. One moment, she could barely stand, let alone hold the massive blade. Then power started creeping along her like an IV in her veins, pulsing through her, a magical fluid flushing through her. Her skin was on fire, in a good way, tingling with raw energy and possibility again. Atticus faltered ahead of her and the fire demon Lord let out a high-pitched squall of delight, going for the killing blow.

Not on her fucking watch. The demon Lord pulled back, letting his fire gather, ready to throw himself into Atticus as she dashed forward with a speed and energy she didn't know was possible. Gilderon sang, a lyrical melody of steel and iron as she closed the distance between herself and the others. As Gulivior came down on Atticus, she darted between them, swinging the scythe like a Reaper, catching the side of the demon with her blade. He screamed, a horrific caterwaul as it cleaved into him, his flames spluttering as she gritted her teeth and yanked it clean through the demon. Hazel dropped the ancient demon weapon with a clatter.

Like a campfire dying out, the demon Lord fell to the ground in two neat pieces, broken, defeated.

Hazel watched the dying embers of the fight dissipate, ash floating away on the wind like cleansing rain. The world felt quieter, smaller now, as they pulled themselves away from the smoky remnants of charred buildings and burned demon bodies. Was the nightmare really over? Had they beaten down the two demons who had threatened to overwhelm them, to kill them all? Had they actually survived? And at what cost?

In a flash of light, the angelic demon and dragon were gone. Atticus and Specter had changed back, the former racing to his brother's side, the cat hot on his heels. *If he could run that fast, why hadn't he earlier when they got separated?* She tried to not sigh in disgruntlement. The worst was over... right?

She stared at the mess that lay before them. Two dead demons. Multiple buildings in ruin. And her friends, though alive, looking worse for wear. Wade still sat over Nox, looking exhausted. Charlotte and Rini had joined him at some point, collapsing on the ground beside them. The fires were out, but the stench of smoke and sulfur filled the air, a reminder of how close they had been to losing everything. Hazel shuddered.

All of this, because she had wanted Lottie to be happy. All of this, because of her actions.

Her body was heavy, sedated, as though she were in a trance as she made her way over to them. Atticus was furiously waving his hands over his brother, audibly frustrated as little sighs and huffs expelled from him. Hazel dropped to her knees beside Atticus. Specter mewled and crawled into Charlotte's lap, and the Witch began to absentmindedly pet him.

Nox looked as bad as when she had left him with Wade. She wasn't even sure he was breathing. Reaching a hand out, she touched him, reached for his fur where the flesh wouldn't be scarred and burned beneath. He was cool to the touch. Maybe he was dead.

"Don't touch him," Atticus gasped. She looked up at Atticus. The Princeling had his shoulders drawn, shaking, his head bowed. He was crying, she realized. She hadn't thought that he could, but here he was, sobbing openly as he stroked his hands over his brother. "Please wake up, Nox. You can't do this to Mother. Or to me."

Without thinking, Hazel wrapped an arm around Atticus, tugging him toward her. Hugging him. Somehow, the demon had become human to her. His kind had always been the worst of the worst to her. The most evil of the creatures she had sacrificed her life to hunting down, to disposing of. But there was something so raw, so young, in the way he sobbed now.

Even more surprising than her reaching out to him, was him reaching back. Atticus wrapped his arms around Hazel, burying his face into her shoulder as he began to sob in earnest. He was so little; how had she never noticed that? He was slight and short, like a child. Logically, she had seen that, but he was so loud and confident she hadn't really noticed it. A sob slipped from her own throat, unbidden, as she remembered Heather and Mama holding her after her parents died. Atticus and Nox had risked their lives to save her, to save them all. And now he had lost someone because of it.

"I'm sorry," Hazel murmured as she held the demon. He squeezed tighter, his body wracked with tears. She glanced helplessly at the others, their own eyes wet at the corners. This was really it. They hadn't all made it out, after all. And Atticus had been the one to lose someone. "He... he didn't deserve this."

Atticus cried harder then, his hands fisting the back of her jacket. What happened when a demon died? They had left the corpses of the others behind. Did they have funeral rites, customs? Did they bury their dead, burn them? Keep them in that weird mountain that loomed over this strange city? Or were there other cities, other places, in this strange world?

Time was a weird thing. Hazel couldn't tell if it was moving fast or slow as they sat there in silence as a group, mourning the dead. Atticus' grip didn't loosen on her as she stared down at the body of his dead brother. Her head was empty as she stared, wishing none of this had happened, that she just had left things alone.

"Son?"

CHAPTER TWENTY-NINE

ATTICUS

While Mother's voice was soft, gentle, comforting like a child's favorite blanket, the same could not be said of Nova. His father's voice wrapped around him like a shroud—a mourning shroud of cold, dark silk.

Atticus froze. If his father could speak to him, that meant he could see him, see him cuddling up to a mortal woman, worse than any fate imaginable. He desperately wanted to scramble away, to put as much distance between himself and the humans as he could. Would his father hurt them, know his sentiment toward them? Would he hurt Atticus for being so pathetic?

"It's okay," Hazel murmured into his hair. "If your daddy wants to pick a fight with you, he has to pick a fight with all of us. So, wipe those tears and get your head up. We've got you, babes."

Babes. That was her affectionate name for humans, and she had called him that without a hint of sarcasm or loathing. Atticus' held back a sniffle. If Hazel could believe in him, then so could he. The Princeling pushed back from her, shooting a wan smile. *Deep breath.* He pulled himself to his feet, frowning at the wet, dirty cuffs of his sleeves. He must have looked a wreck.

He turned to face his father.

Nova was a proud man. Atticus could see why Nox was his heir; they were essentially carbon copies of one another. His father was enormous, tall with wide shoulders, bronze skin dazzling in the moonlight, his long, pale blond hair secured at the nape of his neck with a white ribbon. He was dressed in his Council clothes—long, white robes with intricate gold and silver embroidery in the Old

Tongue, a hidden story woven into the very fibers. Atticus looked like a common street urchin before him, his father unscathed by the events of the day.

There was no way that the 'son' had been addressed to him. That he would ever acknowledge Atticus in that way. He was merely 'the boy' to Nova. The spare, the forgotten one. The odd one out.

Atticus felt a shuffle beside him and was shocked to feel Hazel's arm press against his. "Maybe you need to speak up, talk to him?" she muttered to him, head bowed toward Atticus. He swallowed hard and nodded.

"Father, I..." What was he meant to say? *Father, you knew I was on trial, knew this probably happened because of me. Nox is dead because of me.*

Nox is dead.

And it was all his fault.

"Father, I messed up." He hung his head, his voice barely a whisper. "Nox... Nox was hurt because of me, because of my actions. I take full responsibility. Don't lay the blame on the mortals. They... they were just trying their best to help. Everything broke, Father. Everything just went so catastrophically wrong."

Nova stared down at Atticus, silent for a long moment. He squirmed under the hard gaze of his father. What was he going to say, going to do? Atticus wished he had gotten the others out already, had been able to. "Move aside, Asterius," his Father said finally. Atticus obliged without a word, stepping toward Hazel. Thankfully, the Hunter was aware enough to shuffle aside too.

Nova stepped forward, toward the giant wolf-body of Nox, where his brother lay cold and still since the fighting had ended. He knew Wade had tried, had felt his companion tugging on the bond between them. Maybe magic wasn't strong enough to fix everything. Atticus watched, a hollowness forming in his chest where he supposed his heart was meant to be.

Nova Lyra knelt down beside Nox, reaching a hand out to the burned, sticky flesh of his other son. His real son. Atticus tried not flinch, tried not thinking about that. For what would happen when Nova realized he had no heir without Nox?

"My baby."

Atticus nearly jumped out of his skin, enveloped by the warmth of his mother's voice, of the sea salt scent of her skin. He wanted to melt into her as he turned and saw Aurora's pale face staring at him, her eyes shining with tears. Atticus wanted nothing more than to soak her in, breathe her in. But now wasn't the time. He gave his mother a tight smile, a promise to speak later without words, and returned his attention to Father and Nox. He dropped to his knees beside Nova, who's hands stroked the fur of his brother's true form.

He knew better than to ask anything of Nova, to speak to him until he was spoken to. So they waited in silence. His friends gathered together, shuffling to the side, as Aurora settled beside Atticus, as graceful and delicate as ever as she smoothed out her long, powder blue skirts. His Father broke the silence at last. "What happened, Asterius?"

He was not used to hearing that name so much. It had been so long, and in the span of a day, he had heard it more times than he cared to count. He swallowed. "We... we were caught in a fight with Sporas and Gulivior, sir. They were damaging the Council. Nox filled us in briefly on what had transpired, and we got sweptup in things. Then Nox got hurt."

Hurt because of me.

His Father didn't speak, merely surveyed Nox's broken, burned body. His dead brother. *Dead.*

Atticus had experienced a lot of death in the mortal world. Had lost many a companion to it, even Wade. And that had hurt like a thousand knives stabbing all over his body. Mortals were fragile, breakable. Expected to eventually shuffle off their mortal coil and to the lands that awaited them next.

Daemons, though? Those were a rarer death, an almost unnatural occurrence. He wasn't sure how long his kind lived for, what purpose their long lives truly served. He just knew that Nox didn't deserve to have that cut short, for *any* reason. He'd seen more daemon deaths that day, than in his entire lifetime.

He didn't want to see any more.

Atticus watched, heart heavy, as his father's hands made their way up to Nox's throat. How cold had his brother gotten by now? How had his final moments felt, alone while chaos raged around them? The Princeling hoped that Wade had been on some comfort to his brother, at least. Nova's hands stopped on Nox's neck, and Atticus' heart skipped a beat. This was when Father would work out his brother was dead, that all was lost—

"There it is," Nova murmured, almost to himself. "I can feel your lifeblood pulsing there, my son. Weak as it is, it has not been quashed yet." Atticus' heart skipped another beat. Nox wasn't dead? But he had been so still, so cold...

Nova's hands worked over Atticus' brother, a frown on his face. "You are not far off though, are you?"

He knew he shouldn't speak first, but he couldn't help it. "How can I help, Father? I wish to be of assistance to you, to Nox."

He had expected his father to ignore him, at best. At worst, he expected spiteful vitriol for what he had done to Nox. What he hadn't expected was the gentle sigh that came out of the stern daemon Lord. "Lay your hands beside mine, Asterius. I need all the strength I can acquire. They had your mother and I shackled in iron down beneath the Mountain, and we are still rather weak. I can see you're depleted, but perhaps together, we can assist your brother."

When was the last time his father had said so many words together to him? Several whole sentences that weren't full of mockery and disdain? Was that possible? But he abided, nonetheless. Like a child, tremulous in their movements, he scooted closer to his father, laying his hands over Nox. He could feel what Father meant now that he was closer to his brother's life origin, his heart, where magic and blood pulsed through the daemon. It was a dull flicker, but there it was.

"He is alive still," Atticus murmured. Nova nodded, eyes narrowed.

"His blood is tainted," Nova muttered. "That is why he cannot regenerate on his own. There is too much corrupting it."

Atticus paled. He must have sealed in the damage earlier, when he had healed Nox. He hadn't cleaned out his blood, his veins, his very magic. What a stupid oversight to have made. He cringed. "That would be my fault. He was pierced through by Celestium, and I healed him. I hadn't realized the damage would remain inside."

His father's head shot up. "Celestium damaged him? How?"

Atticus explained the fight with Herstafont, how she had tried to take down Nox with her as she fell. How Celestium had cut Nox, and it had seemed like a fairly superficial wound that hadn't needed more than they'd done. He should have realized the poison would have seeped deeper than skin level. Nova was silent as Atticus spoke, unmoving, his face an impassive mask.

"And I didn't realize that would seal in any of the damage from the blade," Atticus whispered. "He seemed fine."

Nova sighed again, and Atticus had to fight every instinct in him not to flinch as the daemon Lord said, "That is not your burden to bear, Asterius. It is truly something to behold that you were capable of healing the damage of a Daemonic Blade."

Atticus gaped. Was that *praise* from his father? Surely he was mishearing things.

"Right." Nova looked over Nox. "Where did Celestium cut him, Asterius?"

In a daze, Atticus helped move his brother's haunches to reveal the slice on his brother's abdomen. The scar was puckering, bruising, beneath the fur as Atticus brushed it aside. Nova leaned in, his father's scent a mixture of perspiration and smokiness. It was almost like hugging his father, in a way.

"Push his fur aside for me, Asterius, at the wound site." Atticus obliged, and Nova ran a finger over the old cut. Magic crackled from his fingertip as the old wound opened, and black bile began to seep from the wound. It smelled of sulfur and over-ripened fruit, and was gag worthy so close to it. Nox had been carrying that in him the entire time they fought Sporas and Gulivior, too.

"Poison taints his blood and magic now, Asterius. You see it." Atticus nodded. His father's lips pursed tight together. "Cleansing it will be... painful."

Atticus watched the bile and blood, thick and coagulated, drip from his brother's abdomen. "Tell me what to do, and so it shall be done."

His father was right about the pain.

It wasn't just Nox that was experiencing it, however. Cleansing his brother's blood was a straightforward enough process—in theory. Use magic to siphon out the bad like earlier. Not many steps at all. "Asterius, we are going to feed our magic through the wound and clean out the darkness that has tainted your brother. Pull on it, clean out the venom until his blood runs clean and clear once more," Nova had explained. Again, simple enough. Atticus had pulled off a lot harder things that day.

However, what his father had failed to mention was the connection he would feel through his magic to the blood, to the taint. Maybe his father hadn't warned him on purpose, as it was the worst thing that he had ever experienced in all his born days.

Atticus didn't know what *true* suffering was. Not in the way a mortal being tormented by a daemon might, or someone on their death bed might feel. He had been hurt before, certainly. He had experienced a great many things in his existence. Heartache, pain, happiness. But the pain that shuddered through his body as he sent his magic into his brother's open wound was something else, something *indescribable*.

He felt like he was submerged in icy cold water, unable to breathe, it was so frigid. His teeth chattered, pinpricks of pain like little knives all over his body, stabbing him, slicing him apart. Was this the pain that Nox was in as he lay near death on the ground?

In the words of Hazel, *fuck*.

Atticus heard himself gasp for breath as though he were far away. Out of his body. Ah, this is what humans called an 'out of body' experience. He wished he wasn't connected to his own right then. To feel like everything was burning, it was so cold.

"Push through it, Asterius," his father commanded. Were Nova's teeth chattering, too? Atticus couldn't tell where he ended or where his brother began anymore. The taint was overwhelming as his magic dug into it, clawed at it. He could have sworn it was fighting back, growing, trying to make him succumb to it. "Don't let it win."

With a nod, Atticus gritted his teeth. His father was right. He wouldn't let the pain win. Nox hadn't, so he wouldn't either.

Together, they worked silently. The poison whispered dark things to Atticus. Told him he wasn't good enough, to give up, that his brother was as good as dead already. But he wouldn't listen to that. He would never listen to a dark voice again.

Gritting his teeth, he poked and probed with his magic, like an archaeologist excavating a delicate forgotten relic. And soon, his father was right. Nox's blood was clean, and the darkness simply vanished. Atticus gulped down a breath of air, the sulfur and sweetness vanished now.

Nox shuddered as he drew in a breath, exhaling with a deep whine. Atticus could have sobbed in relief. His brother was alive—not well, but alive. They had done it. Everything would be okay.

Atticus collapsed in a heap beside his brother and father, the weariness of the day threatening to drag him under. They had done it. *He* had done it. And they were alive for it.

Chapter Thirty

Hazel

A tticus' father was a formidable man—demon?—but Hazel was used to sticking up to worse. She'd worked with hipsters in the Arts sector, after all.

He towered over them, exuding a regal quality that was palpable. Like seeing a king, or something. When she heard the words 'Demon Lord', this is exactly who she imagined. His father didn't even seem to notice them as he bossed his son around, commanding Atticus to help his brother with him.

So the humans did what they could. They scampered to the side to wait, to see if Atticus' brother would live or die. There was something about the quiet, about finally stopping, that had Hazel unable to keep still. Momentum had kept her going, and she couldn't stop now, or she was worried she'd never begin moving again. She fidgeted beside Charlotte, who slapped her hand and gave her a warning look.

"Stay still, you're not five," Charlotte hissed. Hazel rolled her eyes, but complied.

What were they meant to do, huddled to the side, watching in anticipation? Hazel was a doer, not a waiter. Demon Lord or not, she didn't like submitting to any man.

Still, she waited patiently as he leaned over Nox with Atticus, waiting with bated breath as they worked together on the giant wolf. Would he make it? Hazel had no allegiance toward the demon, but she felt bad. He had tried hard, had done his best to keep them safe. She didn't want him to die. He didn't deserve to.

So, Hazel did something she didn't normally do. She prayed to herself, silently, hoping that if there were something greater, they would listen.

Eventually, Nox began breathing once more, and the two demons pulled away in relief as the humans stood awkwardly to the side. Atticus looked ready to cry again as his father stood, turning toward Atticus' mother. How weird that he had parents, that demons had family. She had just assumed they were creatures that sprang into existence before coming to this place.

"Now," Nova turned to the group of humans at last. "Who in the celestial skies are you five, and what are you all doing here?"

It was the weirdest catch up she had ever done. Each side filled one another on the details of the day, about all the tragedies that had passed.

The coup had started during a meeting, just as Atticus had predicted. It must have been premeditated; they had iron shackles ready to lock down Nova and the others that sided with them, as they prepared for the trial of Atticus and Wade. Nova suspected that the trial was just a convenient excuse for the attack they had planned long before.

Hazel had no fucking clue about demon politics, and she didn't really want to know. It didn't matter, though. All that mattered was that they would get to head home soon enough. And that was good enough.

"Rest for a moment," Nova told them, "as we tend to our son. Then we will make haste to send you back on your way home, mortals."

They sat around the broken square, lumped in little groups, as Atticus and his family had a moment to talk and take care of his brother. That big, looming worry no longer hung over them, a rain cloud that was slowly dissipating. Rini wandered off, telling them she needed a moment, so Hazel stood to the side with Charlotte and Wade.

"Where are they?" Hazel grumbled, patting down her pockets. It had been a long day. She wanted a cigarette.

"If you can't find them, maybe this is the sign that you finally quit for good, hmm?"

"Babes, I love you, but I will light you on fire and smoke you if I have to right now."

Charlotte smirked and laughed. "Yeah, okay. You can try, but I don't think you'll get very far. Besides, don't you wanna do better for others?"

"Huh?"

Charlotte lolled her head toward where Rini had wandered off to.

Rini sat off to the side, on the edge of the broken fountain, hand skimming the water with fascination. She looked like a heroine out of an anime in the soft, twilit moon light.

Charlotte nudged her shoulder into Hazel. Hazel glared at the Witch. "What the hell is that for?'

"Go talk to her, you idiot. We aren't running away from danger now, so go. Shoo. Go see why she followed you to this place. I'm sure she has a good reason."

Hazel rolled her eyes. "Did I ever tell you that you're real fuckin' annoying, babes?"

Charlotte grinned, wrapping an arm around Wade's waist. "All the time." Charlotte reached up, nuzzling the side of his neck. Hazel pretended to gag.

"Ugh, I see your ploy to be rid of me. Fine, bitch. You enjoy being mushy and sappy with your ghost boyfriend." Hazel grinned. Charlotte knew she was joking. She blew sloppy kisses at them as she sauntered over to where Rini sat.

The idol didn't take her eyes off the water as Hazel sat beside her, their heads almost touching. "Today has been so full on, I haven't stopped to consider how magical this place is. Liquid stars? The same time of day, all day? Multiple moons? Where even are we?"

Hazel shrugged. "Wherever demons live." Rini huffed softly, the faintest of laughs.

"Yeah, I guess so."

The two women sat in silence as Rini continued to trail her hand over the water. Hazel watched, mesmerized by the soft ripples caused by the idol's delicate hands. She was so beautiful. Hazel could watch her all day and not get bored. Finally, though, she remembered what Lottie had told her to ask Rini.

"Why did you follow us in?"

The idol finally tore her attention away from the water. Sitting up straight to look at Hazel, Rini raised her eyebrows, a look of disbelief etched across her face. "Are you really asking me that?"

"Uh, yeah?" Hazel pushed her glasses back up her nose, sweat making the bridge of her nose wet. Rini rolled her eyes.

"Because I didn't want anything to happen to you. I like you, that's pretty obvious, I thought. I didn't want the woman I'm falling for with to be maimed or killed before I could even see where things went, y'know."

Hazel didn't hesitate. She leaned in, kissing Rini. Softer, gentler than she normally would. The kind of kiss that you gave someone when you wanted them to feel how your heart felt. Her lips were light as they grazed against Rini's—a promise that they would, indeed, get to know one another better.

"You know," Hazel murmured against Rini's lips, "some people say soul mates are fate, but I believe they're a choice. And you're the choice I am choosing to make."

Rini sighed against her, and finally, time seemed to stand still in the good way.

"It's time to go now."

Atticus' father's announcement was abrupt, interrupting the tender moment between the two Hunters. Reluctantly, Hazel pulled away from Rini, extending a hand toward the idol. "Onward to the future or something then, right?"

Rini giggled, reaching out to clasp Hazel's hand. "Yeah, something like that."

Chapter Thirty-One

Atticus

When the dust settles, a new day comes.

And a new day had come for them all. One that he wasn't sure any of them would get to see. And yet, here they stood. Terra Doerum still blazed with small fires and ash rained down like a blanket of snow. But there they all stood, together, alive. Somehow, they had come out the other end together.

It was almost like a funeral procession as they marched through the broken, rainbow streets of Terra Doerum to House Lyra as a group. Nova led the way with Nox right behind him, as Aurora held Atticus' hand tightly in her own, like he was a child again. The mortals trailed close behind them. A weight had been lifted, replaced by a somber shroud. They were going to go now. They were going to leave him behind.

The city streets lay in various states of ruin as they traversed the broken paths and skittered around debris. He wondered who was going to fix this, and how. It felt to him like this was the precipice of some monumental change. There was an energy to the air, and the shift was coming soon, whether they liked it or not.

Change came for them all, eventually.

Wade moved up beside him. His mother gave Wade a taut smile, but said nothing.

"Are you coming with us?" Wade asked Atticus in a low tone.

He'd been considering this on the entire march back to his home. *Home.* That was such a hollow word. It was a place he had existed at, in various points of his life. Besides his mother, he had never felt at place there, like he really belonged.

But he had a chance to change that. To make it a place where he felt comfortable, accepted, wanted. To make it *home*.

"I have to stay with my family. A lot of damage has been wrought. They will need all the help they can get fixing it, rebuilding it. Who knows how deep the damage and treachery even run? Until things are well and safe again, I must do my duties as a Prince."

Wade gave him a sad, small smile. "I suppose that makes sense. It just won't feel the same without you around."

Atticus felt his mother squeeze his hand tightly. "I suppose not, dear friend. But we all make sacrifices in life, and it is time for me to pay my dues. That is just the nature of things."

Wade's leather shoes clacked against the path, a gentle, rhythmic gait that Atticus knew all too well. He and Wade were so in sync after years spent together, he could tell his walk, even with all his senses muted. That was the thing about having a best friend, he'd come to realize through all the ups and downs—you knew them, good and bad. And they knew you.

And that's why Wade wasn't fighting him, fighting for Atticus to come with him. Because Wade knew when Atticus said he needed to do something, that he had to. Because Wade knew, despite the downs that they'd had, that Atticus wanted to be around Wade desperately, more than anything. For he loved Wade more than anything, more than anyone, he had ever met.

He actually loved Wade, and not the idea of his friendship. Ugly bits and all.

"Wade?"

"Hmm?"

Atticus turned to his mother. "Walk with Father for a moment, Mother. I must speak to my friend."

Another taut smile from Aurora, but she complied, lifting the fronts of her skirts as she hastened toward Nova and Nox. Atticus' hand was still warm from where she held his. He forgot how nice it was to have a mother around, to hold him, to love him.

He wanted Wade to have someone around to love him. The Blythe girl. That red thread that linked the two used to bother him, used to threaten Atticus. But he had come to realize that there were different types of love and care, and that he couldn't give Wade everything he needed, as much as he wished he could.

"I want to release you from your bargains with me. All of them. You are not bound to be my friend, or to share power with me henceforth. I want you to return to the mortal world, and build the life that was robbed of you."

Wade gasped, stumbling. Atticus was quick to reach a hand out and steady Wade. "What do you mean?"

"You missed out on life, dear one. And in no short part thanks to me. Perhaps it was fate; you wouldn't have met your soul mate, otherwise. In any case, this is your chance. And you can't go about beginning that journey while bound to your past."

Wade's eyes welled as they climbed the weaving streets upward. "Do you mean that?"

"More than anything, dear friend."

Wade reached over and grabbed Atticus' hand, squeezing it tightly. "Thank you, friend. You have no idea what that means for me, to hear you say that."

He had some idea—he was the one saying it, after all. He merely smiled at his friend as they continued on their march, hands warm in one another's.

Nova stared at the misfits as they gathered around them in the gardens of House Lyra.

The manor home and its surrounds had thankfully remained by and large untouched by the events that had unfolded. But there was a darkness that loomed over the house that pricked at Atticus as they gathered in the dark, the magical gas lamps still unable to ignite. There was a foreboding energy to it. A great storm was set to come, and they were in the calm before.

Maybe he was reading too much into things.

Atticus let go of his mother's hand as they piled around one of the great pools that served as a fountain in the gardens. He had to be strong for his companions now. For his friends. He was no longer the Asterius that hid behind his mother's skirts. He was Atticus the daemon—friend and fighter.

Aurora leaned in toward him, her mouth brushing over his hair as she kissed him. "Remember that you are my brave child, and you can handle anything that the world throws at you," she murmured.

Nova cleared his throat. Atticus glanced at the others, fully taking in how exhausted they looked now. Even Specter looked bedraggled. The fighting, the fear, the energy that they had let be consumed, had taken its toll on them. His chest tightened. He just wanted them whole and hale once more.

"It is time to send these mortals home," Nova announced.

His father began to weave his hands the way he'd watched the Blythe girl do, murmuring something low, almost as if he were humming a hymn, a melody. It was almost hypnotic to watch his father as he transformed the water of the pool. It was subtle, almost imperceptible. But there it was. The starlight pool began to glow faintly, a shimmer that it didn't possess before. It was a portal now, a way to leave this world and return to their own.

Nova turned his attention to the humans. Inclining his head ever so slightly, he said, "While I thank you for your efforts on this day, now is the time we must close the boundaries between your world and ours, for the sake of both realms, and getting to the bottom of the havoc that has been caused today.

"I beseech you to keep what you have seen on this day to yourself. Mortals cannot handle the knowledge of our world, of our lives. It is best for you, and for us, if it remains between us."

There was a heavy silence then, the implication of his threat weighing on them. Nova was a terrifying Lord for a reason. His voice softened, though, as he added, "But I thank you for your efforts today. With Asterius, with keeping our home safe. You didn't have to, and yet, you did. We will ensure your safety from our kind as our debt."

Atticus desperately wanted to yell at them to not go, to not leave him behind. He wanted them to stay with him. He glanced at each of their faces, one by one. They were done here, he could see it. The exhaustion, the turmoil—it was all taking a toll on their fragile human bodies. He remembered that saying again.

If you love him, let him go.

He locked eyes with Wade. Those sad, gray, stormy eyes. He had seen them sparkle with laughter and tears many times over their years together; had seen the light fade from them. Had seen them cold and glassy in death. Atticus wanted those eyes to remain filled with wonder and happiness, with joy and excitement. And that couldn't happen if he were tethered to the daemon.

He could see that plainly.

Hazel spoke now, brash as ever as she raised her brows and stared up at Nova. "And how are we meant to trust you that your bullshit won't bleed over to us and make problems over the other side? I know your kind can jump back and forth between planes. Look how easy as shit it was for you to make a portal. Who says this isn't gonna happen again?"

Nova stared at Hazel for a long moment, then bowed his head in apology. "I can't promise you that it won't. But I promise I will do my best to ensure your safety. Consider it a bargain."

Atticus gaped. Not only had his father conceded on something, but he had offered her a bargain? Nova had never, not in all of his lifetime, offered a *bargain*. His father was too powerful to gain anything from a mortal. But here he was, offering something that *benefited* her. Hazel considered his father for a moment, before shrugging.

"Yeah, that seems fair enough, I guess. I can't really argue with a Lord from Hell or whatever."

How was she so flippant, so arrogant? Did she not comprehend the power Nova wielded, or did she simply not care? Either way, she astounded Atticus. He would never have the audacity, no matter how much bravado he mustered. His mother stifled a mirthful chuckle as Hazel cracked her hands and neck, as though gearing up for a fight.

Nox leaned heavily against a hedge, watching with calculating eyes. His brother nodded when he caught Atticus glancing his way. Atticus nodded back, unsure of what his brother was thinking. He wasn't even sure of what *he* was thinking any longer.

"It is time for your... acquaintances to leave now, Asterius. They aren't meant to be here, and the longer they're here, the worse it could be for them." His father placed a hand on his shoulder—comforting or threat, Atticus couldn't tell.

"I know," Atticus replied softly. He cleared his throat. "Alright, humans, it's time for you to traipse back whence you came. It has been a delight fighting alongside you, but alas, the world keeps revolving or some such, and we must part for now."

Rini leaned over to Hazel and whispered, not quietly enough, "Is he always like this? Melodramatic and weird?"

"Yeah, it's kinda his shtick."

Atticus sketched a bow and grinned at them. Ever the Princeling, ever the persona.

"I aim to serve, ladies. Now, how about we get you moving along?"

Atticus watched his friends disappear beneath the surface, their existence barely a ripple upon the still waters. One by one, they vanished beneath the night sky, and his heart tugged with each. Wade was the last to go, apprehensive as he eyed off the water. Finally, Wade turned to look at Atticus.

"What about you?" his dear companion asked softly. Atticus smiled brightly, let out a tinkling, soft laugh.

"A daemon always lands on his feet, or something akin to that." Wade looked at him doubtfully. "Oh dearest, I'll be fine. You scamper off home with the others. You'll see me before you know it."

"Goodbye, my friend," Wade whispered as his auburn hair slipped beneath the waterline.

And just like that, they were gone. Atticus' throat bobbed as reality began to weigh in on him, on what had happened. He turned to his family, who waited beside him. "And what do we do now?"

His father gazed at him thoughtfully for a moment. "Well, son. We fix what has happened and we convene to ensure nothing like this happens again." Nova turned to Aurora. "I suppose we hastily call a meeting with the non-traitors and work out where to go from there. The worst of the damage is contained, but we need to know how far the dissent and taint runs."

Son. His father had called him son. Atticus puffed up his chest.

"Allow me to assist you, then."

Chapter Thirty Two

Hazel

Hazel gasped as she poked her head out of the water. Light blinded her vision as she blinked against the orange and lilac of sunset.

The others popped up beside her, drawing in deep breaths as they emerged. It took her a few moments to recognize the pond out the back of Winterbourne, where she used to smoke and watch the ducks. They were home—they were finally, really *home*. Teeth chattering, she began to swim to shore, urging the others to follow.

As if a trance, they trudged their way up to the house, where a shocked Jacob saw them and came rushing out. It was a blur as Gran came to comfort them, and they got cleaned up, and told them what happened.

Umbra Hollow had, once more, been taped off from the public. Somehow, they had found Hazel and Charlotte's stuff there, and deduced what they had been up to, shortly after Rini had followed them in. And they had been spending the time they were missing trying to find them. Gran came out sobbing, holding them all, and telling them to never scare her again.

Time passed in weird ways.

As a child, it was slow, meandering. Long, lazy days filled with potential. When you were depressed, it was also long, but that was more torturous, slow in a 'please-get-to-the-end-of-the-day' kinda way. When you were relaxing, or having fun, or busy—bam, where did it all go?

Time was a strange limbo, a mix of these when they returned home and tried to regain their footing. They had Wade back now, and Hazel wasn't exactly the most cut up about the wrench she had thrown in Charlotte's life. She'd had to break it to Bradley that she wasn't able to see him anymore—what a pity—and it turned out even for the Foundation, having a reanimated, hundred-year-old ghost was difficult. How did they register him? What about his family name, gone from the records?

That wasn't a Hazel problem, she told them. She'd found him and helped drag him back. Someone else who worked in the government could surely forge all that paperwork for him. Celebrities and gross billionaires without the resources Lottie and company had did shadier stuff all the time. They could slip one dead dude back into the system, right?

Rini fell right into place with them. She'd have to go back on tour soon, Hazel knew. But she wanted to enjoy that time with her. To see if things had a chance. At least, that's what Hazel thought. A few weeks after they'd gotten back, their wounds healed, and Winterbourne began to be a flurry of activity once more, Rini approached her.

Hazel was cleaning up after herself, tiding the bedroom that she'd somehow been sharing with Rini every day since they had returned. When had that suitcase gotten there? And the side table was over-ladened with perfumes and creams, and plush toys of anime characters that Hazel had never heard of. Her own table was covered with polaroids and tape that she hadn't gotten to putting into her journal yet. She wished she'd been able to take photos of Atticus' home to add in, of the triple moon and the starlight ponds, of the majestic rainbow city and the mountain that loomed over it.

And she liked it. She liked having Rini there.

She'd just set her photos gently in the cover of her leather-bound journal when Rini slid into the room. She was dressed in a purple and green tracksuit—again, based on a character from an anime that she didn't know about—her hair in a classic side ponytail. Her eyes darted around nervously as she approached the bed, sitting tentatively on the corner, as if worried about putting her full weight on it. "Hey, Hazel? Can I talk to you?"

Hazel stomach dropped. 'Can I talk to you' was never good. Every rom-com in existence made that clear. She forced a smile to her face, even as her heart began to race and her blood thrummed, hot and erratic. "Sure, babes. What's up?"

Don't crack.

"I'm meant to be on tour in like, a week or so," Rini began cautiously. "You remember, right?"

Of course she remembered. How could she forget. Big smile, big nod.

"Well, uh, that would mean leaving here."

That would mean breaking up.

Rini reached for her hair, tugging the silky ends of the strands between her fingers. Rini was nervous, that was apparent. Hazel tried not to grimace as she stared at her soon-to-be-ex-girlfriend. Should she sit while she was being dumped? She'd never been on the receiving end of a breakup. Had they even made it official? She was also more of a text dumper herself—sleep with a girl while in town and move on with your life.

Staying still wasn't something Hazel had really done before. Maybe that's why she'd wanted Wade back for Charlotte. *That's a lot to unpack, and this ain't the time.*

Rini took a deep breath and Hazel's stomach did flips. She braced herself for the next few words out of Rini's mouth. "I want to be around you, like, all the time. You know that, right?"

Had she heard Rini right? That wasn't how a breakup was supposed to go, was it? Was she just being nice before dropping the other shoe? 'Yeah, I totally wanna stay with you, I promise, but also, I'm leaving anyway'? Hazel blinked her eyes as they stung, willing her tears not to come. She just wanted it over and done with.

"I've enjoyed seeing you, and doing other things together but—" ah, there it was, the 'it was nice, but' "—but I need more than that."

Hazel's stomach dropped. "I see."

Rini glanced to the ground. "This is hard."

"I get it." Hazel cleared her throat. "You don't need to say it. We don't have to do the song and dance. You have to go back to work and I have a life to live too. I gotta help Charlotte. We all know Wade can't do it. It's all good, babes. No need for either of us to stress." Oh, she was going to cry if they didn't wrap this up soon.

Rini's head shot up. "Are you breaking up with me?"

Hazel blinked. "You're breaking up with *me*."

The idol shot to her feet, closing the space between them. She was so close to Hazel that she could smell her cherry cola lip gloss. God, Hazel wanted to grab her and kiss her. "What do you mean, I'm breaking up with you?"

Hazel turned her head to the side. She needed to make distance between them, physically and emotionally. "I know it's hard to say, you said it yourself—"

"I want to stay here I don't want to go back to being an idol. I'm getting too old for it to remain popular, anyway. At least, not a full time idol. Touring is... stressful, and hard. I want to make music on my own terms. I want to stay here, to help you and Charlotte. To stay with you. I love you, you stupid idiot."

What did Rini just say? "Huh?"

"I love you." Rini drew the words out slowly, pronouncing them like a tourist in a foreign country. "Can I say that any simpler for you?'

"You love me?" Hazel didn't mean to sound so incredulous, but wasn't she getting dumped?

Rini rolled her eyes. "Yes, I love you. Do you love me?"

She'd never said it to someone romantically before. Her family, and bestie, yeah. Of course she loved them. Charlotte was the sister she'd never had, and Gran was her bonus grandma. She was lucky to have them. And Wade was okay, she supposed. But she'd never told a girl she loved them. What did it feel like?

When she looked at Rini, time seemed to slow down. Her chest ached, and her stomach could never decide if it was excited or if she was going to throw up. The world seemed to spin and all she could focus on was the idol in front of her.

Was that love? If so, she guessed she was head over heels for Rini.

"I've never told someone I love them," Hazel started, choosing her words carefully, slowly. "I'd never really formed attachments before. Seeing you get hurt in demon land, and all the things we went through together... they were different. I was proud of you, but protective of you, and wanted to be around you. I'm not... well, I've never really had to be uh, sincere, with a girl I've slept with before. But I don't wanna slip out in the middle of the night, or make excuses not to see you. I want you here, with me, like all the time. I get stupid in the brain when you're around, and can't think. And if that's love, well, I love you."

Rini didn't hesitate. She threw her arms around Hazel, closing that distance, and they fell into the taste of cherry lip gloss and tentative, tender promises.

She slipped away early in the morning, before breakfast. She left Rini snoozing quietly in her bed, silky black hair trailing behind her onto Hazel's pillow. As the big spoon, she'd gotten used to the idol's hair being in her face ninety percent of the time. She placed a soft kiss to Rini's brow before slipping away, getting dressed in darkness and silence. It had been several days since their confession, since it was official. She guessed they were stuck together, at least for now. And she was more than okay with that.

The early hours of the morning were always her favorite. Was it the quietness, the stillness? Perhaps it was because she was so used to coming out of the darkness at the end of a long night, plagued by monsters, secrets, and summonings. There was something about coming out of a dark tunnel, covered in the muck and goo of the undead and unknown, grabbing an iced, whipped-cream-covered coffee through the drive thru on her way home. It calmed her, knowing it was a fresh day, a fresh start, and the world was a little less filled with darkness.

There was something missing though, in those weeks. Wade might have been back, and things were settling down at Winterbourne once more, as the seasons threatened to change again. It took her a while to realize it, but the energy was wrong, lopsided, out of balance. It was quieter. And it was because Atticus was missing.

She'd gotten used to his energy when they'd been in his world. There was something about him that had initially put her on edge, but now she noticed how hollow it was without it. Like having an extremely irritating little brother or cousin around. They annoyed you when they were there, but you missed them when they were gone.

So that was how Hazel found herself wandering down to the mausoleum at the back of Winterbourne, candles and matches shoved into a tote bag, a pocket knife crammed into her pocket. She made her way into the tiny chapel that housed the toy and memorial for the Blythe and Van Baird families. She hadn't been in there since she'd tried—and failed—to summon Atticus last.

Butterflies fluttered in her stomach as she set up a ring of candles, not unlike the ones in Umbra Hollow before the floor gave out on them. She drew a circle of salt around the candles on the floor; she wasn't taking any chances in case something else came through again. Taking deep breaths, she lit the candles, sitting outside of them and the ring she had created. Then, she reached into the tote bag, pricking her finger as she said, "Asterius, it better be you that comes when I call, or I'll come back there and beat the shit out of you myself."

The candles hissed as she reached into the circle and let the drop of blood fall. She retracted her arm with lightning speed as the flames lengthened and danced in an invisible breeze, shadows twisting along the walls. Had she fucked up? She scrambled back a bit as the candles roared into pillars of flame, heat licking at her face even from a distance. Her heart thrummed as she pulled out her hunting knife from her bag. She'd stab her way out of this if she had to.

Knife poised, ready to slash, she waited with bated breath as the flames died down and a small figure blinked into existence in the middle of the candles. There he was, the angelic, blond hair demon boy, Atticus. His eyes fluttered as he took in the scene around him, before his gaze eventually landed on her. "Oh, the mouthy one has finally deigned to call me, then?"

"Are you going to make me regret that decision right out of the gate?"

Atticus shot her a grin, climbing to his feet. He was dressed the same as ever, nary a wrinkle on him. "It is what it is, I suppose. Is there something I can assist you with? A dark desire that has finally consumed you, mayhaps? What fiendishly wicked things can I assist you with, Hazel?" He paused for a moment, before groaning. "Did you really have to salt me in once more? Have I not proven myself to be more trustworthy than this? What else have you prepared for me, an iron coffin?"

"I can still throw you in one, if you'd like, babes," she retorted. She scurried forward, placing her knife on the ground beside her. "Gimme a sec, I can get you out of there. I just didn't want to be unprepared in case one of those fucking monsters we fought came through." She kicked the salt out of the way, blowing out the candles as she went. She climbed to her feet, where she could look the demon in the eyes.

Atticus eyed her off dubiously, widening as his gaze finally came to rest on the knife. "Were you going to *stab* me?"

"Only if I had to."

"Uncouth creature." He shook his golden hair, his little boots clattering gently against the ground as he shimmied through the salt gap. "This better not burn me, devil girl."

Hazel snorted. "Now that's the pot calling the kettle black, isn't it?"

Atticus stopped in front of her, tilting his head inquisitively. "I suppose it is. So, perhaps you can tell me why you called me here? You and I both know my tether to this plane is tenuous without a contract."

She shuffled uncomfortably. She knew that it was; that he would disappear soon. Now that she knew they could call upon him like this, though, Wade could see his friend. She'd seen him float around the manor. He was doting on Lottie, but none of them were stupid—it was clear he missed his friend, demon or not. "Yeah, that's what I wanna talk to you about."

Atticus said nothing, staring her down silently, cherubic face masking the creature she knew lurked beneath. Shouldn't he have frightened her? She knew what he was capable of. For all her smack talk, she knew he could end her in a moment.

And yet, he chose not to.

"Wade misses you," she began, "despite all the shit you've done. And things feel... weird without you. We know you have your family and you gotta like, fix demon society or whatever. But it'd be nice if you could spend time with your buddy or whatever."

"Wade hasn't called on me to make a contract," Atticus said softly. Hazel blew out a breath.

"Yeah, well, probably because he's an idiot that doesn't like imposing on anyone. I can't even get him to ask me for the bread at the dinner table yet."

"But here you are, brash, and willing to impose."

Gulping, Hazel locked eyes with the demon. "Yeah, that sounds like me. Brash and willing to impose on others. So, I figured, I'd ask. Or something."

Atticus tilted his head back and laughed. It was a melodious cackle. When he stopped, he wiped a tear from the corner of his eye. "Oh, Miss Hunter, you can just say you all miss me and want me around. It's not too big an ask, is it?"

"It kinda is when you have to summon a demon," she grunted. "You know, the effort of summoning you and then—"

"—and then making a deal with a devil?" he finished with a grin, as Hazel rolled her eyes.

"Yeah, that."

Atticus leaned in conspiratorially, azure eyes glinting in the low light. "Would you like to make a deal with me then, Hazel Williams?"

Hazel and Atticus walked side by side out of the chapel after they carefully cleaned up the ritual, a deal sealed between them. She'd gone from wanting to destroy all demons to making multiple deals now. Internally, she laughed. How absurd of her. She wondered how Mama and Heather would feel when she called them later that day. She suspected they already knew, though.

As they crested the grass knoll that led to the atrium at the back of the house, Hazel flinched as Charlotte, Wade, and Gran came into view.

"Uh oh," Hazel muttered under her breath as they began to march toward Hazel and the demon.

"I knew you were up to something when I saw you carrying that bag out of the house, young lady," Gran said, her long, silver braid bouncing on her shoulder. Despite her age, she was so nimble still, possessing a grace and refinement that made her seem much younger than her years. And she looked *pissed*.

"Gran, I can explain—" she began, but Edith cut her off.

"Oh no, you can tell me in full just what you were doing and what you planned *after*. For now, we have a bigger problem to deal with. I told you not to summon devils, did I not? And yet, here you are, doing it again!" Gran turned her chocolate brown eyes onto Atticus.

"You," Gran looked at Atticus, and the demon boy stared at her like a deer in the headlights. "You're the demon they summoned, the one that made sure everyone was returned home safely?"

Atticus' blue eyes were as round as saucers as he stared at Gran. It wasn't often that Hazel had seen the Princeling at a loss for words. He eyed her off fearfully, before nodding. He didn't get to speak a word before Edith Blythe swooped in and pulled the demon into a hug. "I guess that makes you the newest member of our flock then, doesn't it?"

A gasp of surprise slipped from Atticus as his eyes welled up for a moment. Then, cautiously, he wrapped his arms around Gran, leaning into her embrace. "Thank... you?" he murmured against Gran. She reached a hand up to stroke the back of his head.

"Demon, monster, whatever you are, when you are part of this family, you are part of this family. That means you will behave, and not make a mess of things," Gran warned him as she pulled back, placing her hands on his shoulders. "You *will* be a member of this household, and act like it. We Blythes' do not tolerate nonsense. Do I make myself clear? As a new Blythe, you will come to understand what that means."

Atticus seemed lost for words as he choked out, "Yes, ma'am."

"You may call me Grandmother," she corrected him. "Now, let's get inside, it's time for tea and breakfast. Hazel, you can wake dear Rini up. Oh my goodness, all you children and the trouble you cause this old woman." With a shake of her head, a wisp of a smile on her face, Edith marched ahead toward Winterbourne, ushering them up the slope to the house. The group glanced at one another and exchanged shrugs. As Wade and Atticus followed Edith, Charlotte grasped Hazel's arm, holding her back.

"What did you promise him? And why did you make a deal with him?" Charlotte whispered as Atticus walked again, chattering excitedly to Wade. The tall man bent his head to listen to his demon friend. Hazel shrugged.

"Your boyfriend seemed sad his little buddy wasn't there, so we made a deal. You know, the usual. The eternal promise to be his bestie forever. Oh, and he asked for a bedroom. I said you'd hook him up."

Charlotte whipped her head toward Hazel. "You promised him a room, in our house?"

"It's not like you don't have a billion of them spare, babes!"

"And what did *you* ask for, in return?"

Hazel grinned. "I think it's funnier if I don't tell you."

The two bickered and quarreled like sisters are wont to do as they made their way back into the old house as a group, a new path laying itself out in front of them.

EPILOGUE

R ivulets of rain trickled down the windows, tree branches tapping softly against them as a light breeze caressed the browning leaves. It was one of the last sticky rains of summer before it gave way to autumn once more. One of those gentle storms that made the world cozy and magical. The din of voices floated through the winding halls of the great manor home, weaving their own melody.

They gathered around the antique desk, heads low as they pushed for space around the screens. Charlotte sat in her many times over great-grandmother's chair, Wade and Atticus to her right, Hazel to her left. Specter curled up Charlotte's lap, purring softly as the fire crackled, filling the room with cozy warmth. Their chatter was low, excited, as they spoke over one another.

"It needs to be snappier, with more jump cuts and stuff, like a horror film," Hazel said, leaning over Charlotte to grab at the mouse. The other woman scowled and smacked the Hunter's hand away, while the demon child snorted. Hazel's gaze turned to him, withering. "You think you get to have an opinion?"

Atticus straightened, looking the Hunter in the eye as he shrugged with easy nonchalance. "Opinions are subjective, whereas I am always correct."

"And what do you want to do, *your Highness*," Hazel shot back. The demon folded his arms, pursing his lips.

"Obviously you want as much drama and atmosphere as possible. Your audience wants flair and storytelling, not cheap tricks. What are you, a harlot?

Charlotte, don't listen to this imp, she has no taste and certainly no sense of whimsy."

The two began to argue, heated barbs hurled at one another across the table, and subsequently across Wade and Charlotte. The other two shared a look as Charlotte sighed and slapped her hand on the desk, startling both demon and Hunter. The light caught the ring on her left hand as it slammed against the wood, causing the diamond and sapphires to sparkle in the ambient light.

"If you two cannot behave, I'll send you both out into the storm," Charlotte scolded as Wade wrapped a tender, loving arm around her shoulders. She glanced up at him, smiling as he dropped a kiss to her hairline. Charlotte leaned against him for a moment, before continuing her admonishment of the others. "If you recall, this is *my* channel. I chose to involve you both; don't make me regret it."

As Hazel and Atticus shared a look and grunted in agreement, Specter rose from Charlotte's lap, launching onto the desk and settling onto the keyboard. Charlotte reached a hand over and stroked the cat-not-cat.

"Some things never change, do they, Speckles?"

Leaving Charlotte and Wade together to finish the video, Hazel and Atticus slipped from the study. They had places to be, after all. Rain didn't stop them from doing their job.

Rini waited for the Hunter and the demon in the hallway. She was donned in the black leather jacket Hazel had gifted her for their one-month anniversary, her hunting bag slung over her shoulder. She pulled a lollipop from her mouth, offering it to Hazel. The Hunter took it from her girlfriend with a grin, before popping it in her own mouth. Atticus made a disgusted noise.

"I will never, for the life of me, understand the germ sharing you two do."

The girls giggled as they clasped hands. Hazel nodded toward the hallway, to the stairs. "Are we ready to leave? Got everything? We should be back by tomorrow morning at the latest if we get a wriggle on."

Rini nodded, and Hazel glanced to Atticus. Atticus, the Princeling, the demon, the weird child that had somehow turned their hunting duo into a trio. He winked at her, before grinning at the women. "I'm ready to hunt some monsters."

Acknowledgements

Books are such a weird, personal experience.

My first book, *Wraiths and Wanderings*, I wrote entirely alone. I didn't even get eyes on it until multiple drafts in. It was me, in the quiet hours, with my headphones and pumpkin and bourbon scented candle. Too much of it was done alone, and became lonely. And I'm so glad that this book wasn't, in contrast. I got to write it on stream while laughing, making jokes and memes, and spreading my silly characters until they became in jokes. I have so much less doubt, and so much more confidence as a result.

To my husband Sean and my bun buns—thank you for all the love and hot milos. I can't thank you enough for the support.

I feel like a cover of a book really speaks to the soul of the story within. Adara always understands the essence of my stories, of me, and brings that out with her illustrations and designs. *Secrets and Summonings* is no different. Thank you babes, my bestie, for getting me.

Nicole Evans, my illustrious, wonderful editor—thank you for taking such good care of my babies. ElementEds, I owe you more than a candle for making my blurb so crisp. Sonja, thank you for understanding my characters and capturing them in your delightful illustrations (especially all of the Atticus content you create!). And where would be without my ever patient model, our Charlotte? Thank you Julia, for being the star.

To my Twitch community—thank you for keeping me on task, even when my ADHD wanted to go anywhere else. Without you all working with me, laughing with me, and cheering me on, I wonder where this book would be. Probably not finished yet. I might have even abandoned it during my low points.

To my MOTW gang—thank you all for letting my play with my world and characters, and be silly with it. You have indulged me beyond words and measure. I'll make sure to repay you for that.

And you, reader. Thank you for coming on the journey with me.

About E.K

E.K lives in Adelaide with her husband, and now six rabbits: Bugs, Xena, Rain, Cloud, Button, and Twinkles! (Yes, that *is* a lot of bunnies!) She writes on Twitch between mentoring young writers, and giving writing workshops as part of her day job.

When she isn't writing, E.K likes to read, play video games, or work on various craft projects like her cosplays. E.K is also neurodivergent and currently diagnosed with ADHD and OCD (with suspected ASD), and focuses on creating a neuro-divergent friendly co-working space for other writers.

www.ingramcontent.com/pod-product-compliance
Lightning Source LLC
Chambersburg PA
CBHW030603120726
47904CB00006B/1758